MY LOVER, MY ENEMY

"Why would I dream about you?"

Tristan bent until his lips were a whisper away. "I wonder," he murmured, his breath mingling with hers.

Sha'Nara hated the bolt of anticipation that streaked through her body. But most of all, she hated that some inner part of her wanted him to kiss her. "I...I'm not attracted to you." Even though she protested, she didn't move away.

"Yes, you are. You've been dreaming about me." He had the audacity to look smug and Sha'Nara recoiled, shaking her head.

"Tell me about this dream." Though she didn't answer, he obviously guessed what she'd been dreaming from her flushed cheeks. "Do I kiss you?"

He closed the tiny gap between them, bestowing the lightest touch of his lips before he drew back. She needed all her self-control to keep from seeking more.

"Do I touch you?" He traced the outline of her face, her hair, her shoulder, yet didn't actually touch her. When he skimmed the shape of her breast, she bit back a moan.

"Do I make love to you?" He kept his hands by his side, but his gaze caressed her, his eyes dark with intimacy.

Sha'Nara remained still, torn between the aching desire of her body and the rational part of her mind.

"Why would you dream of me like that, Sha'Nara?" he asked quietly.

"I don't want to." She bit back the urge to scream with frustration. "It's wrong. You're the enemy."

Other *Love Spell* books by Karen Fox:
SWORD OF MACLEOD

Somewhere My Love

Karen Fox

LOVE SPELL BOOKS NEW YORK CITY

LOVE SPELL®
July 1997
Published by

Dorchester Publishing Co., Inc.
276 Fifth Avenue
New York, NY 10001

Printed in the United States of America.

To my husband, John, who believed in me even when I had doubts. I couldn't do it without your support.

To my Southern critique groups. Great Expectations—Bobbie Thibodeaux, Sherry Crane and Nancy Burns, and the Sandies—Kathy Carmichael, Rebecca Cox, Jea Dudley and Susan Carter. Thanks for sharing your time, your knowledge, and yourselves, and for reading great chunks in a short time. Thanks, too, to Ginger McSween for not even hesitating when I asked her to read 430 pages in a few days.

And, as always, to the Wyrd Sisters—Pam McCutcheon, Deb Stover, Laura Hayden, Paula Gill and Von Jocks, whose support continues even from across country.

Somewhere My Love

Prologue

He came to her in her dreams, as he always did when she'd had a particularly stressful day.

Teasing her lips with feather-light kisses, he ran his hands over her bare skin, her standard-issue underwear surprisingly gone. Her breasts swelled, anticipating his touch, her nipples hardening into tight little nubs.

He lifted his mouth from hers and smiled—a smile that acted like a supernova on her senses. She looked at his face . . . so very familiar yet totally unknown. Though not overwhelmingly handsome, his features were arresting, with his high brow, sculpted cheekbones, distinct nose, and finely shaped lips.

Though he smiled at her now, she knew—somehow— it wasn't his usual expression. The glimmer of pain and despair buried in the depths of his dark eyes couldn't be disguised.

His straight, black hair blended with the night and fell below his shoulders. As he bent to draw her breast into the warm cavern of his mouth, the silky strands brushed

9

against her skin, creating an erotic tingle that coiled in her belly.

She buried her hands in his hair to hold him close, her pulse racing, her breathing shallow. Though she couldn't say his name, all this was familiar . . . right. She felt no fear, only pleasure, anticipation, and a desire so keen it permeated her being.

He used his hands to trace paths over her body, and his mouth to bring her to the brink of a vast bottomless canyon. Returning to her lips, he made love to her mouth. She could only respond to his thrust and parry and his teasing sensuous touch, her senses caught up in the feel of his mouth, his tongue, his hands.

It was a kiss . . . and much more—a linking of two souls, a melding of perfect counterparts. The innermost reaches of their hearts and minds touched and joined, enveloping her in flames, pleasure, and passion.

The equal joining of their bodies seemed almost superfluous, but she traced the lean lines of his form, drawing him closer. She wanted him, needed him. Only together did they make a whole.

He drew back, only a little, his gaze meeting hers, burning with desire, as potent as any physical touch. His countenance had darkened, casting shadows over the planes of his face. She recognized that expression. Yes, this was who he was.

"You are all I need." His voice, quiet, deep, caressed her like soft velvet.

"Yes." She could deny him nothing.

He lifted slightly, then plunged forward.

The blaring sound of the morning alert jarred her awake. She blinked, reluctant to leave the dream behind. Sitting upright, she found her underwear plastered to her skin, soaked with perspiration. She consciously tried to control her erratic breathing and calm her rapid heartbeat as well.

Why that dream again? Why did this man look so familiar when she knew for certain she'd never seen him before? This erotic fantasy came more often now. Did it mean anything?

She dismissed that thought as quickly as it appeared. No, it was just a dream, nothing more—merely the unconscious desires of a woman too long without a man.

Which didn't mean she intended to look for one either. She had her career, her goals, and her father's expectations to keep her busy.

Crossing the room toward the lav, she remembered her mission for that day and scowled. She knew she'd only received it because of her father's interference. To him, this assignment meant prestige, honor, and glory.

To her, it meant the longest, most boring day of her life.

Chapter One

Tristan Galeron whirled from tending his terrarium, certain he hadn't heard correctly. "You want me to *what*?"

"I want you to kidnap the Director-General's daughter." Mael Ner approached, his age-lined face solemn.

This had to be a joke. Tristan glanced from Mael to his son, Cadell, who remained near the doorway. "Is he serious?"

Cadell nodded. "Very serious." Despite his words, a mischievous gleam danced in his blue eyes, and Tristan knew he wasn't going to get more than that from his friend. He turned his attention back to the older man.

"Why would I want to do something that foolhardy?" Tristan respected Mael's judgment, but this assignment bordered on suicide. "It would mean infiltrating Alliance Headquarters."

The thought of approaching the central seat of power sent nervous trickles along Tristan's spine. Not only could he expect Alliance troops, but the dreaded *brain drainers*, the PSI Police, were based there.

"We can no longer glide through space, hoping to go unnoticed. More and more of our people are finding their way here to the *Hermitage*. It's only a matter of time before the PSI Police do, too." Mael paused and glanced through the port window at the stars gleaming outside. Drawing in a slow breath, he looked back at Tristan, his determination clear. "We shouldn't be held responsible for what our ancestors did. It's time the Alliance accepted us."

"And kidnapping the Director-General's daughter will do that?" Tristan frowned. "Somehow, I don't think that will make the Alliance very happy with us."

"Perhaps not." Mael raised his clenched fist. "But it will show them we mean business."

Tristan responded to the force in Mael's voice. More than once, he'd wanted to destroy the Alliance. If it took a kidnapping to obtain his freedom, the risk would be worth it.

Cadell hurried over. "We won't harm her, Tristan. But Father thinks—and I agree—that the Director-General will be more likely to listen to us if his daughter is our guest for a while."

"Our guest?" Tristan twisted his lips. "Just like we're their guests in the readjustment chamber?" He'd known too many Scanners who had fallen victim to the brain mutilation used by the PSI Police.

"Not like that at all." Cadell scowled. "Father's plan is for a peaceful rebellion."

"There's no such thing." Tristan looked from son to father, uncertain how much of this gibberish to believe. "If we start anything, the Alliance will scream it's the PSI Wars again."

Mael shook his head. "The PSI Wars ended over a hundred years ago. Anyone who participated in them is now dead. With so few of us remaining in the universe, the Alliance can't possibly consider us a threat."

Tristan sighed in disgust. If he and others like him weren't considered a threat, why did the Alliance have an entire directorate dedicated to tracking and capturing them? Probably because Earth had many representatives on the Alliance council and Earthlings had long memories.

They hadn't forgotten the brutal uprising when those individuals with unique mental abilities had tried to control the planet. The Scanners, as they'd been named, had risen to power rapidly and fallen from it even more rapidly, leaving behind a fear of anyone who possessed parapsychic talents.

Most of that group had been destroyed when their rebellion collapsed, but a handful had escaped and fled into space, where they could hide among the varied planets and species. The Alliance had created the PSI Police to find them. Not one Scanner was to be left free.

But they had survived, despite the PSI Police's attempt to wipe them out, strengthening their powers by mating within their race. Yet they never knew peace, could never settle in one place for too long.

Tristan grimaced. Glancing around his quarters, he acknowledged that the three years he'd lived aboard the *Hermitage* were the longest he'd lived anywhere. How long would that last? The mammoth battleship had been decommissioned by the Alliance years ago. Its outdated maneuvering and hyperspeed capabilities made it a sitting duck if attacked by the Alliance's faster, more powerful fighters.

They had to do something. But kidnap someone? Especially the Director-General's daughter?

"Will the Director-General agree to talks?" he asked.

"He will if he wants his daughter back."

Tristan noticed Mael watching him closely. "And you think all we have to do is ask and they'll say all is forgiven?"

"Why wouldn't they?" Cadell asked. "We can prove we're not after power, that all we want is freedom." His gaze darted toward Tristan's terrarium. "And a place to call our own."

Tristan's insides clenched as he looked at his clear globe filled with precious soil and even more precious plants. He'd worked hard to get anything to grow. His terrarium meant more to him than any other possession. It was his piece of land—probably the only piece he would ever own.

Unless Scanners could be absolved of blame for what their ancestors had done.

A brief glimmer of hope flared to life, but he quickly extinguished it. In reality, how likely was it that that would happen?

Tristan turned to Mael. Ever since Tristan had formed his friendship with Cadell, Mael had substituted for Tristan's missing father, slowly becoming one of the few people Tristan trusted. If Mael honestly thought this plan had a chance to succeed, then Tristan should go along with it.

"Tell me exactly how you expect this to work."

"First off, you wouldn't have to go to Alliance Headquarters. I've just received word that the Director-General's daughter is currently residing at the family's home on Tarsus VI, which is why we need to move now." Mael kept his voice quiet, yet managed to convey his urgency.

"Kidnap the daughter and bring her here," he continued. "Then, I'll contact the Director-General to ask for negotiations."

Tristan grimaced. "And you expect him to agree?"

"Is it asking so much to set up a meeting in exchange for his daughter?"

As much as Tristan wanted to believe it could be that simple, he knew better. "What's to stop him from bringing the entire PSI Police army with him to this meeting?"

Mael nodded, acknowledging Tristan's foresight. "If he did, we would know, but I've heard he's a fair man. Though there are many on the Alliance council I don't trust, I believe this man is not one of them."

"What do you intend to ask for?" Tristan still couldn't shake his uneasy feeling. Too many things could go wrong. A brief image flickered through his mind of Mael meeting the Director-General and falling beneath a barrage of laser fire.

Tristan's stomach clenched. Though he'd never been

officially designated the Scanners' leader, Mael acted as the focal point for those who found their way to the *Hermitage*'s drifting haven. What would they do without him?

"I intend to ask for a pardon." Mael's words cut into Tristan's thoughts. "I'm sure the Director-General will see we're not the same as our ancestors and grant us freedom to live without persecution again. We may have to promise never to return to Earth, but I don't consider that a hardship."

Mael smiled. "I also intend to ask for a planet to call our own—someplace where the Scanners can live together in peace."

"They'll never give us that." Tristan desperately wanted to hope, but he couldn't. Having a piece of land to call his own existed only in his dreams.

"Perhaps not, but I still intend to ask." Mael paused. "Will you do it, Tristan?"

"Why me? Why not Bran, who could teleport in and out with no one the wiser?"

"I need someone I can trust. You know how unstable Bran is."

Tristan opened his mouth to offer Cadell's services, but Mael continued.

"I also need your powers. Your psychokinetic abilities are stronger than any other Scanner's."

Tristan grimaced. "How does that make me the best person for this mission?"

"In itself, it doesn't, but combined with your anger, your hatred of the Alliance, I'm confident you will succeed where someone else—less motivated—would fail."

"I thought you wanted this done peacefully." If Tristan had his way, he'd destroy anyone who got in his way.

"I do." Mael touched his son's shoulder. "That's why Cadell would go with you. He would be the diplomat while you provided the necessary force."

Tristan noticed a smile tugging at the corner of Cadell's lips. His even temper had seen Tristan through more than one altercation. Slightly built and shorter than Tristan, with thick blond hair cropped above his shoulders, Cadell said little, but then empaths usually were quiet.

Tristan raised his eyebrows. "What do you think, Cadell?"

The younger man hesitated, as if choosing his words carefully before speaking. "I think anything you and I approach together can only succeed."

Turning away, Tristan stared out his window into the blackness of space. He'd lived so long on the run, in space, he could barely conceive of settling in one place, let alone finding land he could cultivate.

But he wanted that. More than he wanted to see the Alliance destroyed, he wanted that piece of land.

Squaring his shoulders, he faced his friends again. "I'll do it."

Sha'Nara Calles checked her chronometer and sighed for the sixth time that day. Would this assignment ever be over? Pausing, she leaned back against the wall and watched the young woman sitting before a mirror hastily dismiss first one, then another, of the hair designs provided by her maid.

"No, no, Danae, that's not right either." Jacy Vadin frowned at her reflection. "I want to look older, not younger."

Sha'Nara rolled her eyes. All she'd heard all morning were petty decisions over shoes, undergarments, fingernail coloring, and now hair. Judging from Danae's reddening cheeks, the maid was fast approaching the end of her tolerance.

"Mistress, you're only twenty-one. Enjoy your youth while you have it." Danae gripped the strands of honey-blond hair again and wound them into an extravagant coil. Upon pinning the thick twist into an intricate arrangement, she nodded, her satisfaction obvious. "There, Mistress."

The towering coil added height to the petite woman and emphasized her slender neck. Sha'Nara had to admit Jacy's perfect features and flawless ivory skin made any design look good.

Jacy's eyes showed her indecision, and she picked at first one, then another piece of hair. In a sharp movement, she yanked her hair free of the coil. "No, no, that's not right either."

Lowering her gaze, Danae backed away. "Perhaps you should calm yourself before I start again. I will return." She left before Jacy could turn around.

Sha'Nara smothered a smile. The maid had already lasted longer than Sha'Nara had expected.

"Let her go." Jacy stared at her chamber entrance, then swung around to look at Sha'Nara. "You can help me, can't you?"

Indignation formed a steel rod along Sha'Nara's back. "Then you'll wear your hair long," she said, not bothering to keep the coolness from her voice. "I don't design hair."

Why had her father done this to her? True, escorting Jacy to her wedding ceremony would earn political favor, but Sha'Nara hadn't spent a year in training for the PSI Police in order to baby-sit the Director-General's spoiled daughter.

"But your hair always looks perfect." Jacy gazed at Sha'Nara's long woven braid, the envy in her gaze surprising. "In fact, everything about you always looks perfect."

Before Sha'Nara could respond, Jacy burst into tears and dropped her head to the dressing table, cradling it on her arms.

Sha'Nara didn't move, though her eyes widened. She hadn't cried since she was a little girl. Her father had made it clear he would not abide tears. Watching Jacy sob as if her heart would break put Sha'Nara at a momentary loss.

Forcing herself to move, she crossed to the younger woman. "What is it?"

"I can't do this. I can't."

Sha'Nara's chest tightened. "It's too late to back out now."

Jacy shook her head without lifting it from her arms. "I can't marry Devon Zdenek. It's wrong."

So much for political favor. Sha'Nara would never be able to face her father again if Jacy's marriage didn't take place. Too much depended on this union.

"Devon's planet must join the Alliance," she said. "Its magnicite mines make it invaluable."

"Other planets have them, too."

"Only five other planets in the known universe have magnicite stores, Jacy, but all intergalactic ships use it for fuel. Despite its replenishing capabilities, we always need more."

Jacy only shook her head as her sobs continued.

Sha'Nara bit back her irritation. "You agreed to this, Jacy. No one forced you."

"I only agreed so Daddy would treat me as an adult. I've spent my entire life restricted to the estate here or Daddy's quarters on Centralia. I wanted to get out of here." Jacy sniffed and raised her head.

Even crying, she retained her beauty. Her eyelashes, unusually dark on someone so fair, had lengthened with her tears and framed her reddened eyes.

Unfair. Sha'Nara knew she herself didn't look that good, even when at her best. Trying to comfort Jacy, she patted the girl's shoulder in an awkward gesture. "It's just nerves. I've heard brides go through this."

"It's *not* nerves." Jacy met Sha'Nara's gaze. "I just realized this is forever and I can't go through with it. I can't leave here with him, no matter how much the Alliance needs it."

Sha'Nara had received training on how to handle wild-eyes and irrationals. Perhaps that would help now. Pitching her voice to be reassuring, she forced a smile. "You've seen the holos of Devon. You've talked to him via vidcom. He's not a total stranger."

"But he is. I don't know anything about him. Does he like to walk? To talk? To eat frangolies?" Jacy's voice rose as she listed her conditions.

Sha'Nara saw her career fading rapidly. "From what I understand, Devon's father saw your father's holo of

19

you and decided on the spot his son must marry you. That's an honor, Jacy."

"Not to me. I don't want to get married."

Unexpected sympathy swelled within Sha'Nara. She'd decided long ago never to join with any man. Her career as a PSI officer took precedence over any emotional entanglement. Her father often said emotions caused problems, dissent, death.

Sha'Nara preferred to use logic. Logic solved problems, eased dissent, and prevented death. Banishing the small glimmer of sympathy, Sha'Nara sought a rational way to influence Jacy.

"Your father likes Devon. As much as he wants the planet Lander in the Alliance, he never would've agreed to this condition if he didn't think Devon could make you happy." Sha'Nara paused, letting Jacy ponder that statement before adding the final point. "You know your father adores you."

Everyone knew how much Remy Vadin, Director-General of the Planetary Alliance, doted on his only daughter. But while he indulged most of her wishes, he also kept her under constant supervision, unwilling to risk any harm befalling her. No wonder Jacy was spoiled and restless.

"I know Daddy loves me."

Jacy's words brought a twinge of pain, but Sha'Nara brushed it aside. "And he only wants what's best for you."

"Yes."

Sensing victory, Sha'Nara smiled. "Think of this as a grand adventure. You'll have a terrific story to tell your children."

A slow smile crept across Jacy's face. "My children . . ." She swiped at her damp cheeks, nodding decisively. "I'll do it."

Sha'Nara allowed herself a sigh of relief. She still had a career . . . for the moment. "Why don't you get into your dress and finish your hair afterward?"

"It's the most beautiful dress you ever saw." Jacy

jumped from her chair and ran across her chambers. "Daddy had it specially made for me."

Sha'Nara started to follow, until the loud jangle of the vidcom snared her attention. "I'll get that." No doubt Jacy's father was checking on his daughter's progress.

After keying the receive sequence, Sha'Nara caught her breath as her father's image appeared on the screen, imposing in his Alliance dress uniform. "Father."

He didn't waste time on greetings. "Is Jacy almost ready? I trust you allowed time for travel."

"She's dressing now." Sha'Nara knew exactly how long a ship would take to cover the distance between Tarsus VI and Centralia and had allotted plenty of time.

"Dressing?" Amyr Calles arched one of his thick, gray eyebrows, managing to convey his irritation with only one word.

"We had a slight problem." Sha'Nara hesitated, already knowing how her father would greet her news. "Jacy decided she didn't want to marry Devon Zdenek."

Amyr's expression tightened, his thin lips compressed, and his eyes glittered dangerously. "I assumed a PSI Police Commander could handle a young woman's wedding preparations. I would hate to think this assignment was too difficult for your talents. Especially when it would jeopardize what the Alliance has worked so hard to achieve."

Sha'Nara straightened, lifting her chin in defiance. He always managed to make her feel inadequate, no matter what task she took on. Others congratulated her on her achievements, but not her father. He always demanded more. "I have the situation in hand," she said. "Jacy will arrive for her wedding as scheduled."

He said nothing for several moments, but Sha'Nara refused to squirm beneath his interrogating gaze. Finally he nodded. "I trust we will see you shortly. Calles out."

The link closed and the screen went black. Sha'Nara released a long, slow breath and uncurled her fingers, not realizing until that moment that she'd drawn them into fists. She tried so hard to fulfill her father's wishes, but her efforts were never enough.

What did she have to do to earn his approval? Defeat the Scanners single-handedly?

"What do you think?"

She turned at Jacy's question and examined the woman's elaborate gown. Though the white bodice molded to Jacy's slim torso, it was covered with a transparent layer of material that formed the sleeves and train. The skirt billowed out in several heavy tiers, completely hiding Jacy's feet.

Only someone as beautiful and petite as Jacy could wear such a dress and not be overwhelmed by it. Sha'Nara smiled. "You look wonderful." She eyed Jacy's long, full hair as it tumbled down the girl's back. "I don't think you need to do anything else to your hair. It looks fine like that."

"Do you think so?" Jacy went to pirouette before the mirror. "It does look beautiful, doesn't it?"

Sha'Nara didn't feel obligated to answer the rhetorical question. They needed to get moving. "Do you have a veil?"

"No, just this." Jacy lifted a circular headpiece, entwined with white blossoms and ribbon, and placed it on her head.

"Good." Sha'Nara turned toward the communications panel. "I'll instruct the ship to prepare for departure."

She'd barely taken five steps when the door to Jacy's chamber slid open behind her. Sha'Nara whipped around, resting her hand on the laser holstered around her hips. She hadn't heard the entry chimes.

Two men entered, then paused. They wore Alliance uniforms, but Sha'Nara frowned. They didn't *look* like Alliance officers. The slighter of the two appeared too casual, his expression open, his stance relaxed. His bright blue gaze, however, jumped from her to Jacy. Slowly he smiled.

The taller man held himself more at attention, but Sha'Nara sensed a tension about him, as if he kept every muscle ready for action. And he had plenty of muscles. She couldn't resist the urge to scan the lines of his body before fully examining his face. Few Alliance officers kept themselves in such excellent physical condition.

Though he wore his straight black hair tied back, it was still too long to meet regulations. Was he one of those who constantly tested the rules? She'd met men like him before. From her experience, Alliance officers weren't often held to the same rigid restrictions as PSI Police.

His face showed no emotion, but she liked its appearance. Though his chin was too square, the set of his jaw uncompromising and his mouth entirely too sensuous, she liked his high cheekbones and the aristocratic line of his nose. She blinked at a sudden sense of déjà vu. She'd never seen him before, had she?

She met his dark gaze, almost losing herself in black eyes rimmed with equally black lashes and brows. As she stared, awareness dawned and her heart plummeted into her stomach.

By Orion's Sword! It was the man from her dreams.

For a moment after entering the chamber, Tristan thought he'd been hit by a stun beam. One glance at the tall woman standing defensively nearby made his breath catch in his throat.

Her appearance was striking, the type no man could forget. Her hair glowed with dark red color, despite being twisted into a long braid down her back. He had no trouble imagining it unbound, creating a veil around her shoulders.

As he looked into her green eyes, he pictured the two of them together, their clothing gone, their bodies entwined in heated passion. Blood rushed to his loins and he inhaled sharply. What was happening to him?

Unable to stop, he examined her closely. While her figure wasn't too abundant, he wouldn't call it scrawny, either. Her breasts, easily revealed by her snug uniform, would fill his palms, and her hips flared slightly, triggering a jolt of longing for what lay between her thighs.

Tristan held back a groan. This shouldn't be happening to him. Not here. Not now.

Forcing himself to concentrate, he noted the insignia of two planets on her shoulder. An Alliance symbol. Though her style of uniform was unfamiliar, she undoubtedly was an Alliance officer. The cords on her opposite shoulder indicated her rank. Commander. His sudden lust cooled.

"What . . ." She licked her lips, drawing his attention to their lush fullness, and started again. "What's your business here?"

Tristan opened his mouth to speak, but no words emerged from his dry throat. He glanced at Cadell in alarm.

His friend smiled easily, then snapped to attention. "We're here for Mistress Vadin." He looked across the room and Tristan followed Cadell's gaze, noticing for the first time the other woman in the room.

This woman was obviously younger, but even more stunning. With her golden hair and striking features, she should have overwhelmed the red-haired woman. But she didn't. Despite her beauty, Tristan experienced none of the same desire.

"Daddy sent you, didn't he?" The younger girl gave them a radiant smile, then looked at the other woman. "I imagine he thought he was being helpful, Sha'Nara."

Sha'Nara's lips thinned. "I wonder if he thinks I'm not capable enough to get you to your wedding."

Wedding! Tristan exchanged glances with Cadell. They hadn't foreseen this. "We need to leave soon, Mistress Vadin." He motioned toward the doorway. "If you please."

Though he and Cadell wore stolen Alliance uniforms, he expected to be called out as an impostor at any moment. Judging from Sha'Nara's wary gaze, she already distrusted him.

The Director-General's daughter paused in front of Cadell and gave him an impish smile. "Call me Jacy, please." She looked from one man to the other. "Shall we go?"

Tristan felt, more than saw, Sha'Nara move to join them. Keeping his features expressionless, he faced her. "There's no need to accompany us. We'll get Mistress Vadin to her wedding."

Sha'Nara's green eyes snapped with barely restrained anger. "I was given the assignment of escorting Jacy and I intend to finish it . . . whether her father sends extra escorts or not."

She brushed past Tristan and took a position beside Jacy. Tristan grimaced. Just what he didn't need. An Alliance officer. Though they weren't as cold-blooded as the PSI Police, Tristan had no use for the so-called diplomats who meddled in planetary affairs. Even worse, this Alliance officer made his desire surge just by being near him.

Casting an exasperated look at Cadell, Tristan received only his friend's casual shrug in reply. "Shall we go then?" Cadell said. "We need to go to the upper level for departure."

Tristan let Cadell guide the women while he lingered behind, surveying the hallways. As two men approached, he tensed, his initial response to smash them with his psychokinetic abilities. Before he could act, he recalled Mael's final instructions.

Mael had looked directly at him. "No violence unless absolutely necessary and under no circumstances bloodshed."

They were not to create a disturbance or raise an alarm. The plan called for escorting the Director-General's daughter off the planet without protest. By the time she realized she was their prisoner, she'd be far from Tarsus VI.

Tempering his power, Tristan used it to close a door in the hallway and snap off the activation switch. The men wouldn't follow them from that way.

Tristan's group reached the lift without encountering anyone else, then stepped inside. Tristan found himself standing behind Sha'Nara, all his senses instantly on alert. Her gentle fragrance, that of the liliana flower, reached his nostrils and he inhaled deeply. It reminded him of things he would never have—her being chief among them.

She kept her body stiff, her tension obvious, and Tristan clenched his hands into fists to keep from caressing the graceful line of her neck. Her braid hung halfway down her back, and he wanted to run his fingers over that, too. Was her hair actually as silky and vibrant as it appeared?

An urge to taste her, to touch her, permeated his being until he shuddered from the effort of restraining it. Why did she affect him this way? There were women on the *Hermitage*, yet none had ever kindled his desire with so little effort.

He saw her and he wanted her.

If she insisted on accompanying them, she would become a prisoner, too. He could mimic the PSI Police, who thought nothing of taking what they wanted. After all, she was nothing but an Alliance officer.

He immediately discarded that idea, the thought leaving an unpleasant taste in his mouth. The fires on Armaga would burn out before he lowered himself to those standards.

The cubicle lurched as it came to a halt, and Sha'Nara staggered back. Without thinking, Tristan seized her shoulders to steady her.

Mistake.

Desire traveled through his palms and along his nerve endings to his gut, where it whirled in a frenzy before dropping low in his belly. He inhaled sharply, echoing her gasp.

"Are you all right?" He struggled to produce words, his brain fogged.

"I . . . yes . . . I'm fine." She glanced at him over her shoulder, and he could see his reflection in her wide eyes. "You can . . . you can let me go now."

Suddenly aware he still held her, he dropped his hands instantly. No wonder he couldn't think. Touching her was more dangerous than facing an angry Gatorian.

Cadell grinned as he escorted Jacy out of the cubicle,

his hand on her elbow, leaving Tristan to follow with Sha'Nara.

No way would Tristan touch her again. He waited for Sha'Nara to precede him onto the landing strip, thankful for the biting wind that helped restore his coherency.

The Director-General's house, like most others on Tarsus VI, has its own landing pad on the roof. With most of the planet covered with vast seas, space came at a premium.

Sha'Nara stopped beside their six-passenger ship and pivoted to face him, a frown creasing her brow. "That is not an Alliance ship."

"You're correct." Tristan had expected this question. "The Director-General felt it would be better if his daughter arrived without detection."

"For her wedding?" Her voice rose.

The wedding again. Shibit. He thought quickly. "There is always the possibility that someone might want to prevent this marriage. The Director-General is unwilling to take that chance."

She appeared satisfied with that answer, for she moved to Jacy's side and murmured something Tristan couldn't hear. The younger woman smiled as she replied, then reached up to take Cadell's extended hand to board the craft.

Sha'Nara ignored Cadell's hand and climbed the narrow steps unaided. Tristan followed, pausing briefly to survey the area. They'd used an Alliance code to request permission for landing. Thus far, no one appeared to be aware of anything out of the ordinary. They might just pull this off.

He swung into the ship and secured the door latch before meeting Cadell's gaze with a grimace. "Let's get out of here."

"If you'll see to our guests, I'll initiate preflight." Cadell went to the controls without waiting for Tristan's reply.

Tristan would see to the guests, all right. There was one he'd especially like to see to. With an exclamation

27

of disgust, he secured the hatch and went to the rear area, where Sha'Nara and Jacy had settled into passenger seats.

"Do you need any help with the restraints?" he asked, concentrating on Jacy. As much as he wanted to, he didn't dare look at Sha'Nara.

"I think I have it," Jacy replied. "But Sha'Nara can't find her other connector."

Having no option, he turned to Sha'Nara. She didn't look pleased by Jacy's revelation. "I've found it," she said, her tone cool. "But it's stuck."

"Let me help." Tristan bent across her to reach for the restraint. The scent of lilianas caressed his senses as he located the clip and tugged it free. He gave it to Sha'Nara and drew back, his breathing not quite even.

She didn't meet his gaze, and concentrated on fastening the restraint instead, but Tristan noticed the rapid beat of the pulse in her throat. Obviously his nearness affected her as well.

Not altogether displeased with that thought, he took the time to examine a tiny symbol embroidered on her collar, almost indistinguishable against the dark blue material.

He made out a tiny lightning bolt within a circle. His stomach clenched. He knew that insignia—far better than he cared to.

The PSI Police.

Chapter Two

Tristan placed his hands on the armrests, pinning Sha'Nara in her seat. "Who are you?" He didn't try to hide his anger.

Her eyes narrowed and glittered with defiance before she answered. "Sha'Nara Calles."

"And your position?" He waited, hoping he was wrong.

"Commander, PSI Police Division Ten."

Red-hot rage boiled through his veins, and he gripped the armrests so tightly his knuckles whitened. Something must have shown in his eyes for she drew back, her own eyes wide. He wanted to kill her . . . needed to kill her to make up for his parents' deaths, his friends' deaths, his loss of a normal life.

Even through his anger, one thought bubbled to the front of his mind, and he seized it. "Calles?" There couldn't be more than one of them.

"Yes, Calles." Though wary, Sha'Nara didn't show any fear. If anything, indignation shone in her eyes.

"Any relation to Amyr Calles?" All Scanners knew the

name and image of the PSI Police Director, but not that of this woman.

She hesitated before answering. "He's my father."

With a deep-throated growl, Tristan pushed himself away from her seat and whirled toward the control seats. Her father? Tristan didn't think anyone as heartless as Calles was capable of siring children.

He threw himself into his seat, shaking from his pent-up fury. "Take off . . . now!"

Cadell shot him a surprised glance, but quickly lifted the craft off the landing pad. Only when the blackness of space appeared on the view screen did he give Tristan his full attention. "What's going on?" Cadell asked.

"We have to kill her." Tristan kept his voice low but determined. They had no choice. To bring a PSI Police officer to the *Hermitage* intending to let her go was suicidal to them all. She should've stayed behind. Now she had to be eliminated . . . before she destroyed them.

Why rationalize this? A dead PSI officer was one less to torment Scanners. But then he'd never met one who looked like Sha'Nara Calles. Or one who affected his senses so strongly.

"We're not killing anybody." The corner of Cadell's mouth lifted. "Just because she's caught your interest is no reason to kill her."

He had to deny it. How could he be attracted to a PSI Police officer? "She didn't—"

Cadell cut him off. "I know you and that's the first time I've seen you speechless. So she's an Alliance officer. It could be worse."

"It is worse." Tristan ground out the words. "She's PSI Police."

Cadell's features tightened, and he darted a glance at the woman in the back. "You're certain?"

"She told me." Tristan couldn't stop a bitter laugh from escaping. "She's Director Calles' daughter."

"His daughter?" Cadell gave a low whistle. "What a coup. The Alliance will have to listen to us now."

"We can't take her to the *Hermitage*."

"Why not? As long as she doesn't know the coordi-

nates, we're safe. All I sense from her and Jacy is unease, but not fear. They still believe we're taking them
to Centralia. By the time they realize we're not, they
won't know where they are. Release your anger and
you'll see that I'm right."

Tristan tried to cool the raging inferno burning inside
him, but had little success. The image of his mother
pushing him out the rear window as PSI Police rushed
in the front door appeared in his mind. He'd never seen
her again. His parents were either dead or readjusted—
in which case they would be better off dead.

And PSI Police were responsible.

"No." He sliced his hand through the air. "She's a
threat to our plans. I can expel her through the air lock.
She'll die quickly—quicker than one of them deserves."
A momentary unease surfaced, but he thrust it away. A
PSI Police officer never hesitated to eliminate a Scan-
ner. Why should he?

"We're taking her with us." Cadell spoke with surprising firmness. "I know how much you hate the PSI
Police, but killing her would destroy all our chances for
a settlement." He laid his hand on Tristan's shoulder.
"All I sense from you is rage, and that's never yet produced a clear head. When you calm down, you'll see
that I'm right."

"She'll ruin everything." Tristan had seen the intelligence in her gaze and the feistiness in her manner.
Sha'Nara Calles would never be content as their prisoner.

"In a short time she'll be one PSI Officer among two
hundred and fifty Scanners. She'll have no opportunity
to interfere." Cadell paused. "I'm more worried about
her PSI Detector. No officer is without one. She must
not have it activated or it would've alerted on us."

Startled, Tristan turned in his seat and found
Sha'Nara staring at him, unafraid, her gaze curious.
With an effort, he dampened his fury. Ascertaining
what he wanted to know, he gave her a sullen nod, then
faced front again. How could he have forgotten about
her PSI Detector? When activated, the device produced

a steady tone of alert when within a five-meter distance of a Scanner.

She wore the small device on the narrow belt around her trim waist, but obviously it wasn't active. He'd also noticed a laser pistol hanging in its holster. That he'd missed it before only reaffirmed the impact she'd had on him.

"How much longer before we enter hyperspace?" he asked.

Cadell glanced at the controls. "Soon."

As Cadell set the coordinates, Tristan verified them. Though the journey through hyperspace to the *Hermitage* would take slightly longer than that to Centralia, he hoped neither woman would notice the difference until it was too late.

With a grimace, Cadell gripped the control lever and took the ship into hyperspace. The stars blurred together, creating a black field outside their view screen, and Tristan nodded with satisfaction. So far, so good.

Tristan's anger finally cooled enough to allow him to reexamine Cadell's words. Though he didn't like it, he had to admit his friend was right. Despite Tristan's first desire to destroy all PSI Police, to eliminate this one would only cause bigger problems and put any chance of freedom out of reach.

He shifted in his chair to watch her from the corner of his eye. Yet he felt certain she'd be a big enough problem all on her own.

Sha'Nara watched the two men converse between themselves. Though the dark-haired Alliance officer kept his voice low, she had no doubt he'd informed his partner of her identity. She sighed. This wasn't the first time she'd encountered someone with a grievance against her father. He hadn't reached his current position by being nice. He did what was best for the Alliance and the PSI Police Division . . . always.

This officer had probably been denied entry into the PSI Police. Many applied each year, but only a few were chosen. If those passed over held a grudge against her father, they obviously didn't deserve the slot in the first place.

"Sha'Nara."

Jacy's whisper diverted Sha'Nara's attention from her thoughts. "Yes?"

"Don't you think these are the handsomest officers you've ever seen?" The young woman didn't take her gaze off the men as she spoke. "Especially the blond."

"They're . . . tolerable." Sha'Nara still couldn't believe the dark-haired one looked like the man in her dreams. How could she have dreamed of him when they'd never met until today?

She must've seen his holo somewhere, perhaps in an official file, and that had caused the dream. She couldn't deny his striking looks affected her heart rate, so she would've subconsciously remembered him. That was it.

"Tolerable?" Jacy looked at Sha'Nara in amazement. "Have you had your vision checked lately? I wouldn't mind a close encounter with either of them." She smiled as if harboring a secret thought, and Sha'Nara sighed.

"You're on your way to your wedding, Jacy."

"All the more reason to look my fill now." Jacy's smile faded. "Who knows what kind of life I'll have with Devon? He may keep me locked up just like my father did."

"I doubt that." While she didn't know much about the Landerian people, Sha'Nara couldn't see Devon allowing any harm to befall Jacy. Not the Director-General's daughter.

"Do you know their names?"

"No." She returned Jacy's exasperated look. "I don't know *everyone* in the Alliance."

"Then I'll find out." The girl leaned forward. "Could I get your names, please? I'd like to tell my father how pleased I am with the escort he sent."

The blond turned and smiled at Jacy, illuminating his fine features. Sha'Nara conceded defeat. He was gorgeous. She'd have to be dead to deny it.

"I'm Cadell Ner." He motioned toward the man beside him. "This is Tristan Galeron."

Tristan didn't bother to acknowledge the introduction. Instead, he showed a deep interest in the control panel.

Tristan Galeron. Sha'Nara repeated the name to herself. She intended to find out what slight he thought he'd received from her father. His anger had been more potent than most. Perhaps Tristan had been demoted as a result of some careless error. Her father had no patience with those who made mistakes.

"I'm very pleased to meet you," Jacy said with too much enthusiasm.

"The pleasure is mine." Cadell's gaze traveled over Jacy before returning to her face. Sha'Nara's muscles tightened. If she wasn't careful, Jacy would want to run away with this Alliance officer next.

And she'd thought escorting the young woman to her wedding would be boring.

"Will we arrive at Centralia soon?" she asked. The sooner she could deposit Jacy Vadin in her father's care, the better.

Cadell's gaze moved to her, and she caught a glimpse of something almost probing before he blinked and smiled. "Not much longer." He glanced at the control panel. "We should emerge from hyperspace shortly."

She nodded and aimed a warning glance at Jacy. The girl twisted her lips in a chagrined expression, but settled back in her seat, crossing her arms over her chest.

Let her pout. All Sha'Nara wanted was to deliver the headstrong bride to her waiting groom and be finished with any responsibility for her. Sha'Nara's training had taught her how to deal with deadly Scanners, not spoiled children.

Still, she couldn't shake a lingering sense of unease, and searched the close interior of the ship. Tristan and Cadell appeared interested in the controls, while Jacy sulked. Sha'Nara saw no sign of a threat, but the feeling remained.

Sha'Nara scowled. How many times had her father

instructed her to ignore her feelings, to use logic to make decisions? With an effort, she banished the emotional entreaty and sat back to watch the blackness of hyperspace on the view screen.

The vast emptiness offered no consolation, and she found herself watching Tristan instead. Though Cadell was the more stunningly handsome of the two, something about this dark man stirred her senses. Studying the blue-black strands of his hair, she knew instinctively how it would feel intertwined between her fingers.

Jumbled images of her dream filtered through her mind, and she caught her breath. A part of her insisted she knew this man, intimately, yet they hadn't met until today. She'd swear to that. Then why did her skin warm as she watched him? Why did her lips tingle as if anticipating his kiss? As he bent over the control panel, she flexed her fingers, aware of an urge to trace the muscular structure of his back.

Sha'Nara shook her head to clear it of such traitorous thoughts. She had no place in her life for these imaginings, and certainly no place for the angry man at the console.

She leaned back in her chair. Would they ever reach Alliance Headquarters? She stole a quick look at her chronometer and sat upright. They should've reached Centralia sometime ago. Why was the trip taking so long? They'd had no mechanical malfunctions.

As she recalled the men's arrival in Jacy's room without announcing chimes, the unexpectedness of an escort, and the non-Alliance ship, the pieces came together in Sha'Nara's mind. Her stomach sank. She'd been careless. She should've been suspicious before now. Her attraction to Tristan had overruled her logic.

She slowly unfastened her restraints, her gaze focused on the two Alliance officers. Cadell leaned over to murmur something to Tristan, and Sha'Nara froze. When neither man glanced in her direction, she slid the ends of the belt off her lap and placed her hand on her laser. She intended to get some answers.

Before she could stand, the ship emerged from hyperspace. Sha'Nara studied the blanket of stars outside the view screen. Her insides knotted. They were not the stars near Centralia.

A long, narrow object in the distance grew larger as they approached it rapidly. Recognizing it as an old battle cruiser, Sha'Nara jumped her feet. "Where have you taken us?"

She meant to pull her laser, but in one fluid movement, Tristan stood and her weapon flew from her holster to his hand. She stared at her empty holster, then at Tristan aiming the laser at her. The blood drained from her face as she felt suddenly chilled.

Scanners!

And judging from the ease with which Tristan took her weapon, he had tremendous psychokinetic skills. None of the other Scanners she'd encountered had demonstrated such control of their mutant abilities.

The real reason for his earlier rage dawned at once. Sha'Nara couldn't stop the shiver of fear that traced her spine. By Orion's Sword. She was going to die.

Everyone knew how power-hungry and bloodthirsty Scanners were. These people had no morals, no conscience. If not for the PSI Police's readjustment procedure, they'd try to control the universe as they'd tried to enslave the Earth's population over a century ago.

At least with her people, Scanners had a chance. True, many still fought and had to be killed, but those who survived were sent for readjustment. Once that was completed, they could go on to lead productive lives.

As for her, a PSI Officer held prisoner by Scanners had no chance at all. Why hadn't she activated her PSI Detector? Why would she? She'd expected to escort Jacy to her wedding, nothing more. Too late now.

Tristan's dark gaze bored into her. "Sit down. We'll be docking soon."

The iciness of his voice only added to the cold dread filling Sha'Nara's veins. She hesitated, searching the small interior of the craft for another option.

Abruptly, she felt a pressure against her shoulders as if someone had gripped them. The pressure forced her back into her seat despite her resistance, and her belt fastened itself.

She watched Tristan, her eyes wide. He hadn't moved, his hard expression hadn't changed. Terror streaked through her. He'd needed so little effort to use his powers.

"I advise you to stay in your seat." Tristan held the laser loosely, but Sha'Nara saw the threat in his gaze. "Then you won't get hurt."

"Sha'Nara?" Jacy's voice trembled.

Jacy! Sha'Nara looked at the young woman and fought back her rising panic. Jacy was the target, not her. Too late she recalled how the men had tried to get her to stay behind. Naturally, they didn't want a PSI Officer. They wanted the Director-General's daughter.

But for what?

"Don't worry, Jacy."

New determination gave Sha'Nara courage. She'd fight them all before she let anything happen to Jacy. The woman had been entrusted to her care, and Sha'Nara intended to complete her mission. Somehow.

Tristan's fierce glare offered little encouragement. He rested against his chair, still holding the laser, and cast quick glances over his shoulder at the view screen as they approached the large ship.

Now able to see details of the battleship, Sha'Nara recognized it immediately as an old class twelve, capable of holding five hundred people. This level of ship had been declared obsolete over a decade ago. She'd never expected to encounter one in space, especially one that worked.

Her heart hammered at her ribs. Were the weapons functional, too? Was this just one small part of a Scanner armada intent on controlling the universe?

That was why they'd taken Jacy—to force Remy Vadin to give in to their demands. As Director-General, head of the Alliance, he couldn't afford to do that, no matter how much he loved his daughter. Sha'Nara tightened her jaw. Jacy's safety rested in her hands.

A vast door slid open in the side of the mammoth cruiser to reveal a dark, yawning passageway. Their ship flew inside, reminding Sha'Nara of a Shaktor Beast swallowing its prey—a very apt analogy for her circumstances.

Their vehicle skidded to a stop, and a siren blared as lights flickered on around them to reveal a vast landing bay, easily large enough for twenty similar-sized craft. Only one other ship sat in the bay. Sha'Nara frowned. Were the rest already out preparing their attack?

"Where are we?" whispered Jacy.

"You're on board the *Hermitage*." Cadell left his seat and approached, his smile in place. His gaze flickered over Sha'Nara before resting on Jacy. "You have nothing to fear. We mean you no harm."

Sha'Nara released her restraints and stood. Anger mingled with her fear as she faced the two men. "I've never known a Scanner that didn't intend harm."

Tristan pushed out of his chair and came to stand before her, his anger palpable. "I doubt if you've ever really known a Scanner."

"Scanners?" Jacy gasped, her eyes wide and full of horror. She stared at Cadell as if unable to believe it possible.

He extended his hand to help her up. "Don't be afraid." He spoke calmly, with such reassurance, that Jacy placed her hand in his and allowed him to pull her to her feet. "I won't hurt you."

Sha'Nara didn't believe that for a moment.

"Do you promise?" Obviously Jacy did.

"I promise." He continued to hold Jacy's hand as they looked at each other silently, their expressions solemn.

Sha'Nara's heart thudded wildly. What was he doing? Brainwashing Jacy? "A Scanner's promise means nothing," she said in an attempt to break his spell.

It worked. Cadell dropped Jacy's hand and faced Tristan with a wry smile. "Father will be waiting to see them."

Father? Sha'Nara blinked. Somehow she'd never thought of Scanners as having fathers.

Something must have shown in her expression, for Tristan raised one eyebrow. "What's the matter? Do you find it hard to believe we don't come from a test tube?"

Against her will, Sha'Nara's cheeks warmed. She turned away, not wanting Tristan to see how accurate he'd been.

Cadell opened the hatch. "If you'll come with me, I'll take you to my father." He aimed a pointed look at Sha'Nara. "You can't escape, so don't try. It'll only upset everyone."

Don't try. Not farding likely. Sha'Nara let Jacy precede her out of the ship before she followed Cadell. She intended to take the first opportunity to get herself and Jacy away from these dangerous mutants.

By the prickling at the back of her neck, she knew immediately when Tristan fell into step near her shoulder. Even though she knew what he was, her body responded to him with an awareness that defied reason. The sooner she escaped, the better.

Watching closely, she committed their path to memory as they traveled along corridors, ascended in a lift, then made their way to a mid-sized room filled with hovertables and chairs. The outer wall drew her attention first as it contained windows that revealed the vastness of space outside. The interior of the room looked tiny in comparison. Sha'Nara felt as if she paled into insignificance. Perhaps that was the purpose.

"Welcome to the *Hermitage*."

The voice surprised her. Turning, she saw someone standing beside one of the tables. A tall, slim man of fifty or more years, he looked impressive with his mane of white hair only slightly tinged with gray. He wore his hair long, but unlike Tristan, he let it hang loose. No light reflected back from his eyes. She didn't trust any of these people, but with this one, obviously their leader, she had to be especially on her guard.

Cadell stepped forward and introduced Jacy to his father.

"How is she?" asked the older man.

"She's very frightened. We need to reassure her." Cadell lowered his voice, but Sha'Nara caught his words.

An empath. Knowing these men's powers would help Sha'Nara in her escape. She studied the leader. What abilities did he possess?

"Welcome." Cadell's father nodded his head at Jacy, then focused on Sha'Nara. Cadell exchanged glances with Tristan.

With a twist of his lips, Tristan spoke. "Mael, this is Sha'Nara Calles."

"I didn't expect an addition," Mael said.

"It couldn't be helped if we were avoid discovery," Tristan replied.

As one they looked at her. It took all her willpower to keep from shifting in discomfort.

Mael's intent blue gaze pinned her in place. "I see you are an Alliance officer."

Tristan laughed harshly. "She's far more than that. She's PSI Police."

Mael's face tightened. Something flickered in his eyes that frightened Sha'Nara more than if he had screamed ugly curses at her. Her muscles tightened, ready to flee.

"What are you going to do with us?" she demanded, unwilling to reveal her fear.

At first, she didn't think he would answer.

"You'll be our guests," he said dismissively.

"Guests! Hosts don't kidnap their guests. What do you want?"

Mael paused as if considering her words. "We want our freedom."

"Freedom?" That wasn't what she'd expected him to say. The man radiated power. Obviously he would want more of the same. "I know your kind. You're planning to take over the Alliance."

"No." Cadell answered for his father. "We want to be left alone to live without fear. We're no threat to anyone."

"Fardpissle. All Scanners are delusional and power-hungry."

"You're thinking of the people who lived a hundred years ago. We're not them."

They must think she was a Neeban to fall for this stuff. The Scanners were greedy for control and these were the words they planned to use to fool people into thinking otherwise. But they wouldn't fool her.

"Are you the same as your ancestors were a hundred years ago?" Mael asked.

She froze. She knew nothing of her ancestors on either her father or her mother's side. Who were they? What had they been?

Her confusion must have shown, or else Cadell with his emphatic abilities had picked up on it. "Perhaps they were privateers or murderers or worse," he said with a wicked gleam in his eye.

"I think not." Sha'Nara lifted her chin. No matter who her ancestors had been, they hadn't been Scanners. "I've been chasing Scanners for years and all those I've encountered have been just as avaricious as a hundred years ago."

Tristan scowled. "Greedy? Or fighting for their lives?"

"They wouldn't have to fight if they came with us peacefully."

"So they could be readjusted?"

"Of course. Then they would present no threat to anyone."

Tristan turned away as if he couldn't bear to look at her, and Sha'Nara frowned. His slight hurt, surprising her. She had to get away from this man and his irrational affect on her senses.

"When do you plan to contact my father?" Jacy spoke for the first time, her voice barely audible.

"I think we'll wait a day or two," Mael replied. "The delay should make him more receptive to what we have to say."

Jacy looked at Mael, biting her lip, her fear obvious. "What do you plan to do with us in the meantime?"

"We can't give you free run of the ship." Mael gazed pointedly at Sha'Nara. "Tristan and Cadell will watch over you."

"No!" Tristan whirled around, his muscles taut. "I agreed to bring the daughter here. That's the end of my involvement."

Mael grimaced. "Tristan, I need someone I can trust with these women."

"Exactly." Tristan glared at Sha'Nara.

"We can't allow anything to happen to either of them."

"And who's to say I wouldn't be the one to harm them." Tristan ground out his words, and true terror unfurled in Sha'Nara. He could kill her easily and no one here would stop him.

"I know you wouldn't do anything to jeopardize our mission."

Tristan scowled, then turned to Cadell, who shrugged. "It's only for a few days," Cadell said.

"That's a few days too many with her." Tristan focused on Sha'Nara and something akin to excitement—fear?—snaked through her veins.

Sha'Nara strengthened her resolve. They would escape. Soon. She couldn't afford to spend any more time on the Scanner ship, let alone in the company of Tristan Galeron. His presence was as potent as a vat of Tanturian ale.

When Cadell indicated that she and Jacy should precede him and Tristan from the room, she knew she had to act quickly. If they were locked inside a cell, they'd have no chance to escape. As they walked down the hallway, she mentally reviewed the path back to the landing bay. If she could get to the ship. . . .

Just ahead, she spied the doors to the lift. There. If she didn't make her move, she might never get another opportunity.

She concentrated on controlling her emotions before her excitement could betray her to Cadell. Fortunately, she'd learn this control in her training. Breathing evenly, she calmed herself as all the while she planned her next actions.

They walked down the hallway, Tristan at the rear, his tension obvious, Cadell in front of him, his posture more relaxed. Sha'Nara eyed the lift. Would they stop there? What would she do if they didn't?

Before she could consider that option, they paused by the lift and Cadell signaled for its arrival. Sha'Nara struggled to maintain her calmness even as her muscles clenched with readiness.

The doors open and Jacy stepped inside. Sha'Nara hesitated only a moment, then pretended to stumble as she moved forward. Cadell reached for her and she whirled around, planting her foot against his chest in a kick that sent him flying to the floor.

Before Tristan could react, she kicked at him, then swiped her foot behind his legs. He fell hard, crashing his head against the wall.

Sha'Nara didn't wait. If he used his powers, they'd never get away. "Close the door, Jacy." She jumped inside as the doors slid shut and ordered the lift to the lower floor.

Her stomach knotted. Phase I of her plan had been successful. But what of Phase II?

Chapter Three

Tristan sat up, rubbing the back of his head, as Cadell climbed to his feet. Sha'Nara'd caught them off guard. Tristan scowled. He should've known to watch her better.

"Couldn't you tell she was going to do that?" Tristan snapped, as irritated with himself as Cadell. Cadell's empathic abilities had saved them more than once. He'd mentioned Sha'Nara's alarm when it surfaced on board the shuttle. Why not this?

"I felt nothing from her," Cadell replied. "She masked her emotions somehow. It must be her PSI Police training."

"Wonderful." That was all Tristan needed. If Sha'Nara could cover her emotions, he'd have no clue as to her state of mind. In dealing with her, he wanted every advantage he could get.

He rose to his feet. "Computer, stop lift five."

"Lift five has already stopped on Deck J," the computer's feminine voice said from the ceiling speaker.

Tristan exchanged glances with Cadell. "The landing bay."

"They're trying to return to the ship," Cadell said.

Tristan signaled the lift to return to their deck. For once, he wished he had the ability to transport from one place to another in milliseconds. If Sha'Nara escaped, all the Scanners' hopes for freedom would be lost.

He mentally reviewed the security procedures he'd set up as he waited impatiently for the lift to arrive. "Computer, seal the doors to landing bay twenty-nine. Implement security procedure voice command only."

"Unable to implement that procedure. Not activated."

"Shibit." Tristan had concerned himself solely with arranging security to keep people out. He'd never thought about having to keep someone on the *Hermitage*. A mistake he wouldn't make again.

The lift doors opened and the men hurried inside. When they reached Deck J, Tristan squeezed through the parting doors, then took off running. He *had* to stop Sha'Nara.

Could he hold the ship in the bay if she'd already powered it up? He doubted even his abilities could hold back that much force. He pushed himself to run faster, his muscles burning as he raced along the corridor. If he couldn't see Sha'Nara or the ship, he couldn't do anything. His psychokinetic powers only worked on what he could physically see.

The entrance to the landing bay was closed, but swished open as Tristan approached. He frowned at it. If he'd had all his security procedures in place, the door would've been locked.

Pausing just inside, his breathing ragged, he searched the interior of the huge, open bay. Only two ships occupied the vast area. The gray walls reflected the murky light back at him. He saw refueling fixtures and places for mechanics to work, but no sign of the escapees.

Waiting, he listened. Sha'Nara and Jacy had to be there somewhere.

Silence.

Unable to stay still any longer, he approached the six-passenger ship, then froze as he heard footsteps echo across the metal interior. He whipped around and spotted the two women climbing into the smaller two-passenger shuttle.

Relieved that they hadn't left yet, he smiled dryly. Clever. The smaller ship would be much faster and more maneuverable than the larger one. Reluctantly he acknowledged Sha'Nara's intelligence. He wouldn't underestimate her again.

Digging deep within his mind, he gathered his psychokinetic power into a force he could use. He only had to concentrate on what he wanted done and it happened, though it had taken him years of practice to learn to measure the force he applied. For now, he wanted enough to hold Sha'Nara, but not harm her.

He seized Sha'Nara's shoulders with this invisible force and pushed her against the ship's hull, holding her in place as he approached. She struggled fiercely, unceasingly. Tristan's head began to pound with the energy required to hold her there.

"Stop struggling," he ordered.

His only response was an increase in her efforts. She paused once and glared at him. "This is impossible," she said.

"Not for me." Tristan approached, needing to replace his mental hold with a real one. Her struggles forced him to concentrate even more, aggravating his growing headache.

"Jacy, get inside. Start the ship. Get out of here," she shouted.

Jacy hesitated in the vehicle's doorway. "I . . . I don't know how."

Tristan rushed to grab Sha'Nara's shoulders. He regretted it immediately. Even knowing who she was . . . what she was, he responded to her close femininity with an all too potent desire that poured through his veins and made him ache in another place besides his head.

Damn her! He didn't want her. He couldn't.

Yet as she stared up at him, defiance and anger sparking in her eyes, her lips parted while she drew shallow breaths, he had to fight back an urge to taste those lips.

"No!" He shouted the word and dropped his hands from her shoulders.

She darted immediately toward the ship's entrance, but he blocked her path. He didn't dare touch her again, but neither could he let her escape.

He drew in a steadying breath. "You're not going anywhere."

"Let us go." Sha'Nara met his gaze defiantly. "We'll deliver whatever message you want to the Director General."

"I'm sure you will." Tristan could imagine what she'd have to say. "I'm also certain you'd have the entire PSI Police directorate out here in no time to destroy us all."

Her gaze flickered for only an instant. "Of course. That's my job."

Tristan curled his hands into fists. She might be foolish, but she had courage. Surely she knew how easily he could destroy her. He wouldn't even have to touch her. In one mental gesture, he could stop her heart.

"I see you have everything under control."

Tristan greeted Cadell's arrival with relief, horrified by the path his thoughts had taken. No matter what powers he possessed, some things were absolutely, morally wrong. To kill in such a way fell in that category.

With Sha'Nara, he'd rather feel his hands around her neck.

He motioned toward Cadell, hoping he wouldn't be required to touch Sha'Nara again to get her moving. "If you would . . ."

Sha'Nara cast him a dark look tinged with regret before heading across the room. She must've realized he'd be on his guard now. This had been her only chance.

A slight tug of sympathy pulled at him. He would've done the same in her position. Had done the same.

Recalling the one time he'd been captured by PSI Police filled him with dread. Fortunately, they hadn't been prepared for his more developed abilities. His escape had been successful.

Of course, Tristan had known what awaited him—the readjustment center—a punishment worse than death. He watched Sha'Nara join Cadell. She would be set free. He grimaced. Obviously she didn't believe that, and neither would he if their roles were reversed.

Turning, he extended his hand to help Jacy from the ship. "Mistress Vadin?"

She bit her lip before placing her small palm in his. "Are . . . are you going to hurt us?"

"No." He put all his sincerity into that one word. Harming this naive young woman would be the same as stomping a newborn kikta to death. His fight was with the PSI Police. *He* didn't target innocents.

Leading her to the doorway, he kept his hold on her hand. Though she was the more beautiful of the two women, her touch had no affect on him. He didn't know whether to be angry or relieved. Why then did he respond like an oversexed teen to Sha'Nara's nearness?

He glared at Sha'Nara as he reached the doorway. It had to be her doing, her fault . . . somehow.

Cadell gave his warmest smile and took Jacy's hand from Tristan. "Shall we try again to reach your quarters?"

"Our prison, you mean," Sha'Nara said coldly.

"Whatever you want to make it." Tristan motioned her forward. No Alliance prison would be as comfortable as the room they had prepared for these women.

He kept every sense alert as they made their way to the upper decks, but Sha'Nara didn't make any other escape attempts. Evidently she realized the futility of that action.

They paused outside their selected room, and Cadell keyed the door open. Jacy entered immediately, her expression surprised. Spinning around, she examined the interior. "This is nice."

"As Father said, you're our guest." Cadell indicated a door situated in one wall. "The lav is there and a food processor over there. We'll bring you some more appealing meals later, but if you're hungry now, you can obtain food sticks."

Tristan studied Sha'Nara's reaction. She didn't give much away, but he caught a quickly suppressed glimmer of amazement as it crossed her face. He smiled slightly. Maybe she would discover Scanners had some good points.

His smile faded. Right. And the Alliance would be overjoyed to grant the Scanners freedom.

"Do you find it satisfactory?" he asked.

"It'll do." She paused, her unease obvious despite her attempt to mask it. "Will we be locked in there for a long time?"

"Probably a day or so." Keeping her locked up was safest.

She moistened her lips, drawing his attention to their lush fullness. "Could we tour the ship or something?" She met his gaze, her body rigid. "I don't like to be kept confined."

"Does anyone?" Tristan replied, his voice quiet. He'd spent his share of time hiding in tight spaces, and relished the massive interior of the *Hermitage*.

Sha'Nara turned away, her jaw tight as if she regretted her words, but not before he saw a glimmer of trepidation in her eyes. "Of course not."

"I'll check with Mael." Tristan spoke before he thought. Something in her posture told him being locked up bothered her.

He scowled. She was PSI Police. He shouldn't care about her comfort.

So, why did he?

"Thank you." Her words sounded reluctant. Obviously she hated to be indebted to her enemy. She ducked inside the room, and Cadell quickly sealed the door.

He leaned against the wall. "Whew. This isn't going as easily as I'd thought."

Tristan raised his eyebrow. He hadn't expected it to be easy at all. "You've keyed the door?"

Cadell nodded. "If it was just Jacy in there, I wouldn't worry about her anymore, but . . ."

"But we have a PSI Police guest who'll try her best to

get them out of here," Tristan finished for his friend. "We need to keep watch. Which shift do you want?"

"I'll start. We can switch when you bring dinner in about four hours."

"When *I* bring dinner?"

"You can't expect our guests to survive on food sticks?" Cadell's eyes gleamed with mischief.

"It wouldn't hurt them."

"I thought their figures were fine the way they were, didn't you?"

Sha'Nara's image immediately popped into Tristan's mind, her gently rounded curves begging for a man's touch. He swallowed, his throat suddenly dry. "I'll bring dinner."

He hurried away followed by Cadell's laughter.

Tristan took advantage of his off shift the next day to visit Mael, locating the older man at work in the large conference room. Stepping inside, he paused briefly, in awe as always of the vastness of space revealed by the clear wall.

The older man greeted him with a terse smile. "Our guests are well?"

"Cadell senses a lot of tension, but that's to be expected."

Mael nodded. "Everything is going according to plan."

"I wouldn't say that. I didn't plan to have a PSI Police officer involved."

"It couldn't be helped. You managed to capture the daughter without an outcry being raised. That was the primary objective."

In Tristan's opinion, dumb luck had played a role. Learning about Jacy's wedding had changed things. "Did you know why Jacy was at her family home?"

"She retired there to prepare for her wedding." Mael glanced at Tristan. "Why?"

"It would've helped if you'd told us she was going to be married." Tristan didn't understand why Mael hadn't passed on that information. Surely the older man knew that every bit of knowledge would've helped.

"I thought I did." Mael shrugged. "It wasn't important. We had only the one opportunity to find her isolated like that. We had to take the chance."

"If I'd known, I would've been better prepared to deal with a bodyguard. We'd expected Jacy to be alone." To be truthful, Tristan wasn't sure being forewarned would've helped. Sha'Nara had been determined to remain with Jacy.

Tristan shook his head. No doubt Mael had just forgotten to mention it. After all, he'd had to consider the ramifications of this kidnapping and plan for their future meeting with the Director-General.

"You succeeded anyway." Mael gave Tristan a rare smile. "I'm proud of you—especially considering your restraint around this PSI Police woman."

Tristan shrugged. As much as he hated everything connected with the PSI Police, he found himself weakening when with Sha'Nara. "She'll be leaving soon." *Not soon enough, though.* Remembering her earlier request, he voiced it reluctantly. "She wants to tour the *Hermitage.*"

"As long as you stay with her, I see no problem with that."

Tristan stared for a moment. "Are you sure? She'll go back and tell them everything about us."

"What's there to tell? As long as you don't show her our non-existent weapons supply, all she'll see is that we live like other people." Mael placed his hand on Tristan's shoulder. "Don't worry. She's not a threat to us."

How could she not be a threat? Her entire mission in life was to destroy Scanners. Evidently, Mael didn't realize how dangerous she was. "But—"

"I plan to contact the Director-General later. Why don't you take our guests on that tour? Just be careful what you show them. I'll notify you when I'm ready for them." Mael dropped his hand and returned to his view screen.

Though unsatisfied with this decision, Tristan nodded and left. As he made his way to where Cadell stood guard, Tristan puzzled over Mael's lack of concern about these women. Sha'Nara Calles was a threat. She was far too dedicated an officer and too intelligent to be allowed to roam the ship . . . even blindfolded.

Cadell raised his eyebrows in surprise as Tristan approached. "You still have a couple more hours before your shift." Cadell grinned suddenly. "Or can't you bear to be away?"

Tristan aimed a dry look at his friend. "Mael said we could show our guests around the ship if they still want to go."

"Great." Cadell's expression brightened. "I wouldn't mind showing Jacy some back corners."

"She's the Director-General's daughter," Tristan said pointedly. When Cadell appeared unfazed, Tristan sighed. "She's supposed to get married, you know."

"She's a sweet, beautiful young woman." Good humor danced in Cadell's eyes. "What's the harm in enjoying her company? Oh, I know. That leaves you with the other one."

"I don't trust Sha'Nara." Tristan ignored his friend's attempt to bait him. "How do we know this tour won't lead to another attempt to escape? Her fear of being confined could be a lie."

The amusement left Cadell's face. "Maybe, but I know the tension level in there is very high—much higher than I'd expect at this point in time."

"She can mask her emotions."

"Mask them, but not change them. It's impossible for her to transmit something she's not feeling."

Tristan hesitated. The wise thing would be to leave the women in the room until time for Mael's call to the Director-General. So what if she didn't like being locked up. She wasn't being mistreated.

But the brief glimpse of trepidation Tristan had seen in Sha'Nara's eyes tugged at him. A short tour couldn't hurt. As long as he remained alert, she'd have no chance to escape. He'd ensure she saw nothing of importance.

He gave in reluctantly. "Open the door and scan her for me. If the fear is real, we'll take a walk around B and C decks." As the door slid open, he searched the room for Sha'Nara.

He didn't need Cadell's terse nod to confirm what he could see for himself. Sha'Nara stood in the center of the room, her arms wrapped around her torso, her face pale and beaded with moisture, her eyes wild. The pulse point in her throat throbbed erratically.

Tristan stilled his first instinct to go to her and drag her into the hallway. Though she looked like she needed more oxygen, the air in the room and hallway was the same. He remained frozen in the doorway as she slowly looked at him.

Their gazes met, and he saw the panic in hers before she blinked and stiffened with defiance. Good. She hadn't given up. The thought was irrational, but he didn't want her to lose her fighting nature.

"Did you want something?" She spoke as if forming the words took effort.

Jacy approached Tristan, her face concerned. "I think Sha'Nara's sick. She won't sleep or eat."

Tristan nodded to acknowledge Jacy's words, but kept his gaze on Sha'Nara. "We have time for that tour . . . if you like."

Apprehension mingled with gratitude as Sha'Nara came closer. "That would be nice."

Tristan stepped out of the room and watched as she followed him into the hallway. She gulped the air, and his stomach twisted into a tight knot. Her fear was very real. That she'd managed to keep from screaming for release only attested to her courage.

Leaving Cadell to tend to Jacy, Tristan extended his arm down the corridor. "I thought we'd start with the cafeteria. You might want to have a meal there."

Sha'Nara gave him a wan smile—the first he'd seen from her—and it impacted against his chest like a laser beam. Fortunately she started walking, and didn't notice how he fought to drag in a new breath. With an effort he made his way to her side, grimacing as he heard Cadell chuckle behind him.

As much as Tristan trusted Cadell and his empathic

powers, there were times when his friend was just too damned observant. No doubt Tristan would hear about this later.

They reached the large cafeteria, and Jacy gave a cry of awe as they entered. Designed to hold two hundred people, the room contained several hovertables and chairs. Many of the chairs were filled with Scanners eating.

Tristan felt their curious gazes as he led Sha'Nara to a table. Though the cafeteria menu offered limited fare, at least it presented alternatives to the inexpensive but tasteless food sticks. "Can you eat something?" he asked. Color had returned to Sha'Nara's cheeks, but dark circles remained under her eyes.

She hesitated, her gaze wary. "A bowl of soup, please."

Seating her with Cadell and Jacy, he reached out with his mind to select a soup from the automat and bring it to the table. As an afterthought, he added a spoon, then looked up to find Sha'Nara frowning, anger flaring in her eyes.

"What?" What had he done? "The soup is safe."

Her expression tightened. "You just have to flaunt your powers, don't you?"

"Flaunt my . . ." He trailed off, realizing what he'd done. He hadn't used his kinesis purposely—more because he didn't want to leave her. Pride swelled within him and he straightened. "It's what I am."

"It's *unnatural*."

The word punched him in the gut. "My brain is more developed. Everyone has the potential for these powers, but usually that part of the brain remains dormant." He leaned closer. "Even you."

She recoiled as if he'd struck her. "I'm nothing like you."

"That's obvious." He leaned back in a slouch and glowered at Sha'Nara. Evidently she felt much better.

Cadell cleared his throat and smiled at Jacy. "Can I get you something to eat?"

Tristan shook his head. Leave it to Cadell to try and to lighten the moment.

"I'm fine." Jacy paused, her gaze searching his face. "What . . . what powers do you have?"

"I'm empathic."

"Empathic?" Jacy's eyes widened, her expression horrified. "You can read minds?"

Resisting the urge to roll his eyes, Tristan sighed. Why did people always assume that Scanners could read minds?

Cadell laughed. "No. I sense people's emotions, which sometimes gives me a clue as to what they're thinking."

"Then you know what I'm feeling?" When he nodded, Jacy drew back. "I don't like that. Turn it off."

"I wish I could." He smiled wryly. "As a child I felt constantly bombarded by everyone's emotions. I've since learned to filter them, but they're always there."

Tristan exchanged glances with his friend. Though he'd missed Cadell's childhood, they'd gone through enough together for Tristan to know Cadell underexaggerated what he suffered. Even now, Cadell couldn't visit the medical wards. The intense emotional suffering and pain were too much for him to handle.

Unable to completely comprehend carrying anyone's emotional baggage, Tristan appreciated his friend's lighthearted manner. They all had their methods of dealing with reality. Cadell had chosen to take life lightly, whereas Tristan saw it as a battle to be won.

"And what powers does your father have?" Sha'Nara asked Cadell suddenly. Her expression was casual . . . too casual.

Tristan tensed. Sha'Nara didn't need to know that information. Even among Scanners, Mael was unique.

"He's . . . his abilities are different." Cadell cut his words short, then gazed around the room. "I'm sensing some hostility other than at this table." He focused on Sha'Nara. "If you don't intend to eat your soup, I think we should leave."

Acknowledging Cadell's observations, Tristan stood. The curious gazes had become filled with anger and hatred. Though Sha'Nara's dress uniform wasn't obviously PSI Police, word of her position had probably made its way through the ship by now. He should never have brought her among the others.

"Let's go." Tristan ushered them from the room and a good distance down the corridor before he spoke again. "I think we'll avoid people if possible."

"Good idea." Cadell touched Jacy's elbow. "Would you like to see our hydroponic gardens? They're fantastic."

"I'd like that." She returned his smile with no sign of her earlier hesitation. "What do you grow?"

"Fruits and vegetables, of course, but many types of plants and flowers, too." He darted a glance at Tristan. "It's the only way we have to duplicate living on a planet."

Tristan's insides clenched. He usually avoided the hydroponics. His terrarium was big enough to hold his dreams. To walk through the massive gardens made him want too much.

"I'd rather not go there," Sha'Nara said, verbalizing his thoughts.

"As you wish." Cadell shrugged. "I'll take Jacy and we'll meet up later."

"No, wait."

Cadell guided Jacy into a nearby lift before Sha'Nara could utter more than a couple of words. She hurried after them, but the doors shut in her face.

She whirled on Tristan. "I need to stay with her."

"Cadell won't harm her."

"That's not what I'm afraid of."

"Me either." When Sha'Nara gaped at him in surprise, Tristan held back a grin. Cadell could take care of himself. Tristan had the bigger problem on his hands. "Where would you like to go?"

"The armory, your guidance center, your engineering section."

"Good try."

"Your ship repair?"

Tristan only stared at her.

"Your medical wards?"

He nodded. She'd see nothing useful there except some injured Scanners who'd recently arrived at the *Hermitage*. It would do her good to see the results of PSI Police persecution.

After taking the lift to the lower deck, Tristan steered Sha'Nara toward the vast wing that held the medical wards. He refrained from touching her. Her presence filled the corridor, enticing him, as her vague liliana scent teased his senses. He struggled to control his response. Perhaps her scent had been created to achieve this type of reaction. If so, it worked.

He released a sigh of relief upon spotting the entrance. "The medical ward starts—"

"So this is the PSI Police bitch." Bran Mastis materialized in front of them, a deadly sneer on his face.

Without thinking, Tristan placed himself between Bran and Sha'Nara. Bran's anger operated on even a shorter fuse than Tristan's and rarely followed any logic. Tristan was half convinced each of Bran's teleportive hops damaged parts of the man's brain. No wonder he had no real job on the ship.

"This is a guest, Bran," he said in a warning tone.

"A PSI Police officer?" Bran moved closer. "I don't think so."

Tristan kept Sha'Nara behind him as he shifted position so that he faced Bran. "Leave her alone."

"You surprise me, Tristan." Bran circled them, his eyes glittering dangerously. "Haven't you always believed the only good PSI officer is a dead one?"

Tristan frowned as Sha'Nara gasped quietly. He did believe that, but Sha'Nara was different. As much as he hated to admit it, he saw her as a person—one he couldn't casually destroy. "She's under my protection." He didn't hide the threat in his voice. Bran knew the extent of Tristan's powers.

"You'd protect her? After what they did to your parents?" Bran suddenly blinked out of sight, then reappeared behind Sha'Nara, a dagger in his hand.

Before Bran could plunge the weapon into her back,

Tristan mentally seized the man's wrist, tightening his grip until the dagger clattered to the floor. At the noise, Sha'Nara whirled around, then backed up until she collided with Tristan.

He placed his hand on her shoulder in a reassuring gesture as he gathered his strength and mentally threw Bran against the wall. The man slid to the floor. He glared up at Tristan and Sha'Nara, but didn't try to stand.

"I meant what I said. Get out of here, Bran."

The younger man staggered to his feet, one hand held against his shoulder. "There's no place here for PSI Police," he said, each word bitter. "And no place for those who protect them."

Before Tristan could respond, Bran vanished.

Tristan waited, searching the vast empty corridors, but they remained empty. Evidently Bran had learned his lesson . . . this time. Something had to be done about him or Sha'Nara would never live to leave the *Hermitage*. Tristan made a mental note to talk to Mael about the teleporter.

Tristan eased his guard, but couldn't erase the tension invading his body—a tension that had nothing to do with Bran and everything to do with Sha'Nara.

Warmth traveled up Tristan's arm from Sha'Nara's shoulder, creating a dizzy sensation in his head, but he didn't release her. He couldn't. The softness of her body felt right where it pressed against his.

Desire pounded in his loins. Need swelled, so powerful he wanted to drag Sha'Nara into a nearby room and bury himself in her. His body shook. Fardpissle, what was wrong with him?

With an effort, he turned her around to face him. "Are you all right?" His words emerged rougher than he'd intended.

Her cheeks flushed as she nodded. "Thank you. I didn't expect you to act as my protector." She placed her hand on his chest, and he felt her palm burn its imprint into his skin through the material of his form-fitting black suit.

A lump blocked his throat, and he swallowed hard. Wisps of hair had escaped her braid, softening her appearance. Without forethought, Tristan lifted his hand to smooth them back, then instantly regretted it.

He wanted to keep touching her.

She met his gaze as he lightly ran one finger along the curve of her cheek, then paused to trace the outline of her lips. He dropped his gaze to her mouth. For a moment, he felt certain she wouldn't protest if he claimed her lips. He ached to kiss her.

He ached to take her. He ached as something new, indefinable exploded in his chest, frightening him more than facing an entire squadron of PSI officers. In a panic, he stepped back.

The moment vanished.

She blinked, looking as stunned as he felt, before her guard returned. He could see her straighten her shoulders before she spoke. "What did he mean about your parents?"

His parents. Old anger replaced his desire. He studied her face, wanting to watch her reaction. "PSI Police stormed where we stayed when I was a boy. My mother helped me escape and told me to run, so I did. I don't know if she intended to follow or not, but she never appeared." His bitterness coiled into a hard ball in his gut. "I never saw either of my parents again."

Sha'Nara didn't flinch, but sympathy appeared in her gaze. "How old were you?"

"Twelve."

"You should've stayed with your parents. After readjustment, you would've been allowed to live together."

Tristan gave a short laugh. After readjustment, he wouldn't have cared who he lived with. "Readjustment is not an option."

She opened her mouth, no doubt to pursue the issue, but Mael's voice blaring from a comm in the ceiling cut her off.

"Tristan, Cadell, I need you and our guests in the control room as soon as possible. I'm putting through the call to the Director-General."

Chapter Four

Sha'Nara's heart thudded against her ribs as she entered the bridge of the massive battleship. If Mael intended to contact Remy Vadin, she had to find a way to let the Director-General know their location. But how?

Staring out the enormous view screen dominating the deck, she tried to place the stars, but failed. Only one constellation looked familiar, and she could be mistaken at that. These Scanners had obviously found an uncharted part of space to hide in.

She darted a glance at Tristan beside her, and acknowledged her pounding pulse wasn't entirely due to her apprehension about this communication. For one crazy instant, she'd thought he intended to kiss her. Worse, she'd wanted him to.

She drew in a deep breath. How could she even consider such an action? These mutants were the enemy. They'd kidnapped her and Jacy. They planned to take over the Alliance.

Jacy and Cadell stood beside Mael. Jacy looked different. With a start, Sha'Nara realized the young woman now wore a plain blue jumpsuit.

"Where's your dress?" she asked.

Jacy blushed. "I felt uncomfortable wearing it. I mean, it was my wedding dress. Cadell located this for me. It fits perfectly."

"We produce our own clothing here." Cadell's gaze softened as it lingered on Jacy. "It was a simple matter."

"Good, you're all here." Mael nodded toward a woman sitting before a wide console. "Complete the connection."

Sha'Nara's muscles tightened. She had to do something. Searching the room, she noticed familiar gauges on one of the panels—the positioning coordinates.

While all eyes focused on the vidcom screen as it crackled with static, she slowly maneuvered within reading distance of the panel. The coordinates were unfamiliar, but she committed them to memory. Now she knew their position.

But how to pass on that information?

Mael would cut her off if she tried to do so openly. Rejoining the group, Sha'Nara planned her words carefully. The PSI Police had certain code phrases. The trick was combining those with the coordinate information in apparently innocuous statements.

The screen erupted into the visage of the comm room receptionist, who met Mael's gaze blandly. "Alliance Central. How I may direct your communication?"

"Mael Ner." He held himself erect, his posture proclaiming his importance. "I want to speak to the Director-General."

Sha'Nara grimaced. Mael would never get through to him that way. The receptionist apparently agreed. She frowned at Mael. "I'm afraid all calls must be routed through—"

"This concerns his daughter."

The receptionist paled. Obviously news of Jacy's disappearance had spread. The receptionist bent toward her console, and the screen's picture changed to that of Remy Vadin.

Worry showed in the etched lines of his face and dark circles beneath his eyes, but anger shone in his gaze. "Who are you?" he demanded. "Where's my daughter?"

"She's here and safe."

Sha'Nara realized Mael must have the vidcom configured to show only one individual at a time, as she and Jacy stood only a short distance from the man. Without thinking, she stepped forward, but Tristan touched her shoulder, freezing her in place.

She glared at him, but his dark countenance didn't waver. "Remy will want to see us," she said.

"That is for Mael to decide."

Aware of Tristan's powers, Sha'Nara knew she had no chance to burst into the viewer area. Releasing an angry sigh, she crossed her arms and waited.

Remy's wrath echoed hers. "Who are you?" he demanded again, his voice cold.

"Mael Ner." Mael paused before adding the final blow. "I represent the organized Scanners."

"Scanners!" The Director-General visibly paled, his face revealing his inner struggle to control his emotions. He leaned closer to his viewer. "What do you want?"

"A chance to meet, to talk, nothing more."

Remy's gaze narrowed with suspicion. Sha'Nara nodded to herself in satisfaction. Good. Despite his worry, he was acting cautiously. He had every right to be suspicious. No sane person would trust these mutants.

"What else?" Remy asked.

"All we want is a chance to plead our case, to convince you we are not the threat you have made us out to be." Mael sounded so sincere Sha'Nara was half-tempted to believe him.

But she knew better.

"You kidnap my daughter and say you're not a threat? I find that hard to believe."

"Your daughter is our guest. She'll be returned unharmed when we meet. You must come alone."

"And if I don't meet with you?"

Mael stiffened and appeared to grow taller. "Then she

will become our *permanent* guest." A shiver of apprehension traced Sha'Nara's spine.

Remy swallowed, but didn't look away. "I want to see her, talk to her."

"As you wish." Mael stepped from the view area and touched Jacy's shoulder. He stared at her silently, then urged her forward. "Please assure your father that you're well."

She nodded and ran into position. "Daddy!"

"Jacy!" Remy lifted his hand toward the screen as if he might touch her. "Are you all right?" Sha'Nara watched as he tried to temper his concern.

"I'm fine, Daddy. Everyone here has been wonderful to me." She smiled radiantly. "I'm having an adventure."

"An adventure, eh?" The Director-General attempted to smile, but failed. "I've been worried about you."

Jacy sobered. "I know." She looked down at her feet, then back at her father. "Was Devon upset?"

"Of course. He expected a marriage, not this."

She bit her lip. "Daddy, I . . . I don't think I want to marry him after all."

Remy looked genuinely surprised. Obviously Sha'Nara had been the only one to hear Jacy's doubts. "We'll discuss that later . . . when you're home."

"Yes." The word emerged as a whisper.

Mael guided Jacy from the viewer area and took her place. "As you can see, she is being well cared for."

"What about her escort?" Remy sounded apprehensive, and Sha'Nara guessed he didn't want to give away her position.

"You mean the PSI Police officer?" Mael's voice grew cold. "She is our guest as well."

"Can I speak with her?"

"Is that necessary?"

The Director-General's face tightened. "As she is a PSI Police officer, I believe it's very necessary."

Mael turned toward Sha'Nara, and she struggled to calm her nervousness. She couldn't have Cadell give away her plan to pass information to Remy.

Placing his hand on her shoulder, Mael stared at her with the same intensity he'd given Jacy. Sha'Nara couldn't look away. His dark, bottomless depths drew her in as if peeling away layers to look at her soul. He frowned, and a sudden wave of dizziness washed over her.

She brought her hand to her head, almost stumbling as he released her. "It's your turn," Mael said.

Staggering into position, she looked at Remy. "Sir."

"Are you all right?"

She opened her mouth to utter her well crafted phrases, but they stuck in her throat. Instead new words emerged. "I'm fine. Everyone has been kind to us."

Stunned, she touched her throat, her eyes wide.

"And all is well?"

A code phrase. He wanted to know what she could tell him. Again, she tried to use her words. Again, false platitudes sounded. "Of course. I suggest you meet with these people and listen to what they have to say."

Remy blinked. "You believe them?"

She couldn't even shake her head. "What they say has merit." Frustration brought tears to her eyes. She didn't believe that, didn't want to say it. Unwilling to lie any more, she turned to face Mael. "Wha—?"

Before she could say more, he yanked her from the viewing area. She glared up at him, curling her hands into fists. "What did you do to me?" Her own words emerged hoarsely as if torn from her throat.

He said nothing, dismissing her as if she didn't exist, and resumed the prominent position. Sha'Nara glanced at Tristan to find him looking stunned, almost alarmed. Before she could question him, Mael spoke. "They are both safe. Will you meet with us?"

"I can't make that decision without talking to the council."

"Very well." Mael concluded the conversation with a wave of his hand and the screen went dark, eliminating Remy's face even as he opened his mouth to protest.

Mael turned to face them. "I think we'll wait several

days this time." He didn't look pleased. "Escort our guests back to their quarters."

Cadell stared at his father, his expression confused, before he nodded and took Jacy's elbow. Tristan approached Mael. "You go ahead. I'll catch up," he said to Cadell.

Coldness filled Sha'Nara's veins as she watched Tristan and Mael. What were they plotting now? Anger mingled with her terror as she comprehended the extent of Mael's power.

He'd possessed her mind.

Somehow he'd made his words come out of her mouth. How was that possible? No other Scanner had demonstrated anything even remotely resembling that ability.

Cadell nudged her forward. She joined him and Jacy with reluctance. Though she walked through the vast corridors, her mind remained fixed on what had just happened.

No wonder Mael presented such a powerful image. With his mutant ability, he could control anyone . . . everyone. Doubts blossomed. What were her real thoughts and what were his? Had her attraction to Tristan been planted?

Her dream!

With certainty, she knew Mael had sent the recurring dream of Tristan. Where else could it have come from? Probably to make her more pliable, ready to fall into Tristan's arms, and less likely to create trouble during this diabolical plan of theirs.

She pressed her lips together firmly. Obviously they didn't know her.

At the room she shared with Jacy, she hesitated, her old fears rising. She knew they wouldn't keep her locked up forever, but her rational mind couldn't overcome her emotional response. Just standing in the doorway made her pulse rate increase and a cold sweat bathe her body.

Jacy entered the room, then looked back at Sha'Nara. "Are you going to be all right?" the girl asked.

Pressing her lips together, Sha'Nara inhaled slowly, then turned to face Cadell. He appeared the more easygoing of her captors. Could she reason with him? "I know you've been posting a guard. I've heard someone out here."

He nodded, but said nothing, watching her.

"Would you be willing to leave the door unkeyed? You'll still have your guard to keep Jacy and me from escaping."

"I'd like to think you've given up any thoughts of escape."

Sha'Nara wouldn't . . . couldn't give him that assurance. "Will you do it?"

For several long moments, Cadell remained silent. Was he scanning her emotions? Sha'Nara wished she could hide her unreasonable fear or do away with it altogether. Her previous night in this room had been torture.

"Very well."

Relief eased her tense muscles. She smiled at Cadell with honest warmth. "Thank you."

"However, there will be a guard."

"I know." Sha'Nara entered the room and found that she didn't jump when the door sealed behind her. Just knowing it would open if she needed it to was enough. "Though I can't think why I should trust the word of a Scanner," she muttered.

Jacy's look held reproach. "Cadell wouldn't lie."

"He's a *Scanner*, Jacy." Sha'Nara couldn't put enough emphasis on that vile word. She didn't need this girl to align herself with one of the enemy. They had enough problems.

Instead of Jacy reacting with a stubborn avowal of Cadell's innocence as Sha'Nara expected, the young woman met Sha'Nara's gaze, her expression defiant. "He's a person."

She turned away to prepare for sleep, but Sha'Nara stood frozen. A person. With horror, she realized she had begun to see Cadell and Tristan as separate individuals. She couldn't allow that. They were part of the whole—Scanners.

And all Scanners were evil.

Tristan waited for Sha'Nara to leave before he confronted Mael. When he'd first seen her lift her hand to her head, Tristan had wondered. When she'd returned from the viewer, lost and confused, he'd known.

"You implanted her," he said, unable to hide his anger.

Mael didn't try to deny it. "I had to."

As far as Tristan knew, Mael was the only Scanner with the ability to read minds and implant thoughts. Implanting was forbidden. It fell into the same moral category as Tristan using his power to crush a man's heart. Implanting was . . . wrong.

"But why?" As Tristan argued with his mentor, he tried to rationalize Mael's actions and failed. Sha'Nara was their prisoner, a PSI Police officer, but her frightened expression had touched him. Tristan couldn't imagine how it would feel to find foreign words emerging from his mouth.

"When I scanned her mind, I discovered she planned to convey our position via coded sentences. I couldn't allow that." Mael spoke calmly, cooling Tristan's anger.

Tristan could believe that of Sha'Nara. Glancing at the nearby locator panel, he grimaced. And he knew where she'd discovered their position, too.

"Still, to implant her." The idea left an unpleasant taste in Tristan's mouth. "Couldn't you have refused to let her talk?"

"Not and satisfy the Director-General. Once he realized we knew she was PSI Police, he had to talk to her. I'm sure he expected that we'd killed her."

As Tristan had originally wanted to do. He grimaced, glad that Cadell has persuaded him otherwise. By sparing Sha'Nara, they'd proven they could be trusted. But implanting words in her mouth had probably doubled her hatred of them. "I trust you won't be doing this again?" he asked, even as he wondered why her hatred should bother him.

"There should be no reason to." Mael gave him a fatherly smile. "I dislike it as much as you, Tristan. Believe me. It was necessary." He glanced at a nearby chronometer. "Weren't you taking the first shift at guard?"

Tristan nodded and sprinted toward Sha'Nara's room. Though he didn't like what Mael had done, he saw the reason for it. But he doubted Sha'Nara would understand.

Sha'Nara sat up in the darkened room, her pulse racing. Gasping for breath, she tried to ease the pulsing ache centered between her thighs. That dream.

Even as she slept, a part of her mind knew Mael had to be causing it, but that didn't stop her dream self from responding to Tristan's caresses. Now her body yearned for, wanted what she shouldn't have.

She slid quietly from the bed. She had to escape before she completely lost track of reality. Everyone would be lax while they waited to contact Remy again. She tugged on her uniform and sealed it closed before her gaze found the door. Was it unlocked as Cadell promised? And who stood guard outside?

Crossing to the door, she keyed it open, her heart lodged in her throat. Cadell pushed away from the wall to look at her, blinking sleep from his eyes. "What's wrong?"

She thought quickly. "Can you get me some water, please?"

"Doesn't the dispenser work?"

"No." Her heart still beat wildly from her dream. "I . . . I had a bad dream. All I want is a drink." She tried to look sleepy, no threat to anyone. Would he believe her?

"Let me look at it." Smothering a yawn, Cadell entered the room.

Sha'Nara wasted no time and delivered a precise blow to the back of his neck. He barely had time to gasp before he slid to the floor. After verifying that he was unconscious, she went to shake Jacy awake.

"Jacy, come on. We're getting out of here."

"What?" Jacy sat up slowly and stared at Sha'Nara.

"We're escaping. Get dressed." Sha'Nara tried to keep her voice a whisper, but it rose in volume as the urgency of their situation struck her. She had no idea when a new guard would take over. They had to hurry.

"We don't need to escape." Jacy rubbed at her eyes. "They're not going to hurt us."

Sha'Nara expelled an exasperated breath and threw back Jacy's covers. She didn't have time to argue. "Come on."

"You go ahead." Jacy smiled. "This is my first adventure and I want to enjoy it."

"Enjoy it?" Sha'Nara nearly shouted the words, then caught herself. "They'll probably kill us."

Shaking her head, Jacy stood up. "Cadell wouldn't hurt me." She stopped abruptly at seeing his figure on the floor, and knelt down beside him. "What did you do?"

"He's just unconscious for a while." Sha'Nara wanted to throttle the young woman. "We have to get out of here."

Jacy ignored her and stroked Cadell's hair away from his face. "Cadell?"

"Arrgh." Sha'Nara whirled around and fled the room. Leave it to her to be saddled with someone too dense to know she was in danger. What now? She couldn't leave Jacy behind. The *Hermitage* would merely change position and they'd never find her.

But she could notify the Alliance of their present location.

She made her way to the control deck with little problem, and found it almost deserted. One young man sat before the main console, his head bowed, obviously asleep. Sha'Nara used one sharp blow to render him unconscious.

Standing before the communications panel, she studied the myriad of controls. The comm systems she'd used had been on a lesser scale, but that didn't mean she couldn't figure this one out. She cast an anxious glance over her shoulder, unable to shake the compelling urge to hurry.

How much time did she have?

Sha'Nara ran from Tristan, outdistancing him even as he implored her to stop, to stay with him. He tried to grab her, but failed. She slipped away into the darkness.

An immediate sense of loss permeated his soul. She was gone.

"No." Tristan awakened abruptly, startled by his own voice, and glanced at the chronometer. He still had another hour before his shift started.

The memory of his dream lingered and he frowned. Why should he care if Sha'Nara left? She meant nothing to him.

He sat up. He'd reluctantly agreed with Cadell's decision to leave the door unkeyed, knowing his friend provided a reliable guard. Yet Tristan couldn't escape the feeling of losing something . . . someone important to him.

A sense of urgency pulled at him. Since he was awake, he might as well check on Cadell and relieve him early. He yanked on his suit and hurried to the room.

Even in the dimmed nighttime lighting of the corridor, Tristan noticed the door open while he was still some distance away. A fist squeezed his heart as he ran to the entrance.

One glance told him what he needed to know. Jacy sat on the floor, cradling Cadell's head in her lap. She murmured soft, encouraging words that reassured Tristan his friend still lived. As he expected, Sha'Nara was gone.

He dashed instantly for the lift, intending to catch her before she reached the landing bays. Entering the lift, he paused, the words for Deck J on his lips.

Jacy was still in the room.

Already he knew Sha'Nara would never leave the young woman behind. She wasn't stealing a ship. Then

70

where was she? What would she do that didn't involve Jacy? She'd tried to send a message earlier and Mael had stopped her. Would she try again?

"Lift, Deck A."

He knew she was there—knew it before he saw her silhouetted against the white static of the view screen. She hadn't established a link yet . . . or was he too late?

As he approached, the screen flashed to life, revealing an Alliance operator. Panic drove him to close the distance between them.

Sha'Nara didn't wait for a greeting. "Sha'Nara Calles," she snapped. "Take down these coordinates."

Tristan reached out with his mind and flicked the switch, breaking the link and bringing Sha'Nara around in alarm.

"No!" Anguish filled her cry.

She snatched a nearby reader and threw it at him, but he deflected it easily. Her rage was obvious as she searched for more weapons. He tried to catch her arm, but she swung at him with her arms and legs until he was forced to wrap his arms around her and pin her between his body and the wall.

His physical reaction was immediate, and her squirming to free herself didn't help. "Stop it," he ordered.

She continued to fight and he pressed closer, leaving her in no doubt of her effect on him. She froze. Frustration and anger vied for control in her gaze. "Let me go."

"I don't think so." Her soft curves fit his hard angles perfectly, the juncture of her thighs cupping his swollen member, her breasts flattened against his chest. Desire flamed through his blood.

Lifting one hand, he cradled her face and ran his thumb over her cheek and mouth. Her lips trembled and a new emotion—passion?—flared to life in her eyes. He bent his head closer, admonishing himself as he did.

He knew what she was. He shouldn't want her. But he did. He wanted her with a need that threatened to drive him insane. He brought his lips within a breath of hers, waiting for her protest—a protest that never came.

Her rapid pulse throbbed beneath his fingers where they curved around her neck. Her hands on his shoulders no longer tried to push him away, but instead pulled him nearer as if she had no more control over the situation than he.

For a brief instant, his lips brushed hers.

"I see you found her."

The dry humor in Cadell's voice made Tristan step back immediately. His friend and Jacy stood in the entrance to the control deck. Despite the dimmed lighting, Tristan could see Cadell's wide grin.

Embarrassment at being caught and anger at being interrupted sent heat up Tristan's neck. He glanced at Sha'Nara to find her watching him closely, her breathing not quite even and her eyes staring. What was he to do with her?

He reached out to snag her wrist within his long fingers. "You're coming with me."

Her muscles tightened. "I'm not—"

Tristan ignored her protest and pulled her with him, pausing briefly by Cadell. "From now on, you watch over that one and I'll be responsible for this one. Maybe that will cut down these escape attempts."

Cadell blinked, then flashed a wicked smile. "Whatever you say."

"Good." Tristan started to leave, then stopped again, needing to wipe the smile off Cadell's face. "You know, you deserved what you got for agreeing to unkey the door."

"I know." His friend remained cheerful. "That'll teach me to be an obliging host." He waggled his eyebrows at Sha'Nara. "Now you're in for it."

His words only stirred Sha'Nara to try again to pull away. With an angry exclamation, Tristan picked her up, throwing her over his shoulder, so that her torso fell along his back. Aiming one last dark glare at Cadell, Tristan hurried down the corridor to his quarters.

He used his mental powers to open his door, then waited for it to seal behind him before he set Sha'Nara on her feet. She immediately backed away as far as his limited space would allow.

"I want to return to Jacy." She lifted her chin defiantly.

"What you want doesn't matter anymore," he replied, biting off each word. He'd known this woman would be trouble from the beginning, and thus far she'd proved him right. Her attempt tonight had almost achieved success. They couldn't afford that.

But what angered him most was his irrational response to her nearness. He didn't need it, didn't want it, yet when he looked at her, hot need burned through his loins.

He dropped his gaze and concentrated on removing his boots. "You obviously can't be trusted. In order for me to keep an eye on you, you'll have to stay here with me."

"In your quarters?" Her voice rose.

"Yes."

A loud crash followed, and he jerked his head up to see her pick up an Alderian statue off the nearby ledge and examine it before she smashed it onto the floor beside its mate. "I won't stay here with you," she shouted.

She next seized his reader, studied it, and tossed it, apparently relishing the sound of breakage. "I know what you have in mind."

Finishing with the ledge, she started in on his collection of books, glancing at each one, then hurling it at him with fierce rage. "I won't let you use me."

He dodged the books and used his powers to ease them to the floor. Old-fashioned bound books were a scarcity in today's world. "I have no intention of using you." He'd never forced a woman in his life and didn't intend to start with this one, no matter how great her influence over him.

"And why should I believe that?" She continued to toss whatever she could reach. "I . . . I felt . . . that." She gestured toward his groin.

73

"That was a natural reaction to being in close proximity to a woman," Tristan said. "It had nothing to do with you personally." Now that, he admitted to himself, *felt* like a lie.

"You can't make me stay here." Sha'Nara threw his pillow next as she made her way along the edge of the room.

Tristan grinned. "But I can."

As she lifted his terrarium and examined it, everything inside him froze. For a moment, he couldn't breath, couldn't speak. Fear stabbed his soul. At last, he forced harsh, cold words from his throat. "Don't do it."

Chapter Five

Sha'Nara froze. The panic in Tristan's voice stopped her in place. She weighed the terrarium in her hands, stroking the glass, as she considered his words. She'd thought nothing affected this man's emotions, yet for the first time, he appeared strangely vulnerable. Her rage dissipated as her curiosity grew.

She glanced at the terrarium. The clear globe wasn't very large, and held only dark soil and a collection of plants. What made this so special to him?

Tightening her grip, she met his gaze. "Why?"

The rigidity of his muscles sent a frisson of fear along her spine. She was definitely courting trouble, but she had to know what could cause a dent in Tristan's hardened shell.

"It's mine. Put it down."

She shook her head. "Not until I know why this matters to you."

He tugged at the globe with his kinesis, but she'd expected that and refused to relinquish her hold. "Sha'Nara . . ." His voice held a warning note.

"Why should you care about this? It's only a pile of dirt."

"But it's my dirt." He approached slowly. "It may be the only land I'll ever have to call my own."

Land? Sha'Nara looked the terrarium again, but saw nothing out of the ordinary. "You call this land?"

"Yes." He moved quickly, catching her unaware as he placed his hands over hers. "Set it down."

She let him guide the terrarium to a nearby table, too aware of the warmth traveling up her arms from his touch. Her dreams had apparently achieved Mael's intended result, she realized, as she found herself unable to shed her attraction to this man.

Once the globe sat in its rightful place, he pulled her hands free and held them in his as he faced her. "Never touch that again." His dark eyes bored into her.

Sensual heat radiated from his body, reminding Sha'Nara of her earlier fear that he'd planned to ravish her.

She didn't believe that now. At this moment, he appeared more . . . human. She didn't look away or try to extract her hands. "I don't understand," she said quietly.

"No, you wouldn't." He released his grip and turned away, leaving Sha'Nara feeling oddly bereft.

Without thinking, she followed him across the room and tugged on his arm so that he looked at her again. "Then help me to understand."

He sighed and ran his hand through his hair. The simple gesture touched Sha'Nara's heart. Whatever he planned to say, he obviously didn't find it easy.

"I've spent my entire life on the run." He smiled dryly. "Trying to stay one step ahead of the PSI Police. I've never had a place to call home."

Though Sha'Nara knew her companions had only done their jobs, a niggle of guilt raised its head. She nodded at him to continue.

"What I've always wanted is to stay in one place, to put down roots, to work with the soil." He gave a short laugh. "Which will never happen as long as we're hunted."

He motioned toward the terrarium. "That represents the land I want to have someday." He paused. "Or it may be the only land I'll ever have." He looked at Sha'Nara as if daring her to speak. "It depends on whether the Alliance accepts our proposal."

"And what is your proposal?" For the first time, Sha'Nara wanted to hear what the Scanners planned to tell Remy Vadin.

"If the Alliance agrees to grant us freedom from persecution and call off the PSI Police, we'll promise to stay out of political affairs or any other power struggle."

Despite the nonsense of his words, Tristan's passionate sincerity nearly convinced Sha'Nara to believe him. Yet everything she'd been taught said Scanners only wanted power and control. How could she believe him?

Tristan must've seen her doubt, for he gripped her shoulders. "All we want is somewhere we can live, undisturbed, in peace. I want to be able to travel safely in space, land on a planet, walk into a bar, and not have to constantly watch my back. Is that asking too much?"

His intensity made Sha'Nara want to tell him no, it wasn't too much, but it was. The Scanners asked for the impossible. After the killing and chaos during the PSI Wars a hundred years ago, the Alliance couldn't chance that happening again.

To allow Scanners to gather in one area where they could breed and strengthen their abilities would invite another power struggle. Already Sha'Nara had seen more developed skills among the Scanners on this ship than any she'd encountered in her entire career. For the first time she realized that those Scanners the PSI Police had captured had been in the lower rung of development.

How many more Scanners existed with abilities as finely honed as Tristan's? The thought alarmed her.

"It'll never happen, Tristan." She spoke softly, trying to lessen the blow. "It can't. Scanners are too dangerous."

Pain flickered across his face before he hardened his expression. "You only know what you've been told. You don't really know us as people." He searched her face. "Do you think I'm dangerous?"

"Very much so." Not only dangerous physically, but emotionally.

"But have I hurt you?"

Sha'Nara hesitated. He'd bruised her pride, but never actually harmed her. In fact, he'd protected her from Bran. "No," she said. Thinking back over the Scanners she'd encountered since her arrival, she had to admit that while they'd all been antagonistic toward her, no one but Bran had tried to hurt her.

"How do you think of me?" Tristan asked. "As a Scanner or Tristan Galeron?"

Earlier she'd considered him a Scanner first and foremost, but lately her focus had blurred. It had to be that farding dream. Now when she studied his familiar face, his dark eyes, his sensuous mouth, her stomach knotted and liquid fire spread through her veins. How *did* she think of him? As her lover?

Inhaling sharply, Sha'Nara twisted away. "I don't know."

He remained silent until finally she had to turn back to see his expression. His eyes had darkened further, and something akin to sympathy flickered in their depths.

Sympathy? For her? She wasn't the one who kept dirt in a globe and called it home. She had homes at her family's house on Octurus and her father's quarters at Centralia.

Yet neither place would provide her a warm welcome. Sha'Nara shrugged that thought aside. Her family had never been affectionately demonstrative. It wasn't their way.

Tristan lowered his gaze. "Be sure to tell me once you do know." Turning toward the large bed dominating the room, he unsealed the top of his suit, revealing his broad chest etched with well-defined muscles and covered with dark hair.

Sha'Nara's breath caught in her throat. "What are you doing?"

"It's the middle of the night." He gave her a bland look. "I'm going back to sleep."

Moistening her lips, she searched the room for another bed. "Where am I to sleep?" She dreaded his answer despite the quickening of her pulse.

"I guess we'll have to share." His expression revealed nothing of his thoughts.

Sha'Nara's sudden rush of anticipation terrified her. Whirling toward the door, she tried to key it open, her fingers flying over the keypad. Old fears returned to mingle with her new apprehension. Her breathing grew shallow and rapid as cold sweat collected first on her palms, then spread to cover her body.

She continued to try key combinations, her actions growing more frantic. She couldn't stay here. She couldn't. Her stomach clenched as her muscles tightened. The door had to open. She had to get out.

With a cry of anguish, she pounded on the door, but only succeeded in bruising her fists. Struggling for control, she buried her face atop the back of her hands. Somehow she had to conquer this fear.

"Sha'Nara." Tristan spoke her name gently before he touched her shoulders and turned her around. "I won't harm you. I swear it."

Her chest rose and fell with each ragged breath. She refused to meet his searching gaze. "Unkey the door, please."

"I can't while you're here. Surely you know that." He extended his hand and softly brushed the loose tendrils of her hair away from her face. "Why are you so afraid of being locked up?"

She'd been afraid for so long, she didn't remember . . . didn't want to remember how it had started. "Something happened. A long time ago."

"Tell me about it." He sounded so kind, so gentle, that she had to look up to check his sincerity. Only concern showed in his eyes, not the mockery she'd expected.

"It'll help if you talk about it." His grin illuminated his features. "Or at least that's what my mother always told me."

A thick lump blocked Sha'Nara's throat as old memories climbed to the surface of her mind. She swallowed, her mouth dry. "I . . . I was seven."

He waited, his expression expectant, but said nothing.

"As discipline, my father would lock me in my bedroom and leave me there to think about what I'd done wrong." At first she'd played in her room, but as time passed, she would consider her actions and believe her father no longer cared about her, that he would leave her there forever. "Usually after an hour or two, he let me out."

"And this caused your fear?"

"No. Yes." That day came into sharp focus, as if she hadn't tried to banish it a million times. "One day after he'd locked me in, something happened, an emergency at work, and he left." She met Tristan's gaze, needing his strength to continue. "He didn't return for three days."

"Three days!" Tristan's jaw dropped. "But surely your mother . . ."

Sha'Nara shrugged, trying to dismiss the incident, but even now she recalled her horror when darkness fell and still the door remained locked. She shivered, and Tristan wrapped her in his arms. "She never paid much attention to me. Since she and my father don't get along very well, she's always kept to her own wing of the house. I don't think she knew I was there."

But Sha'Nara remembered her cries, her screams, her tears as she pounded on the keyed door. Why hadn't someone heard her? "I was so thirsty, so hungry," she murmured into Tristan's chest. "And afraid. Every noise became a goblin waiting to eat me up."

Tears welled in her eyes, but she blinked them back. She hadn't cried since that time, and didn't intend to start now. "I soiled myself because I couldn't get to the lav. I broke one of my mother's beautiful vases to get the water from inside. I thought Father would be angry with me."

"Angry with you?" Tristan repeated incredulously.

"Then I feared he was never coming back. That he'd given up on me and left forever as he'd threatened to do."

"By the stars!" Tristan pressed her closer to him, and she savored his nearness, his warmth.

"But he did return and let me out." Sha'Nara couldn't keep her voice from trembling. "I was very ill. I'd had no food and little water during that time. I think I almost died."

"I always knew your father was a bastard, but how could he do that to a child?"

"He never keyed me in again after that," she said, rising to her father's defense. Of course, he'd never needed to discipline her again. She'd done her best to obey his every command as efficiently as she could. Sha'Nara grimaced. She was still trying.

"I always knew the man was merciless, but I never thought it extended to his own family." Tristan ran his hand over Sha'Nara's hair, and she breathed deeply of his unique masculine scent. Closing her eyes, she nestled closer to his bare chest.

For the first time in her life, she felt safe.

Her eyes flew open. Safe?

Pushing away from Tristan, she staggered backward, staring at him. How could she have forgotten who he was—for even a moment?

He looked as startled as she felt. Clearing his throat, he tried to act casual as he dropped his arms to his side. "Does it bother you to have the door keyed even though I'm with you?"

"Yes." She needed only a moment to consider that question. Though her fear wasn't as acute with Tristan present, she still couldn't open the door, couldn't step outside if necessary. "What if you died?"

His lips twitched in the beginnings of a smile. "Only if you kill me."

She found herself smiling in response. That was true. She'd never met anyone so virile, so alive, so less likely to die.

He hesitated. "If I unkey the door, will you give me

your word that you won't try to escape?" He shook his head when he finished speaking, as if he couldn't believe he'd said the words.

Sha'Nara had difficulty believing it herself. "My word? Do you trust it?"

"Can't I?" he countered.

If she agreed, she'd limit her escape options, but knowing the door was unlocked would give her a good night's sleep for the first time since her arrival. And she needed sleep. Maybe then she wouldn't be so easily affected by Tristan's masculinity.

"Yes," she said firmly. She'd find another opportunity to flee the *Hermitage*. "I won't try to escape from this room while the door is unkeyed."

He grinned. "That's precise." Crossing to the keypad, he lifted his hand, then paused. "I must be insane," he muttered quietly, then danced his fingers over the keys.

"There." He faced her again. "It's done."

Aware of his gaze upon her, Sha'Nara approached the door and signaled for it to open. It did. For a moment she stared into the dimly lit hallway, aware of her tension easing and something else less definable wrapping around her chest.

She closed the door and smiled at Tristan. "Thank you."

"Don't make me regret this." He studied her face, then gestured toward the bed. "Take the bed. I'll sleep over there." He indicated a spot on the floor.

Sha'Nara almost protested, but stopped herself. She didn't want him in bed with her. Did she?

She waited for him to make up his pallet and signal the lights to dim before she climbed into the bed, unfastening her jumpsuit, but not removing it. The vast bed dwarfed her, and she snuggled deep into its softness, bringing to mind Tristan's comforting touch.

No, not that. Anything but that.

"Sha'Nara?" Tristan's voice drifted out of the darkness.

"What?"

"I need one more promise from you." He sounded worried.

"What's that?" She sat up in the bed, gazing in the direction of his voice.

"Don't tell Cadell I did this."

"I won't." She lay back down, considering the seriousness of Tristan's tone. What would Cadell do if he knew? Recalling Cadell's casual innuendoes and mocking manner, she knew immediately what he'd do.

An unfamiliar sensation rose in her throat. She tried to stop it, but couldn't.

She giggled.

The dream captured her within its hold again. Sha'Nara's heart pounded rapidly as Tristan stroked the lines of her body, pausing only to caress the swells of her breast and rub his thumb over her already taut peak. Her body burned with need, her longing so strong it threatened to overpower all logic.

His body lay partially over hers, their legs intertwined, as he bent to seduce her mouth, his kiss demanding yet tender, giving yet taking. He left no doubt of his desire.

And she wanted him, too.

Seizing his shoulders, she pulled him fully on top of her, his muscular body pressing her deeper into the softness of the bed, his rigid length pulsing against her thigh. She returned his kiss, conveying her willingness.

He left her lips and trailed kisses along the line of her throat and over her chest until he drew her breast into the warm cavern of his mouth. Sha'Nara gasped, her insides so tight they threatened to tear her apart, but she didn't pull away. Instead, she arched her back, allowing him complete freedom to continue, to take all she had.

He used his tongue to torment her nipple into an aching nub and Sha'Nara moaned low in her throat. She never would've thought a Scanner could be such an accomplished lover.

A Scanner!

Sha'Nara came awake instantly, but the sensation didn't fade. She still felt a mouth upon her breast, her body clenching for release. Her throat tightened. Was Tristan . . . ?

She glanced down, but even in the dimmed light she could see no one near her. But she felt it. She tried to sit up, but couldn't. An invisible weight kept her pinned to the bed.

Her breathing grew shallow, and she tried to fight the fever of need overwhelming her body as the mouth left one breast and moved to the other. She watched as her thin T-shirt molded to the crest, the nipple tightening beneath an unseen assault. Potent desire traveled along every nerve and she rocked her hips in an instinctive reaction. She wanted . . . she needed. . . .

Struggling to retain coherent thought, Sha'Nara turned her head toward where Tristan lay on his pallet. He had to be doing this to her. How dare he!

Teeth grazed her sensitive peak and she gasped aloud. Tristan moaned and turned on his pallet, enabling Sha'Nara to see he still slept. By Orion's Sword! He did this to her in his sleep. How powerful was he?

"Tristan." Sha'Nara forced his name through her constricted throat. The sensual assault on her body continued, making it difficult for her to draw a breath. She tried again with more force. "Tristan. Wake up."

He stirred, and abruptly all sensation stopped. Freed of the restrictive weight, Sha'Nara leapt to her feet and kicked at Tristan's form.

"How dare you!" Her reaction to his touch alarmed her. How could she submit so easily? "I knew Scanners couldn't be trusted."

He came awake instantly and rolled out of reach before jumping to his feet. "What are you talking about?"

"You molested me while I slept." Her fury mounted, directed as much at herself as him. She'd only responded so fervently because he'd caught her vulnerable from the dream. He still had no right.

"I never touched you." Indignation filled his voice.

"Yes, you did." She cut him off when he would've protested further. "With your mind."

Confusion crossed his face. "I . . . dreamed, but I've

never used my powers in my sleep before."

"You did this time. I felt you . . . your mouth . . ." Sha'Nara motioned toward her chest, then trailed off as Tristan's gaze followed her movement. Her nipples, still aching from their earlier teasing, hardened immediately beneath his gaze. Her jumpsuit was still opened. Her T-shirt hid nothing.

Her throat went dry as an all too familiar longing surged through her veins. Unbidden, her gaze dropped to his loins, clad only in a pair of micro-briefs. The material hugged the length of his erection. A shiver—half fear, half desire—ran through her as she realized her predicament.

They stood only an arm's length apart in the dimly lit room. His need was obvious. No one would hear her if she screamed. No one would come to her aid if they did hear her.

But would she scream? Her body longed for what she knew he could give. In trepidation she lifted her gaze to meet his. He held himself stiffly, his tension clear. For a moment, they stared at each other—neither moving nor speaking. A fire blazed in the depths of his eyes, frightening Sha'Nara with its intensity.

"I'm sorry."

She jumped at his unexpected words. "What?"

"I apologize." He spoke as if each word had to be dragged from his throat. "I thought I was dreaming. I never before . . . I didn't realize. . . ." He inhaled deeply, then stepped closer.

Sha'Nara put out her hand to stop him, her fingers splaying across his chest. Heat traveled along her fingertips to ignite the stoked blaze low in her belly. She knew she ought to drop her hand, but she couldn't. Staring up at him, she waited, frozen, caught between the demands of her desire and her mind.

"I apologize for touching you against your will," Tristan continued, his voice low and husky, reaching inside her like a caress. "But I won't apologize for having my dream." He slid his hand behind her neck and ran his fingers through her unbound hair before cradling her head. "I enjoyed it."

Bringing his mouth within a whisper of hers, he used the thumb of his other hand to trace the outline of her lips. "Sha'Nara."

He said her name reverently, as if she mattered. Something deep inside her loosened. Had she ever mattered? To anyone?

When he finally claimed her mouth, she didn't protest. Her entire body trembled beneath his kiss as her lips softened under his gentle tutelage. As she responded, he wrapped his arms around her, drawing her close, molding her to his hardened length.

Deepening the kiss, he ran his tongue along her lips, teasing, taunting, until she allowed him admittance. He parried skillfully, seducing her tongue into a symbolic mating with his. She shivered, her blood so hot the air seemed cold.

She'd thought the kisses in her dream potent enough, but they paled to insignificance beside this. She couldn't think . . . didn't want to think . . . only to feel.

Still caressing her lips, Tristan brought his hand between them to cup her breast. Gently he rolled her taut nipple between his thumb and finger, and Sha'Nara gave herself up to the stabs of delight with a throaty moan.

Her heart pounded so hard in her chest, she felt sure it would rip itself free. Gasping for breath, she broke free of the kiss. "Tristan."

He paused, his hand still holding her breast. His gaze captured hers, so familiar, so full of passion, she felt it as a tangible presence. "Tell me to stop now or let me finish," he said, his voice ragged.

She tried to think, needed to think. Tristan brushed his thumb over her nipple and need, strong and undeniable, erased any misgivings. "Finish," she breathed.

With a groan, Tristan eased her back onto the bed, then stretched beside her, taking her lips again. His gentleness gave way to the fierceness of passion as he pushed her suit further open and slid her shirt up, his hands burning paths along her skin. He broke his kiss in order to pull her shirt over her head, then paused, silent, to look at her.

Sha'Nara couldn't control the rapid movement of her chest nor the way her nipples hardened, begging for his touch. "This is better than my dream," he murmured. Almost as if in awe, he stroked the sides of her breasts, then bent to press a kiss on the tip of first one, then the other. "Much better."

With a cry, she arched against the bed, wanting more. He quickly complied, enveloping one peak within his mouth, taunting her nipple with his tongue. Sha'Nara clutched at his bare shoulders, dimly aware of the play of his muscles as he moved.

Sensations of need washed over her until she thought she would die. She'd never imagined such a pleasurable pain. Weaving her fingers through his long, silky hair, she held him close, lost to the expertise of his mouth and hands.

She never wanted him to stop, yet to continue would surely destroy her. The coil within her abdomen drew tighter as he ran his hand over her skin and beneath her underwear. He paused, his hand resting possessively over her mound, and she rocked against him, urging him to continue.

She'd never imagined any man, let alone a Scanner, could have this power over her.

Man? Scanner? Power?

She froze, alarm overcoming her desire. Mael's brainwashing did this to her. Otherwise, she'd never respond to a Scanner.

Tristan lifted his head. "Sha'Nara?"

"I . . . I can't. . . ."

"Tristan. Tristan, are you there?" The communications speaker in the wall blared to life.

Tristan tensed, not looking away from her gaze. "I'm here, Mael," he replied finally.

"I need to meet with you and Cadell. If the Director-General refuses to talk with us, we must go over our strategy."

"When?"

"As soon as possible."

He sighed with resignation. "Very well."

Tristan straightened and rose to his feet. Sha'Nara breathed a sigh of relief. Despite the tingling of her body, the thought of what she'd almost done filled her with horror. How could she consider for one moment mating with a Scanner?

Tristan turned toward the lav, then smiled back at her. "We'll have to finish this later."

"No, never." Sha'Nara drew the covers around her. "Mael's doing something to my mind. You're a Scanner. I can't. . . ."

Tristan's face hardened. "Yes, I am, a very foolish Scanner, who thought for a moment you were different from other PSI Police." He clenched his jaw before continuing. "My mistake."

Without another word, he entered the lav.

Sha'Nara wrapped her arms around herself, all too aware that her body still quivered with need. Locating her shirt, she dressed quickly, then paced the room, regretting her impulsive promise not to flee. She had to escape and soon, even if she had to force Jacy to accompany her.

How could she consider betraying her fellow officers, what she'd trained for, worked for? Her mission required her to capture Scanners and take them for adjustment. Yet at the moment, remembering the passion of Tristan's kisses and heat of his touch, she had a difficult time seeing him as a Scanner.

And that frightened her most of all.

Chapter Six

Tristan sat in a hoverchair and looked toward Mael at the head of the conference room table, but his mind remained focused on the woman he'd just left. Since he and Cadell were needed at the meeting, he'd left Sha'Nara and Jacy in a room guarded by two Scanners, but he hadn't locked the door. After hearing Sha'Nara's story the night before, he couldn't bring himself to lock her in. He shook his head. How foolish could he be?

The sooner they returned Sha'Nara to Centralia, the better. As far as Tristan was concerned, she'd become a bigger danger than that represented by her PSI Police status. He didn't want this attraction to her, yet knowing that didn't overcome it. He hadn't lost control over his kinetic abilities since he was six years old, but he didn't think she was lying either when she accused him of touching her in her sleep.

Even worse, she made him want her, want things he knew he'd never have—a home, a family, peace. For those brief moments when he'd held her, kissed her, touched her, he'd believed anything was possible. That the Alliance would grant Scanners freedom, that he had a future, that he'd found the woman to share that future.

Tristan grimaced. He should've known better. He had no future, and definitely not one that included Sha'Nara Calles.

"We need to consider our options." Mael started speaking, and Tristan dragged his thoughts back to the subject at hand. "I didn't expect the Director-General to balk at meeting us. This raises the possibility that he may not agree at all."

"What happens to Sha'Nara and Jacy then?" Cadell asked the question uppermost in Tristan's mind.

"As I see it, we have three choices. We can set them free, keep them here, or kill them."

Tristan clenched his fist. None of those choices met with his approval.

"No killing." Cadell spoke emphatically, his expression more serious than Tristan had seen it in a long time. "If it comes to that, I suggest we keep them here."

"Sha'Nara will never stop trying to escape," Tristan said. He knew her well enough to be certain of that. Though she raised his frustration and anger to new levels, he couldn't help but admire her spirit. If their places were reversed, he'd do the same.

"Then we'll let her go free," Cadell said.

Tristan hesitated. "She knows too much. If we set her free, we'll have to move the *Hermitage* to another corner of space."

Cadell glared at him. "So you want to kill her? I thought you might've forgotten the fact that she's PSI Police."

If only Cadell knew how close Tristan had come to forgetting that fact. "I don't want to kill her," he said, suddenly aware of the truth behind those words. "But she may force us into it."

His stomach knotting, Tristan looked to Mael. "I still think the Director-General will agree to meet with us. I doubt he'll give us our freedom, but he'll meet. He wants his daughter back."

Mael studied Tristan, his gaze dark, his face inscrutable. "I'm counting on that. I'll contact Remy Vadin in another day or two. Perhaps then he'll be ready to talk." He turned to face the windows revealing the vastness of space. "Until then, I'll need both of you to continue your watch over these women." He glanced back over his shoulder. "I trust you're not having any problems?"

"No." Cadell and Tristan answered together, then exchanged wry smiles. If Mael only knew the problems . . .

Two more days in Sha'Nara's company would definitely test Tristan's control. His body played traitor whenever she was near. He'd have to count on his mind to remember who and what she was.

"Mael." A young man appeared in the doorway, obviously agitated. Tristan frowned. What now?

When Mael turned and nodded at the young man, he continued. "We're docking a Scanner transport. It contains some of our people from the moon at Aktion. The moon is under attack by PSI Police."

Mael hurried forward. "Did everyone escape?"

"No. They didn't have enough time to get everyone aboard their only spaceship. Their pilot says at least thirty people remain at the moon."

Tristan went to Mael's side, anger brewing in his gut. Aktion's moon sheltered several families. Yet when had the PSI Police ever cared about families?

Cadell followed, his concern obvious. "Are they wounded?"

"Yes." The young man glanced at Cadell. "I've notified the healers and they're on their way to the docking bay."

"Were these people followed?" Tristan needed to oversee security. He'd been so distracted by Sha'Nara, he hadn't finished implementing his procedures. Now was not a good time to battle PSI Police, but the Scanners would fight if they had to.

"So far, we've seen no other signs of spacecraft. The bridge is still monitoring the area."

"Good." Tristan started for the bridge, then paused as his name emerged from a ceiling speaker.

"Tristan, they've escaped."

He bit back an oath. He didn't need to ask who. Pivoting, he glanced back at Mael and Cadell. "I'll stop her."

He ran toward the lift. Since Sha'Nara had Jacy with her, he knew exactly where she was headed—the docking bay. Did she know the Scanner ship was arriving? She couldn't, but she'd certainly picked an apt time to make her move. The bay would be in chaos with the healers helping the wounded.

If he didn't hurry, she might succeed.

He skidded to a halt just inside the docking bay's door. As he'd expected, the place vibrated with turmoil. The newly arrived Scanners debarked steadily from their ship, calling for help as needed. Tristan recognized several healers already at work, using their particular parapsychic skill to treat wounds.

Navigating through the crowd, he searched for Sha'Nara. She had to be here. This incoming ship provided the perfect opportunity for her to mingle and make her way to one of the smaller craft.

His gaze caught on one of the wounded, a young woman, her face covered with blood. As he watched, the healer attending her raised his hands and shook his head.

Tristan ground his teeth together. The PSI Police had claimed another victim in their senseless war. Sha'Nara had been right. Scanners would never be free as long as PSI Police existed.

Pushing his way through the swarming arrivals, Tristan made his way to the smaller of the parked craft. He quickly checked the interior. Nothing.

The crowd started to thin—many of the newly arrived Scanners no doubt taken to quarters or medical—as he strode to the shuttle. Though he searched every corner of the craft, he found no sign of his quarry.

He stood in the doorway, clenching his fists. She was here. He knew it. But where?

The larger transport ship appeared almost empty. Only a few individuals remained nearby, immersed in conversation. As the hatch began to slide closed, a figure appeared and jumped out.

Jacy!

Tristan reached her side in three quick strides and grasped her arm. "Where's Sha'Nara?"

Jacy's eyes widened. "In . . . inside. I don't want to go."

The door continued to close. Once it was sealed, Sha'Nara would have the advantage. Without hesitation, Tristan shoved Jacy at a nearby Scanner. "Take her to Cadell."

In one fluid movement, he leapt through the remaining space and slid painfully along the metal floor to an abrupt stop. He'd only risen to one knee when the hatch sealed behind him and the spacecraft roared to life.

The departure from the landing bay was quick, crude, and unexpected. Tristan flew across the entry platform, thrown against the ship's side by the rapid acceleration. Seizing a nearby rail, he clung with both hands until the pressure eased enough for him to regain his footing.

"Damned woman." He could tell by the sound of the engine that she was pushing the craft to its maximum level. With his luck, she'd blow them both up into neutron particles.

Using the rails to maintain his balance, he fought his way to the front cabin, then hesitated before activating the door. His first instinct said to rush in and yank Sha'Nara from the controls, but the tiny bit of wisdom that remained warned him that that action could get them both killed. He had to ascertain whether she'd started a hyperspace jump before he took control.

Then he'd deal with Sha'Nara Calles.

Sha'Nara struggled with the unfamiliar controls, her gaze darting from the view screen to the numbers before her. She'd set the hyperspace coordinates, but still hadn't found the optimum jump window. If she didn't find it soon, she'd jump regardless and take her chances. The worst that could happen would be a longer ride and a slight miscalculation in her exit point.

At least, she'd be away from the Scanners.

The door slid open and she released an exasperated breath. "I told you to strap in, Jacy. This isn't going to be a fun ride."

"I tend to agree."

Her heart skipped a beat at the sound of Tristan's tightly controlled voice, and Sha'Nara slowly turned her head to look at him. Anger radiated from him in waves, the fury in his gaze hot enough to set off fire alarms.

The farding Scanner! Couldn't she ever escape him?

In desperation, she reached for the hyperspace lever, but he caught her hand with his kinetic ability before she could pull the lever back. Leaping forward, he pried her hand off the lever.

As Sha'Nara cried out in frustration, he erased her carefully programmed coordinates. She wouldn't be jumping to hyperspace any time soon.

She shoved him away and leapt to her feet, feeling at a definite disadvantage as he towered over her. "I *will* escape," she vowed.

"I know."

The very quietness of his voice added impact. He straightened from the controls and turned to face her. The darkness of his gaze drove daggers into her chest. Was this the same man who'd so tenderly kissed her this morning?

"When I first found out who you were, I wanted to throw you out the airlock." Tristan approached slowly, and despite her inner admonition to remain firm, Sha'Nara found herself backing up. "I'm beginning to think that might have been the wisest course of action."

Her heart rose to her throat, and she had to swallow before she could speak. "You'd never have a chance for peace then."

"Which is why you're still alive."

His coldness sent chills along her nerves. "Then you have to keep me alive." She clung to that thought. "You need me and Jacy."

"We need Jacy." Tristan assumed her vacated seat and turned the craft toward the *Hermitage*.

Sha'Nara approached stealthily from behind. All she needed was to deliver one blow—one blow and she'd regain control. Before she reached him, he extended his arm and his kinetic push caught her full in the chest, knocking her back and pinning her against the wall. Air escaped from her lungs in a whoosh.

He glanced at her briefly. "Don't try it, Sha'Nara. You'd gain nothing. Jacy is still on the *Hermitage*."

On the *Hermitage*? Sha'Nara remained against the wall even after Tristan released her, her hopes diminished. She'd been determined to escape this time. So determined that she'd followed the instinct that had told her to go now even though she'd planned to wait for a more opportune time. She'd had to down the guards and drag Jacy to get away, but when she'd reached the bay and found it a mass of confusion, she knew she couldn't have asked for a better opportunity. Her father would have lectured her on obeying an instinct, but this one had paid off . . . until Tristan showed up.

"But I fastened Jacy into a seat myself," she protested. She wanted to believe he was lying, but why would he at this point?

"She jumped off the ship just before you left." He gave her a brief smile. "*She* likes us."

"She's a young woman who's been sheltered her entire life. She doesn't know what you really are, so she's letting herself be swayed by Cadell's seductive charm."

He turned in his seat to fasten his gaze on her. "And you'd never be affected by anything like that, would you?"

The memory of their encounter that morning leapt vividly into her mind. Sha'Nara lifted her chin. "No, I wouldn't." He was seductive, all right, but never charming. Her body had betrayed her only because of the dream—the dream caused by Mael.

"I thought not." Tristan returned to the controls and opened a channel. "This is Tristan. I have Sha'Nara in custody and am returning to the landing bay."

"Wait, Tristan." Mael's voice crackled over the communications line. "Do not return to the *Hermitage*."

Sha'Nara frowned. Why not? A sense of unease crept along her spine. Did Mael intend to keep her separated from Jacy? Tristan had already confirmed that Jacy was important to them. Sha'Nara wasn't.

"What is it?" Tristan asked, his irritation clear.

"Apparently some Scanners are still alive on Aktion's moon. I need you to help them escape."

Tristan started to nod, then jerked his head around to focus on Sha'Nara. "I can do that, Mael, but let me drop off Sha'Nara first."

"There's no time. Take her with you."

Sha'Nara could see Tristan's muscles tighten. "I don't think that's wise. The PSI Police are there."

"I trust she won't get near them." Mael sounded so confident, so calm, that Sha'Nara wanted to throw something at him. He obviously didn't know her very well.

"Very well." Tristan didn't look pleased, but he closed the channel and started configuring the controls. "Sit down and fasten your restraints," he ordered.

She slowly approached the chair beside his. "Did he say Aktion?"

"Yes."

Her interest caught. She knew Aktion. A PSI Police division resided in that quadrant of space. "Why there?" She tried to keep her tone casual, but judging from the look Tristan threw her way, she didn't succeed.

"Did you notice the Scanners who came off this ship?"

She hadn't paid much attention to them at first. They'd merely been a convenient mob of people covering her escape. But when she'd seen a man stained with blood, she'd had to look. "I saw some of them," she admitted. "They looked hurt."

"I saw a young woman die while looking for you." Tristan kept his focus on the controls, his voice so cold Sha'Nara shivered. "Do you know how they came to be injured?"

Sha'Nara's defenses kicked in. "I suppose you're going to say it's my fault."

"Indirectly. Hold on." He drew back a lever and the ship melted into blackness of hyperspace. Sha'Nara couldn't change their direction now.

As he turned to look at her, his expression angry, her stomach knotted. "They were attacked by PSI Police," he continued. "A Scanner community lived beneath the surface of Aktion's moon. Apparently they were discovered. Their injuries resulted from the *brain drainers'* usual persuasive methods."

Sha'Nara balled her hand into a fist. Just like a Scanner to blame everything on the PSI Police. "They probably injured themselves in their attempts to flee. Our procedures call for talk first."

"I know how you talk—one order to evacuate or die. Some choice." Dark lights flashed in his eyes. "If these police followed the usual procedure, they gave these people five minutes to surrender, then began bombing." His fingers curled around the edge of the control panel, his knuckles white. "Several families live on Aktion's moon."

"You're assuming this patrol knows that. That outpost could have just as easily contained fifty armed men."

"I doubt if PSI Police care whether it's one or the other. After all, your main goal is to capture all Scanners, isn't it?"

Sha'Nara hesitated, then drew herself up straight. "Yes. Scanners are too powerful, too unpredictable, too dangerous to be allowed to roam free. You're a perfect example of that."

Tristan released a sound of disgust and threw himself from his chair. "You're just afraid of anything you don't understand."

He was the one who didn't understand, she thought. He had the power to touch her while he slept, and he thought she shouldn't be afraid of that? "We're not totally uncaring," she said. She stood to face him. "We always offer readjustment first. You force us into killing you."

"Better dead than readjusted."

"At least you'd be alive."

"I don't consider that living."

"How can you say that?" Sha'Nara approached him. "Are you so afraid of losing your powers that you can't live without them?"

"I'm not afraid of losing my powers." He jabbed his finger toward his head. "I'm more afraid of losing my mind."

"Your mind?" What did he think readjustment was?

Tristan paused, his gaze searching her face. "What is readjustment to you, Sha'Nara?"

"It's a procedure performed on Scanners in which the parapsychic part of their brain is deactivated. After this procedure they are reintegrated into society to lead productive lives." She'd quoted the definition without missing a beat. After all, she'd heard it since her first contact with the PSI Police.

"Have you ever been present for this procedure?"

"No." That wasn't part of her job. She merely captured and delivered the Scanners. Others handled them from there.

"Have you ever seen a Scanner after this procedure?"

She thought for a moment before replying. "No." Some hesitation crept into her answer, and she hated herself for it.

"Do you know where these readjusted Scanners are relocated?"

Again she had to think. "Relocation doesn't fall into my division. I have no need to know, but I imagine they're reintegrated throughout the galaxy."

Tristan sighed, and a touch of sadness entered his gaze. "They've been lying to you, Sha'Nara."

"You're telling me everything I believe is a lie?" She laughed dryly. "I'd sooner believe my people than you."

"Of course you would. How else can they brainwash you into killing us?" Tristan ran his fingers through his hair in obvious frustration.

"Brainwash?" Sha'Nara's voice rose. "If anyone's brainwashing people, it's Mael. I know he's been making me have this dream."

Tristan raised one eyebrow. "Dream? What kind of dream?"

"About you and me . . . we . . . we're . . ." Heat flooded her cheeks as she trailed off. She mentally shook herself. She couldn't let this man intimidate her. "That's the only reason I let you kiss me. Because I'd just had the dream again."

"Again?" Doubt flickered across Tristan's face, and Sha'Nara congratulated herself. She had to make him see Mael's dishonesty. How could Tristan trust a man who did this to people?

"I . . . I've had them for a while."

"Since Mael touched you during the transmission to Remy?"

"No, before that."

"How long?" He sounded deceptively cool as he stepped closer, his body radiating heat.

"Three—no—four months now." Refusing to move back, she met his gaze defiantly.

A strange gleam flickered in his eyes. "You've been dreaming about me for four months? You didn't know me then."

"I know, but it was you."

He stood in front of her, their bodies almost touching. An instant response stirred in Sha'Nara's belly, but she tried to ignore it. She refused to be attracted to this . . . this Scanner. Her body only reacted to Mael's implanted suggestions.

"Mael isn't giving you the dreams. He couldn't."

Tristan's self-assurance shattered her illusion. She stiffened. "What?"

"You just met Mael two days ago."

"I'm sure his powers are more extensive than I've seen."

"Not this much." A ghost of a smile played around Tristan's lips. "He has to touch a person to read their mind or implant thoughts, and then the implant wears off quickly."

Her brain refused to grasp his meaning. "But this dream . . ."

"Mael isn't causing it. You are."

"Why would I dream about you?"

He bent until his lips were a whisper away. "I wonder," he murmured, his breath mingling with hers.

She hated the bolt of anticipation that streaked through her body. She hated the way her breasts tightened. Most of all, she hated it that some inner part of her wanted him to kiss her. "I . . . I'm not attracted to you." Even though she protested, she didn't move away.

"Yes, you are. You've been dreaming about me." He had the audacity to look smug, and Sha'Nara recoiled, shaking her head.

"Tell me about this dream." Though she didn't answer, he obviously guessed what she'd dreamed from her flushed cheeks. "Do I kiss you?"

He closed the tiny gap between them, bestowing the lightest touch of his lips before he drew back. She needed all her self-control to keep from seeking more.

"Do I touch you?" He traced the outline of her face, her hair, her shoulder, yet didn't actually touch her. When he skimmed the shape of her breast, she bit back a moan.

"Do I make love to you?" He kept his hands by his side, but his gaze caressed her, his eyes dark with intimacy.

Sha'Nara remained still, torn between the aching desire of her body and the rational part of her mind.

"Why would you dream of me like that, Sha'Nara?" he asked quietly.

"I don't want to." She bit back the urge to scream with frustration. "It's wrong. You're the enemy."

"Maybe your subconscious knows more than the lies you've been fed by the Alliance. Maybe some part of you realizes we're . . . I'm not the enemy."

"The Alliance hasn't lied to me." Why would they?

He stepped away from her, and a chill traveled over

her heated skin. Disappointment, sharp and keen, cut through her.

"They have lied to you." Tristan turned to check the controls. "Constantly."

Battling for self-control, Sha'Nara grabbed the back of her chair. She knew better than to believe him. "What kind of lies?"

His glance traveled over her quickly, then dismissed her. "You're not ready to listen."

"Try me." She wanted to know what he considered Alliance lies. The information might prove useful.

He straightened. "Scanners are not a threat. We haven't been a threat since the PSI Wars ended a hundred years ago."

She opened her mouth to protest, but he didn't let her speak. "Think back. Do you know of any instance in which Scanners have caused problems? Without being provoked first?"

His condition made her review the long list of Scanner episodes in her memory. Try as she might, she couldn't think of a single instance where the uprising hadn't broken out after the arrival of PSI Police. Wait, there was one. . . .

"What about that Roget person on Miniva Three? He was a Scanner who tried to take over the government there." She didn't bother to hide her triumph.

"One Scanner in the past hundred years. What about Manderling, a human who tried to take over the government on Delinor? Or Treadwell, a human who actually enslaved an entire planet for a period of time?" Sha'Nara's triumph faded at the mention of two notorious episodes in recent history. He grinned and held up his finger. "Oh, and Smytheson on Earth, no less, who led a revolt against the Alliance. Why aren't normal humans on the extermination list? They're more out of control than we are."

She scowled. "Those were just isolated incidents. Sometimes people just go crazy."

"Then wouldn't the Roget incident fall in that category?"

"Possibly. But I refuse to admit Scanners aren't dangerous. Look at what Mael can do, what you can do."

"Sha'Nara, I could've killed you ten times by now if that was my intention. What do I have to do to make you understand all we want is peace?"

"Let me go." She didn't have to think about that answer.

He faltered and looked away. "We will. Eventually."

What else did she expect? That he'd tell her the truth. "You're going to kill me, aren't you?"

"What?" He jerked his head up. "No."

"I know where your ship is located."

"We'll move it."

"I know your weaknesses."

"You only think you do." Tristan extended his hand and caressed the side of her face, his touch surprisingly gentle. "We won't kill you. That would defeat our purpose."

Sha'Nara's throat went dry. Just his palm against her skin set off hormone alarms. She swallowed—twice—before she could speak. "What . . . what else is a lie?"

As she'd hoped, he dropped his hand. His face clouded. "Readjustment." He spat out the word as if it were a disease.

"It's the best thing for all—"

He sliced his hand through the air. "It's complete, total destruction of the mind." For a man who'd been so gentle only a moment ago, he now radiated violence. "Scanners who live through this readjustment process are trapped forever within themselves. Most are vegetables. Some relive pain and terror continuously. None go on to lead productive lives."

"But—"

"Don't believe me. I'm only a Scanner. Once you return, see for yourself. Then decide who's been lying." He whirled away.

For the first time doubt seeped into her mind. She could easily verify what he said. Centralia had a readjustment chamber on the premises. If he'd lied, that would be no more than she'd expected, but if he told the truth . . . Her chest felt suddenly too small. No, it couldn't be. Surely she'd know if something like that was taking place.

"I *will* check," she said finally.

He didn't look around. "Good."

Approaching him slowly, she caught herself before she touched his shoulder. "Have you seen any of these readjusted people?"

"More than I ever cared to." He sounded weary, almost broken.

Against her will, she wrapped her fingers around his arm. "If this is taking place . . ." She caught herself. What if it was true?

"What?" He glanced at her then, and she caught a glimpse of his carefully hidden pain. "To you, we're only animals, better off dead. What will you do, Sha'Nara Calles?"

Her heart rose to fill her throat. Somehow, without her realizing it, she'd come to see these people as more than animals, as individuals who lived, who felt, who hurt. When had that happened? Why did the thought of a Scanner having his brain destroyed fill her with horror?

"If it's true, I'll stop it." She didn't flinch beneath the intensity of his gaze. She meant her words, and had the authority to carry them out. After all, she was Amyr Calles's daughter.

A brief buzz drew Tristan's attention to the control panel, and he brought them smoothly out of hyperspace. A large gaseous planet filled the better part of the view screen, but Sha'Nara found her gaze drawn to the orbiting moon.

Even from this distance she could see the flashes of low-level bombs on the surface. "Aktion's moon," she murmured.

"And the PSI Police." Tristan's expression revealed nothing of his thoughts. "What do you plan to do now?"

Chapter Seven

Sha'Nara slowly turned to look at Tristan. "What options do I have?"

"Not many. I intend to take this ship into the Scanner camp and help the survivors escape. I can either tie you up and leave you in here while I do that, or you can help me. Your choice."

Some choice. She certainly didn't want to be tied up—not this close to her comrades. "I guess I'll help."

Tristan watched her closely, but she didn't look away. "I'll be nearby," he said finally.

She accepted his warning for what it was. If she had a chance to escape, she had to make sure this psychokinetic Scanner was nowhere in sight.

"Fasten yourself in." Tristan slid into his chair and took over the controls. "We're going in fast so we won't be spotted."

"How will you be able to get in when my people couldn't?"

"I know what to look for."

Sha'Nara had barely fastened her restraints when

Tristan accelerated the engines, tossing her back into her seat. Though she didn't dare say anything, she found herself holding her breath as they blazed through the thin atmosphere at a speed far too fast for a safe landing.

Avoiding the area obviously occupied by PSI Police, Tristan aimed the craft for a large, dark crater on the back surface of the moon. Sha'Nara wrapped her hands around her armrests. What was he doing? They'd crash.

With impact only seconds away, she saw the opening, nearly invisible against the darkness of the crater. After one sharp turn, Tristan guided the large transport into the corridor and eased the power. They slid to a stop within a large bay, surrounded by rock walls. Her breath shuddered from her in relief, her muscles momentarily weak.

As Tristan cut off the engines, the entire area resounded with an explosion, and rock fragments pelted the spacecraft. He frowned. "I doubt we have much time." Rising from his chair, he glanced back at Sha'Nara. "Work with me here."

She nodded and followed him to the hatch. Since he grabbed no breathing gear, she assumed none was needed. If she remembered correctly, Aktion's moon had a breathable atmosphere, though one very thin with oxygen.

The hatch slid open as another explosion rocked the area. Frightened screams echoed down a tunnel leading away from the bay. Without hesitation, Tristan went into it. Sha'Nara hurried to keep up with him, her attention caught by the intricacy and scale of the underground dwelling. No wonder she had such difficulty locating these people.

Rounding a bend, Tristan froze, and Sha'Nara nearly ran into him. She followed his gaze and gasped. The corridor opened into a large cave, which clearly at one time had held several homes. Most of the dwellings were now rubble. Even as she watched, the ground shook and a large portion of the rock roof crashed down.

But the destruction was not the worst of it. Entwined among the debris were people, some buried beneath the fallen rock, some trying to help, others trying to flee. Screams and crying blotted out all other sound, traveling along Sha'Nara's nerves straight into her heart.

"Grab people and get them into the ship." Tristan moved even as he spoke. "This entire place is ready to collapse."

Sha'Nara hurried to obey. Why were her comrades still bombing? Surely they knew the damage they'd wrought by now. Procedure called for an initial bombing followed by invasion. Couldn't they find an entrance?

Skirting around the shattered remains of homes, Sha'Nara spoke to everyone she passed and directed them toward the transport. The level of destruction shook her. It was one thing to order the elimination of a group, another to witness it.

She saw little evidence of parapsychic powers. Some individuals were attempting to use psychokinesis to move rocks, but none of them possessed Tristan's dexterity or level of strength. Pausing, Sha'Nara swept her gaze over the cavern until she found him heading into the corridor, a child in each arm.

Was he an anomaly even among his own people? Or was his power just more developed? She'd seen evidence of much greater control over PSI abilities among Scanners on the *Hermitage*, yet this settlement displayed nothing more extraordinary than what she'd previously encountered in her PSI Police duties.

Was that why they were in this predicament now? Sha'Nara searched for some evidence that these people were fighting back, but found none. As far as she could tell, they presented no threat at all. Everyone she saw appeared more concerned with survival than trying to fight back.

She doubted the Scanners on the *Hermitage* would react in the same way. When the PSI Police finally located and captured that battleship—and they would—the fight would be long and costly.

Loud agonizing wails pierced Sha'Nara's thoughts, and she ran toward a screaming woman. Snagging the woman by the shoulder, Sha'Nara pointed her in the direction of the transport. "We brought a ship. Go to it now."

"I can't. My children . . ." The woman gestured behind her, her eyes wild.

Sha'Nara looked where the woman indicated, and sucked in her breath. A small hand stuck out from beneath a pile of rubble. Even as she bent to check, she knew she'd find no pulse. Tears stung her eyes. "By Orion's Sword." She'd known there were children among the Scanners, but she'd never encountered them herself. To find one like this . . .

A brief flicker of doubt crossed her mind. Could she justify killing children? "From little Scanners come adult, more dangerous Scanners." She could hear her father say the words.

She started to rise, then checked her movement as she heard a moan from beneath the rock. Was someone else under there? Jerking upright, Sha'Nara grabbed at the boulders and tossed them aside. If another child still lived . . .

Upon lifting several stones, she spotted a thin arm. Before she could touch it, the fingers moved and Sha'Nara's heart leapt into her throat. She whirled around, looking for help.

"Tristan, here, help me."

He joined her at once while the mother stood behind them, crying, her wails impacting on Sha'Nara's heart. Working together, Tristan and Sha'Nara managed to uncover a young girl wedged into a space between several large rocks. Though she appeared unconscious, she moaned softly when Sha'Nara brushed her arm.

One massive boulder pinned the child in the opening. Sha'Nara raised her gaze to Tristan's. "If I can lift it, can you get her out?" he asked.

She nodded and crouched beside the child, ready to spring into action. Tristan not only wrapped his arms around the rock, but apparently used his kinesis as well

107

to move the heavy weight. The strain showed clearly on his face as he held the boulder back.

Not waiting, Sha'Nara squeezed into the opening and encircled the child in her arms. She'd just started to wiggle out when another explosion shook the cave. Smaller rocks flew around them, and Tristan groaned as the rock trembled in his grasp.

Sha'Nara didn't hesitate. Oblivious to the scrapes on her arms, she yanked the child free and fell backward. Immediately Tristan released the boulder and it crashed back into place.

"Get her to the ship," he ordered through uneven breaths.

Sha'Nara nodded. With the child's mother at her elbow, she carried the little girl to the transport. After settling the mother and child as comfortably as possible, Sha'Nara glanced around. Already the ship was nearly full with people . . . Scanners.

For a brief moment, Sha'Nara considered fleeing with the transport, but discarded the idea. She was heavily outnumbered, even if a large portion of those aboard were injured. As she disembarked again, she wondered if her decision came from logic or the heart-wrenching feeling that these people had suffered enough.

More Scanners streamed into the bay, and she directed them inside. At this rate, the ship would soon be loaded to capacity. How many were left?

She'd never seen so many women and children among the Scanners before. In fact, she'd rarely thought of them as having families, relationships.

The main cavern vibrated again beneath another bombing, and Sha'Nara clenched her teeth. Enough was enough. She had to stop this.

When Tristan went with a small group into the corridor, Sha'Nara bolted down another tunnel. Surely somewhere she'd find a passage to the surface.

One path was blocked with fallen debris, forcing her to change direction. The groaning of the unstable structure spurred her onward. She no longer heard cries from the Scanners, but the bombings sounded closer.

A blast knocked her off her feet and she huddled into a ball, her heart in her throat, as rock rained around her. Maybe this wasn't the right thing to do. She couldn't shake a persistent feeling of danger, trouble.

She shook her head. Feelings had no meaning, only logic. Her comrades were out there . . . somewhere. She had to reach them. Once the dust cleared, she climbed to her feet and started again.

Rounding a corner, she paused. Light streamed in through a narrow opening. Though it didn't look as if the opening had been planned for this spot, it did provide access to the surface . . . and the PSI Police.

After a quick glance over her shoulder, Sha'Nara dashed to the surface. She stopped for only a brief moment to get her bearings, then hurried toward the encampment in the distance.

With the moon's thin atmosphere, the surface was rocky, and Sha'Nara stumbled over the uneven ground in her haste. She kept expecting Tristan to materialize at the last moment to stop her.

She concentrated so intently on watching for his presence that she literally ran right into the arms of a PSI Police officer. He gripped her shoulders and jerked her away from him.

"What's this? One of the creatures has bolted." The smile on his face held no warmth.

Sha'Nara shook her head, anxious to set him straight. "No, I'm Sha'Nara Calles. Commander, PSI Police Division Ten."

To her surprise, he laughed. "That's good. You mutants are becoming more clever all the time." He pulled her toward a small group. "Look here. This one says she's a PSI Police Commander."

Anger pulsed through Sha'Nara and she held her head high. "I am a PSI Police Commander. I'm Director Calles' daughter."

All the men laughed now. "I never thought I'd hear one of them claim that," said one man.

"Release me at once and let me call the director," Sha'Nara said. "That will clear this up."

The man holding her shook his head. "Not a chance. If I disturb the director for something as foolish as this, he'd have my head."

Sha'Nara sputtered with frustration. "I am Sha'Nara Calles. Look at my uniform." She stopped abruptly, remembering too late she'd agreed to change into a clean Scanner suit. Why hadn't she held out for another day?

Before anyone could respond, another missile sailed into the air, a streak of light against the sky, before it dove into the surface, shaking the ground. All the men turned to watch it, then grinned at each other in satisfaction when it landed.

The quivering beneath her feet reminded Sha'Nara of why she'd climbed to the surface. "You can stop the bombs now," she said, using her best authoritative tone. "I just came from down there and it's a shambles. You can begin invasion now."

Her captor looked at her in amazement. "A shambles is what we want." He nodded toward the missile operator standing near them. "Keep them coming."

"But you'll kill everyone." Didn't he know proper procedure? She searched his uniform for a sign of his rank. Lieutenant. That explained it. She had yet to meet one of these lower-ranking officers who wasn't out to prove himself.

"A Scanner is better dead than alive," he replied.

"Procedure calls for transporting captives for readjustment."

"Saves everybody a lot of time if they're dead." He yanked her hands behind her back and linked cuffs around her wrists. "And I do have you." His gaze traveled the length of her body, and Sha'Nara fought an urge to gag. "Whether you live to go through readjustment is up to you."

"I am *not* a Scanner."

He tapped the detector on his belt. "This says you are."

For the first time, she noticed the steady beep of alert

emitted by the device and scowled. "It's faulty. Other detectors have done the same thing."

"It's fine. You're the one that's faulty, mutant. Come on." Uncaring of how she stumbled, he dragged her to where two ships were parked, then pushed her to the ground beside one of them. "Now sit and think about the trouble you're in, Scanner."

He gave her a smile that chilled her blood. "And think about how friendly you're willing to be to get out of it."

Sha'Nara blinked, unable to believe she could be in this position. Once she found her way out of this farce, she'd end this lieutenant's career. Sooner or later she'd have to encounter someone who knew her, who could identify her. "Where will you take me?"

"Nearest readjustment center's on Toblerone."

His answer didn't reassure her. She'd never been to the Toblerone outpost. It sat outside her jurisdiction.

The painful reality of her situation crept in. What if no one ever did recognize her? What if she was put into readjustment? Wouldn't someone realize at that point that she wasn't a Scanner?

Tristan's words took on new significance. What if minds really were being destroyed? Panic built up in her chest, and she searched the surrounding terrain for some sign of help.

For the first time she wouldn't mind if Tristan decided to stop her.

Tristan searched the interior of the cave dwellings once more. Everyone was out—at least everyone alive.

Another shudder shook the ground, and a large portion of the ceiling crashed atop the already shattered homes.

Whirling around, Tristan hurried for the transport. And none too soon either. The entire structure would collapse within minutes. They had to get out of there.

As he climbed into the transport, he glanced over those individuals who'd made it. Many emitted quiet moans. Others stared at a sight only they could see. He saw one healer trying her best to help the wounded.

But he didn't see Sha'Nara.

He'd last seen her carrying the injured girl to the ship. Locating the girl's mother, he ascertained that Sha'Nara had left them here and returned to the cave.

A brief flash of panic made his blood run cold. Had she been buried by one of the cave-ins?

Tristan whirled back toward the hatch, the urge to search for her overpowering. The mental image of her body lying bloody and broken sent stabbing pain into his gut. Wrapping his hand around the edge of the door, he squeezed tightly.

If she was dead, so much the better. Logic dictated they were better off without her, but something deep inside him discarded that thought instantly. He had to find her, had to bring her back.

As another explosion rocked the bay, he glanced over his shoulder at all the Scanners depending on him. He couldn't desert them. A lump grew in his throat until he could barely swallow. He couldn't desert Sha'Nara either.

Turning, he faced the ship's occupants. "Can anyone fly this ship?"

Two men held up their hands. The younger one cradled his arm close to his body, while the other had a bloodstained bandage encircling his skull. Neither was a good choice.

Tristan nodded at the healer, and she went to the men immediately. After a few moments, she came to Tristan. "The arm was broken, but I've accelerated the healing properties. He should be fine soon. The head wound is more serious. I've stopped the bleeding, but he'll need more attention."

"Thank you." Tristan gave her a weak smile before he approached the younger man. "I need your help. I have to search for the . . . my . . . ." He trailed off. How did he describe Sha'Nara? His prisoner?

"The woman who was with you?" the man offered.

"Yes." That summed it up. Tristan led the man to the front controls and set the coordinates for the hyperspace leap to the *Hermitage*. "I want you to get this ship out of here. Go into hyperspace as soon as you can. These coordinates will take you to safety."

"What about you?"

"I'll be fine." Tristan didn't believe that, but he had to offer some encouragement. "Give me a few minutes to get clear, then take off."

The man extended his good hand. "Thank you for this. And thank your friend, too, when you find her."

Tristan nodded, surprised by the ache in his chest. "I will."

He hurried away from the bay and into the central cave. Total collapse was imminent. If Sha'Nara was here, he had to find her . . . fast.

As he frantically searched the piles of rubble, he called her name. A small part of him waited for a reply, a moan, something. All he received was the crash of falling rock.

At each site of destruction, he dreaded seeing the fiery red hair visible beneath the boulders, and felt his stomach tighten when he didn't. Another explosion triggered more collapse, and Tristan dashed for the more sturdily built corridor.

He couldn't look here any longer. He'd run out of time.

Moving as quickly as the atmosphere would allow, he continued to scan the tunnel for Sha'Nara even as he made his way to the surface. When he located an opening, he took it, then huddled close to the ground as he viewed the area.

The PSI Police were easy to spot. They made no attempt to hide themselves, confident of their superiority. Disgust rose in his throat. He could kill them all from where he crouched.

Temptation wrapped its alluring arms around him. They'd taken how many lives with their uncaring bombing? Didn't they deserve to die?

For several long moments, he considered it, but his argument with Sha'Nara kept playing in his mind. She believed what she'd been taught. No doubt these officers did, too. They were wrong, very wrong, but would killing them change things?

Tristan grimaced. It would make him feel better.

With a sigh, he focused his attention on the missile launcher. He needed only one powerful push to flip the device on its side. The crunch of breaking bone and an agonizing scream told him he'd managed to land it on the operator. Okay, that made him feel a little better.

Working his way closer, he counted the number of officers. Nine including the one injured. There should be one more. These destroyers always traveled in packs.

As he counted, he realized he was still searching for Sha'Nara. Though she'd been working with him for a change, he wouldn't put it past her to escape. He turned his gaze on the two space cruisers. Was she even now inside relaying the coordinates of the *Hermitage* to Centralia? Would the ship that just fled the moon arrive in time to be captured?

He had to know.

Most of the officers had been diverted by the broken launcher and its injured operator. Tristan easily made his way to the back of the ships. Before he could formulate a plan for getting inside, he heard a familiar voice and froze.

"I'm Commander Sha'Nara Calles. If you'd just let me open a comm channel, I can prove I'm not a Scanner."

Tristan heard the exasperation in her voice. They thought she was a Scanner? He grinned. How fitting.

"I'll say this for you, you're consistent." A male voice answered her, and Tristan knew he'd found the missing officer.

"I'm telling the truth." Anger colored her words. "And once I reach Alliance headquarters, you're going to be out of a job."

"I'm real scared," the man drawled. "Especially since you're not getting anywhere near Centralia. The nearest readjustment center is on Toblerone and that's where you're going."

"I have the right to request a meeting with the PSI Director."

"Scanner, you have no rights at all."

Tristan had to admit to a certain satisfaction at this moment. Sha'Nara Calles was being held as a Scanner. Even her own people didn't believe her. Maybe now she'd have some idea of what Scanners suffered.

Pressed against the side of the ship, he considered his next move. He could leave her and let the PSI Police take the responsibility for her destruction. A bitter taste filled his mouth. Readjustment. What would it do to someone who didn't have parapsychic abilities?

The thought of intelligent, feisty Sha'Nara with her mind erased twisted his gut. As much as she probably deserved it, he couldn't let that happen.

He tried to rationalize his driving urge to rescue her. If somehow she did make these officers believe her, she could destroy everything Tristan, Cadell, and Mael had worked for. Tristan couldn't take that risk.

Maybe she'd learned a lesson and would work willingly with him to achieve Scanner freedom. Tristan grimaced. Yeah, when the Centurian sun burned out.

He studied the PSI cruisers and recognized the model. He'd be able to pilot one of them without difficulty. Backing away from where Sha'Nara and her captor stood, Tristan worked his way to the hatch of the opposite craft, then slipped inside.

His muscles tensed as he paused, waiting for someone to call out an alarm, but evidently all the officers were involved with the bombing. He found the controls and swiftly set the coordinates for a hyperspace leap. He had a feeling he wouldn't want to linger in space once he left this place.

With everything ready for a quick departure, he returned to the hatch. From this angle, he had a good view of Sha'Nara on the ground beside the other ship and the PSI officer who stood nearby. She didn't look pleased. Tristan's lips twitched with amusement.

He needed to be closer to release her cuffs. He ducked behind the ships again and approached as close as he dared. By peeking around the edge of the cruiser, he could see Sha'Nara's hands where they were locked behind her back. Using his kinesis, he had no difficulty in lifting the code key from the officer's belt and applying it to the cuffs.

Sha'Nara's startled expression told him when the cuffs opened. To her credit, she didn't immediately leap up. Instead a calculating look came into her eyes, and Tristan hesitated. What if she'd set up a trap . . . for him?

Sliding along the edge of the ship, she slowly rose to her feet. The officer turned to look at her. "What do you think you're doing?" He came over to put his hand on her shoulder.

"You wanted to know how friendly I was willing to be." The silky smoothness of Sha'Nara's tone warned Tristan, but the officer bought into it, a lecherous smile crossing his face. "I'd like to show you," she continued.

Before the officer had a chance to react, she slammed her fist into his face. Blood spurted from his nose and he staggered backward, his hands to his face. "You . . . you . . ." he sputtered.

Sha'Nara kept her fists ready. "You farding pig. I'll make you regret you ever laid eyes on me."

"And she can, too." Tristan slipped from his hiding place and snared Sha'Nara's wrist. "Time to go."

For a change the look she gave him held warmth and relief, making Tristan catch his breath. When he tugged for her to accompany him, the warmth faded. "I need to use the comms," she said.

"You know I can't let you do that." Forestalling argument, he flung her over his shoulder, then paused to smile at the PSI officer. "I'm sure Director Calles will be interested to hear how you actually had his daughter safe in your custody for a while. Too bad you messed up."

Not waiting to see how his words were received, Tristan bolted for the other spacecraft and tossed Sha'Nara inside. He jumped in after her, then sealed the hatch and pulled her with him to the control chairs.

"Hang on. This is going to be quick and dirty." He

fired up the engines. As he expected, the noise attracted the other officers, who came running.

He only waited to make sure Sha'Nara sat before lifting off the moon's surface. Pressure pushed at his chest, but he managed to whip the craft out of the shallow atmosphere and into space.

As he headed for the optimum launch point, he reverified the coordinates. He couldn't wait to get out of here.

"They didn't believe me." Sha'Nara said finally, her words bitter.

"So I saw." Tristan gave her only a cursory glance. "How does it feel to be treated like a Scanner?"

"I didn't like it."

She spoke so quietly, he wasn't sure he heard right. He turned to look at her in disbelief. "Did you think *we* did?"

"No." She hesitated. "I've never worked with the division in this part of the galaxy. I didn't realize they were . . . that they . . ." Her gaze held defiance. "I've never ordered bombings to continue like that."

"But you still restrained Scanners, took them in for readjustment."

"Of course. That's my job."

"So what's the difference? They're either dead from the bombings or brain-dead from the readjustment." He couldn't contain the anger that rose whenever he thought about this subject. "I'd prefer dead."

"I . . ." Sha'Nara stopped herself, her gaze focusing on the view screen over Tristan's shoulder.

Whirling around, he recoiled, the impact of the image before him equivalent to a kick in the stomach. A PSI Police battleship hovered just ahead of him . . . and it didn't look friendly.

"Perhaps I can bluff my way past." He leaned toward the communication panel, but before he could open a channel, the battleship fired. The beam streaked just in front of his ship. "Or maybe not."

Seizing the controls, Tristan immediately changed

course and applied full power to the engines. He needed to enter hyperspace . . . now.

"Maybe I can talk to them," said Sha'Nara.

More laser beams streaked in their direction. "I don't think they're in the mood to talk." Tristan barely managed to avoid being hit. He couldn't wait any longer.

Gripping the hyperspace lever, he started to pull it toward him. The stars had just begun to fade when the back of the cruiser shuddered, followed by an explosion. The ship spun wildly. Flames erupted at the rear.

Tristan leapt from the controls. Seizing an extinguisher, he concentrated on the fire. To his surprise, Sha'Nara joined him with another extinguisher. In moments, only the acrid odor of smoke lingered in the air. After he vented the smoke into space, he and Sha'Nara exchanged uneasy glances.

As one they returned to the control panel. The view screen showed the blackness of hyperspace, but one look at the controls confirmed that they couldn't maintain this course for long. The engines were failing, their fuel leaking steadily.

Filled with a sense of hopelessness, Tristan faced Sha'Nara. "We're in big trouble."

Chapter Eight

Sha'Nara agreed with Tristan's summation. "We have to get out of hyperspace," she said as she resumed her seat.

"If we *can* get out of hyperspace." His tone was grim. He probably knew as well as she did that the damage to their engine could leave them permanently cast in this blackness until the fuel ran out and the ship disintegrated from the impact of colliding with real space at too slow a speed.

"I know this ship better than you do." Sha'Nara reached for the controls, then glanced at Tristan. "Let me try."

He hesitated for only a moment, then nodded. "Do it."

Of all the Alliance ships, the cruiser was best designed for quick entry into and reentry from hyperspace. If the thrusters lasted long enough for one major push, they had a chance of survival.

With the preset coordinates now useless, Sha'Nara erased them and adjusted the fuel flow. The level dipped steadily. They had to take action now . . . or never.

She turned to Tristan. "Here we go." Something glimmered in his eyes, causing her heart to pound even more rapidly, but his only reply was a tight smile.

Gripping the lever, Sha'Nara drew in a long breath, then eased the ship out of hyperspace. The cruiser vibrated wildly from the unevenness of the thrusters, the hull groaning beneath the pressure. Suddenly the view screen revealed stars, and she could breathe again.

"We're out," she said, surprised that she had succeeded.

"Good job." Tristan kept his attention on the controls. "But we're not safe yet. We'll have to land soon. I'm looking for . . . there, a G-type planet with a breathable atmosphere about fifteen microns ahead. Can we get there?"

Sha'Nara hadn't gotten this far only to give up now. "I can try." Changing direction, she fired one main thrust, then tempered back the engines and let the ship coast through space toward the planet. Landing would be tricky, but not impossible. If only she had more time to assess the level of damage.

As if reading her mind, Tristan went to the rear of the ship and surveyed the burned compartment.

"What do you think?" she asked.

"We have two more burns maximum." He gave her a wry smile. "Make them count."

Two more. Not enough. She needed one to position the craft for entry into the planet's atmosphere and another to guide them down. Without another thrust, how would they stop?

Badly.

Tristan's expression as he rejoined her told her he'd reached the same conclusion. He cast one glance at the planet growing larger in the view screen, then extended his hand to caress her cheek, his gaze solemn. "It's been fun, Sha'Nara."

Her stomach clenched as he leaned closer, but she didn't evade the touch of his lips. Releasing her fears, she responded to the fire he ignited deep inside, her mouth alive beneath his. Desire, full and potent, erupted low in her belly as she wound her hand into his hair.

He broke away too quickly, but continued to hold her chin, his thumb caressing her bottom lip.

"Tristan—" She stopped, uncertain of what she wanted to say. That maybe she didn't hate him after all. That if they'd been different people at a different time, a different place, that maybe . . . What did it matter? She couldn't change anything now.

Turning to look at the planet, she straightened. "We're not dead yet."

Making an instant decision, she fired the engine, swinging the ship around for entry, then blasting into the atmosphere in one movement. Tristan slammed back into his seat and fumbled for the restraints. "You might've warned me," he muttered.

"I'm not sure this'll work, but it's worth a try." This atmosphere was thicker, richer than the one they'd just left. She could already feel the friction against the ship as it burned its way in.

The engines sputtered. *Please, hold. Just a little longer.*

They broke through the cloud cover. She could make out an uneven surface decorated with thick vegetation. If she angled the ship just right . . . Could she use the vegetation to slow them down? Without tearing the ship apart? Did she have a choice?

She cut the thrusters. The ship continued to shudder. Moisture beaded on her forehead. Jerking the craft around, she found a flight path that skimmed the surface of the forest. If she could maintain this altitude for just a little longer . . .

No such luck. She needed more power—power she didn't have. She wiped her moist palms against her legs. The ship dipped into the treetops and the buffeting began in earnest. Through a gap, she spotted a flat opening ahead. They needed to reach that.

Following her instinct, she fired the engine once more. The craft lifted slightly. Just a little further. She could see the wide, flat plain more clearly now. They could slide for some distance without hitting anything. Perfect.

Abruptly the engine died. The ship sank again into the trees. Sha'Nara fought for control, but had none. All she could do was stare at her approaching doom. Between the flurry of leaves and branches she saw a wide tree trunk directly in front of them. She had no slowing thrust left.

They were dead.

She cast a last agonizing glance at Tristan. Then stared in disbelief. He had his hands linked together and extended in front of him as a buffer. His face reflected his concentration. A vein throbbed in his forehead.

He was using his psychokinesis. Did he think that would save them?

They appeared to be slowing. But not enough, not soon enough. Tristan groaned. Sha'Nara rocked back in her seat as something pushed against the front of the ship. Tristan?

No more time.

The ship met the tree, burying its nose into the wood. Sha'Nara jerked against her restraints as she flung her arms in front of her face. She couldn't scream. Her throat was too tight for any sound to emerge.

The control panel crumpled. The sound of tearing metal filled the air. Shattered pieces of the supposedly indestructible view screen showered upon her. Her seat shuddered from the impact. Her breathing came quick and uneven. She waited for the ship to crunch around her.

Then it all stopped.

Silence.

A quiet more unnerving than the previous noise surrounded them. Her body still tense, Sha'Nara slowly lowered her arms and risked a deep breath. She was alive.

Glancing up, she gasped. The tree trunk now inhabited the space formerly occupied by the view screen.

The arms of her seat were embedded into the control panel, neatly trapping her in the chair.

Tristan! She turned and saw him dangling forward in his restraints, obviously unconscious. "Tristan." Her heart skipped a beat. She had to help him.

Unfastening her belts, she managed to wiggle into a standing position on her chair. She jumped to the floor, then froze as the ship quivered beneath her.

How far up the tree trunk were they? At this point, she didn't want to know.

She went immediately to Tristan and released his restraints. He sagged back against his seat. Was he dead? No. He couldn't be. Her heart clenched.

Upon seeing no blood, she felt for his pulse, then released her breath upon finding it. He lived. But was he hurt? How could she tell?

Cradling his cheek in her palm, she examined his face—a face she now knew as well as her own. Who was this man? What part did he play in her life? On impulse, she pressed a light kiss against his lips.

He remained immobile, and she began a systematic search for injuries, running her hands over his shoulders and arms. As she touched his chest, she couldn't stop the shiver of awareness that traveled along her nerves. Even unconscious, the planes and muscles of his body were beyond compare. She traced the flatness of her abdomen, then paused, her hands poised above his loins.

"Touch me there and you'll have my complete, undivided attention."

She jerked her head up to meet Tristan's dark gaze. A half smile framed his lips.

"I was . . . I was just checking for injuries." Heat flooded her cheeks.

"By all means, please continue." He closed his eyes again. "Right now, every place hurts."

Sha'Nara took a step back. "You sound fine to me."

"You're not looking at it from my point of view." Tristan winced as he sat up straight, and she instantly touched his shoulder.

"Are you all right?"

"I think so." He stretched, testing every limb. "It's just my head." His eyes widened as he spotted the tree trunk. "I tried . . . I'd never . . . I guess it worked."

"Did you try to slow us down?" Though she found it hard to believe he had that much power, she knew they should both be dead.

"I tried." He brought his hand up to his head. "Now I'm paying for it with the worst headache of my life."

She placed her palm against his forehead. "Can I help?"

"I feel much better already."

"Oh, you . . ." Pulling her hand away, she jumped back.

Again the ship shuddered, then slipped, the front sliding an arm's length along the tree trunk. "I think we need to get out of here," she said, her pulse racing.

"I couldn't agree more." Tristan started to stand, but the ship trembled again, dropping rapidly. They were falling! With one swift movement, he grabbed Sha'Nara and pulled her on top of him in the chair, wrapping his arms around her securely.

She buried her face against his shoulder, expecting the final impact on the ground to achieve what the first one hadn't. As abruptly as the fall started, it ended with a roaring jolt. Tristan groaned as Sha'Nara bounced against him, and she tightened her hold around his neck.

Slowly she lifted her head. "Are we on the ground?"

"I think so." Tristan studied the tree trunk. "Evidently we weren't up very high."

"That's all right with me." Sha'Nara tried to rise, but Tristan tightened his arms, holding her in place. She met his gaze and shivered from the unshuttered longing she saw there.

"What's your hurry?" he asked quietly.

"Tristan—"

He cut her off with his lips, seizing the words from her mouth even as he sought her tongue. Her body shuddered with response as rational thought fled beneath his persuasive kiss. He made love to her mouth, nipping, teasing, tantalizing, making her want more . . . much more.

He kept his arms entwined around her, yet his kiss touched every secret curve of her body. Heat flared to life, then burned paths along her nerves before lingering to boil low in her belly.

Entwining her fingers in his hair, she pursued the kiss, following his lead, stroking, caressing, seducing. Her breath came in gasps, her breasts crushed against his chest.

She shifted in his lap, aware only of wanting his touch. Instantly she noticed his erection beneath her. She needed to touch him, to find relief for this inner ache.

His masculine scent fueled her already heightened senses. He ran his tongue along her lower lip, and she moaned from mounting desire. Leaning back, she welcomed his lips along her throat, his teeth gently nipping at her pulse.

Easing his hold, he brought his hand up to cradle her breast. Even through the material of her suit, her nipple responded to his light caress. Her breasts tightened and swelled, aching for more. Sha'Nara moaned low in her throat and shifted again. This was wrong. This position . . . this . . .

This was wrong.

Realization filtered through her passion-glazed mind, and she jerked away as if burned. Caught by surprise, Tristan didn't stop her as she regained her footing.

"What's wrong?" he asked, his gaze wary.

"I can't. . . ." Her breath came in short, uneven gasps as she struggled for control.

"You didn't object when I kissed you before."

"Then I thought I was going to die."

"I see." His expression hardened. "A Scanner will do in pinch."

"No, I . . ." What? She'd craved his kisses, his touch, until she'd remembered what he was.

Tristan stood, his desire still evident. "You may find

your options limited, Sha'Nara." He waved his hand toward the destroyed control panel. "I think we're going to be here for a while."

The seriousness of the situation hit her. Though they'd both survived the landing, they had no ship, no communication equipment, no food or water.

No one knew where they were.

Sha'Nara swallowed. She was stranded on this planet with a Scanner . . . and rescue could be a long time arriving.

Tristan watched the panic cross Sha'Nara's face, and grimaced. He should've kept his mouth shut. He hadn't meant to break the news so bluntly, but her withdrawal had touched something deep within him. Though she represented everything he detested, he wanted her. Now that he knew the taste of her lips and curve of her breast, he had to have her.

Inhaling sharply, he turned away. He should be thankful that she'd stopped him. What good could come of a mating between a Scanner and PSI officer?

"We need to check the comms," said Sha'Nara, her voice unsteady.

Tristan grimaced, but ducked down to peer beneath the control panel. His first glance at the smashed equipment offered no indication for hope, but as he dug deeper he found the basic components still intact. The crystals had suffered the worst damage.

Holding the fragments in his palm, he extended his hand to Sha'Nara. "You wouldn't happen to have some spare crystals on you, would you?"

Her grim look answered him.

"No crystals, no comms." He let them fall to the floor and turned toward the hatch. "Let's see where we are."

Sha'Nara trailed after him. "Didn't you check the identifier when you found this planet?"

"I looked long enough to find out what I needed to know. This planet had an atmosphere and it was close." He opened the hatch. Hot, moist air immediately flooded the cabin. For a moment his lungs refused to inhale the thicker mixture. Then the tightness eased and his breathing became regular again.

He gave Sha'Nara an encouraging smile. Her struggle to filter the air exaggerated her chest movements, triggering desire that lay too near the surface for Tristan anytime she was near. He swallowed and turned back to the hatch.

"I think it was called Perdidum," he added.

"Perdidum. I'm not familiar with it."

"Me either." He searched the thick forest outside the ship for signs of life. Nothing moved. "You stay here. I'll see if it's safe."

"I'm coming, too."

"We have no idea what's out there. I want you to stay here." He'd make better time if he didn't have her to worry about.

"Too bad." As Sha'Nara crossed to a panel and opened it, he sighed. He should've known better than to try. Maybe she should come along. He'd worry about her if he left her behind, too. She retrieved two lasers and Tristan tensed.

What did she plan to do with those? She could temporarily get the upper hand—for all the good it would do her.

To his surprise, she crossed the floor and handed one to him. "We might need these."

A strange warmth filled Tristan's veins. Extending his hand, he accepted the weapon, then met Sha'Nara's gaze. For once her eyes held no anger or distrust.

"In this situation, working together helps both of us," she said, keeping her chin high.

"Yes." Tristan couldn't stop the smile that rose to his lips. "Besides, you owe me one."

Before Sha'Nara could protest, he tested the ground outside the ship, then started through the brush. Though he tried to clear a path, more than one branch snapped back as he passed.

"Watch what you're doing." Her grousing carried over the breaking of branches as she followed him.

Good, things were back to normal. The warmth and

camaraderie they'd shared made him uneasy. He had to remember what she was. Her people had ruined his chance for a normal life.

The greenery ended abruptly as Tristan reached the edge of a vast barren plain, rimmed on one side by several jagged rocks. Isolated bursts of smoke rose from random positions on the plain, but he couldn't see their source. The forest ran along two sides, meeting a large body of water in the distance.

Water. Good.

Sha'Nara stumbled into place beside him. "This is where I'd hoped to land."

"Almost made it." Tristan pointed toward the water. "Let's head there. Any form of life, whether civilized or not, should be nearby."

"Do you think there's civilized life here?"

"Could be." He stepped onto the plain, then stopped as his foot sank slightly into the fine white granules. Stooping to sift the grains through his fingers, he searched for the proper word.

"It's sand." Sha'Nara grinned. "Haven't you ever seen it before?"

"No, not like this." He eyed the vast area. "Not so much at once."

She started walking. "I've been to a planet that's nothing but this. Trust me, a little bit goes a long way."

After they'd covered the distance to the water, Tristan agreed with her. His leg muscles ached from the way his feet slid on every step, and aside from the peculiar bursts of smoke near the rocks, it all looked exactly the same. He reached the water with relief.

He immediately bent to cup some in his hands.

"Wait. What if it's contaminated?"

Good point, but he hadn't thought to bring a water tester with him. "It is or it isn't." If not, best they found out right away. He took a cautious sip, then spat it out. "Salty."

"Which might explain why there's no signs of life." Sha'Nara indicated the pristine sand nearby. No footsteps marred the flat surface.

Tristan stood and looked over the water. He couldn't make out an opposite shore. For all he knew, it could cover a major portion of this planet's surface. To survive here, they didn't need salty water, they needed drinkable water.

To his right, the forest lined the shoreline. To his left, he saw sand and rock. Jagged and black, the rocks varied in width and height from waist-high to treetop level. Their obsidian quality appealed to him. "Let's try over there first."

"Why that way? The trees are a more logical choice."

She made sense, but he still wanted to try the rocks first. "I want to see what's on the other side," he said finally. "My instincts tell me there's fresh water nearby."

Sha'Nara shrugged and fell into step with him. "Are you psychic as well as telekinetic?" She sounded curious rather than taunting.

He paused for only a moment. "No, but I got you moving."

Instead of the anger he'd expected, she gave him a wry smile that shot straight to his heart. "I should've known," she said. "Never trust a Scanner."

"I wouldn't say that."

"*You* wouldn't."

Though their words followed the set pattern, they lacked the underlying anger. Instead they held an almost bantering quality. Tristan's chest tightened. He didn't want this feeling of warmth and desire.

Shibit, who was he kidding? He wanted it all too much.

"Be careful, Sha'Nara," he murmured. "You might forget you hate me."

Her gaze hardened. "Not in this lifetime."

"Good." He resumed walking, unaccountably depressed. For some reason, he felt as if he'd destroyed something precious, unique, but he'd had to do it. He knew how to deal with this cold Alliance officer Sha'Nara.

The other Sha'Nara—the one who looked at him with trust and returned his kisses with passion—terrified him. She could destroy him without even trying.

Upon reaching the wall of rock, Tristan stopped to study it. A quiet sense of power radiated from the reflective surface. Perhaps he didn't want to scale it after all.

He spotted a narrow path of sand between two large groupings, and started for it. Sha'Nara didn't move, and he turned back to her. "Come on."

She wrapped her arms around herself as she stared at the rock. "I don't like this. Let's go back."

Her words made him pause. She sounded so certain. "Who's psychic now?" he asked, trying to break her concentration.

It worked. She focused her gaze on him, her lips pressed tightly together. "I just think we should try the forest instead. We're more likely to find water there."

"I want to follow this path. You can wait for me here."

"No." She joined him. "We're staying together."

She wasn't psychic. Probably the dark rocks had spooked her. Yet her concern had affected him. Tristan increased his pace, wondering why he found it so important to see beyond this ridge.

Emerging from between the rocks, he caught his breath. Maybe that was why. A mid-sized lake stretched out below the gentle slope he stood upon. Even from this distance the light danced on the blue-gray surface, inviting them nearer.

Sha'Nara gasped. "Fresh water."

Green grass surrounded the shore, dotted with short trees and even shorter bushes. As Tristan watched, a small furry animal scampered to the edge of the water and drank. "I'd say so."

Impulsively he caught Sha'Nara's hand and started down the slope. With fresh water they could easily survive being stranded here. He tightened his hold on her fingers. Being marooned might not be such a bad thing after all.

He glimpsed movement from the corner of his eye, and came to a sudden halt, steadying Sha'Nara with his arm. As he focused on the large creature approaching in the distance, a cold chill permeated every cell of his body.

Sha'Nara recognized it at the same time. "Thorgs." Her voice held the horror he felt.

"Back up," he ordered. "Let's get out of here."

She didn't hesitate, and he followed on her heels. By the time they reached the path through the rocks, both of them were breathing hard. "Did he see us?" she asked.

"I don't know." Tristan threw frequent glances over his shoulder. Of all the species he'd encountered in his travels, none were as bloodthirsty or ruthless as the armor-plated Thorgs. Slightly taller than an average human, they had a humanoid structure, but far greater strength and a taste for destruction.

Some planets used Thorgs as mercenaries—a task well suited to these beasts, as their armor deflected most laser bursts. They had no feelings, no morals.

Sha'Nara paused as she reached the flat plains again. "Are they coming?"

"I don't think so." Tristan saw no sign of anyone following.

"This isn't their home world."

"They must be visiting." Which meant they probably had a ship. Once he had Sha'Nara safely back at their crumpled ship, he'd try to scout the terrain and see what they were up against. With the element of surprise on his side, he could handle two, maybe three of the creatures . . . if he was fast and his kinesis worked flawlessly.

He touched Sha'Nara's elbow. "Let's get back to the ship."

She didn't move. "No."

"Sha'Nara, we can't stay here."

"I know what you're thinking, and you're not going without me."

Why had he ever thought her intelligence a good thing? Tristan scowled. "I'm just—"

"You're just going to tuck me safely away, then come back to steal a Thorg ship." Her eyes flashed with anger.

"I'm a PSI officer, Tristan. I can take care of myself."

Trouble was, he didn't see her as a PSI officer. She looked all too vulnerable—and desirable. Tristan knew what Thorgs did to women. Death usually came as a relief. He wasn't about to let Sha'Nara anywhere near them.

"You're not—"

She stabbed her finger into his chest. "Oh, yes, I am." Whirling around, she pointed to a tall rock a short distance away. "Let's climb up there and see if we can spot the Thorgs."

Tristan opened his mouth, then shut it. How was he supposed to handle this? Carrying her back to the ship over all that sand would take every bit of strength he had left. Even if they made it, she probably wouldn't stay put.

Grinding his teeth together, he followed her. He'd play it her way . . . for now. But once he decided to take action, he'd tie her up before he let her go with him.

She'd only gone a short distance over the sand when she stopped abruptly. "Tristan, look at this." She waved at him.

At her obvious excitement, he hurried to her side. A mound, with an opening slightly wider than a man's head, jutted out of the ground. The sand around it was black, but amidst the discoloring sat several brilliant crystals in assorted shapes.

"Look, crystals." She started for the mound. "We might be able to make them work in the communications equipment."

As she bent to gather the crystals, a tiny wisp of smoke drifted up from the hole. Recalling the previous bursts he'd seen, Tristan didn't hesitate. He leapt forward, catching her around the waist and rolling them both away from the mound.

In the next instant a pillar of fire exploded from the hole, reaching for the sky with long, deadly arms for several moments, then withdrawing again, leaving nothing but smoke.

Tristan stared at it, his heart hammering against his

ribs. Slowly he became aware of softness beneath his body. Sha'Nara lay under him, her breasts crushed against his chest, her hips cradling his already swelling member, her lips only a murmur away.

Her eyes widened as he hardened against her, but he gave her no time to protest, seizing her lips with a fierceness that proclaimed his passion, his need for her, and his centuries-old male ego that demanded he protect her. He was tired of fighting his lust for this woman. He ached with a need to make love to her and he would . . . as soon as they were safe.

He broke the kiss and stared at her, his breathing uneven. "That's only the beginning." The words emerged raspy from his thick throat.

Her tongue darted out to moisten her kiss-swollen lips. Her eyes had darkened with desire. He recognized it, reveled in it. She would be his.

Her eyes widened suddenly as she gazed over his shoulder. "Tristan!"

He started to turn his head, and caught a glimpse of a Thorg as it swung its fist toward him. Before he could move, the blow impacted with the back of his head.

Dizziness descended. He fought it, struggled to stay conscious . . . and failed.

Chapter Nine

Sha'Nara struggled within the Thorg's grasp as he dragged her with one arm around her midriff to his camp. Despite the fear clogging her throat, she hammered on his armored chest and kicked at his tree-trunk legs, all to no avail.

Terror, unlike anything she'd ever experienced facing the Scanners, swelled within her. She couldn't even talk to these creatures. They refused to listen, and her universal translator couldn't handle their language of grunts and growls. Not that she could sway them anyhow. Thorgs did as they pleased, which usually involved inflicting pain.

She looked for Tristan, and found him flung over another Thorg's shoulder, still unconscious. No help there. Panic squeezed the air from her lungs. What chance did she have against these oversized, super-strong beasts?

At the Thorg camp, her captor dumped her on the ground near one of the stubby trees. She sat where she'd been dropped and assessed the situation. The

Thorg threw Tristan down some distance from Sha'Nara, and she winced at the thud as his body hit the ground, then remained still. The Thorg's blow to Tristan's head had been powerful. Had it killed him?

Her breath caught at the sudden jab of pain in her chest. No, this Scanner couldn't be killed as easily as that.

Searching the area, she spotted two Thorg fighters parked a short distance away. If she could get to one of them, she might have a chance to escape. She counted the Thorgs as they grunted to each other, waving their long, thick arms in punctuation.

Four. Which was four too many.

But she had to try. The Thorgs kept her alive for only one reason—their sexual appetites were as voracious and violent as their lifestyles. Though fighting would do her no good, she didn't intend to cooperate. She hadn't survived kidnapping by Scanners to be destroyed by Thorgs.

Rising slowly to her feet, she kept her gaze focused on the four Thorgs in the center of the camp. From their angry snorts and wild swinging arms, she assumed they were arguing. Over her, no doubt.

That thought didn't give her any comfort.

She took one step backward, then waited to see whether they'd noticed. So far, so good. If she could slip behind this tree, she'd be within reach of the ship. But what about Tristan?

She couldn't abandon him to certain death, but if he were dead already, how could she discard a possible chance to escape? She wavered in indecision.

Her hesitation cost her.

The Thorgs advanced on her as a group, dragging her away from the tree to surround her. Sha'Nara clenched her fists, her muscles tense with anticipation. Swinging her head around, she tried to watch each of the beasts at once.

They towered over her, their black eyes glittering with an emotion she didn't want to define. Their leathery faces resembled that of an ape's which had been smashed in, with prominent nostrils and a wide mouth filled with incisor-like teeth. Their hot breath pelted her from all sides, almost as foul as their body odor—a smell similar to garbage left too long outside. Each of the creatures was as wide as two Tristans. Despite their armor-plated torsos, a combination of a leathery skin and coarse fur covered their limbs.

One standing behind her extended his enormous hand and grabbed her braid, jerking her head back. She tried to pull away despite the pain as he yanked her plaits free of their restraint. Terror welled up inside her, and she struggled to catch a deep breath. She swung at the beast, landing a blow that sent tremors of pain up her arm, but had no noticeable effect on the creature.

Two Thorgs, one on each side of her, seized her arms and held her in place. Panic erupted, fear shuddering through her veins as her heart raced and her mouth went dry. She twisted frantically in an attempt to free herself.

For some reason, her hair fascinated the creatures. The one behind her ran his three fingers through her tresses, uncoiling the braid. As he raised her hair to his nose, Sha'Nara cried out, rising to her tiptoes to ease the pain. He rubbed the strands against his cheek, then growled something to his two nearby companions, who still held her arms perpendicular to her body.

In response, they each grabbed a handful of her hair and brought it to their faces. Agony reverberated through her scalp as Sha'Nara found her head tugged back and forth by their grasps. Tears sprang to her eyes, but she angrily blinked them away.

"Let me go," she ordered.

They ignored her, grunting between themselves in obvious pleasure.

The sudden painful squeezing of her breast brought her gaze quickly to the front. The remaining Thorg stood before her, his massive hand mauling her through her uniform. Sha'Nara kicked at him in a rage, releasing a stream of curses that would've shocked her father. She wasn't about to let these creatures have her.

The beast smiled, if the revealing of his oversized teeth could be called that, and tugged at the front opening of her suit. The Stik-Tite gave at once with a ripping sound that acted as fuel to Sha'Nara's horror.

She couldn't help it. She screamed. But her fear only made the beast grin again. Gripping the front of her T-shirt, he tore it open, then reached for her bare breasts.

"Leave her alone." Tristan's voice sounded weak but defiant, and Sha'Nara looked in his direction, hope springing to life.

He stood shakily, his anger apparent as he stared at the Thorgs. The creature in front of Sha'Nara suddenly jerked backward and fell to the ground. Surprise rushed through her. Even in his weakened state he possessed powerful kinesis. But did he have the strength to fight them all?

The remaining Thorgs deserted Sha'Nara to advance on Tristan. She immediately resealed her uniform, then backed away, her heart pounding so loudly she could barely hear Tristan's words.

"Get out of here, Sha'Nara. Run."

She started to turn when a high-pitched humming filled the camp. A Thorg held a small square device in his hands, his grotesque smile in place. Sha'Nara winced. The shrill noise irritated her ears and pulsed through her head.

Tristan's reaction stunned her. He cried out in obvious agony, clamping his hands over his ears as he sank to one knee.

Sound. Sha'Nara stared at him in disbelief as the full import hit her. The Scanners could be hurt with sound waves. So simple, yet the PSI Police had never thought of it.

With Tristan disabled, the Thorgs attacked. One rammed his meaty fist into Tristan's stomach, and Sha'Nara winced at Tristan's gasp. More blows fell upon him. She felt each one as if it impacted on her.

She had to do something.

With the Thorgs intent on Tristan, she ran to the closest spaceship and leapt inside to search for some type

137

of weapon. Spotting the control panel, so easily accessed, she hesitated. She could escape now and they'd never catch her.

No. She dismissed that thought instantly. Tristan had saved her from her own people despite the risk to his own life. She could at least do the same for him.

A large full-barrel laser sat in a rack on one wall of the ship. Sha'Nara had never seen anything like it. Perhaps here was one weapon even the Thorgs couldn't shrug off. She staggered under the weight of the laser as she removed it. It had obviously been designed with Thorgs in mind.

A quick scan of the weapon gave her a clue as to how it worked. She had no time to waste. Jumping from the craft, she ran back to the camp, slowed by the weapon's heaviness.

Tristan's groans reached her ears, mingled with the beasts' laughing grunts. Despite her pounding head, fiery hot anger burned in her veins, and she raised the laser into firing position.

Her first shot seared through the back of one Thorg and he fell instantly. Before she could rejoice at that small victory, the others turned on her. Firing steadily, she concentrated on missing Tristan while destroying these monsters.

One shot hit a Thorg's shoulder, while another disintegrated one creature's head. The remaining beast ran at her with a horrendous scream. Sha'Nara didn't flinch. She fired.

At first, his armored chest appeared to deflect the blast. Then suddenly he stopped and collapsed to the ground only an arm's length away.

One more shot destroyed the high-pitched sound box. Sha'Nara swallowed hard and hurried to where Tristan tried to stand up. Blood trickled from cuts on his face and lips, and his slow movement indicated internal pain as well. She wanted to wrap her arms around him in an attempt to stop the pain—a totally illogical action.

Instead she gripped his shoulder and helped him to his feet. "Can you walk?"

He nodded, a slight movement of his head, and started forward. After a few steps, he staggered, and Sha'Nara had to drop the laser in order to position herself beneath his arm and support his weight. She hated giving up her only advantage, but helping Tristan was more important.

"Come on. We're getting out of here."

They made slow progress toward the fighter. As they neared the hatch, the back of her neck prickled with warning. Glancing back, Sha'Nara saw one of the Thorgs getting to his feet.

Shibit, she should've made sure she'd killed them, but she'd been more concerned about Tristan. Now she wished she had found a way to carry the heavy weapon and help him.

"Hurry up." She pushed Tristan into the fighter and jumped in after him. After sealing the hatch, she steered him toward the two seats, one in front of the other, by the control panel. Though the seats reflected the Thorgs' larger size, the overall interior of the ship was more cramped than either craft she'd flown in thus far.

"Can you fly this thing?" Tristan muttered as he sank into the rear seat.

"Don't know, but one ship's pretty much like the other." Sha'Nara faced the controls. "How difficult can it be?"

Very.

The labeling of controls bore no correlation to anything she knew, and the oversized levers and buttons could activate anything. She studied the panel, looking for something familiar. Tentatively, she turned a switch and was rewarded with the engine's roar.

Maybe she could do this after all.

A loud blast against the side of the ship caught her complete attention. The laser gun! The farding Thorg must've found it.

Sha'Nara inhaled sharply. No time to study the controls now. Gripping what she hoped was the correct lever, she eased it back. The fighter headed for the sky at a speed that tossed her against the seat.

As they reached the starry blackness of space, she released the breath she'd been holding and looked back at Tristan. "We made it."

"Good." His wan smile made her ache for him. "Can you figure out the hyperspace controls?"

"I can try." She saw a place to enter coordinates, but the numbering system didn't correspond to anything she knew. In frustration, she spun one of the dials to something similar to Centralia's coordinates, but were they? A slight mistake could put them in another part of the galaxy. Or worse, in the center of a star.

"Set them for the *Hermitage*," said Tristan. When she didn't reply, he leaned forward, his pain obvious at the slight movement. "Do you intend to turn me in to the PSI Police? Why bother to save me then? I'll be killed or readjusted anyway."

"I . . ." How could she explain? She'd saved him because she couldn't bear to see him hurt, couldn't leave him behind to die. But she had to return to Centralia and get help to rescue Jacy.

Even if it meant delivering Tristan to be readjusted?

Her stomach clenched. If what he'd told her was true, she'd be condemning him to a mindless existence. How could she do that to someone so vital, so alive?

But he could be lying to her. Readjustment was probably just what she'd always been told it was—an elimination of the PSI ability from a Scanner's brain. Why should she believe Tristan over her father?

"I'm doing what I have to do," she said finally.

"Sha'Nara—" The anguish in his voice wrapped itself around her heart. He cut off with a groan and sank back in his seat, apparently unconscious.

"This is what's best." She said the words out loud as if convincing herself. Best for whom? For Jacy, who wanted to remain with the Scanners? For Tristan, who could be a prisoner or lose his mutant abilities? For her?

Sha'Nara paused. What did she want? Her job dictated she return to Centralia and procure help to lead an attack against the Scanner battleship. She'd always worked hard, followed the rules, used her logic to deal with any difficult situations.

Except lately, logic hadn't worked very well. Logic had nothing to do with the twist in her gut when she looked at Tristan's bloodied face. Logic would banish her attraction to this Scanner and keep her focused on the mission at hand.

With a shake of her head, Sha'Nara started to set what she hoped were the final coordinates. A nearby blast distracted her as the reverberations shook the fighter.

Unable to discern the blips on the monitor, she tried to bring her craft around. Though only partially successful, she saw enough. The Thorg had evidently recovered enough to follow her in the second fighter. Since he knew how to handle his ship, this could be a very short battle.

A missile streaked past on Sha'Nara's view screen, and she snapped to attention. One of these buttons had to fire the weapons. She pressed one after another with no apparent result.

Suddenly, the sound of the engine changed and Sha'Nara glanced up. "By Orion's Sword." She'd done it now. The view screen revealed the blackness of hyperspace.

And she hadn't a clue as to where they were going.

Unable to determine anything more from the settings, Sha'Nara threw herself back in her chair in defeat. Even if she knew how to bring them out of hyperspace early, she'd run just as big a risk. Better to wait and see where they emerged.

She turned her attention to Tristan. He hadn't moved since he'd lapsed into unconsciousness. How badly hurt was he?

Her insides knotted as she climbed to her feet. Did this ship have a medtech unit? She refused to think about Tristan dying because she didn't have help for his injuries.

A thorough search turned up a rectangular-shaped

object she thought could be a medtech unit, but when she tried to activate it nothing happened. Just as well. With the differences in Thorg physiology, the device probably wouldn't work on Tristan anyway.

She did locate some moisture pads, and used those to clean the dried blood from Tristan's face. As the gash on his cheekbone became visible, she blinked in surprise. She could've sworn this had been a gaping wound, but now the edges were knit together, already showing signs of healing.

The cut on his lip had disappeared. Sha'Nara finished her cleansing, then studied his features. Though his cuts appeared to be healing, he still wore large bruises on his cheeks and jaw.

Her heart felt too large for her chest. He'd been trying to save her. Had saved her, in fact. If he hadn't intervened, she would've suffered the proverbial fate worse than death. Remembering the grasping Thorgs, Sha'Nara shuddered. That cliche didn't feel too far from the truth.

She ran her palm gently along the contours of his face, then jerked her hand back. Cold. His skin was so cold. Was he alive? Locating a thready pulse in his neck, she breathed a sigh of relief. He lived . . . for now.

She had to get him warm.

Recalling the discovery of an insul-bag during her earlier search, she hurried to pull it out. Though the area behind the seats was limited, she found enough floor space to stretch out the bag and activate it. Now to get Tristan into it.

As she struggled to get his limp form out of the chair and onto the bag, she wished for a portion of his kinesis. Anything had to be easier than this.

He outweighed her by several kilos, but she'd handled problems tougher than this. Though he probably gained more bruises in the process, she managed to drag him onto the bag and fasten it around him. Gasping, she collapsed beside him.

Why go through all this for a Scanner? She frowned.

Because he mattered. Somehow the farding man had managed to make her care about him.

Illogical. Caring for him went against everything she believed in. Yet somehow it felt so right.

She sighed and sat up to study his face. So familiar, but still a stranger. They had nothing in common, yet his kisses made her forget that, forget everything except the unfurling knot of desire deep inside.

On impulse she pressed her lips to the bruise on his cheekbone. "Don't you dare die on me, Scanner," she murmured. The slightly salty taste of his skin drew her back for more, and she gently kissed his scraped jaw. With his lips only a breath away, it felt natural to brush them with her own . . . until they suddenly moved beneath hers.

With a start, she jerked away, her eyes wide. Laughter danced in Tristan's now alert gaze. "I'm already beginning to feel much better."

"You!" Relief mingled with her embarrassment. "I thought you were dying."

He pushed himself into a sitting position. "It wasn't that bad. I just needed to shut down for a while and try to heal."

"Are you a healer, too?"

"Not in the usual sense. I can't heal anyone else. It takes everything I have to heal myself. As it is, I only took care of the major injuries. I can live with the aches and bruises." Before Sha'Nara could move, he took her hand in his. "But thank you for your concern."

He kissed the back of her hand, sending her hormones into a frenzy, then met her gaze, his expression solemn. "It's not what I'd expect from someone who plans to turn me over to be killed."

She jerked her hand away. "They won't kill you."

"Yes, they will. One way or the other." A sense of inevitability colored his words, and a chill danced along Sha'Nara's nerves.

Opening the insul-bag, he gingerly climbed to his feet, then looked at the view screen. "Hyperspace. Where are we going?"

He kept his tone even, but the tenseness of his shoulders alerted Sha'Nara to how much her answer mattered. "I don't know."

"Sha'Nara . . ."

"I *don't* know," she repeated, anxious that he believe her. "The Thorg started attacking us before I set the coordinates. I tried to fire the weapons, and put us in hyperspace instead."

Tristan studied the controls. "These numbers are gibberish. We could end up anywhere."

"That's what I'm afraid of." Sha'Nara joined him. "I have no idea how long it'll take either."

"Do we have food? Water?"

She nodded. "I found some water packets earlier and—I think—some food pouches. Since it's Thorg food, I'll have to be pretty hungry before I try it."

"I agree." Tristan stared at the black screen. "I hope it doesn't come to that."

Sha'Nara couldn't stop herself from touching his arm. Neither could she explain the feeling that they would survive, that all this was right. "We're going to be fine."

She shook her head as Tristan turned to face her. At least her father wasn't here to witness how easily she'd lost her grasp of logic.

"I actually believe you when you say that." Tristan gave her a half smile that didn't reach his eyes. They had darkened, and searched her face for an answer she couldn't yet give.

When he extended his hand and gently caressed a strand of her hair, she realized it still hung loose around her shoulders. After the Thorgs, his touch should've alarmed her, but it didn't. Instead, a slow heat spread insidiously throughout her body.

She raised her hands to her hair in a sudden panic. "I . . . I need to braid it again."

"Don't." Tristan spoke so quietly she barely heard him. "It's beautiful this way."

She'd never thought of her hair as beautiful. A nuisance, perhaps. Definitely the worst possible color in the galaxy. "It's—"

"It's so much like you." He slid his fingers through it, slowly, with a sensuousness that added to the ache growing inside her. "Untamed, fiery, and beautiful. So very beautiful."

His gaze said he spoke of more than her hair, and Sha'Nara's throat tightened. He held the side of her face in his palm, his fingers extending beneath her hair.

"Did they hurt you?" he asked abruptly.

She knew immediately what he meant. "No, not really. They didn't have time." If it hadn't been for him . . . "Thank you."

He lowered his hand. "I don't want your thanks." His voice sounded colder, restrained, and she frowned. What had she done?

Curling his hands into fists, he stepped back, then met her gaze with his own. She recoiled from the heat in its depths, her heart skipping a beat. "Tristan . . ."

"I want you, Sha'Nara." He didn't look happy about it. "Whatever this is between us is insane. It's a death wish, but I'm tired of fighting it. I want you so badly I can hardly stand."

Her breasts swelled as the fire in her belly blazed higher. She was tempted, so tempted. "And if I say no?"

"Then I expect this'll be a long, painful trip for both of us." Not looking away, he peeled open his flight suit and removed it and his boots.

He stood before her, vulnerable and proud, wearing only his micro-briefs, which did little to disguise his obvious desire. "It's your move, Sha'Nara. Am I wrong in believing you feel this, too?"

She had to swallow twice to ease the dryness of her throat, her gaze riveted to his erection. The fire within her begged for fuel, the ache between her loins screamed for satisfaction, for Tristan. A brief memory touched her mind—of sweaty closeness, touching and kisses, a mating that was more than physical.

Without hesitation, she opened her suit and stepped out of it and the tattered remains of her undershirt.

When she bent to remove her boots, Tristan knelt before her. "Let me."

He easily slid first one boot, then the other off her feet. But he didn't release his hold on her leg. To her surprise he kissed the hollow of her knee, and she gasped at the bolt of need that speared her.

With agonizing slowness, he continued to press kisses as he rose—along her inner thigh, atop the mound barely covered by her underwear, in the indention of her belly, at the valley between her breasts. By the time he reached her lips, Sha'Nara could barely stand, let alone breathe.

"This is . . ." She wanted to say wrong, but couldn't. How could anything that felt this wonderful be wrong?

"Beautiful." He raised his hand to cup her breast and tease the peak with his thumb. "So beautiful."

She tensed at first, remembering the Thorg's painful grasp. Then she relaxed, her tension melting beneath his gentle touch. His lips moved upon hers. He pressed his hips against her, enticing her with his rigid erection, until she stumbled against the control panel.

He caught her easily, wrapping his arm around her waist. "This ship isn't designed for this," he murmured. "Fortunately, we don't need a lot of room."

Without loosening his hold, he guided her to the back and eased her down onto the insul-bag. Its softness acted as a cushion on the metal floor, but Sha'Nara barely noticed as Tristan stretched beside her, his lips finding hers again.

Gaining admittance to her mouth, he seduced her with his tongue, stroking, plunging, promising. When he caressed her breast, tormenting her already firm nipple into greater prominence, she couldn't hold back the moan that rose from deep inside her.

Tristan chuckled, the sound apparently pleasing him. "Just let go, Sha'Nara." He trailed kisses along her neck, then nipped gently at the base of her throat. "Just feel."

Feel? Her body burned with sensation, with wanting. How could she possibly feel more than this?

He drew her breast into his heated mouth, and she

cried out. The coil in her belly contracted even more. She wrapped her fingers in his hair, pulling it free from its ponytail until it framed his head and played erotically over her skin. His masculine scent surrounded her, escalating her already heightened need for this man.

As he suckled, nipping gently with his teeth, she arched against the floor, the ache between her thighs threatening to tear her apart. "Tristan, I . . . I . . ." How could she put it into words, this demanding need?

As if he understood, he eased his hand beneath her underpants, exploring with his fingers until he located one special spot amidst the moist folds. He stroked only a few times before her body tensed, then exploded in ripples of pleasure that traveled from one end to the other.

"Oh." No wonder people sought this mating. Sha'Nara relaxed briefly as the ripples eased.

Tristan brushed her lips with his. "That is only the beginning."

"There's more?" How could anything compare with such pleasure?

"Much more." He quickly removed their underwear, then began again, using his hands and mouth to build her tension to a new peak. She hadn't believed it possible.

As he explored every inch of her skin, flashes of her dream arose, mingled with the moment, then disappeared, until nothing remained but the reality, the feeling, the rightness. In a brief moment of sanity, Sha'Nara realized she'd never dream that again. Not now.

His erection pulsed against her thigh, and she rocked toward it. Tristan groaned, adding to her pleasure. She reached between them to touch his organ, but he snatched her hand away.

"Don't." He could barely speak. "I can't wait much longer."

"Then don't." She slid her hands over his chest.

"I want to be sure you're ready." He drew his tongue

over the taut tips of her breast, and she inhaled sharply, the pressure inside her threatening to explode once again.

"I doubt I could be more ready."

He gently suckled at one nipple, and she squirmed beneath him, unable to breath, unable to think. "Tristan, now."

With surprising gentleness, he knelt between her thighs and began to move. Slowly. He entered slightly, then withdrew. Too slowly.

Sha'Nara's tension grew.

He probed further, then withdrew.

She groaned with frustration. She needed him, all of him. The next time he moved, she wrapped her legs around him and thrust her hips up to meet his.

A brief sensation of pain gave way to the fullness of him, to the rightness of their joining. The tightness of his muscles showed his strain as he remained still. Unwilling to wait any longer, she began to move along his rigid length.

With a groan, he took control, thrusting deep, filling her. New sensations replaced the old, even stronger, more overpowering than before. Impossible. Wonderful.

The need low inside her wound even tighter, tinged with steady swirls of pleasure. A sense of forever surrounded them.

Tristan gripped her hips and plunged even deeper. Sha'Nara shattered around him, dissolving into spasms of pleasure so intense she cried out, gripping his shoulders even more firmly. A short moment later, he pulsed within her, adding to her slowly fading shivers of delight.

As he collapsed on top of her, she stroked his long dark hair and marveled at the experience. No dream could begin to compete with this. She'd never taken a lover, and now wondered why she'd resisted. How could she have lived this long without knowing of this ecstasy?

Yet no one had appealed to her, stirred her desire,

until Tristan. For the first time she felt as if she'd found the place where she belonged, really belonged.

She tried to picture their future, her by Tristan's side, and saw them running, shot at, discarded. Her father's face appeared in her imagination, condemning her, pointing an accusatory finger at Tristan. "Are you willing to give up everything for a Scanner?"

Reality intruded like a harsh slap. Sha'Nara dropped her hand. Orion's Sword. What had she done? Her job called for her to capture Scanners, not make love to them. Already she found it difficult to see the people as the powerful evil she knew them to be. How could she face Tristan now and see him as the enemy?

As if sensing her withdrawal, Tristan rolled away from her and propped his head on his hand. "Are you sorry?"

Sorry? That she might never have known this pleasure made her sorry. If only he were someone else. "No, just realistic." She sat up, pulling her knees to her chest and wrapping her arms around them. "This can never happen again."

"Because of who I am?"

"Because of who I am." She was a Commander of the PSI Police. How could she have forgotten that? Her job meant everything to her. Could she discard it so recklessly for a few moments of ecstasy?

Tristan touched her knee. "What is it? You've gone pale."

She stood instantly and went to pull on her clothing. "Never again. Never." She had a duty to uphold. As she dressed, she tried to impose logic over her unsteady emotions.

"Sha'Nara—" Tristan approached her, fastening his jumpsuit.

Before he could finish, a loud wail sounded and the ship jerked once. Looking at the view screen, Sha'Nara saw they'd emerged from hyperspace.

In an instant, she recognized the stars, the planet

barely visible to one side. Not Centralia, but Hyperion, home to one of her PSI Police Divisions.

The comms sounded with a hail at the same time a ship came into view—a PSI Police ship.

Chapter Ten

Tristan waited, watching Sha'Nara intently as he finished dressing. Though wary, he saw no immediate danger. The PSI Police had no idea who was in the Thorg fighter. Did she plan to turn him in? Could she, after what they'd just shared?

His senses still reeled from the passion of their joining. He'd hoped that making love to her would stem the desire she created within him, but touching her, tasting her, sharing with her only made him want more. Why her of all women? She had to be the worst possible choice in the entire galaxy . . . and he still wanted her.

He'd never experienced such a complete feeling of blending, becoming one before. They each gave and took, their bodies matching perfectly in rhythm and desire. He shook his head. Her PSI Police status had become merely incidental. That he could forget that at all was an indication of how much she affected him. Watching her, he couldn't stop the warmth that flooded through him.

He wanted to take her in his arms, inhale her mes-

151

merizing scent, and mold her soft curves along his body. If she growled gibberish into the comm channel, the PSI Police would consider them Thorgs and leave them alone. No one started a fight with a Thorg if he could help it.

Then Tristan could try to deal with her rapid withdrawal, her sudden coolness. Yes, they had differences, but his desire failed to consider that.

After all, she appeared to be changing from the rigid officer he'd first met. She'd actually taken the time to help him escape the Thorgs. She'd moaned beneath his lips, his hands, and begged for more.

His body hardened, just remembering. How could he be ready to make love to her again so soon? She finished closing her jumpsuit, hiding her perfect breasts, and he nearly groaned at the deprivation.

The hail continued over the comms, and Sha'Nara leaned forward, her palms on the panel, her face almost touching the view screen. Her body tensed. Tristan didn't doubt this type of decision was hard for her, but she was coming around to their side. If she intervened for them with the Alliance . . .

She glanced over her shoulder at him, her internal struggle evident. "I . . ." She bit her lip, then met his gaze. He barely had time to read her confusion before her expression hardened. "I have to do this." Trepidation rose as he registered her look.

She turned and suddenly activated the comm switch. "This is Commander Sha'Nara Calles. You must rescue Jacy Vadin." She spoke rapidly, her words tumbling over one another, affecting Tristan like a physical blow. The immediate sense of betrayal stunned him.

"She's on a battleship. Forty—"

He disconnected the communications with a thought, then hurried forward to pull her away from the panel. As he gripped her wrist, he had to fight his first urge to hold her close. She whirled around, her color heightened.

"I had to do it." Her pulse beat rapidly at the base of her throat. "I have to save Jacy."

"I can't let you do that." Didn't she yet realize she couldn't fight him?

Her gaze turned defiant. "You can't keep me prisoner forever."

A chill colder than space poured through his blood. He should've known better. PSI officers didn't change, couldn't change. If he'd thought with his brains instead of his passion, he'd have realized that.

"Try me," he muttered. Jerking Sha'Nara into the rear seat, he quickly studied the controls. He knew where he was. By comparing the Thorg coordinates with those he knew to be true, he translated their method of measurement.

He had only moments to get them into hyperspace again. He spun the coordinates to match his calculations for the *Hermitage*, then searched for the hyperspace lever. None existed.

The PSI ship fired a warning laser across the bow. They wouldn't destroy the fighter, not with Sha'Nara aboard, but they could disable it. He pushed frantically at the buttons on the panel, all the while keeping one ear focused on Sha'Nara.

He heard her rummaging through the various storage units in the back, but couldn't take the time to stop her. They had to get out of here. Now.

"Get away from there." Her voice held a slight tremor that captured Tristan's attention.

He looked around and inhaled sharply. She'd managed to locate a Thorg sound box, and held it in her hands. A quick jab of fear overrode his initial disappointment.

She knew the one weapon that could destroy Scanners, and obviously meant to use it. He'd been a fool to think she might be different from the other PSI Police. Rage burned low in his gut. Her response to his kisses had no doubt been a ploy to lull him into a false sense of trust. He wouldn't make that mistake again.

"Do you intend to use that?" He kept his voice calm, but his anger seeped through.

"If I have to." Though her voice wavered, she approached him slowly. From the way she held the box, Tristan knew she didn't have a clue as to how it operated. "Get away from the controls and open the communications channel," she ordered.

"No." With one strong kinetic movement, he tore the box from her hands and smashed it on the floor. She cried out in protest as it broke into pieces. He ignored her and returned his attention to the control panel.

He finally found the right button. The sudden jump to hyperspace threw him into his seat. Gripping the chair arms, he leaned forward to double-check his settings. If his haphazard calculations were correct, they should return to the *Hermitage*.

Now to deal with Sha'Nara.

A bitter taste lingered in his mouth as he stood to face her. She sat on the floor, where the abrupt leap had thrown her, but quickly scrambled to her feet. Though her expression showed only defiance, he caught a glimmer of trepidation in her gaze. Good.

The sound box provided a satisfying crunch beneath his boots as he approached her. He stopped in front of her, curling his fists.

"What did you hope to achieve with that stunt?" he asked. "Wasn't your betrayal complete enough?"

"I . . ." She swallowed. "I'm a PSI Police officer." If possible, she stood even straighter, her shoulders square. "I have an obligation to protect Jacy, even if you don't like it."

"You weren't thinking of Jacy a short while ago." Against his best intentions, his bitterness seeped out.

Though a flush rose in her cheeks, her expression didn't change. "That was a mistake."

"Obviously." Tristan berated himself again for giving in to his attraction to her.

"I didn't think." She moistened her lips in a nervous gesture, and Tristan held himself rigid, fighting the urge to cover her mouth with his own. "I've erred in letting my feelings control my actions. It won't happen again."

"That's right." He gave her a mocking grin. "Cold, orderly, logical. That's how you like it, isn't it?"

"Yes."

Her feeble reply didn't sound convincing. He raised one eyebrow.

"Yes." She repeated it more firmly. "That's how I like it."

"Then live with it." He whirled around, unable to bear her closeness any longer. As the shattered box crunched again under his feet, he bent to lift one of the pieces.

"Do you know what this was?" Against all reason, he hoped she didn't, that she only knew it could hurt him, but not how.

"I believe it uses sound waves," she said evenly. "These waves hurt Scanners."

His hopes sank, and he tried to forestall the damage. "They only hurt me."

"I doubt that."

Damn her intelligence!

"The Thorgs wouldn't carry around these boxes on the off chance they would meet you," she said. She took the broken piece from his hand and studied it. "Whatever this is can hurt all Scanners."

She met his gaze steadily, though she had to realize what she'd just said. Tristan returned to his seat, unwilling to look at her any longer. She'd just sealed her own death.

Mael could never let her leave the *Hermitage* knowing about the effect of sound waves on Scanner brains. Though Sha'Nara wouldn't have a sound box to show her people, she could describe it and they'd devise one as quickly as possible.

How would Scanners have any chance once PSI Police carried these devices? No matter how well developed Tristan's kinetic ability was, he had no defense against this. To his knowledge, only the Thorgs had learned that high-intensity sounds waves caused Scanners debilitating pain. No doubt they'd come upon that secret in one of their torture sessions. But Thorgs didn't share, thus keeping this information to themselves.

Now Sha'Nara knew, which meant eventually the entire Alliance would have this secret if she lived to tell it. The Scanners would be doomed.

With a sigh, Tristan tried to concentrate on the foreign controls. He'd need to know what he was doing when it came time to dock the fighter. *If* his coordinates were correctly set.

If not—if they emerged only to plunge into the gaseous center of a star, then they would die. At least it would quick and relatively painless, and perhaps the best solution in the long run.

Sha'Nara had been made his responsibility. How could he face Mael with this information? What would he do if Mael directed him to kill her? Could he? At one time, maybe, but not now. He'd lost a part of himself when they made love. He could regret their joining. Part of him could want to kill her. But he couldn't do it.

The minute he touched her, he'd be lost.

He wove his fingers through his hair. "Shibit."

"You have to kill me now, don't you?" Sha'Nara spoke quietly as she sat in the rear seat.

"I should." Tristan glanced back at her. "But I won't."

"I didn't ask to know this. It was handed to me."

"You don't have to tell the Alliance either."

"Yes, I do."

Her lack of hesitation tore at him. She was an officer doing her duty. What did he expect?

"Well, that should be an honor," he said dryly, returning his gaze to the controls.

"An honor?"

"You'll be singly responsible for wiping out an entire race of people. You should make the Alliance history records, at least." His gut churned.

"Extermination isn't our intention. Readjustment—"

He whirled on her. "Don't give me that. Readjustment is a death sentence. Only in some cases, it's a living death."

She stiffened. "I have no reason to believe you. Confusing me is in your best interests."

"Yeah, so's living."

Before she could retort, the alarm wailed and the ship

slid out of hyperspace. Tristan checked his chronometer. A fast ship made a difference. Even if this was a Thorg vehicle, it would make a good addition to the tiny Scanner fleet.

Almost afraid to look, he searched the stars. He'd barely registered the familiarity when the *Hermitage* appeared on the view screen. Uncurling his fingers from his chair arm, he grimaced.

They'd made it back, but now what?

Activating the comms, he signaled the battleship. "Tristan Galeron requesting permission to dock."

"Permission granted."

"Did the transport arrive from Aktion?" In all the ensuing commotion, he'd almost forgotten about the injured Scanners.

"They made it. Everyone's been transferred to medical or quarters."

"Tristan, we were worried about you." Mael's voice replaced that of the comms operator. "How did you end up with a Thorg ship?"

"It's a long story." Tristan cast a quick glance at Sha'Nara. "I'll tell you later."

He closed the channel and played with the controls in an attempt to guide the fighter into the docking bay. Though it was far from smooth, he managed to steer the craft to a safe landing.

After cutting the engines, he stood and gazed down at Sha'Nara. "Let's go."

She rose slowly. "Now what?" If not for the tiny quiver in her voice, he would've believed her defiant attitude.

"You realize we can't ever let you go now."

Her eyes widened. "What about Jacy?"

"She can return . . . if you don't pass on what you know." He waved for Sha'Nara to precede him off the ship.

"I won't stay here." She paused as the hatch opened and glared at him. "I'll keep trying to escape."

"I know." Sadness filled him. "And one of these times

the only way to stop you will be to kill you. And that's where it'll end."

The color drained from her face. "I might be successful."

"I doubt it."

She swung at him with her fist, but he caught it and pulled her into his firm embrace. "I hate you," she said angrily.

Her words said one thing, her body another. Tristan's own senses alerted instantly to the way her nipples tightened against his chest, to the softening of her curves, to the sudden rush of pink to her face. Her parted lips begged for his kiss.

Releasing her fist, he smoothed her hair away from her face. "No, you don't." He understood her feelings. They mirrored his own. "You only wish you did."

She jerked away from him, and he released her without a word. At the entrance to the docking bay, she hesitated. "Where now?"

He remained by the fighter. "Go where you will. You can't escape and we have no more secrets."

Her face reflected her surprise, but she didn't argue. Instead, she stepped through the sliding door and hurried away.

Tristan curled his fingers around the edge of the hatch. He ought to follow her, keep her out of trouble, but he couldn't. Not right now.

"Did I just see Sha'Nara going down the hall?" Cadell burst into the docking bay, his customary smile in place. "Aren't you planning to stop her?"

"You go after her." Tristan wandered to the computer terminal in the corner. "I want to upgrade the security for the bay first." He had a feeling he'd need it . . . soon.

Sha'Nara couldn't get far enough away from Tristan. She followed one corridor, then another, not caring where she went. Just so long as that farding Scanner didn't come near her, didn't touch her.

Despite her attempt to fuel her anger, fear trickled in. When he'd held her close, when she'd felt his erection hardening, her body had betrayed her. She'd wanted him.

Insanity. Impossible.

She walked rapidly, trying to burn off her anxiety. When he'd told her she had to remain a prisoner forever, her first thought had been of whether he would still be her captor . . . if she'd still be kept in his quarters . . . in his bed.

If he kept her prisoner, forced her to have sex, it wouldn't be her fault. But her guilt wasn't so easily absolved. He wouldn't have to force her into his bed. All he had to do was kiss her again, and she feared her defenses would shatter.

Even worse, for one brief instant, the thought of staying here with Tristan had created excitement, not anger. Sha'Nara blew out an exasperated breath. What was wrong with her?

He was the enemy, a Scanner. How could she consider staying here on a ship full of Scanners, a ship full of . . . people. Images from Aktion's moon filled her mind. None of the Scanners had looked like the enemy then.

She shook her head. An illusion. Everything Tristan did was designed to keep her off balance, to make her doubt her entire life's teaching.

Had making love to her been part of his plan?

Her stomach clenched. During that wonderful moment when they'd joined, shared in all they were, she'd felt as if she'd come home, as if she'd belonged, as if their mating had been preordained and nothing she could've done would've stopped it.

Foolishness. All Tristan's actions were planned, and despite his protests to the contrary, she still believed Mael had planted her erotic dream. After all, it made her more pliable, more easily swayed by Tristan's seductive masculinity.

From now on, she'd only give heed to her logic, not these rampant feelings, uncontrollable emotions. Yet she found it difficult to maintain her logical shell.

She'd had to force herself to contact the PSI Police

ship when the Thorg fighter had emerged from hyperspace. Such a decision should've come naturally, without thought. Instead she'd agonized over it for several precious seconds, unwilling to betray Tristan, yet obligated to protect Jacy. That she'd even hesitated alarmed her. How could a few days aboard a Scanner battleship destroy the defenses of a lifetime?

"Sha'Nara."

She turned to see Cadell at the far end of the corridor, and took off running. She didn't want to see Cadell and listen to his mocking innuendoes. She didn't want to face anybody. Not right now. She might've shown a tough exterior to Tristan, but she'd never felt more vulnerable in her life.

Rounding the corner, she saw several doors on one side of the hall, but only one on the other side. Darting to one of the many doors, she opened one, then closed it without entering and ran instead to the doorway on the opposite wall. Maybe she could confuse Cadell and force him to check all the rooms.

She had to press twice to activate the door, glancing over her shoulder for Cadell as she did. When it slid open, she dashed inside and sealed it shut again.

Flattening against the wall, she waited until she heard his footsteps in the hallway, then the sound of a door opening. Good, it had worked. She'd wait until he went inside another room, then take off again.

A low moan came from nearby and Sha'Nara jumped, looking for the first time at her surroundings. The room was dimly lit. As her eyes adjusted, she noticed beds lining the walls. Some people filled the beds, while others roamed aimlessly in the room.

She moved closer, intrigued. Was this the medical ward? If so, it didn't say much for the Scanner level of care. Where was someone to watch over these people?

Mostly men occupied the beds. With one exception, they all lay unmoving, their eyes open, but unseeing. The remaining man sat up in his bed, his arms linked around his knees, his eyes closed as he rocked back and forth in a repetitious manner.

What was wrong with these people?

A nagging voice inside told her to get out, but she ignored it. No one appeared dangerous. In fact, no one appeared to be much at all.

One woman wandered the width of the room, traveling to one wall, turning, and retracing her footsteps. Another woman stood in the middle, tearing at her hair, her mouth open in a soundless scream, her eyes terrified by something only she could see.

Crying came from a far corner, a quiet steady noise. Moans emitted from several individuals. Though everyone appeared oblivious of her presence, the back of Sha'Nara's neck prickled.

She didn't like this.

She backed toward the entrance, then gasped when it flew open and Cadell burst in. "Sha'Nara, come on. You need to—" He cut off with a cry of pain and fell to his knees.

"Cadell?" His sudden agony baffled her. Was there a sound device at work in this room?

He brought his hands to his head, mimicking Tristan's earlier action, and a moan escaped his lips.

Something was terribly wrong. Sha'Nara knelt before him and touched his arm. "Cadell, let's get out of here."

He looked at her, but didn't focus. Words—gibberish—emerged. "No. No. Arrgh. Pain. Alone. No. Stop." He screamed as if he were being torn into pieces.

Sha'Nara's heart hammered in her chest and she tugged at him again. "Cadell."

"Alone. Pain. Kill me. Kill me. Kill me."

One of the room's occupants echoed Cadell's scream, and Sha'Nara jumped to her feet as realization dawned. Cadell was picking up these people's emotions, their pain.

She stared at him as he rocked back and forth, the words giving way to crying and moans. She had to get him out of here.

Moving into position behind him, she linked her hands under his arms and dragged him backward toward the door. Though it was slow, she made steady

161

progress until she collided with someone.

She turned to find a woman standing behind her, her face, already marred by a large red birthmark, frozen in an expression of terror. Startled, Sha'Nara recoiled, but the woman made no attempt to touch her. She just stood there, blocking the doorway.

"Can you move?" Sha'Nara asked.

No response, but she hadn't realistically expected one. She gently took the woman's shoulders and pulled her away from the door. Drawn by the contorted face, Sha'Nara finally forced her gaze back to Cadell.

She bent to grasp his arms again, then stopped as a long-ago memory surfaced. Unable to help herself, she went to look at the woman again. Something about the face looked familiar, as if Sha'Nara knew her.

Sha'Nara suddenly gasped, the air freezing in her lungs. She looked again, hoping she might be mistaken by the expression, but how many people had that birthmark? She brought her hands to her mouth and backed away, trying to banish the recollection.

But she couldn't. She couldn't deny it.

She'd captured this Scanner over a year ago. And delivered her alive and healthy to be readjusted.

Sha'Nara looked at the room's occupants again, horror squeezing her in its grip. These people weren't sick, not in any sense that could be cured.

They'd been readjusted.

Tristan had told the truth.

"No!" Pain pierced her. She'd done this. She'd sent these people into this mindless hell.

She wanted to flee, to run, to deny it all, but an agonizing moan from Cadell made her remember his presence. He appeared almost catatonic, his eyes glazed.

What was their pain doing to him?

With a surge of strength, she pulled him into the hallway and sealed the door closed. "Tristan!" She called to the transmitters she knew lined the halls. "Tristan!"

What was she to do? How could she help Cadell? Kneeling beside him, she cradled his head and shoulders in her arms. Though out of the room, he continued to twitch and moan.

Her fault. It was all her fault.

"Cadell, what can I do?"

He caught her hand in his and for a moment, his gaze cleared. He opened his mouth as if to speak, but only sounds emerged.

"I'm sorry," she murmured. "I'm so sorry."

Though it felt like ages before Tristan appeared in the corridor, Sha'Nara knew it had only been minutes. "Sha'Nara?"

"Here." She welcomed his presence. He'd know how to help his friend.

"Cadell." Tristan knelt beside them and touched Cadell's shoulder. "What happened?"

"I . . . I went in there," she said. She indicated the doorway with her head. "And he followed me."

Tristan's expression tightened. "Shibit, not that room. Was he there long?"

"A few minutes." Sha'Nara looked at him, expecting accusation. "Will he be all right?"

He looked back at her with nothing more than concern for Cadell. "It's hard to tell right now. We have to get him to his room as quickly as possible." He blinked and reached out to touch her cheek. "You're crying."

"I don't cry," she said automatically, but Tristan's finger showed dampness when he withdrew it. Lifting her hand, she found her face bathed in tears. "I don't cry," she repeated.

Tristan didn't say anything, but squatted to lift Cadell in his arms. Sha'Nara stood as well, trying to help. She found it difficult to met his gaze, but forced herself to. "Those people . . . I . . . I didn't know."

He glanced from her to the sealed door, then back. His expression softened, and he opened his mouth twice before he finally spoke. "Now you do."

Without another word, he started down the hall, carrying Cadell as if he were only a child. Sha'Nara caught up with him, and activated the lift and door to Cadell's room.

As Tristan placed Cadell on his bed, Sha'Nara examined the room. Though it contained the usual furniture, several strange statues lined the shelves and a thick, bumpy material hung over the walls.

She motioned toward it. "What is that?"

"Shidas wool. It helps keep out some of the emotional bombardment."

"You mean he's never away from it?" She tried to imagine feeling other people's emotions continuously, and failed. She had a hard enough time with her own.

"Never." Tristan draped a small blanket of the same coarse wool over Cadell's forehead. "Come back, my friend."

His voice contained a husky note that intensified Sha'Nara's guilt. He obviously cared about his friend. What if she was responsible for destroying Cadell, too?

"But you seem able to turn your power off and on."

Tristan didn't look at her. "I've learned how to control it, that's all. My kinesis is always with me. Many times I use it without thinking."

As when he'd touched her while sleeping.

He turned toward her, and she saw by his expression that he remembered that night as well. "But usually while I'm coherent," he added.

Heat rose in her cheeks. That night seemed like a long time ago. She'd stopped him then. Now that she knew how wonderful making love with him could be, would she stop him again?

She moved to Tristan's side. She wanted to touch him, but didn't. "What can I do for Cadell?"

"Getting him away from there is all we can do. With this wool and some quiet, he should recover."

"I'm sorry." She could barely speak through her constricted throat. "I never meant . . ."

"You didn't know." Tristan stood up, his body almost touching hers. His nearness kindled a hungry yearning, one only he could satisfy. "There's a reason Cadell avoids the medical wing. I should never have sent him after you."

"Why did you?" Sha'Nara asked the question without

thinking, the ache deep in her belly overriding her mental abilities.

"Because I was too much of a coward to go after you myself." He grimaced, as if afraid he'd said too much. He raised his hand toward her face, then dropped it again. "What am I to do with you, Sha'Nara?"

She leaned toward him, wanting his touch, his caress. In his arms she could lose this guilt, the pain.

"Out."

The word came from Cadell, and they both turned to look at him in surprise. "Cadell?" asked Tristan.

"Get out." He spoke slowly, tiredly. "If you're going to fill my room with sexual tension, either get out or find Jacy for me."

"You're going to be all right," Sha'Nara said. Relief flooded her as she touched his hand.

He gave her a wan smile. "Eventually." He squeezed her fingers. "Not your fault. Mine. I knew better." He closed his eyes again. "Now out."

Tristan led Sha'Nara from the room, dropping his hand from her arm the moment they reached the hallway. His unwillingness to touch her stung, though Sha'Nara knew they were both better off if he didn't.

"Can I see Jacy now?" she asked.

"That depends."

"On what?"

"On how much you intend to tell her." He paced two steps, then turned back. "Will she learn how to destroy Scanners, too?"

Chapter Eleven

Sha'Nara hesitated. Should she jeopardize Jacy's freedom? "I promise I won't tell her about the sound waves." Especially since she wasn't sure herself what to think anymore.

"This way." Without hesitation Tristan started down the hallway.

Sha'Nara hurried to catch up with him. His immediate acquiescence took her by surprise. Either he'd accepted her promise completely, which she found hard to believe, or he planned to spy on her and Jacy. Probably the latter, but at this point she didn't care. She not only wanted to verify Jacy's safety, but she also needed some time to sort out her emotions—time away from Tristan Galeron.

No guard stood watch by Jacy's room. Instead of unkeying the door, Tristan chimed and Jacy admitted him. Sha'Nara raised her eyebrows.

"She isn't as inclined to leave us as you are," he murmured.

"Sha'Nara." Jacy enveloped Sha'Nara in a hug.

"Jacy." Sha'Nara returned the embrace with a smile, startled by the warmth it generated within her, surprised at how glad she was to see Jacy again. "Are you all right?"

"I'm fine. Are you? Tristan looked very angry when he went after you. Did he harm you?" Jacy studied Sha'Nara, her gaze so intent Sha'Nara felt certain the younger woman saw all her secrets.

Sha'Nara shifted uneasily. Tristan hadn't hurt her, not in the physical sense. His damage had been more emotional. She darted a glance at him and he gave her a mocking smile. "We . . . ah . . . I managed," she said finally.

His grin widened even further. "I have to go." He directed his words to Sha'Nara. "I'll leave the door unlocked, but I advise you to stay put. I've activated new security procedures around the docking bays. If you run, I'll know."

"All I intend to do is sleep." At that moment the last thing Sha'Nara wanted to think about was escape. Maybe after she'd rested . . .

Tristan's eyes darkened, a flicker of desire in their depths, as he looked from Sha'Nara to the two beds in the room. "Rest well."

He left, but Sha'Nara still felt his potent presence, her body pulsing in response to his gaze. Swallowing hard, she turned to face Jacy. "What have you been up to while I was gone?"

"Not a lot. Cadell showed me around the ship. It's mammoth, even bigger than that luxury cruiser Daddy took me on once."

Sha'Nara started to mention what happened to Cadell, then stopped herself. Jacy would only want to see him, and Tristan had said Cadell needed rest away from people right now. Better to wait until later. She glanced at her chronometer. The hours left for sleep were disappearing quickly enough.

As Jacy continued to talk about her time on the *Hermitage,* Sha'Nara prepared for bed, noting at the same time how often Cadell's name appeared in Jacy's sentences. "You sound like you've spent a lot of time with Cadell."

"I have." Eyes dreamy, Jacy sat in the middle of her bed, her legs crossed. "He's so interesting. Because of his empathy, he really knows how I feel about things. He listens to me. He's the most caring man I've ever met."

Sha'Nara sank onto her bed with a sigh and stretched out. Weariness immediately poured through her. "Be careful, Jacy. Next thing you know you'll fall in love with him."

"I have."

Her weariness vanquished, Sha'Nara sat upright. "Jacy, he's—"

"Don't tell me he's a Scanner. I know that. I also know what type of man he is." Jacy met Sha'Nara's stare, her expression placid. "He has no wish to harm anyone or assume any kind of power. All he wants is a quiet life . . . with me."

Sha'Nara's fears fed her anger. "He's using you, Jacy. He'll—"

"He's not. I've given him plenty of opportunity, and he refuses to take advantage of me." She smiled slightly. "I even asked him to make love to me, and he refused. He loves me, too, Sha'Nara. He won't take the chance of becoming part of my life until he knows he has a future."

Yet Tristan hadn't hesitated to make love with Sha'Nara. She grimaced. Somehow their mating had seemed inevitable. Dumbfounded, Sha'Nara tried twice before she could speak. "What about Devon?"

"I'll have to speak to Daddy about him after I return. I couldn't possibly marry Devon now."

Jacy's confidence astounded Sha'Nara. What had happened to the flighty woman she'd brought here? "Are you sure?" she asked.

"I'm very sure." Jacy leaned forward. "Cadell is everything I've ever wanted in a man and more."

"Your father isn't going to be happy about this."

Sha'Nara lay back down. And neither would her own father.

"If my happiness matters as much as he says it does, he'll come around."

"And if he doesn't?"

Jacy didn't reply right away. "I . . . I hope I don't have to choose."

Sha'Nara looked at her, noticing the tears gathering in her friend's eyes. Unable to provide any reassurance, she gave Jacy a wan smile, then closed her eyes. "Lights off."

However, once darkness enveloped the room, she stared at the ceiling. How was she supposed to handle this? She wanted to believe Tristan and Cadell had planned this, that they'd intended all along to make both women care about them, but she couldn't.

Once her father heard about Jacy's feelings, Sha'Nara knew who he'd blame. Her. As if she had any control over Jacy's heart. Sha'Nara sighed. As if she had any control over her own.

Logically she should want to destroy the Scanners, but now they had faces . . . names. The frightened little girl clutching her mother's neck as rubble fell around her. The young man taking time to help another to safety despite his injuries. Cadell and his easygoing manner. Tristan and the way he could make her body come alive.

She now had the knowledge to disable them all, but could she? Especially after discovering her father had lied to her, to everyone. Readjustment was not a painless procedure that allowed Scanners to lead productive lives. It mutilated them far more than any parapsychic ability they'd received at birth. How was this better than killing them outright?

With a sigh, Sha'Nara let tiredness drag her into the edges of slumber. One last thought caught and held as she drifted away. If her father had lied to her about this, what else had he lied about?

*   *   *

Tristan stood beside Mael and watched Sha'Nara enter the bridge. Though she was accompanied by Cadell and Jacy, the sight of her made Tristan's stomach clench. He'd missed her.

Since he'd left her in Jacy's room, she'd stayed there, even declining Jacy's invitation to accompany her on walks with Cadell. Avoiding *him*, no doubt. Which was for the best. It just didn't feel that way.

As she glanced at him, he caught a brief glimmer of light in her gaze, but it faded quickly. Her only acknowledgment of his presence was a short nod.

What had he expected? That she'd reward him for making love to her, for destroying her innocence? That she might want him even half as much as he craved her? That her feelings had been affected as much as his? Not likely.

Mael motioned the others to join him. "It's time to contact the Director-General again. I trust he'll be more willing to talk at this point."

"He's also going to have a tracer ready to leap on this signal, so keep it short," Tristan said.

"Of course." His manner calm, Mael signaled the comms operator to open a channel.

Was Tristan the only one nervous about this encounter? He glanced at Cadell and Jacy. They held hands, something they'd done often lately, their expressions tight. Only Sha'Nara appeared detached, her gaze focused on Mael.

Of course, she believed she had no future, that she'd be forced to remain on the *Hermitage* forever. Tristan clenched his jaw. He'd hated telling Mael about what Sha'Nara now knew, but he couldn't betray all Scanners because of his desire for this woman.

To Tristan's surprise, Mael hadn't ordered her immediate destruction. Instead he'd nodded thoughtfully and thanked Tristan for telling him.

"The Director-General's office is coming through now," said the operator.

The woman at the reception console barely glanced at Mael before switching him into Remy Vadin's office.

The Director-General appeared on the view screen, obviously affected by the past few days of silence. Large dark circles rimmed his eyes, and his face looked drawn and tired as if he hadn't slept in that entire time.

He didn't waste time with preliminaries. "I'll meet."

"Thank you, sir. I appreciate that." Mael gave no sign of his earlier unease over what Remy's answer would be.

"My daughter?"

"She's right here. Her companion, too." Mael motioned for the operator to widen the viewing area to encompass the entire group.

Jacy stepped forward, her eyes damp. "Daddy."

"Jacy, are you all right?" Remy's voice wavered slightly, his concern evident.

"Daddy, I'm very all right." She darted a glance from him to Cadell, then back. "We need to talk when I return."

"Of course." The Director-General focused again on Mael. "I assume you want to coordinate this rendezvous."

"If you don't mind. I would like to suggest a meeting in three hours time on Alpha Station Six."

Three hours? Tristan looked at Mael in surprise.

"Three hours?" Remy echoed Tristan's amazement. "That's impossible. I can't—"

"You can't possibly put together an attack team in that amount of time. I agree." Mael stood even straighter. "I am relying on your word. We have no plans for violence, and I trust you don't either. All we want to do is talk."

Remy stiffened. "As you wish. Will my daughter be present?"

"No." As the Director-General opened his mouth to protest, Mael continued. "As a sign of our good faith, I will release her and Officer Calles immediately. They should arrive at Centralia shortly after your arrival at the station. I trust that will meet with your approval."

Tristan froze. Release Sha'Nara?

171

"Yes." Remy gave a weak smile. "I look forward to meeting you, Mael Ner."

Mael nodded. "And I you. In three hours then." He closed the channel and turned to face the others. "Mistress Vadin, Officer Calles, I suggest you gather together anything you need. You'll be leaving shortly on the transport ship."

"We're going home?" Jacy asked.

"You're setting me free?" Sha'Nara sounded equally incredulous. Tristan didn't blame her. He tried to catch the older man's eye, but Mael ignored him.

"That was always our intention. Your kidnapping was merely a means to get the Director-General to listen to us."

Cadell stepped forward. "I'll fly the transport."

"No. Dar is returning the women." Mael gave his son a sympathetic smile. "I will need you with me for the peace talks. You, too, Tristan."

Tristan had barely opened his mouth when Mael cut him off. He wanted to accompany Sha'Nara back to Centralia. This was all too sudden.

"If you will hurry," Mael said to Sha'Nara and Jacy.

They exchanged stunned looks, then started for their room, Cadell with them. Tristan caught Mael's arm. "Why so quick?"

"This is the only way we can keep the Alliance off balance. They have no time to prepare an attack on us at the station. If all goes well, the Director-General will arrive willing to talk."

"What about Sha'Nara?" Though he didn't want to admit it, Tristan had hoped she wouldn't be set free, that she'd have to remain on the *Hermitage*. "What about what she knows?"

"I'll erase it from her memory."

A chill surged through Tristan's veins. "Can you do that?"

"If necessary." Mael met Tristan's gaze. "The other alternative for Officer Calles is much more final."

Tristan swallowed. Sha'Nara could lose a part of her

memory or die. Some choice. "Is it . . . is it like read-justment?"

"No, not at all. She'll only lose that memory. Nothing else will be affected."

"I . . ."

Mael smiled wryly. "I thought this would be a pre-ferred solution for this problem. Am I mistaken?"

"No." Tristan turned away. "I'll go prepare the trans-port." He paused. "Why that ship? Why not one of the faster ones?"

"There is always the possibility that the ship will not be allowed to return. I'd prefer not to lose one of our better ships if that's the case."

"I see." Tristan headed for the lift, his steps heavy. Sha'Nara would return home. This was good. This was what he'd wanted . . . once.

Until Mael had uttered the words, Tristan hadn't re-alized how much he'd counted on Sha'Nara remaining. In the back of his mind he'd thought he might have a chance to make her see the good in Scanners, to con-vince her that . . . He hesitated. To convince her of what? That they had a future together? Not unless the Alliance changed their attitude. Even though the Direc-tor-General had agreed to the meeting, Tristan still doubted he'd give the Scanners any kind of reprieve.

No, this was better. Sha'Nara could return to her home, to her own people, to hunting Scanners. She had no future with him. His desire for her warped his logic.

He had the docking bay open and the ship readied when Dar arrived to assume the controls. Though the man was a qualified pilot, Tristan still found himself explaining how everything worked and how to negoti-ate air space around Centralia.

Dar placed a friendly hand on Tristan's shoulder. "Don't worry. I'll take good care of them." He swung inside, then motioned over his shoulder. "Here they come. I'll get the engines going."

As Tristan went to meet Sha'Nara, Jacy, and Cadell, his heart sank to his stomach and sat there. Cadell's face mirrored what Tristan felt. He'd obviously fallen for Jacy and fallen hard.

Tristan grimaced. Another doomed relationship, though Cadell had the advantage that Jacy returned his affection, if the way she threw her arms around his neck and kissed him was any indication. Tristan shifted his gaze away. This parting belonged to the two of them. However, the only other place to look was at Sha'Nara.

She looked uncomfortable, too, though Tristan didn't doubt that was anger smoldering in her eyes. She couldn't be pleased about Jacy and Cadell.

He drank in the sight of her, well aware he'd never see her again, except maybe at the other end of a laser. With her thick red hair restrained in its typical braid and her PSI Officer dress uniform, she looked exactly as she had on the day he first met her, yet different, too.

He'd noticed her curves then, but now they appeared softer, more generous. Recalling how smooth her skin felt beneath his palm, he curled his hand into a fist. He'd wanted her then, too, but not like this, not with a longing that permeated every pore of his being.

She lifted her gaze and met his, her face unreadable. He couldn't look away, didn't want to look away. After a moment, her gaze softened and he caught the unmistakable flare of desire in her eyes.

Hope surged, then centered in his loins. He stepped closer. "Sha'Nara." He couldn't keep the huskiness out of his voice.

In reply, she extended her hand. "Good-bye, Tristan."

Despite the sadness of her words, Tristan accepted her warning and only wrapped his fingers around hers. "Good-bye."

He didn't release her right away, nor did she try to pull her hand free. Her liliana scent teased him, triggering memories better left forgotten. Giving her a weak smile, he broke contact.

"Is everyone ready?" Mael entered the docking bay, followed by a young man carrying a portable vidcom.

Tristan frowned and went to meet Mael. "What's that?"

"I'm sending the Director-General a live transmission of his daughter's departure so that he knows we are keeping our end of the bargain."

"Is that wise?" Tristan scanned the interior of the bay. What secrets could the Alliance learn from seeing it?

"Don't worry. We're keeping the view window tight." Mael smiled and approached the two women. "I hope you will return and speak warmly of your stay here."

"Of course." Jacy accepted Mael's outstretched hand. "I intend to tell my father how well I was treated." Her gaze returned to Cadell. "And how much I hope peace is achieved."

"Thank you, Mistress Vadin." Mael faced Sha'Nara. "And you?"

"I have found it informative." She eyed his offered hand. "Do you plan to make me say wonderful things?"

"Not at all. An implant only lasts minutes. I would achieve nothing."

Though obviously wary, she placed her hand briefly in his, then snatched it away. She darted a look at Tristan, and he forced a reassuring smile. Had Mael had enough time to wipe the information about the sound box from her mind? What if he'd failed?

When Sha'Nara turned to enter the transport, Tristan went to touch Mael's arm. The older man smiled and gave a short nod. He must've been successful. Tristan breathed easier. Though Sha'Nara had become somewhat more accepting of Scanners, she was still a PSI Police officer. They couldn't take any chances.

Sha'Nara paused in the hatch and looked back at him. As their gazes caught, he inhaled sharply. He'd never see her again. She disappeared into the ship, and his insides burned with a pain more intense than any laser burst.

He'd known it would hurt, but not this badly. Turning away, he watched Cadell suffer similar agony as he escorted Jacy to the ship. Since the vidcom captured their movements, they refrained from one last kiss, but Tristan could tell it wouldn't take much for either of them to give in.

After Jacy entered the transport, Cadell turned to Tristan, his expression reflecting a deeper anguish than he'd shown thus far.

"Let's move to the bridge and finish from there," said Mael. He left quickly, taking the vidcom operator with him. Slowly Cadell and Tristan followed.

As they headed for the lift, Bran hurried by them without a word of greeting. Tristan lifted an eyebrow. "What's he doing here?"

"Probably cheering that Sha'Nara has left." Cadell smiled dryly. "I can't tell if you're feeling as badly as I am or if that's my emotions covering yours."

Tristan couldn't reveal his suffering, not even to Cadell. It was too deep, too intense. He hadn't expected this. "We both knew not to get involved with these women."

"Knowing and doing are two separate things." They entered the lift and rose to the top level. Cadell lifted his tormented gaze. "I love her, Tristan."

Love? Desire was one thing, but love? "You knew who she was."

"I knew her father's position, but once I knew her, I couldn't help it. She has a sweetness, a caring, that destroyed my defenses."

"She was leaving for her wedding when we kidnapped her, Cadell."

"It was arranged by her father. She doesn't love him." Cadell's expression softened. "She loves me."

"Wait a minute." Tristan stepped off the lift, then paused to face his friend. "Are you actually considering a future with her?"

"It's possible," Cadell replied defensively. "She intends to talk to her father about us, about Scanners. If she can make him understand . . ."

"It's not going to happen." Tristan hated to ruin Cadell's hopes, but they were futile. Tristan knew. He'd been over them a dozen times himself. "The Director-General is coming to this meeting already angry with us. I can't think of any reason why he'll want to remove us from the endangered-species list."

"Father thinks he'll be able to persuade the Director-

General into seeing our side of it. We used no violence. Jacy wasn't harmed. Neither was Sha'Nara and she's a PSI officer."

Tristan shifted uneasily. How did Cadell define harm?

His friend must've sensed Tristan's discomfort, for his gaze sharpened. "She wasn't harmed, was she?"

"Of course not." Tristan started down the hall, evading the subject. Did Sha'Nara believe she'd been harmed? If she returned and told a tale of being attacked by Tristan, they'd believe her. A thick lump formed in his throat. In that case, the stars would cease to shine before Scanners ever received a reprieve.

Sha'Nara actually sympathized with Jacy when the younger woman burst into tears soon after boarding the transport. Without hesitation, she enveloped Jacy in a hug. "I know. It's hard."

"What if I never see him again? I couldn't bear it." Jacy twisted to eye the open hatch. "Sha'Nara, I don't want to go."

"We have to, Jacy. If we don't return, Cadell and the others won't have even a slight chance to gain their freedom." As the words left her lips, Sha'Nara froze. Why should she care whether these people had their way?

"I plan to ask Daddy to forgive them." Sniffling, Jacy stepped out of the hug. "Will you help me?"

Sha'Nara hesitated. If she spoke in the Scanners' defense, she'd jeopardize her entire career. Their plan had no chance of success. She'd have thrown away everything for nothing. "I can't do that," she said finally.

The wounded look Jacy gave her sliced into Sha'Nara's chest. "Didn't you learn anything while you were here? These people aren't dangerous."

But they were. At least one was. Tristan created emotional havoc in her despite years of tight control. He made her think. He made her feel. He made her want.

The engines roared and Jacy jumped. "I can't go," she cried.

Sha'Nara caught her arm. "We have to."

"It's not right. I belong here." Tears streaked down her cheeks.

"We—" Sha'Nara cut herself off, suddenly aware of a sense of wrongness, of impending danger. A tiny voice deep inside screamed to leave the ship, to go . . . now.

She shook her head. Though she'd had hunches before, her father had always told her to follow her logic, not her emotion. Logic said they needed to return to Centralia. Nothing remained for them here.

Except Tristan.

The voice screamed louder, and a shiver danced along her spine. She'd never felt anything this strong. Despite her father's commandments, she actually considered obeying it.

"Buckle up back there." The pilot's voice floated back to them. "We're taking off."

With definite trepidation, Sha'Nara watched as the hatch door began to slide shut.

Tristan paced the entire length of the bridge. He didn't want to watch the transport vanish into hyperspace, yet that aching part deep inside longed for one last look at Sha'Nara.

As he waited for the transport to appear on the view screen, he noticed the vidcom was still transmitting everything to the Director-General. Tristan grimaced. Though he doubted Remy Vadin truly appreciated it, he gave Mael credit for this idea. The man couldn't say his daughter hadn't been safely delivered to him.

"There it is." Cadell moved closer to the screen as the transport appeared. He extended his hand as if to touch it, then drew it back.

Tristan remained frozen, unable to look away from the ship as it neared the optimum launch point for hyperspace. One minute, maybe two, and she'd be out of his life . . . forever. Why didn't that thought please him?

Another object appeared at one edge of the screen and he stepped forward. "What's that?"

It moved closer to the transport, and Tristan recognized it immediately. "Thorgs." His heart rose into his throat. They must've followed him back here.

He rushed to the weapons operator. "Fire on it. Shoot it down. Now!"

Even as he spoke, the Thorg ship fired at the transport. A collective gasp rose from the room. Tristan offered thanks to Dar's piloting skill as the man managed to evade the blast.

The weapons operator struggled frantically to lock onto the Thorg ship. "I'm getting it. I'm getting it," he muttered, his fingers flying over the controls.

Tristan's chest ached until he realized he was holding his breath. The Thorg fighter continued firing. How long could Dar avoid the laser bursts? He had to go into hyperspace.

Unable to stand it any longer, Tristan pushed the operator out of the way and slid into his place. The battleship's lasers only worked erratically. Let this be the one time they did. He fired.

And missed.

The Thorg fired.

And the transport exploded into a blinding flash of light.

"No!" Anguish filled Tristan's cry as he fired again and again at the Thorg ship.

Success.

The ship dissolved into a bright blur, then faded from the sky.

Only floating debris filled the view screen. Tristan stared at it, numbly. She couldn't be dead. She couldn't.

Unfortunately, the evidence said otherwise.

Chapter Twelve

Tristan stood slowly, a numbing chill permeating every pore as he continued to stare at the view screen. Dimly, as though from far away, he heard Cadell murmuring *no* over and over while Mael signaled the Director-General. This wasn't possible, couldn't be possible.

A thick band tightened around his chest. Had he been responsible for bringing the Thorg ship here? Had they followed his escape? Had he killed Sha'Nara?

He couldn't breathe. Staggering to the edge of the window, he hoped by some miracle all the debris would disappear. "Sha'Nara." He could barely speak through his closed throat.

"What's going on there?" Remy Vadin's anger carried through space as he appeared on the comm view screen.

Tristan turned slowly to watch as Mael replied. "You saw what happened. I regret . . . at this point it looks as if there are no survivors."

Remy's face paled even more. "My daughter?"

"I'm sorry."

"You did this! You—"

"You saw the transmission. We had nothing to do with this tragedy. We lost one of our own people, too. Surely you recognized the Thorg ship."

"Yes." The Director-General ran his hand over his eyes before looking up again. "I can't meet with you now."

"Now? Or ever?" The casual tone of Mael's voice caught Tristan's attention. Would all their plans be ruined?

Tristan had to remind himself to inhale. Did he even care any more?

"Not now." Remy's pain sounded in the broken words. "Contact me later." He broke the transmission, and Mael gave a quick, dry smile of satisfaction.

Tristan turned away. He had to get out of this room before he lost what little control he had left. A small part of him had foolishly believed that he might see Sha'Nara again, but not now . . . not ever.

"Tristan, wait." Cadell joined him as he reached the doorway. "I can't . . . I want . . ." He struggled to hold back his obvious grief. "I need to take the ship out, to check."

"Cadell, they can't—"

His friend cut him off. "I have to do something."

Tristan nodded. "Let's go." Sha'Nara and Jacy couldn't have survived that explosion, but he understood Cadell's frustration. They should've been able to do something, should've stopped this from happening.

Illogical hope flickered in Tristan as they made their way to the docking bay. Maybe the women had gone into an escape craft when the attack began. Maybe the craft had survived. He clung to that illusion, needing it to hold back the pain that threatened to overwhelm him.

He glanced at Cadell. For his friend's sake, Tristan needed to keep a rein on his own turbulent emotions. Already Cadell displayed an irrational manner brought on by his own agony. Tristan didn't want to add to that, but he couldn't control the razor-sharp grief tearing through his gut.

Upon reaching the docking bay, he started to key in the security sequence, then realized he'd never set it upon leaving. Had he been so distracted that he forgot? Of course, Sha'Nara had been the main reason he'd locked the door.

Or had he subconsciously left it unkeyed in the hope she might change her mind and decide to stay? He hadn't wanted her to leave. He hadn't wanted her to die.

Tears pricked at the back of his eyes, but he blinked them back and entered the bay. He approached the six-passenger shuttle. They'd need the room if they found any survivors.

If.

He gripped the edge of the hatch, bowing his head as a sob threatened to rip from his chest. Caring hurt. He'd learned that when he lost his parents. How had this fiery PSI officer crept under his skin? He hadn't asked for it, hadn't wanted it, yet she mattered.

And he'd killed her.

For one wild moment, he hoped more Thorgs lingered outside the *Hermitage*. He wanted a chance for revenge, to release this guilt and anger that boiled in his gut. Slapping his palm against the ship's hull, he looked back at Cadell. "Come on. We might find something."

Cadell stood frozen in the middle of the bay, his head cocked as if listening. He gave no sign he heard Tristan's words.

Alarmed, Tristan approached his friend. Because of his empathy, Cadell felt his own emotions more strongly. Had this blow on top of his earlier encounter proven to be too much? "Cadell?" He touched the younger man's shoulder.

Cadell lifted his gaze, a brilliant light in his eyes. "She's here."

"What?" The words hit Tristan like a blow to his chest.

"Jacy's here." Cadell searched the dark corners of the vast room.

Tristan joined him. Had Jacy left the ship once again? Had she survived while Sha'Nara died?

"Jacy." Cadell raised his voice. "Jacy, please, if you're alive, tell me. Don't let me suffer like this."

"Cadell." She ran out of the shadows, tears covering her cheeks, and flung her arms around his neck.

Closing his eyes, Cadell wrapped his arms around her tightly as if he never intended to let her go again. "Jacy." He breathed her name like a prayer, then bent to kiss her.

Tristan tried to summon joy for his friend's happiness, but failed. If only Sha'Nara . . .

A quiet footfall caught his attention, and he jerked to attention as another figure emerged from the dimly lit corner. His heart surged once, paused, then jumped into a rapid rhythm. "Sha'Nara."

He hurried toward her, driven by a need to touch her, hold her, to verify that she lived. He stopped short, feeling her anger as surely as if he'd been empathic. Her gaze bore into him. Obviously she wasn't as happy to see him.

"Was that your plan all along?" she asked quietly.

"Plan?" Tristan could only stare, convinced he'd missed something.

"To let us think we were going home, then kill us."

He stiffened and frowned. "We *were* sending you home. Safely. It was a Thorg ship that attacked the carrier. They must've followed us here."

Her expression only tightened even more. "That was our Thorg ship." She pointed across the docking bay. "Bran came in after you left and took it."

Tristan turned in the direction she indicated. The Thorg craft they'd returned in was gone. He sucked in his breath. "Orion's Sword." It hadn't been a random Thorg attack.

Fury replaced his pain, burning hot in his veins. "Bran." He spat the name out, clenching his fists.

As a teleporter Bran could've jumped back to the *Her-*

mitage before his ship exploded. If so, Tristan would find him . . . and kill him. He looked back at Sha'Nara to find her watching him intently. Curiosity temporarily distracted him from his anger. "How did you know not to go?" he asked. "Why did you stay?"

He wanted her to say she'd realized she needed him. She didn't.

"I . . . I had a hunch."

"A hunch?"

She frowned in obvious confusion. "Almost like a voice, telling me to get out, that it wasn't safe."

"And you listened to it?"

"I almost didn't." She said the words so quietly he almost didn't hear them.

He smiled in relief. No matter what the reason, she was alive. Joy surged through him, lightening his mood so much he couldn't resist teasing her. "Are you sure you're not psychic?"

As he expected, she tensed. Her glare would've wounded a lesser man, but only made his grin broaden. "I followed a hunch." She brushed past him, the brief touch of her body igniting all Tristan's senses.

Reacting instinctively he snared her shoulder, holding her hip against his. Her eyes widened, emotion churning their depths—desire as well as alarm. Her lips parted, lips that begged him to taste them. "We didn't try to harm you, Sha'Nara." He couldn't stop himself from bending close to her face. "If anything, Bran acted on his own."

She swallowed, the movement of her throat drawing his gaze. "I . . . I can't allow myself to believe you. Not any more."

His grip loosened as her words penetrated his consciousness and she tugged away to join Cadell and Jacy. Tristan followed, his steps slower. The division remained between them. Why had he expected things to be any different?

At least Sha'Nara lived. Whatever it took, he'd do his best to ensure she stayed that way.

*   *   *

Sha'Nara was only too aware of Tristan following her. Her first reaction upon seeing him had been to throw herself into the safety of his embrace, but she couldn't.

They'd almost been killed. If not for listening to that sudden urgent voice . . . She shuddered.

After Bran had left in the Thorg ship, she and Jacy had come out of the shadows to watch as he followed the transport ship and fired on it. When the transport exploded, she'd felt the impact almost as keenly as if she'd been there. The Scanners never intended to let them leave here alive. Using the Thorg ship only helped convince the Director-General that their deaths had been the result of a surprise attack.

Seen as innocent in her death, the Scanners would still get their meeting with Remy Vadin even as they secretly rejoiced over her destruction. With her knowledge of their secrets, she'd been surprised they would let her leave. Now she knew they'd never intended to.

Yet she found it hard to believe Tristan could be so deceitful. His surprise at seeing the Thorg ship gone had been real, his anger at Bran almost palpable. Her body screamed at her to trust him, but her body had already proven it wouldn't be bound by logic. Otherwise she never would've made love to the man. Otherwise she wouldn't still want him.

Jacy twisted in Cadell's arms to face Sha'Nara, her expression that of a woman who'd been thoroughly kissed. "We're safe now, Sha'Nara."

"No, we're not." The back of her neck tingled with an awareness of Tristan pausing behind her, but she focused her attention on Cadell. "Who told Bran to shoot us down?"

"Bran?" Cadell immediately looked to Tristan, who must've indicated the empty space where the Thorg ship had sat, for Cadell turned to look at it. "By the stars! Father needs to know of this."

"No," said Sha'Nara. The fewer who knew she and Jacy lived, the better. Cadell's stunned surprise mirrored Tristan's. Had they honestly been kept in the dark about this obvious plan?

"But Jacy's father, we have to tell him you're alive," Cadell said.

"No." Sha'Nara ignored the stricken expression on Jacy's face. "I . . . we can't trust anyone here. Not now."

"We can trust Cadell." The loving gaze Jacy bestowed on the man only reemphasized her youth and naivete.

"Can we?" Sha'Nara shifted her position so she could see Tristan as well. "Can we trust you?"

Tristan held his body still, his muscles tensed. "Only you can answer that."

She wanted to trust him. Against her will she had trusted him until this. Lifting her chin, she studied both men. Tristan could stop her in an instant, no matter what she did. She had no choice . . . for now. "I intend to take Jacy home in the fighter ship. If we can trust you, you'll make sure no one comes after us."

"I'm not sending Jacy off without me again," said Cadell, hugging her even closer. "I'll take you back."

"As will I." Tristan's gaze locked with Sha'Nara's and her heart thudded wildly in her chest. "If Scanners intend to shoot you down, they'll have to kill us as well."

He would sacrifice himself for her? Sha'Nara couldn't believe that. "Maybe the other Scanners will rest assured that you and Cadell won't let Jacy and me reach our destination alive."

Cadell released Jacy and went to stand before Sha'Nara. For the first time since she'd met him, she saw anger blazing in his eyes, on his face, in his stance. "I would never do anything to purposely harm Jacy. Never." He stared at her with such enmity Sha'Nara wanted to cringe. "I thought even you would know that."

"I do know that." Sha'Nara would have to be blind to miss the devotion between her friend and Cadell. "I'm sorry."

The tension eased from his body. "I know it's galling, but you can trust some of us, Sha'Nara."

"Apparently I have to." To be truthful, she was relieved to be forced into this position. She wanted Tristan beside her, no matter how illogical. "Let's go now then."

Tristan shook his head. "We need to tell Mael."

Sudden panic blossomed. Trusting Tristan and Cadell was one thing. Trusting any other Scanner was another. Someone here wanted her dead, and she didn't think it was only Bran. "I don't want anyone else to know we're alive."

"He's my father, Sha'Nara," said Cadell. "We can trust him."

"He'll be able to help us," added Tristan.

Sha'Nara grimaced. She didn't like this, but even Jacy added her nod of agreement. "Very well, but don't tell him over the comm circuits."

Tristan approached the comm panel by the door. "I'll have him come here. Is that satisfactory?"

"Yes." She wanted to see Mael's face once he realized she was alive.

Triggering the comm, Tristan signaled for Mael. The man responded at once. "Mael here."

"Mael, it's Tristan. I'm in the docking bay. Can you come here?"

"I'm in the middle of—"

"It's important."

Obviously Mael caught the seriousness of Tristan's tone. "I'll be right there."

As Tristan rejoined her, Sha'Nara wished she could discard her doubts as easily as Jacy and go into his arms. But she had to remain logical. Jacy's life—her own life—depended on it. No matter how she looked at it, Tristan remained a Scanner with a very powerful ability—who could've killed her a long time ago if he'd wanted to.

She gave him a hesitant smile. "Thank you."

He only nodded in reply, though his dark gaze didn't waver from her face. The intensity of his stare increased her already erratic pulse and created a tight knot deep in the pit of her stomach. Why couldn't he be someone else?

187

Would she still feel this attraction if he were?

Cadell kept his arm around Jacy as he led her toward the shuttle. "I'll make sure everything's ready for departure."

He'd just reached the spacecraft when the door to the bay slid open and Mael entered. The older man must've spotted Jacy, for he stopped abruptly, then swung his gaze toward Sha'Nara.

She almost smiled at the sheer amazement on his face. For once the unflappable leader was unprepared. Obviously he hadn't expected to see them alive.

To give him credit, he recovered quickly and came over to join Sha'Nara and Tristan. "This is most fortunate. How did you manage to avoid leaving with Dar?"

Sha'Nara saw the sparkle of amusement in Tristan's eyes as she replied, "We . . . ah . . . decided to catch the next shuttle."

Mael stared at her for so long, she had to resist the urge to squirm. Could he read her mind without touching her? She felt just as reluctant to admit to him that she'd followed a hunch as she would be to tell her father. Neither man would understand.

"All the better for us," said Mael finally. "I need to notify the Director-General. He'll be most pleased."

Shaking her head, Sha'Nara glanced at Tristan for assistance. Mael didn't like her. She didn't like him. They needed an intermediary.

"Cadell and I are taking Sha'Nara and Jacy back to Centralia," said Tristan.

"That's out of the question. I can't afford to lose both of you," Mael said.

Cadell crossed the distance between them. "After what just happened, I'm not trusting anyone else with Jacy's safety. I'm taking her home."

"I know you're upset, but if we wait, reconsider . . ."

"No." Sha'Nara didn't want to spend another moment on the *Hermitage*. "We're leaving now—with or without an escort."

"At this point, you might as well pilot yourselves." Mael frowned. "You already know our location."

"No." Tristan moved closer to Sha'Nara, not touching her, but close enough that she felt the heated masculine aura that surrounded him. Her body tingled in response, but she forced herself to concentrate on the subject at hand. "Cadell and I are going with them. We kidnapped them. We'll take them back." His tone made it clear he didn't intend to change his mind.

"I see." Mael studied them, then smiled dryly. "Very well. This changes things. I would hate for either of you to become property of the PSI Police." He focused briefly on Sha'Nara, and she lifted her chin defiantly.

"That won't happen," she said. "As our escorts, they'll have a flag of truce."

"A flag of truce means nothing to PSI Police." The coldness in Mael's voice sent a shiver beneath Sha'Nara's skin. "I know this from experience."

"I won't let it happen." Sha'Nara surprised herself at the vehemence of her words.

Mael raised one eyebrow. "So you say." He paused. "Would you be willing to deliver a message to the Director-General for me? Since he has delayed our meeting, this may provide the perfect opportunity to get our message to him."

"What kind of message?" Sha'Nara wasn't about to stand before Remy Vadin and ask him to give the Scanners their freedom. He'd laugh at her.

"I have a scroll imager. It's old, but still works. I can record my message on that."

She nodded. As long as she didn't have to pretend she believed in their cause. "We want to leave now. How long will it take to record your message?"

"Not long." He moved as he spoke, heading for the door. "I'll return shortly."

Silence sat heavily on the group after he left. Unable to stand it any longer, Sha'Nara raised her gaze to Tristan's.

"Will we be allowed to leave Centralia?" he asked.

"You have my word." He'd accepted that once. Would he do so again?

"That's good enough for me." Cadell gave her an accepting smile, and Sha'Nara found herself returning it. "Now let me try again to get the shuttle ready."

He hurried back toward the ship as Tristan stepped even closer to Sha'Nara. Only a slight wisp of space separated their bodies. If she swayed the slightest bit, they'd touch. Swallowing hard, she fought the temptation to do just that. "And you?" she murmured.

"I've played the fool several times for you already." His lips hovered over hers. "Why not again?"

She moistened her dry lips, then regretted the action as his gaze focused on them. "Is that your way of saying you trust me?"

"It's my way of saying I have no choice." He casually brushed the back of his fingers across her cheek. "But then, neither do you."

Was he speaking of trust? Or something more? Something like the desire that surged between them? She wanted his kiss, his touch. His body heat had already stirred banked embers of passion. Did she have a choice when it came to her irrational attraction to him?

Yes, she did.

Before she could submit and lean forward for his kiss, she inhaled deeply and stepped back. He tensed at once. "We'd better get ready to go." Her words sounded inane in the charged air between them.

"I'll help Cadell." He whirled away from her, his back straight, his strides long and purposeful.

She released a long breath and brought her hand up to touch the rapid pulse in her throat. The sooner she returned to Centralia, the better. If Tristan kept up this sensual attack, she'd succumb—and she couldn't allow that to happen again.

Mael returned more quickly than Sha'Nara expected, carrying a long, narrow canister almost the same length as his arm. A scroll imager. She'd seen holos of them, but they'd given way to vidcoms several years ago.

"How does it work?" she asked.

"This equipment is very old. I'd rather not strain it." He held out the device, but Sha'Nara didn't take it.

"If I can't see the message you're sending, I'm not taking it." For all she knew, Mael could be issuing a declaration of war.

His lips thinned. With a snap of his wrist, he caught the tab along one side of the canister and drew it up. Three thin strands fed from it forming an open tent. "First, set the imager." He indicated a button at the end. "You start and stop the recording here."

As he pressed the button, the device sputtered once, then a miniature hologram of Mael appeared within the open tent. "Greetings, Director-General. I am Mael Ner of the Scanners. I regret detaining your daughter, but it appeared to be the only way we could get your attention. Now that I have it, I'd like to discuss the possibility of peace between the Scanners and the Alliance. We—"

Sparks shot from the tent as it crackled ominously. Mael instantly pressed the button to stop the image. "As you can see, this device is less than reliable. I'd prefer my message made it to the Director-General."

Sha'Nara nodded. She'd seen enough to know Mael spouted the same nonsense as Tristan. Accepting the canister, she felt as if she'd taken on a far heavier load than the few kilos it represented. "I'll see that Remy gets it."

"Thank you." Mael glanced toward the shuttle. "Have a safe flight."

She grimaced. "I hope so." Turning, she started for the craft.

"Officer Calles."

Pausing, she glanced over her shoulder at Mael. He seemed to radiate malevolence, his flowing white hair forming a cloak around his shoulders, his dark piercing eyes probing her secrets. Against her will, she trembled. "Yes?"

"I want my son back."

"You'll get him." Tearing her gaze away, she rushed the remainder of the distance and swung into the shuttle. Once she reached the relative safety of the interior, she glanced back.

Mael still stood there, an ominous sentinel.

Disturbed by her nervous reaction, she slapped the control to the hatch and the door slid closed. "Let's get out of here."

Cadell and Tristan occupied the same control seats as they had on the fateful day when they'd brought Sha'Nara and Jacy to the *Hermitage*. But this time, instead of unease and fear, she felt secure, safe. These men would get her to Centralia.

Jacy left Cadell's side and took a passenger seat. Without hesitation, Sha'Nara sat beside her. "Ready?" Sha'Nara asked.

"If I have to go back, I'm glad it's with Cadell," said Jacy.

"You know he can't stay," Sha'Nara said. She would do what she could to make sure Cadell and Tristan left Centralia safely. But if Cadell insisted on staying, she had no hope of keeping him free.

"I know he can't stay." Jacy bit her lip. "I want Cadell safe more than I want him with me."

Astonishing. Sha'Nara sat back before her jaw could drop. This wasn't the same young woman she'd helped prepare for her wedding. Which wasn't necessarily a bad thing.

Cadell looked around. "Are you both strapped in?"

"We're ready."

"Then we're out of here." He touched the controls as he spoke, and the shuttle swung around in the bay. With another short movement, they blasted into space.

Sha'Nara watched out the front window as the *Hermitage* became smaller, expecting at any moment to be confronted by another ship or attacked by a laser beam from the battleship itself. The peaceful glide into optimum launch position, followed by the smooth transition into hyperspace, felt almost anticlimactic.

Once in the blackness, she released her restraints and joined the men by the control panel. Jacy followed, and perched on the edge of Cadell's seat.

"Where are you planning to emerge?" Sha'Nara asked as she sought out the preset coordinates. Recognizing the numbers, she turned to Tristan. "Those aren't the coordinates for Centralia."

"You're right." Tristan's lips twitched as if daring her to challenge him. "After all that's happened, we decided it would be better to reenter at the outer edge of that star system and approach Centralia in the normal traffic lanes."

That made sense. All space traffic emerging from hyperspace near Alliance headquarters was carefully scrutinized, while that using the regular routes escaped such notice, usually because the heavily traveled traffic lanes didn't go near the Alliance complex. Of course, she could direct them in.

She glanced again at the coordinates on the panel, trying to figure out why they looked so familiar. "Why did you chose there?"

"It's on the outer edge of the star system, and the trade planet Bazzar is nearby. We intended to blend in with the large amount of traffic it creates." Tristan frowned at her. "Why?"

"What star charts are you using?"

Cadell looked concerned now as he indicated the star charts programmed into the console. Sha'Nara skimmed them, then grimaced. "These are over five years old."

Tristan's expression hardened. "Is that a problem?"

"It could be." Sha'Nara paused. Did it matter at this point whether she and Jacy returned via a PSI Police patrol or with Cadell and Tristan? Yes, it mattered. "The PSI Police have built a mammoth station on Bazzar with a large space patrol."

"Our ship is unmarked," said Cadell. "They'd have no reason to bother us if we stay in the traffic lanes."

Again Sha'Nara debated on how much to reveal. Could she give away one of the PSI Police's best-kept secrets? The Scanners trusted her with their secret.

No, they didn't. They'd tried to kill her.

Still, she couldn't let Tristan and Cadell be captured. Perhaps they could avoid any PSI Police and she wouldn't have to reveal this closely kept knowledge.

"You're right," she said finally. "Keep to the space lanes and avoid any large PSI Police cruisers and we should be fine." Feeling the impact of Tristan's gaze boring into her as if he knew she had more to tell, she backed away and returned to her seat.

They should be fine.

Then why didn't she believe it? If they were stopped, she and Jacy would come to no harm. They'd simply be returned to Centralia. But Cadell . . . and Tristan . . .

She shouldn't care what happened to a couple of Scanners, but she did. She liked Cadell. He obviously cared about Jacy, and he'd always treated Sha'Nara fairly and with kindness, even after she'd knocked him unconscious and led him into the readjusted Scanners' room.

And Tristan. Did she like him? That word didn't have enough strength to define the emotion he evoked. Her body yearned for the touch of his, but more than that, she appreciated his intelligence, his deep friendship with Cadell, his tenderness at moments when she least expected it. Against all reason, she respected his willingness to follow through on this ridiculous quest for freedom. He had no chance of success, but never gave up trying to find a way to get the land he wanted so badly.

As if feeling her gaze, he turned and gave her a slow, warm smile that twisted the knot low in her belly even tighter. Her throat closed. Breathing became difficult. He started to stand, and she gripped the armrests in a panic.

Not now. She didn't want him near while she was struggling to remember why he was the enemy. He could—too easily—make her forget all of that.

He paused, glanced at the view window, then sat again, returning his attention to the controls. Sha'Nara released her pent-up breath. To her surprise, the shuttle emerged from hyperspace and she glanced at her chronometer in disbelief. How could the time have passed so quickly? All she'd done was think of Tristan.

Spotting a PSI Police battleship at the edge of the

space lane, she leapt to her feet. Who was she fooling? Herself? She did trust Tristan. She trusted him with her life. It was time she showed that.

"Move to the far side of the traffic. Now." She hurried to the front and grabbed the back of Tristan's chair.

"What?" Cadell looked up in confusion, but Tristan immediately took control of the craft.

"The battleship is equipped with a new device that can detect Scanner brain waves within passing spacecraft." Cadell's face paled as she continued. "We've caught several Scanners with it. I'm always amazed at how many are willing to venture into this star system."

Tristan expertly weaved the shuttle through the thick trader traffic, but not in time. As Sha'Nara spotted two small fighters deploy from the battleship, she leaned forward. "Land on the planet as quickly as you can. They've spotted us."

"Land? Are you crazy?"

"You haven't a chance in space in this thing. I know some people down there. We can hide."

He turned his gaze to study her for a brief moment, then gripped the controls even more tightly. "Where do I go?"

Sha'Nara placed her hands over his. "I can do it faster than I can explain."

His hesitation lasted only a second. Then he pulled his hands free and vacated the chair. "Do it."

Assuming his place, Sha'Nara prepared the shuttle for a quick entry into the planet's atmosphere. Their tracking equipment indicated the PSI fighters were closing the distance between them. She only had one chance.

And she couldn't afford any mistakes.

Chapter Thirteen

Tristan gripped the back of Sha'Nara's chair as she aimed the shuttle toward the large planet. Despite Cadell's worried frown, Tristan knew he'd made the right decision in letting Sha'Nara take control. She hadn't given up her knowledge of the PSI Police device in order to see them captured.

In fact, right now she represented the only possible way Tristan and Cadell could avoid becoming PSI Police prisoners.

From the angle of their approach, he could tell they were in for a bumpy landing. Touching Jacy's arm, he led her back to the passenger seats. Before he could sit, Cadell joined him.

"You belong with Sha'Nara," he said. "And I belong here." Not waiting for Tristan to answer, Cadell slid into the seat.

Tristan gave Jacy a dry smile, then lurched as the shuttle entered the atmosphere. Stumbling forward, he pulled himself into Cadell's vacated seat and secured his belts.

The control levers vibrated within Sha'Nara's grasp as the ship burned through the cloudy layers. He glanced at the long-range tracker. "The fighters have fallen back," he told her.

"They'll probably notify the ground station instead." She didn't look at him as she spoke. "Even though we'll be landing some distance from the station, they can travel quickly. We'll have to move fast."

"Where are we going?"

"A small outpost in the badlands. I know some people there."

"And they'll hide us?"

"I hope so." She faced him then, her expression grim. "I haven't spoken to them for some time."

Tristan tried to tell himself that the sudden leap of his pulse came from a certain amount of trepidation, not the need to pull Sha'Nara into his arms. "Who are they?"

Her gaze flickered. Then she smiled slightly before returning her attention to the controls. "Smugglers."

"Smugglers?" Whatever he'd expected, it hadn't been that. Before he could question her further, the shuttle punched through the last layer of clouds and sailed over the rocky terrain. If Bazzar had not become a trade planet, it never would've survived based solely on its natural resources. Water went at a cost equivalent to gold.

Though Tristan couldn't make out any sign of civilization, Sha'Nara kept the ship on a steady course. When she dropped over a flat plateau rimmed by rugged hills, his muscles clenched in response. "What are you doing?" If they landed there, they'd have no place to hide.

In reply, she activated a low-range comm channel. "Ducares, this is Commander Calles. Request permission to land immediately."

A low, throaty voice replied immediately. "Commander. This is unexpected."

"I need to hide my ship and all my passengers."

Though Sha'Nara kept her voice even, Tristan heard her worry. Obviously this Ducares did, too.

"We're opening the cave now. I'll see you soon." The channel closed and Sha'Nara dove the shuttle toward the ring of jagged mountains.

As they drew closer, Tristan could make out a small gathering of buildings. Surely she didn't expect them to hide there? He opened his mouth to ask, then closed it again as an opening suddenly appeared in the side of one mountain.

He blinked. It hadn't been there a moment ago.

Sha'Nara directed the shuttle toward it, banking the engines so that they glided slowly into the dark hole. The shuttle barely cleared the entrance before the opening slid closed behind them.

Lights flickered on around them, and Sha'Nara settled the shuttle gently on the surface. Cutting the power, she released her restraints, then faced Tristan. "We're here."

Tristan could sense her nervousness. Apparently Sha'Nara was no more certain than he what kind of reception to expect.

When she headed for the hatch, he moved to her side. Whatever she faced, she wouldn't face it alone.

"It'll be all right," she said, but she sounded as if she were trying to convince herself as well as him.

The hatch opened and a woman stepped forward. Tristan caught his jaw before it could drop. In all his travels, he'd never encountered a woman like this before.

She stood taller than he, and appeared even more so with the bright orange hair piled high atop her head. Tightly muscled with a big-boned structure and well-proportioned curves, she gave new definition to the word voluptuous, especially when the tiny scraps of cloth fitted over her chest and hips barely covered those curves.

"Ducares, thank you." Sha'Nara greeted the woman by placing her hand over her heart.

Ducares returned the gesture, her full lips, painted

the same color as her hair, curving in a smile. "I am glad to return a favor. Come, your ship is hidden here. I have food waiting."

"You always seem to have food waiting."

"My men are always hungry."

Tristan moved to Sha'Nara's side, noticing now the dagger hanging from the thin rope around Ducares's hips. "How many men do you have?" he asked. Better to know what to expect.

"Thirty, perhaps forty." Ducares lifted one shoulder in a shrug. "I keep them busy." Her gaze lingered on Tristan, the gleam in her eye giving her words a purely suggestive meaning. "Would you like to join them?"

Stunned, he could only stare. Was she asking him to join her harem? Tristan turned to Sha'Nara. As far as he was concerned, he wanted only one woman.

Placing her hand on his arm, Sha'Nara answered for Tristan. "No, he wouldn't."

"Too bad." Ducares gave Sha'Nara a warm smile. "You have excellent taste for a PSI Police officer. I never would've expected it of you." She looked toward the hatch as Cadell and Jacy emerged, and her eyes widened. "Another one."

"He's taken, too." Sha'Nara smiled, and Tristan allowed himself to relax slightly. Apparently Ducares solicited every male she saw. Or did she? What was going on here?

"Pity." Ducares waved her hand toward the back of the cave. "Follow me. I believe the food should be ready by now."

When Sha'Nara would've removed her hand, Tristan trapped it beneath his. "Who *is* this woman?" he asked.

"Ducares. She's the smugglers' leader."

"Smugglers' leader?" He couldn't keep the disbelief from his voice. That woman was a smuggler?

"The thirty or forty men are her partners."

"Oh, I thought she meant . . . that they were her sexual partners."

Tiny spots of color rose in Sha'Nara's cheeks. "Many

of them are that, too. She runs a free-love type of community here."

"How did you meet her?" Ducares and Sha'Nara were complete opposites—the smuggler and Alliance officer. "And why didn't you arrest her?"

"It's a long story." Sha'Nara slid her hand free of his hold and hurried after Ducares, her discomfort obvious.

Grinning, Tristan waved at Jacy and Cadell, then followed. Before they left this planet, he intended to hear that story.

After descending several roughly cut steps, they emerged from the mountain interior onto the plateau. Tristan saw a large fire burning in the center of the circle formed by several rickety shacks. As Ducares led them between the buildings, he noticed many men and women waiting by the fire, their gazes expectant.

He swallowed. The majority of them towered over him, though none of the other women reached Ducares's statuesque height. The women wore the same brief clothing as Ducares, while the men were clad only in tight pants. Sexuality oozed from the entire gathering. He shook his head in bemusement. These people were smugglers? How did they get any work done?

Several children came running through the adults to Ducares, who gathered them in a group hug.

"Are all those hers?" asked Tristan in amazement.

Sha'Nara smiled. "Not all." Some of the older children left Ducares and approached Sha'Nara with their hands held out. She laughed and welcomed them into a hug as well.

Tristan's breath caught in his throat at Sha'Nara's laugh. The lighthearted musical quality touched him deep inside. After just a few days with this career-minded PSI Officer, he knew her laughter didn't come easily.

Yet he enjoyed listening to her as she dealt with the many questions thrown at her, her expression warm, her voice filled with amusement. Obviously many of the children knew her from her previous visit—a visit he intended to know more about.

As he watched her, his chest tightened. He could love this woman.

He inhaled sharply. Love? Where had that come from? He had no place for love in his life, certainly not now, and even more certainly not with a PSI Police officer.

As one of the men approached Sha'Nara, shooing the children away, Tristan stiffened and stood as tall as he could. Acting on impulse, he placed his hand on Sha'Nara's waist and drew her closer to his side. To his surprise, she allowed his hand to remain as she greeted the blond-haired giant.

"Beduar, it's good to see you again."

"It is more than good to see you."

Tristan bristled as the man's gaze roamed freely over Sha'Nara.

"I didn't expect you to return here," Beduar added.

"It was a last-minute decision." Sha'Nara shifted nervously, and Tristan tucked her more firmly against his side.

Beduar smiled slowly, his expression hungry for more than food. "Perhaps we can spend some time together while you are here."

Enough! Tristan swung Sha'Nara partially behind him and faced the smuggler, though he had to look up to meet the man's gaze. "She's with me," he said firmly.

"And you do not share?" Beduar actually sounded stunned.

"Not farding likely." Tristan curled his hands into fists, ready to fight if necessary.

"As you wish." The man bobbed his head once and moved away, apparently unconcerned.

Anger bubbled through Tristan, though he wasn't sure where to direct it. No one could make him desert Sha'Nara so easily. Realizing the direction of his thoughts, he groaned. That didn't mean he loved her.

He swung around to face her and drank in her freshness, her quiet sensuality, which appealed to him much more than the blatant sexuality surrounding the smuggler women. Shibit, he wanted her with every fiber of his being.

"Who was that man?" he demanded, hating the way he sounded, yet unable to hold back the words.

She studied him. "I met him the last time I was here."

"And he propositioned you?"

A slow grin lit up her face. "All the men propositioned me. That's part of who they are. Beduar was a little more persistent than the rest."

"But you didn't give in?" He knew she hadn't. After all, Tristan had been her first. That thought sent heat racing through his blood. Why had she made love with him?

"I have no time for a man in my life." She lowered her gaze. "My career is what's important."

Tristan reached out to cup her cheek in his palm, bringing her startled gaze back to his face. "And is your career still what's important?" He wanted her to say no, to give it all up. Then maybe . . .

"Yes." She whispered the word as conflicting emotions appeared in her eyes. "My career is very important to me."

A slap couldn't have been more effective. Tristan dropped his hand and turned away. "Of course. You need to return to your PSI Police position so you can continue to capture and readjust Scanners. If you're good enough, you might even take your father's place someday."

He heard her intake of breath, but didn't look back. Instead he strode into the midst of the smugglers. He should've known better. It had to be the aura in this encampment that made him think for one mad moment they might actually have a chance.

Two women approached, and made it clear from their blatant touches and husky murmurs that they would be glad to satisfy his need, but he refused. He couldn't deny that he ached with desire, but they couldn't relieve it. Only one woman could do that.

"Tristan."

Hearing Sha'Nara's voice behind him, he spun around to face her. Her eyes glowed with anger. Her rigid stance, hands on hips, legs apart, invited a fight. "You have no right to berate me because I want to have a career. I may leave the PSI Police, but I still intend to remain in the Alliance. It's been my whole life. It's part of who I am. I haven't asked you to give up being who you are, have I?"

"That's because I can't give up who I am, what I am." He stopped in front of her, unable to believe she'd even voice such a ridiculous request. "And I'm not about to undergo readjustment . . . not even for you."

The air crackled between them as they glared at each other, until Sha'Nara's eyes widened as if she finally grasped the importance of his words. Confusion shimmered in her gaze, and her jaw worked twice before words finally emerged.

"Tristan, I—"

"We have company." A man ran into the group, pointing skyward.

Looking up, Tristan spotted the all too familiar shapes of PSI Police cruisers approaching. Sha'Nara seized his arm. "Come on. We have to get inside the mountain again. They won't be able to locate us there."

"No time." Ducares joined them with Cadell and Jacy in tow. "They'll be landing in moments. Don't draw attention to yourselves, but come with me. I have a place you can hide."

Tristan could barely maintain an even stride as he walked with Ducares into one of the larger tumbledown structures, the sound of the cruisers drawing ever closer.

The inside of the building was dotted with large tables placed atop stone pedestals and an assortment of chairs. At Ducares's signal, two men pushed one of the tables aside to reveal a hatch in the ground.

Ducares bent to lift the hatch, motioning them forward. "These spaces are rather small. Only two of you will fit in one. Hurry now."

Jacy pulled Cadell to the front. "We'll take this one."

Karen Fox

"Jacy. . . ." Cadell pulled his hand free of her hold. "It might be better if Sha'Nara went with you. With the emotions I've been sensing from these people, I may not be able to keep my promise to you."

She smiled broadly. "Good. I never asked for that promise." Before he could object further, she climbed into the hole.

"You'll find a glowstick and mats inside," said Ducares. "We've had to hide people here before."

Cadell gave Tristan a wan grimace, then followed Jacy into the darkness. The smugglers immediately replaced the stone table over the closed hatch.

They'd previously moved another table aside, and Ducares went to lift the revealed hatch. "Hurry now."

Sha'Nara hadn't moved from the moment the hatch had first been revealed, and the color drained from her face. Tristan couldn't allow her to hide in these caves. With her fear of locked doors, she'd never make it.

"Will we be in there long?" he asked.

"It may be a while," replied Ducares. "The last time we were so honored with a visit by the PSI Police, they stayed several hours."

Tristan went to the edge of the hole. "Can't Sha'Nara stay outside with you? They're not about to arrest her."

"I can't do that." Sha'Nara spoke finally. "If I'm found, it'll be a signal that you're here and will hurt Ducares as well." She brushed past him and stepped onto the ladder leading downward. As her head drew even with the floor, she hesitated, then inhaled sharply and vanished into the darkness.

Tristan followed quickly, descending the several narrow rungs into blackness. He'd barely touched the rocky floor when he heard the sound of the table scraping into place above him. Pausing, one hand holding the ladder, he tried to see into the darkness.

"Sha'Nara? Feel around. Ducares says there are glowsticks."

No response.

His heart surged. "Sha'Nara?" Running his hands over the nearby stone walls, he located the short tube-

204

like glowstick and activated it. A dim light emerged from the stick, and he held it high as he searched for Sha'Nara.

Unable to stand straight, he advanced further into the hollowed-out tunnel. "Sha'Nara?"

He found her huddled on a wide thick mat, her arms wrapped around her legs, her head buried atop her knees. His gut twisted at seeing her, and he instantly dropped to his knees beside her.

"Sha'Nara, it's all right. They'll let us out again."

"I know that." She lifted her head and gave him a weak smile, but the sweat beaded on her forehead and the pallor of her face only reinforced what Tristan already knew. Being locked in here terrified her.

Reaching out to brush her cheek, he drew back his hand in alarm. "You're like ice."

He settled into a comfortable position, then pulled Sha'Nara onto his lap and wrapped her tightly within his arms. "We're not trapped here, you know."

She looked at him dubiously. "Oh, really?"

"I can move that rock if I have to." He wasn't sure that was a true statement, but he made it sound as if it was. "I wouldn't let them keep you trapped."

"You'd move the rock?" She smiled fully this time. "I know what you're trying to do."

He tried to look indignant. "You doubt me?"

She slid her hand behind his neck, and all his senses kicked into instant alert. "Of course not," she murmured. She'd relaxed slightly, but fear remained in her eyes, visible even in the dim light of the glowstick.

Tormented by the feel of her soft curves cradled on his lap, unable to think with the touch of her hand on him, Tristan gave in to the urge he'd fought all day. He kissed her.

Gently at first, he probed her lips, nibbling on the softness, tracing their outline with the tip of his tongue until she opened to him with a sigh and he delved deeper, ensnaring her even tighter within his arms. Her response fueled his inner fire, sending hot desire

205

throughout every pore of his being. Beneath where she sat, he grew hard . . . very hard.

She had to feel him, for she grew suddenly still and broke off the kiss. Staring at him, her breathing uneven, she shifted slightly, rubbing her bottom across his erection. He grimaced beneath the painful onslaught of need.

"See what you do to me," he said with a rueful smile. "I want you, Sha'Nara. More than I've ever wanted any woman."

"Tristan . . ." She moved again, and he couldn't hold back his groan. Concern crossed her face as she traced the outline of his mouth with her fingertips. "We shouldn't." She didn't sound any more convinced than he felt.

"Then tell me no and let me get to the other side of this cave before I decide to ignore what you say and listen to what your body tells me instead." He hadn't missed the return of color to her cheeks, nor the rapid rise and fall of her chest. "Or say yes and let me make love to you."

Though her eyes darkened, she slid from his lap. He wanted to scream with frustration. He'd hoped . . . Before he could move, she pressed his shoulders back to the mat until he lay flat. "Last time you took over," she said quietly. "This time I have control."

Anticipation tingled along his nerves as he watched her carefully. "What do you want me to do?" His voice emerged in husky tones.

"For now, nothing. Just stay still." Running one finger along the seam of his flight suit, she unsealed the Stik-Tite and peeled back the material until she had it off his shoulders.

He barely had time to realize his arms were trapped in the material before she leaned forward to kiss him, sliding her tongue into his mouth to explore with more and more boldness. Her first hesitant strokes sent new ripples of pleasure coursing through his body. When she finally grew brave enough to sensuously tease his tongue, the ache in his gut grew even tighter.

As she continued to drive him mad with her kiss, she moved her hand over his bared chest to brush his nipple. It stiffened immediately, and Tristan gasped as a lightning bolt of desire shot through him.

She drew back, amusement dancing in her eyes. "I like it when you touch me there," she said. "Do *you* like it?" Without waiting for a response, she put both her hands into motion, caressing his chest hair while she brushed feather-light kisses along his chin, down his throat, and over the broad expanse of his chest. She paused to suckle his hardened nipple.

Tristan grew rigid from head to toe, need pounding so hard he could hear it. "If this is a wicked plan to kill me, it's working."

Her low laugh only added to the sensual blanket of longing she'd wrapped around him. Moving with more confidence, she peeled the flight suit off his shoulders and down the length of his body. He twisted as needed until she'd managed to remove his boots and suit entirely.

Rocking back on her heels, she looked at him. His erection grew even more beneath her gaze. "You are . . . impressive." She ran her palm over the ridge in his briefs, and he groaned again.

"Sha'Nara . . ." His voice held a note of warning. He couldn't take much more of this.

She grasped the edges of his briefs and slid them down his legs. Freed, his erection jutted upward, throbbing with want. When she wrapped her warm fingers around him, he rocked his hips forward. He couldn't maintain control much longer. It felt so good . . . too good.

"I need to touch you," he gasped, raising his hands.

"Keep your hands down," she admonished while her fingers caressed his shaft.

Unfair. The cords in Tristan's neck tightened from the strain. Suddenly he remembered—he didn't have to use his hands.

Sha'Nara jumped when he used his telekinesis to unbraid her hair, and she looked at him accusingly. "I'm not moving my hands," he replied with a satisfied smile. "And I like your hair free. It matches this wanton side of you."

When she didn't object, he proceeded, unsealing her suit and sliding his mental hands beneath her undershirt to caress her breasts. The sudden hitch in her breathing told him he'd caught her attention, and he concentrated on caressing her budded nipples.

She squeezed him more firmly, and he lifted off the floor. "Sha'Nara, please. I want to touch you myself, with my hands, skin against skin."

Her chest rose unevenly as she nodded. "Yes, Tristan, please—"

He moved with a speed he hadn't known he possessed, rolling her beneath him, seizing her lips even as he slid her suit along her curves until it spilled over her boots. Anxious to reach her breasts, he yanked her undershirt off, then filled his palms with her softness.

Better, so much better than anything he could do mentally. Brushing the hardened tips, he reveled in her moans of pleasure. Heat radiated from her body. Or was it his?

Lowering her gently to the mat, he released her mouth only long enough to finish undressing her. Kneeling by her feet, he examined her long seductive length. He could no longer ask himself why her. With a fated inevitability he knew she was the one . . . for now . . . forever.

The taut, tender skin over her abdomen invited teasing nips, the shallow hollow of her belly button a thorough exploration with his tongue. When he drew her breast into his mouth, she arched again, her hips rocking against him, her moans adding to his pent-up desire.

He left that breast, scraping his teeth along her tender nipple, then paused to blow on it, surprised when it hardened even further. After giving her other breast equal attention, he left a trail of kisses en route to her mouth, and captured her lips.

Her passionate response thrilled him. She gripped his

shoulders, pulling him close, pressing his chest firmly against hers. The pebbled tips of her breasts brushed against him and he drew back.

"Tristan." She moaned his name and he plunged into her, forcing himself to remain still as she immediately shuddered around him. As the tremors eased, he began to move with sure, solid strokes, filling her, melding with her, becoming one.

Gathering her buttocks in his hands, he raised her hips so he could delve deeper, giving all of himself. "Sha'Nara . . ." *I need you. I want you.* All of that and more. Words he could never say. But he could show her, and he did. Only when he felt her shudder again did he surrender and pour his seed into her.

Nothing in his entire life had been this good. Nothing ever would again.

He rolled to lay beside her, and struggled to regain control of his erratic breathing. She propped up on one elbow to look down at him.

"This was my dream," she said softly. "I recognize it now."

"Your dream?" He remembered her accusations that Mael had caused a dream. "Mael couldn't have known about this."

"It's not Mael." She smiled sadly. "I don't know what it is, but this was it."

He propped up on his elbows. "How do you know?"

"Because I felt it. . . ." She hesitated.

His mouth went dry as he waited for her to continue. "We're linked, Tristan. I don't know how or why, but I know with you it's right. I become whole for the first time in my life."

"I know." If his life depended on it, he couldn't force any more words through his thick throat right now.

"It's insane." She waved her hand at him. "You're a Scanner." She glanced down. When she lifted her head, her eyes glistened with unshed tears. "Yet it's wonderful. I never knew I could feel like this."

He still didn't move. There was more. Whatever link

they shared told him that. And he didn't want to hear it.

"And it's the most painful experience of my life." A tear rolled down her cheek. "We can't be together, Tristan."

Her tear landed on his chest, burning into his skin as he felt a prickling at the back of his eyes. He couldn't disagree. What kind of life could he offer her?

A life on the run, a life where they had to constantly look over their shoulders, a life where the PSI Police would become her enemy, eager to make retribution for her apparent desertion. No life at all.

He sat up, turning his back to her as agony speared his chest. "You're right, of course."

She came to wrap her arms around his neck from behind, pressing her body along his back. Fresh desire erupted, and he closed his eyes to hold it back. "Maybe you'll get your freedom," she said.

"Only if the Alliance ceases to exist." This plan for freedom had been foolish from the onset, but now . . . now it mattered even more. He twisted to face her. "Sha'Nara—"

She placed her fingers over his mouth, stopping his words. "I know. This shouldn't have happened."

Even so, he wanted her, needed her desperately. "I—"

"No words," she whispered, and kissed him gently. She then gave him a sad smile. "Don't say it. Just show me."

Without hesitation, he sought her lips. That he could do.

Chapter Fourteen

When they finally dressed again, Sha'Nara allowed Tristan to cradle her within his arms, her head resting against his chest. A bittersweet melancholy surrounded her. She would never share this intimate pleasure with him again.

"Are you going to tell me now?" he asked quietly.

Tell him what? Her pulse jumped. She'd all but admitted she cared for him, foolish as that was. To say anything more would be too difficult, too painful. "What?"

"About how you know these smugglers. Somehow I can't see you socializing with this crowd."

She smiled slowly. "That's true."

"How long have you known them?"

"About a year now. I'd been chasing Scanners through the trade corridor and they damaged my ship. I half-landed, half-crashed on the rocks near here." She paused, remembering the waves of pain. "I was seriously injured. Ducares and her people found me and brought me back here."

Tristan tightened his hold around her and she found it easier to retrieve the memories. "She doesn't have access to the latest medical tools, so my recovery took a while. By the time I learned what she did for a living, I couldn't very well arrest her. She'd saved my life."

"And where does this Beduar come in?"

The defensive note in Tristan's voice made Sha'Nara smile.

"All the men issued invitations to lay with them. That's their way of life here. I refused them, but Beduar didn't give up. I think he took my refusal personally." Beduar had actually tried to woo her—a pleasant experience, but a futile one for him. She'd felt no desire for him. "Once I'd recovered enough to travel, Ducares notified the PSI Police station to retrieve me."

"And you resisted Beduar only because of your career?" Tristan idly curled her hair around his finger, but his casualness didn't fool her.

"Mostly that, plus it would've been foolish to get involved with a smuggler. It was better I just left."

"Yet you let me make love to you—a Scanner."

His words cut into her, and she shifted away from him. "I guess I save my foolishness for something truly unreasonable."

Before he could reach for her, she rose to her feet and left the dim light of the glowstick to stand in the darkness by the ladder. Strange, she hadn't been afraid since Tristan touched her. Even now, surrounded by blackness, aware of the massive stone table weighting down the hatch, she experienced no shortness of breath or sweaty palms.

Gazing up at the hatch, she experienced a surge of strength—a strength she knew she'd need upon her return to Centralia. Especially if she intended to take the Scanners' side when they asked for freedom.

She caught her breath. When had she made that decision? She closed her eyes, contemplating the anger she'd encounter. Apparently her foolishness was boundless.

Yet she knew Tristan, knew Cadell. Their quest for

peace was sincere. After all her time on the *Hermitage* among the Scanners, when they'd known who she was, only Bran had tried to harm her. She could no longer see them as the bloodthirsty, power-hungry race she'd been led to believe. They were families, children, individuals who wanted a place to call home, a piece of land.

Remembering Tristan's terrarium brought an ache to Sha'Nara's chest. She had to help him find that land of his own he desired so much.

"What do we do now?" His voice came through the darkness, a blend of macho and uncertainty that tugged at her heart.

Before she could reply, she heard the sound of the stone sliding above her head, and waited until the hatch opened, blasting the blackness with a shaft of brilliance.

She blinked, blaming the watering of her eyes on the sudden light. "We go to Centralia."

Saying good-bye to Ducares and avoiding the PSI Police as they left the planet was easy for Sha'Nara compared to the thick tension inside the shuttle. Jacy and Cadell had emerged from hiding unusually solemn, with Jacy constantly on the brink of tears. Sha'Nara had no doubts the younger woman had consummated her relationship with Cadell.

Remy Vadin was not going to be very happy with them. Sha'Nara shuddered to think of her father's reaction. He would consider sleeping with the enemy an act of treason. If he found out, her career would be finished entirely, if it wasn't already.

Watching the stars glide by the view screen, she inhaled deeply. She'd just have to make sure he never found out. It wasn't as if she'd ever see Tristan again after he left her at Alliance headquarters. That thought only brought depression.

Tristan sat in the other pilot's seat while Cadell and Jacy cuddled together in the rear of the ship. As Centralia grew to fill the view screen, the green-blue swirls taking on shape, he turned to her. "Do you know an easy way in?" Though he kept his expression emotionless, his dark eyes glittered with pain.

"Yes. There's a coded entry corridor that leads directly to the Alliance building." She didn't dare look at him as she leaned forward to issue the proper code. Before they arrived, he'd know all the Alliance secrets.

As she expected, a shimmering corridor displayed on their flight screen and Tristan guided the shuttle into it. As they drew nearer to the planet's surface and the mammoth Alliance complex, Sha'Nara sensed Tristan's rising tension. He'd probably find it easier to face an entire den of Thorgs than to fly right into the central meeting place of his people's greatest enemies.

The complex stretched below them, easily the size of a small city, and as self-contained as one, too. Several long narrow buildings stretched away from the middle circle, and a particularly large square building sat along one side. Designed to withstand any attacks, the fortified white buildings had only small black windows and no observable doors. The only adornment was the large black dome on the circular portion that covered the Director-General's central meeting room.

Keying in another code, Sha'Nara bit her lip. "This will let us into the landing bay." She glanced at Tristan. Would he use this information later against the Alliance?

At the moment he showed no interest in the series of numbers, his concentration centered on steering the shuttle into the opening that appeared in one side of the cube-shaped section. "What will we find in there?" he asked, his features tight.

"We probably won't even be noticed. This is the main transport area. Ships come and go constantly." Sha'Nara resisted the urge to smooth away his lines of tension with her fingers. "Just leave this code in there and you'll be able to leave again once Jacy and I are off the ship."

He jerked around to look at her. "You expect me to just leave you in the bay?"

"Of course." She frowned. "It's safest for you and Cadell."

"No." He paused as if reconsidering. "No. I'm taking you to the Director-General myself."

Insanity. Didn't he realize what they'd have to go through first? "You can't. I can't guarantee your safety if you do."

"I'm not worried about that." The clenching of his jaw belied those words. "I intend to speak to the Director-General. As long as we're here, I might as well deliver our plea myself."

"I have Mael's scroll imager." Sha'Nara's heart hammered in her chest. She couldn't let Tristan into the central chambers. He'd never make it out alive.

"You can take that, too." He guided the shuttle into the landing bay, easing the engines. "I need to do this, Sha'Nara. Maybe I can make him understand. . . ."

She understood his need to make a personal plea, but doubted Remy would be in any mood to listen. "It isn't wise."

He smiled at that. "I know, but I've been doing some foolish things myself lately. I have to try, Sha'Nara." He glanced at her, his gaze so heated that she caught her breath beneath a sudden onslaught of desire.

Docking the ship, he cut the power and swung around. "We're here." His words fell heavily in the silence.

Cadell jumped to his feet. "I'm escorting Jacy personally to her father."

Sighing, Sha'Nara faced them. "If either of you leave this ship, you're putting yourselves into a position where I may not be able to help you."

"I'm willing to take that chance." Cadell drew Jacy to her feet and wrapped his arm around her. "I have to make sure nothing happens to either of you between here and there."

"This is my territory now," Sha'Nara replied. "Nothing will happen to Jacy and me."

"Then stop arguing." Tristan slapped his hand against the hatch control. "We're going."

The hatch slid open, revealing the organized chaos of the transport wing. Alliance pilots of all ranks and divisions milled about on the narrow guideways, exchanging flight information, maintenance requirements, tales of their fearless exploits.

Other personnel worked on the multitude of spacecraft parked in the bay. Sha'Nara knew each bay held at least twenty ships and hundreds of these bays filled the transport wing. Stepping from the shuttle, she held her breath. If someone shouted an alarm, they'd be overpowered in moments.

Thankfully, no one paid any attention as Sha'Nara led the others from the bay and into the transport wing's central corridor. Avoiding the usually packed shuttle, she instead sought the less jammed moving walkway. This method of travel would take more time, but they'd run into fewer people.

The PSI Police occupied an entire wing of this complex. It wasn't uncommon to find them throughout the structure . . . and most of them wore Scanner detectors. Fortunately, a good number left the detectors off while in the headquarters. After all, no one ever expected Scanners to make it inside . . . on their own.

She glanced at Tristan beside her. The tenseness with which he held himself signaled his anxiety. On impulse, she touched his arm and gave him a half smile.

His return smile was even more wan. "This is . . . overwhelming. I'm amazed you don't get lost."

"Visitors always do. That's why they're usually assigned guides." The turnoff for the central circle was approaching. Sha'Nara swallowed hard. "Are you sure about this, Tristan?"

"I'm sure. Unless you don't trust me near your Director-General."

She widened her eyes. To be honest, she hadn't once contemplated that Tristan would do harm to the Alliance leader. Obviously she'd lost her objectivity. Still, Tristan wouldn't try to kill Remy Vadin. She knew it, felt it. "I trust you."

He smiled with more warmth. "Thank you."

At the crosswalk, they turned and entered the center of the Alliance. All the directorate heads had offices in this massive circular building, as well as the Director-General. Her father's office was here. Sha'Nara brushed past that thought. She'd see him soon enough.

They made it to the interior without incident. Fortunately, Tristan, Cadell, and Jacy wore neutral jumpsuits, while she had her dress uniform. Without a Scanner detector, no one would know Tristan and Cadell weren't Alliance officers. Thus far, no one had recognized her or Jacy, but that wouldn't last much longer.

Her stomach rolled as they paused outside the door leading into the Director-General's suite of offices. She couldn't afford to panic now. "We'll have to move fast to get you to Remy." Her gaze touched briefly on Jacy and Cadell, their hands clasped tightly together, their unhappiness apparent on their faces, before she looked at Tristan.

As usual, his expression gave nothing away, but deep inside she felt her connection to him—a connection she didn't want, but couldn't avoid. "Let me do the talking. You men get on either side of Jacy like you're escorting her. Then follow my lead."

Everyone nodded and she raised her hand to the door control, her pulse racing. As the door opened, she dashed inside. "I need to see the Director-General."

Remy's assistant, a capable older woman, merely raised one eyebrow. "I'm afraid he's tied up in a meeting now."

Good, the conference room. Sha'Nara knew where to go. Motioning the others to follow her, she strode toward the conference room entrance with false confidence. When the assistant started to rise, her hand moving for her weapon, Sha'Nara waved at her impatiently, but didn't stop moving.

"I have Jacy Vadin. He'll want to see her now."

Jacy even mustered a smile for the woman as Tristan and Cadell dragged her past. "Hello, Mistress Helios."

Mistress Helios dropped her jaw.

Sha'Nara activated the doorway and rushed inside.

Immediately seven gazes turned her way, gazes she recognized as belonging to the directorate heads. Her father jumped to his feet, but had no chance to say anything as Jacy and her escorts piled in behind Sha'Nara.

"Jacy!" Remy rushed forward to envelope her in a hug, looking up to wave Mistress Helios back to her desk. Only after the door sealed shut again did he release his daughter and turn to Sha'Nara.

"Officer Calles, I thought . . ."

"I know." She had to smile at his obvious relief. "Jacy and I got off the transport before it left the Scanner ship."

"Thank the stars." Remy's gaze moved to Tristan and Cadell, who stood nearby. His eyes widened and he set Jacy away from him. "And you are?"

"Daddy, this is Tristan Galeron." Jacy waved her hand at Tristan, then moved to touch Cadell's arm. "And this is Cadell Ner."

"Ner?" Remy inhaled sharply. "The Scanner."

Cadell gave a brief nod. "My father."

"Scanners!" Instantly Amyr Calles drew his weapon.

Her heart in her throat, Sha'Nara stepped in front of Tristan. "Father, no."

At the same time, the weapon flew from Amyr's hand, then landed softly at the far end of the table behind Remy. Seeing Tristan's kinesis at work, Sha'Nara twisted to give him an inquisitive look.

Tristan didn't acknowledge her, his gaze pinned on the director of the PSI Police. "Director Calles," he said coldly. "I won't say it's a pleasure."

A flush of anger filled Amyr's face. He pointed his finger toward Sha'Nara. "You brought them here."

"I know what I'm doing." Sha'Nara faced Remy. "They wanted to make sure we arrived safely and Tristan wants to talk to you."

The Director-General's features showed his doubt, but he faced Tristan. "What do you have to say?"

Tristan straightened his shoulders. "We haven't come for violence, we've come for peace."

"And that's why you kidnapped my daughter?" An undercurrent of anger entered Remy's calm voice.

"I regret having to do so, but we knew if we simply requested a meeting with you, it wouldn't happen." Tristan kept his tone quiet. "By inviting Jacy to be our guest, we thought you might be more open to agreement."

"They didn't hurt me, Daddy," added Jacy.

As if suddenly realizing Jacy still stood beside Cadell, Remy grasped her wrist and pulled her behind him, his gaze still locked on Tristan. "You're here. I'm listening. What do you want?"

Sha'Nara closed her eyes as disappointment filtered through her. Remy wouldn't agree. She knew already. Nothing Tristan could say would make a difference.

"We want freedom from persecution."

"Freedom?" Amyr pushed from his chair and started toward them. "Freedom to take over and destroy, you mean."

Tristan's mouth tightened, but he didn't glance away. "We're still being blamed for what our ancestors did a hundred years ago. We have no desire for power or to destroy. All we want is to be left in peace to pursue normal lives."

"Normal lives." Remy repeated the words slowly. "But you're not normal, are you?"

"We're normal for who we are." Tristan's voice rose slightly. "You don't hunt down the Rondovals, who can mutate into different shapes. You don't kill the Gregorians, who have the capability of breathing fire. Yet you seek to destroy us simply because we're humans with highly advanced mental abilities. Why?"

Remy hesitated and Sha'Nara rolled her hands into fists. Would he consider Tristan's request?

Amyr pushed his way forward. "We hunt you because you've proven time and time again that you can't be trusted, that you live only to achieve dominance over the rest of the humans who don't have your mental abilities . . . your mutant abilities."

"None of that is true," Tristan protested, but Remy

had heard Amyr. The Director-General's face set into firm lines.

"I can't grant your request," he said. "It's impossible."

"But—"

"You kidnapped my daughter. I thought she was dead." Remy didn't try to disguise his anger now. "Now you come to me wanting to be friends? It doesn't work that way."

Cadell stepped forward. "Please don't make an impulsive judgment." He held out the scroll imager. "My father sent his own message. Listen to him first. Think about it."

"There's nothing to think about," snapped Amyr. He tossed the scroll imager onto the table, then lifted his hand. "Signal the guards. Throw these Scanners in the restraining cells."

"No." Jacy and Sha'Nara cried out together.

"I promised them safe passage for bringing us here," added Sha'Nara, focusing on Remy.

Tears streamed down Jacy's cheeks. "Please, Daddy, don't."

Remy paused, searching first his daughter's face, then Sha'Nara's, before moving on to the implacable features of Tristan and Cadell. "Very well." He lifted his arm when Amyr would've protested. "They did bring my daughter safely back to me. Grant them safe passage out of our star system."

"Thank you, sir," Tristan said stiffly. "We won't bother you anymore."

As he turned toward the door, Sha'Nara's heart plummeted to her stomach. He was leaving and she'd never see him again. "May I escort them to their craft, sir?" she asked impulsively. "To ensure they have no problems?"

Remy nodded.

"May I go—"

Remy cut Jacy off before she could finish. "You're not going anywhere," he said firmly. "Until I have an escort to take you to your quarters. I'll be there as soon as I finish up here."

"But . . ." Jacy looked at Cadell in a panic.

"I'm not about to risk losing you again." The Director-General touched a comm panel on the table. "Please send an escort for my daughter." He glanced up at Tristan and Cadell, his gaze lingering a moment longer on Cadell. "You may go now."

Tristan spun around, the stiffness of his shoulder indicative of his bottled frustration. As Sha'Nara hurried to open the door, she caught the agonizing looks exchanged quickly between Jacy and Cadell, and she ached for them. "This way," she murmured.

"I want to see you when you return, daughter," said Amyr.

A chill spread through her body as she nodded. Already she sensed his displeasure and dreaded the meeting. First, as her superior, he would berate her for failing to destroy the enemy, even worse for bringing them into the complex. Then he would shred her emotions as only a father could do, making her feel completely inadequate.

Leading the men out of the central circle kept her alert as they passed several groups of Alliance officers. She wouldn't put it past her father to order an attack on the Scanners despite Remy's orders.

Tristan said nothing, but despair etched his features. Everything he'd worked toward, hoped for, was gone in an instant. Though Sha'Nara had always felt certain Remy wouldn't grant the Scanners their freedom, she had believed he'd at least consider the idea. The man had come into his position because of his unbiased fairness to the many races that made up the Alliance.

Maybe Cadell's empathic abilities made him radiate his feelings, because Sha'Nara couldn't walk beside him without feeling a small measure of his pain. She wanted to comfort him, but couldn't. No words would replace what he was losing.

Or what she was losing.

Studying Tristan, she tried to imagine her future without him, but came up blank. She hadn't wanted to care for him, to share this passion. Perhaps once they were separated she'd escape this unwanted attraction.

She grimaced. She doubted it.

"I'm sorry," she said quietly.

For a moment she thought he wouldn't answer. Then he looked at her, his gaze filled with bitterness and pain. "It isn't as if you hadn't predicted this." His words emerged harsh, clipped. He hesitated, then spoke again, his voice warmer. "I apologize for all you've gone through . . . both you and Jacy. We should've known better than to hope."

"I'm not sorry for that." Cadell's raspy words drew Sha'Nara's attention to his grief-stricken face. "I never would've met Jacy if we hadn't embarked on this."

"If you'd never met her, you wouldn't have fallen in love with her," snapped Tristan. "You wouldn't be hurting now, knowing you'll never see her again, knowing she's to marry another man."

"What we've shared is more important than any pain I'm suffering now." Cadell smiled slightly. "She will always be a part of me."

Tristan shook his head as if his friend had no sense, but Sha'Nara drew in a deep breath. Cadell's words touched a nerve. After making love to Tristan, she knew she'd never be able to lie with any other man without remembering the Scanner.

"I haven't given up all hope," added Cadell. "The Director-General still has Father's scroll imager. He may listen to it and change his mind."

"The fires on Armaga will burn out first." Tristan's mouth twisted. "He doesn't want to listen."

A sudden sense of panic jumped to life in Sha'Nara. Why? What did it mean? Would Remy destroy Tristan?

As they reached the point where they'd have to change walkways, she stopped, frowning. The panic wasn't associated with Tristan. A vague picture formed in her mind, and she closed her eyes to see it more clearly.

"Sha'Nara, are—"

Cadell stopped speaking suddenly, as if silenced by

Tristan, but she paid him little notice, all her attention focused on the object taking shape.

The scroll imager.

Her muscles tensed, the urge to run almost over-powering. Her sense of urgency grew. As she continued to concentrate, the imager became clearer, the picture larger.

The conference room.

Remy lifting the imager off the table where Amyr had thrown it and studying it.

Remy starting Mael's message.

All the directors watching it.

A thoughtful expression on Remy's face.

A . . . an . . . explosion!

Sha'Nara's eyes flew open and she grabbed Tristan's arm. "We have to go back." She started running along the walkway before she finished speaking.

To their credit, Tristan and Cadell didn't hesitate, but joined her. "What is it?" asked Tristan.

"The scroll imager is going to explode." Saying the words out loud made them sound ridiculous. How could she know that? Yet the panic, the urgency grew even stronger.

"You can't know that," exclaimed Cadell.

"I don't know." Sha'Nara drew in more air, not slow-ing even to speak. "But I feel it."

"Another hunch?" Tristan's voice held no ridicule, merely curiosity.

"I . . . yes . . . a hunch." She couldn't explain, didn't know what to call the shimmering image that had ap-peared in her mind. Her only awareness was of the need to run faster . . . faster. There wasn't much time.

As Tristan ran beside Sha'Nara, he wondered why he believed so easily in her hunches. True, her previous hunch had saved her life. But to know specifically that the scroll imager would explode? He studied her as she ran. If he didn't know better . . .

Getting through the Director-General's office wasn't as easy as the first time. They burst through the outer door to find two lasers pointed at them. Sha'Nara stopped, bouncing on the balls of her feet.

"I have to get in there," she told Mistress Helios. "It's urgent."

"He's not to be disturbed." The woman pinned her with an icy glare. "Especially not by them."

Sha'Nara gave Tristan a panicky look that begged for his help.

He hesitated. Thus far, he'd only used his psi ability once within the complex. To do so again would only invite trouble. As far as he was concerned, it might be better if the scroll imager did explode and destroy the entire Alliance leadership. They certainly meant nothing to him.

But they meant something to Sha'Nara. Her alarm reflected in her wide eyes, the tightness of her jaw. Her father was in there. He might be Tristan's worst enemy, but Amyr Calles *was* Sha'Nara's father.

Would the death of the Alliance council help matters any? Or make things worse? Remy Vadin had, at least, listened to him. If the man hadn't been so upset about Jacy, he might've been willing to talk further. Though Tristan hadn't received the answer he wanted, he still didn't see the Director-General as a bad man.

Apparently unwilling to wait, Sha'Nara bolted toward the door, ignoring the lasers trained on her.

"Stop. Now." The guard by the door showed no qualms about firing on a fellow officer.

Before the guard could react, Tristan mentally snatched the laser from his grip and gave it Cadell, then snared Mistress Helios's laser for himself. Sha'Nara didn't hesitate, and Tristan fell in behind her as she opened the conference room door.

The scroll imager was engaged, the holographic figure of Mael issuing a plea for peace. As the directors turned to stare at Sha'Nara and Tristan, the imager suddenly sputtered, sparks flying from its base.

Tristan didn't hesitate. As crazy as it sounded, he knew Sha'Nara had been right. Seizing the device with his kinesis, he threw it up and through the clear dome covering the room. In a matter of seconds, the sound of an explosion rocked the room and the remaining glass in the dome showered down upon them.

Reacting quickly, he threw himself over Sha'Nara and rolled them both under the table. From the cries of pain, he gathered several directors moved less rapidly.

Chaos erupted. Cadell ran into the room followed by several guards. They froze at the sight before them. Then a guard signaled for a med team. Directors called out for help.

As Tristan emerged from beneath the table, he heard the Director-General's voice, and was surprised to feel relief that the man survived. Before Tristan could move to offer assistance, Amyr's voice rang out above the turmoil.

"Arrest the Scanners! Now!"

"No." Sha'Nara cried out as Tristan turned, glimpsing a swift movement before something crashed against the back of his head.

Chapter Fifteen

"You can't do this." Sha'Nara's protests fell on deaf ears as Tristan and Cadell were dragged away, Tristan still unconscious. She whirled to confront her father across the long glass-littered table. He must've ducked beneath the table as well, for he had not a scratch upon him. "He saved your lives. You can't arrest him for that."

"It was his device that almost killed us all. The only good Scanner is one that's been readjusted, which is what those two will be very soon." Amyr started for the door, and Sha'Nara caught his arm, her chest tight.

"Father, you can't."

The glare he gave her could've frozen water. "Those men are our enemies. Do your job, Sha'Nara. You arrest Scanners. We readjust them. They'll be better men for it."

"They'll be zombies for it," she retorted, fear for Tristan mingling with her anger. When Amyr raised his eyebrows disdainfully, she continued. "You've lied to me about readjustment. I know now what it really does to them."

"Oh? And what is that?"

"It ruins their minds. When you remove that portion of their brain that makes them special, you destroy everything else, too."

"Special?" He locked onto that one word, frowning at her. "You consider that mutant ability special? I thought you knew better than that."

At once, she felt like a child again, not measuring up, never good enough. For a brief moment, her resolve faltered. Then she lifted her chin and met his gaze. "Their abilities do make them special."

As his expression grew colder, she knew her career in the PSI Police was over. Just as well. She couldn't capture Scanners any longer. Reckless now, she continued. "And they don't deserve to have their minds erased. It's wrong."

She might as well been talking to an asteroid. Amyr glanced at his chronometer. "Be in my office in an hour."

When he went to move away, she tightened her grip, holding him in place. She had to make him understand.

His entire body stiffened and he looked pointedly at her hand on his arm.

"Please, listen to me." She hated the begging tone in her voice. Why did he reduce her to this? "I've learned so much about them."

"I'm sorry for you, daughter," he said coolly, his voice indicating just the opposite. "I'd thought you were stronger than that."

"Stronger than what?"

"Strong enough to resist brainwashing." As she recoiled, remembering Mael's ability, he tugged his arm free and made his way to the door. "I only hope you can be redeemed."

"Where you are going?" Her mind reeled from the impact his statement. Had she been brainwashed?

He paused, his gaze sweeping over her, his features indicating he didn't care for what he saw. "I intend to schedule your Scanner *friends* for readjustment immediately. The one's psychokinesis is too powerful for us to keep him contained long." With a last, distasteful look, he left the conference room.

Sha'Nara sagged against the table. When Mael had put words in her mouth, she'd known at the time that wasn't her. Wouldn't she know if her thoughts weren't her own?

In confusion, she turned toward the Director-General. "Sir?"

"Not now, Officer Calles." Blood soaked his shirt from a cut in his shoulder, but instead of tending his own wound, he was bent over another director who'd been much more seriously cut by the falling glass. As if realizing the sharpness of his reply, he gave her a slight smile. "Later."

Dazed, Sha'Nara wove her way through the arriving medtechs and out of the central office. She hadn't been brainwashed. All her decisions came as a result of what she'd seen and experienced while with the Scanners.

And your closeness to Tristan.

Doubt over her dream surfaced again, but she dismissed it immediately. Mael hadn't caused her to dream of Tristan. That came from someplace deep inside her—someplace she was just beginning to discover.

What she shared with Tristan had been real. What she felt for him could not be induced.

She clenched her jaw and her fists. She *hadn't* been brainwashed. Mael might've been able to put words in her mouth, but her thoughts were her own.

Scanners did not deserve readjustment.

Pausing in the corridor, she debated where to turn. She had to free Tristan and Cadell. But how? Appealing to her father obviously wasn't going to work, but could she persuade Remy?

She glanced back toward the central office. Once Remy saw the others into medtech care, he'd probably return to his suite.

Jacy.

Leaping into action as soon as the thought hit, Sha'Nara headed for the Director-General's rooms, eager to see the young woman who'd become her friend. Jacy would understand. Together they'd convince Remy to release Tristan and Cadell.

To her surprise, Sha'Nara found the entrance to the suite guarded, and skidded to a halt at a distant corner, sizing up the two young men standing outside the door. Though they both presented the epitome of professionalism in their blue Alliance uniforms and short haircuts, she'd be willing to bet they were new recruits.

They stood rigidly at attention, their gazes darting constantly, their hands too near their lasers. Sha'Nara bit back a smile. She should have no trouble gaining admittance.

She straightened her uniform, ensuring her rank showed clearly, lifted her head high, and approached as if she had every right to be there. Executing a snappy salute, she gave both guards a careful look. "Commander Calles to see Jacy Vadin. I have some questions for her."

The young men exchanged glances. The taller of the two spoke. "We were told no one is to enter or leave until the Director-General orders otherwise."

"Then why did he tell me to get these answers for him?" Sha'Nara rolled her eyes. "You have heard about the explosion in the conference room, have you not?"

"Explosion?"

"Conference room?" Complete confusion covered their faces.

"The Director-General thought his daughter might have some insight into the device that exploded." Sha'Nara indicated the door. "May I?"

"Certainly." After unkeying the door, they saluted again as Sha'Nara walked in.

As the door slid closed behind her, her smile emerged. Easier than setting a trap for a Neeban.

"Daddy." Jacy came running into the main room, then stopped abruptly as she spotted Sha'Nara. "Sha'Nara. What are you doing here?" Her eyes watered dangerously. "Is Cadell gone?"

"Worse." Sha'Nara faced the younger woman. "The

scroll imager exploded and Tristan and Cadell are being blamed for it."

"Cadell. No." Jacy's eyes grew wide. "What about Daddy? Is he . . . ?"

"I think he's fine. As far as I could tell only one of the directors was seriously hurt." Pausing, Sha'Nara regrouped her thoughts and continued. "My father has arrested Tristan and Cadell. He's scheduled them for immediate readjustment."

"Readjustment?" Jacy frowned, obviously not as familiar with the term as Sha'Nara. "Isn't that where the psi ability is removed from their mind?"

"Actually it amounts to the removal of almost their entire mind."

If possible, Jacy's eyes widened even further and the color drained from her already pale face. "You have to stop it."

"I can't make my father listen to me. I thought, with your help, we could persuade your father to let them go."

"Yes." Nodding her head, Jacy paced back and forth. "I'll beg him. Daddy loves me. He'll listen to me."

"Daddy will what?"

Both women whirled around to see Remy standing in the doorway and he didn't look happy. He speared Sha'Nara with his gaze. "May I ask what you're doing here, Officer Calles?"

Sha'Nara swallowed. "Sir, Tristan and Cadell had nothing to do with the explosion. I swear it. Tristan *saved* you."

"They also gave me the device." Remy proceeded into the room, and Sha'Nara could see he'd had his shoulder bandaged. "What happened? Did they change their minds?"

"They didn't know it was going to explode." Sha'Nara paused. Had Mael known when he gave her the imager? He couldn't have. What purpose would it serve to kill the Director-General? "Mael gave it to me. At the time, he mentioned the device was old and unstable. Probably something shorted out."

"Then why did you come back to the conference room?" Remy narrowed his gaze. "I assumed they'd told you about the bomb. How else would you have known to return?"

Sha'Nara's heart skipped a beat. Explaining a hunch to Tristan was one thing, but making Remy understand was another. He'd probably send her off for a mental evaluation. "I . . . ah . . ."

Jacy jumped into the conversation. "Actually Cadell gets these visions sometimes. Of the future. Sha'Nara just mentioned how he made them turn around to save you." As Jacy went to wrap her arms around her father, Sha'Nara nearly swallowed her teeth.

She'd expected many things from Jacy, most of them foolish, but this . . . this was totally unexpected. She gaped at the woman, and was rewarded with a wink.

"You're not going to allow Cadell to be readjusted, are you?" Jacy continued.

"I believe readjustment will be the best thing for both of them." Remy released Jacy and studied her face. "Obviously you think highly of these young men. If they no longer have their Scanner powers, I may be able to find a place for them here."

His words triggered fresh alarm in Sha'Nara. "You don't know about readjustment, do you?"

He frowned. "What do you mean by that?"

She bristled at his accusatory tone. "Have you ever watched a Scanner being readjusted? Do you know what really happens?"

"No, but I believe what I've been told by my PSI Police Director—your father."

"I used to, until I saw what remained of these people after readjustment. It doesn't delete just the psi portion of their brain. It wipes out nearly their entire brain. If you let this happen to Tristan and Cadell, they'll be nothing more than walking vegetables."

Jacy gasped. "Daddy, you can't—"

He held up his hand, his gaze never leaving Sha'Nara. "Officer Calles, where did you learn about this?" She flushed and he answered for her. "From the Scanners

231

themselves. Wouldn't it be to their advantage for you to believe such a thing?"

She shook her head. "I saw these people. Tristan had been telling me and telling me about readjustment, but I wouldn't believe him . . . until I saw these people." Remembering Cadell's ordeal, she shuddered. "It was awful."

"Officer Calles, I've worked with your father for many years now. I trust him." Remy gave her a tense smile. "I can't call him a liar because someone who's been held captive by these people says differently. You know how reports say captives often end up admiring their captors." He looked pointedly at her, then Jacy.

"We weren't captives, Daddy," said Jacy. "We were guests."

"Guests who almost died." His tone indicated his finality on the subject, but Sha'Nara couldn't give up.

"Sir, if I can prove what I've just said, will you call off the readjustment?"

He watched her silently for several moments, but she refused to flinch. "If you can prove it to me . . ." He hesitated. "I'll consider it."

"Thank you, sir." She had no time to lose. Accepting a vidcom from Jacy, she left the suite and hurried for the readjustment center. She'd never been to that section of the PSI Police wing, and had to turn around twice before she finally located the correct area tucked in the far end away from any random traffic.

The door had no sign beside it, but this had to be the place. She signaled the door to open, but it remained shut. Noticing the keypad on the wall, she entered her officer security number. Still nothing. Obviously she had no reason to be inside and hadn't been granted access.

But her father had to have access. He was the director.

She hesitated. She'd come upon his officer security number by accident several months ago. It could be different by now. She glanced down the hallway. No one else was sight.

Without hesitation, she keyed in her father's number. The door slid open.

Barely daring to breathe, she entered the room. At first glance, she assumed she'd found the wrong place. An unmanned access terminal sat in the tiny entry chamber, its screen blank. The walls held no ornamentation, no indication of what existed here. Surely the readjustment center would have a guard.

Or would it? This was the PSI Police wing. Everyone here worked toward the common goal of eradicating the Scanners. They'd never suspect one of their own of thinking otherwise.

Sha'Nara turned to the other door leading from the room. It opened easily . . . and revealed a modern-day torture chamber.

For several moments she forgot to engage the vidcom as she stared at the six chairs filling the room. With straps on the legs and arms and a clear dome hanging over each chair's top, they more resembled ancient electric chairs than anything else. Why not? They were just as deadly.

As she watched, three PSI officers wrestled a middle-aged man into one of the chairs, more concerned with securing him in place than Sha'Nara's presence. The man shrieked in desperation, jarring her out of her trance and into action.

Swinging the vidcom up, she darted into a dark corner and started recording.

Once the Scanner was fastened in the chair, the PSI officers relaxed, even joking among themselves as if destroying a man's life was nothing. But to them, this wasn't a man. This was a Scanner.

A wave of self-loathing washed over Sha'Nara. Not so long ago, she would've believed the same thing.

The Scanner continued to tug at his bonds, his movements growing more frantic, his cries of distress louder as the clear dome lowered into position over his head. One of the officers fastened electrodes to the man's head, not just over the brain section housing the psi abilities, but over the entire brain web.

Unmindful of the man's pleas, the officer joined the others by a large console against the far wall. Sha'Nara's heart rose into her throat.

With a movement reminiscent of swatting a fly, the officer flipped a switch on the panel, creating an immediate reaction in the bound Scanner. He stiffened, his fingers digging into the seat arm, his legs nearly lifting him up. Then he screamed as if his soul was being ripped from within him.

Sha'Nara lowered the vidcom and started forward. She had to stop this.

Too late.

She'd only taken three steps when the man collapsed, his chin dropping to his chest. The officer flipped the switch again and Sha'Nara froze in place. He motioned to the others to help him and approached the chair again.

Shaking badly, Sha'Nara lifted the vidcom again.

The officers continued to joke as they unfastened the restraints and lifted the man out of the chair. He'd obviously wet himself during the torture, but Sha'Nara didn't let her gaze linger there. Instead she sought his face, then wished she hadn't.

His mouth hung open, drool leaking from the corner, and his eyes held no sign of intelligence, barely any sign of life. When the officers released their hold on him, he sank into a pile on the floor.

One of the offices nudged the man with his toe. "Was this another one of those empaths?"

Another nodded. "Think so."

The first one shook his head. "They always turn out like mush. Have you noticed?" He prodded even harder, but still received no response. "Take him to the holding room with the others. We'll release them on Damnine tomorrow."

Damnine. The planet was still wild, overrun with voracious beasts. One colonization attempt had been totally wiped out. Normal men couldn't survive there. Readjusted Scanners had no chance at all.

Sha'Nara didn't realize her cheeks were wet until she

lowered the vidcom. Remaining motionless, she watched the officers drag the Scanner into an adjoining room. This couldn't be allowed to continue. If Remy didn't do something, she'd blow up the place herself.

Returning to the entry chamber, she paused by the access terminal. It would take time to make her way back to Remy's quarters. Time she might not have.

She put in the code to contact Remy's suite, then held her breath until Jacy's face appeared in a corner of the screen. "Sha'Nara? Did you get it?"

"Is your . . . ?" Sha'Nara struggled to speak through her clogged throat. "Is your father there?"

"He had to leave. I don't know where." Jacy's features reflected her concern. "Is it true?"

"It's true." Sha'Nara swiped her hand across her eyes. "It's too true."

"Download what you recorded and I'll make sure he sees it."

Sha'Nara connected the vidcom to the transfer port, then pressed what she thought was the transfer command. Instead of beginning transfer, a document appeared on the screen. Ignoring it, she tried another command and the video began transferring.

While she waited for the process to complete, she glanced at the document, noticing upon further examination it was a schedule . . . a schedule of readjustments. Skimming down the page, she found what she hadn't wanted to see—Tristan and Cadell, listed as priority.

A time was posted beside their names. Glancing at her chronometer, she gasped. That time was less than half an hour away. She couldn't wait for Remy. She had to take action now.

"Jacy." The channel was still open, but she received no reply. Instead she heard heart-wrenching sobs in the background. Evidently Jacy had decided to watch the video as it came through. Sha'Nara should've warned her. "Jacy." She called again, louder.

Again no reply.

Sha'Nara couldn't afford to wait for the woman to

pull herself together. "Jacy, they've scheduled Tristan and Cadell in less than half an hour. I have to get them out of here now. I can't wait for your father."

Leaving the vidcom connected to the terminal, Sha'Nara rushed out of the room and down the corridor. She already knew her destination—the holding cell, which was unfortunately close to a heavily traveled corridor. However, she hadn't a clue what she was going to do once she arrived there.

Her career was all but over as far as her father was concerned. If she was lucky, she might retain a desk job in the Alliance. If she freed Tristan and Cadell . . .

Sha'Nara continued to hurry, unwilling to examine that option. Life had been much simpler before she met Tristan Galeron.

It would never be that simple again.

Tristan blinked rapidly, trying to bring things into focus. He could make out a ceiling and walls, but they were fuzzy around the edges. His head pounded in a rhythm to match his pulse, making it painful to concentrate.

With difficulty he managed to recall the last few moments before his unconsciousness. Shibit, that had been some blow.

He attempted to move, then discovered his hands . . . and feet were bound. Blinking more, he brought his surroundings into clarity, then wished he hadn't.

The sheen of a laser barrier indicated he was in some type of cell. That would fit. He vaguely remembered Amyr ordering his arrest.

"Cadell?"

"Over here."

Struggling into an upright position, Tristan spotted his friend occupying an adjacent cell. Only Cadell's wrists were bound. Obviously the PSI police thought an empath less a threat than someone with kinesis. Tristan tested the strength of his bonds. As if these would hold him.

"Are you all right?" asked Cadell.

"I've been better." The throbbing at the back of his neck could only be surpassed by the pain from a Thorg sound box. "Guess we're in trouble now."

"Jacy and Sha'Nara will help us."

Tristan wasn't as confident. "I don't think they're viewed with much esteem right now." Recalling how Sha'Nara had supported him, Tristan didn't know whether to rejoice or mourn. She'd learned to see Scanners as more than animals to be hunted down, but now she'd lost the respect of the entire Alliance directorate. Her career, which she valued so highly, would be only a shadow of its former glory . . . because of him.

"We've been scheduled for immediate readjustment." Cadell's words cut through Tristan's thoughts.

"Immediate? How soon is that?"

"Sooner than I care to contemplate." Cadell shook the metal cuffs around his wrists. "Could we get out of here now? If you have nothing better to do?"

Though Cadell kept his tone light, Tristan sensed the underlying urgency. Past time to leave this place. Despite his aching head, he managed to release the locking mechanism on his cuffs. It took him more time without access to a code key, but produced the same result. His leg bindings followed, and he rose unsteadily to his feet, wrapped in a wave of dizziness. He put out one hand to steady himself.

"All right?" Cadell came as close to the laser barrier as he dared without searing off a part of his anatomy.

Tristan waited for the dizziness to pass. "I'm really tired of getting whacked in the head. I never got hit this much before I met Sha'Nara."

"Guess she brings that out in a guy."

Tristan aimed a poisoned look at his friend, then approached the edge of his cell. They were closed in a small room containing only the two cells. No guard. With this laser setup, their captors obviously thought they didn't need one.

As he expected, he saw no sign of controls for the laser barrier. That would be too easy. Any Scanner with psychokinesis could break out that way. But how many could get behind the laser beams and cut them off?

Grateful for his more advanced power, Tristan began work. Though he couldn't actually see the wiring behind the laser portals, he knew what it looked like. He mentally sought, then disconnected the correct wires, and the barrier faded.

Cautious, he removed his boot and tossed it through with no apparent damage before he dared step out of the cell. As he pulled his boot back on, Cadell waved at him from within his cage. "My turn now?"

"Your turn." Tristan released Cadell's cuffs, and had barely started to work on these laser portals when the door flew open. Stepping back, he curled his fists, prepared to do serious damage to whoever tried to stop him.

"You're out." Sha'Nara's look of surprise would've made him laugh at any other time. She glanced from him to the cuffs lying on his cell floor, then back. "I should've expected as much."

His pulse increased dramatically upon seeing her, and it took him several breaths in order to speak. "What are you doing here?" He narrowed his eyes. "Are you taking us for readjustment?"

She recoiled as if he'd hit her, and he instantly regretted his words. "I've come to set you free," she said. Noticing that Cadell remained within his cell, she moved to slide the code card into the lock switch and deactivate the barrier. "Though I guess I'm not really needed, am I?"

Cadell came forward to squeeze her arm. "I, for one, am very glad to see you. Even if we manage to get out of this holding area, I haven't a clue how to find our ship."

Her wan smile tugged at Tristan's heart, and he stepped toward her, eager to make amends. She met his gaze briefly, then turned away. "Come on. You're scheduled for immediate readjustment."

"That word again—immediate. How immediate?"

"Any minute now."

A chill he recognized as stark fear uncoiled through

his body, and he didn't hesitate to follow her through the door. Seeing the two PSI officers lying unconscious on the floor, he looked at her in surprise.

In reply, she demonstrated a kick that he recognized from the time she caught him off guard by the lift. The woman was dangerous in more ways than one.

She started for the outer door, then paused to retrieve a laser from one of the fallen officers before continuing. Motioning for quiet, she activated the door, then stood framed within the entrance as she glanced up and down the corridor.

"It's okay for now," she said quietly. "I want both of you to put your hands on the back of your neck and get in front of me. If we're asked, I'm taking you for readjustment."

Her voice trembled slightly, betraying the risk for them all. Unable to help himself, he touched her cheek in a gentle caress. "I'm yours to command," he whispered.

Her eyes widened and her lips parted, begging for his kiss. He inhaled sharply, wanting to do just that. Time froze around them as he leaned nearer her luscious mouth.

The sound of Cadell clearing his throat shattered the moment, and Tristan slid past her into the hallway, placing his hands upon the back of his neck. Cadell joined him, but not without first giving him a mocking look from beneath raised eyebrows.

So this wasn't the time to exchange kisses. Tristan had the stomach-wrenching feeling that he wasn't likely to find any good time before he was forced to flee this monstrosity of a building.

Sha'Nara nudged them into movement and he went, feeling extremely vulnerable. Surrounded by people who wanted him dead, scheduled to have his brain fried, a laser pointing at his back—no wonder his chest felt too small.

They'd almost reached the moving walkway to the transport area when a voice called out behind them. "Stop."

Tristan tensed, ready to do whatever it took to protect Sha'Nara and ensure his escape.

"Wait for me."

At those words, they all looked around to see Jacy running toward them. She threw herself into Cadell's embrace as she gasped for breath.

"What are you doing here?" Sha'Nara didn't sound pleased.

"I'm going with Cadell." Jacy gave Sha'Nara a defiant look despite her tear-streaked face. "I refuse to remain here where people like Cadell are so casually destroyed."

"Has your father seen the video?"

"Not yet, but—"

Sha'Nara released an angry exclamation. "If he sees it, if you talk to him . . ."

"You talk to him." Jacy clung even tighter to Cadell's arm. "I'm going with Cadell." Some of her defiance faded as she glanced up at him. "Can I?"

He looked torn. "Jacy, I . . . we . . ."

"Do you love me?"

"You know I do."

Tristan could feel his friend's anguish in those words. He shared it. Glancing at Sha'Nara, he caught a glimpse of her pain as it swiftly crossed her face.

"Then I'm coming with you." Jacy cast a glance over her shoulder. "Let's get going. I . . . ah . . . locked my guards in the suite, but I'm sure they've found a way out by now."

"Orion's Sword." Sha'Nara waved them ahead of her. "Come on. Hurry. They'll be looking for us soon."

They ran along the walkways, thankful for the absence of people, pausing only at the entrance to the transport center. Sha'Nara holstered her laser. "We need to split up here. Tristan and I will go first. Cadell and Jacy follow after a minute or so. I think we'll be less noticed that way."

Tristan hesitated. By walking beside him, she put herself in danger of being fired upon. Didn't she realize that? The glimmer of trepidation in her eyes told him she did. "Sha'Nara, if we don't make it . . ."

"We'll make it." Steely determination filled her voice. "I don't give up." She allowed a faint smile to escape. "I've been told it's because I'm so farding stubborn."

He had to agree with that.

After a brief nod to Cadell and Jacy, they entered the terminal. The place reverberated with the same loud cacophony as when they'd first passed through. Nothing sounded different, out of place. In fact, no one appeared to notice them.

When they reached the shuttle without anyone stopping them, Tristan released the breath he hadn't realized until then he'd been holding. Opening the hatch, he leapt inside and dragged Sha'Nara after him. He wanted to hold her close and kiss her until both of them were gasping for air.

Before he could draw her near, she slipped out of his grasp and approached the controls. "My code is still programmed in here. Use that to get out through the tunnel, then jump into hyperspace as soon as you can. I think you'll make it."

You? Not we? A blow to his gut couldn't have stunned Tristan as effectively. "You're coming with us, aren't you?"

She hesitated, then turned to meet his gaze. "No, I'm staying here."

"You can't be serious. Your career is over. They'll destroy you." Fear on her behalf rose to flood his senses. From the moment she'd shown up to free them, he'd assumed she would leave with them. To stay was insane.

"My career may be over," she admitted, then tightened her jaw. "Or it may not. I have a video now to show Remy." She came to face him, her excitement rising. "I think I can talk to him, make him listen. He may be willing to give you another chance."

Another chance? Dimly he realized she meant freedom for the Scanners. He'd already given up on that. "And what if the Director-General doesn't listen to you? What then?"

"Then I'll deal with it." Defiance gleamed in her eyes. "I have to stay here, Tristan. I just might make a difference."

"But—" Before he could protest, Cadell climbed into the shuttle, then turned to help Jacy.

"We made it." The combination of Cadell's smile and his hold on Jacy only added to the pressure inside Tristan's chest.

"Not yet," said Sha'Nara. "But you will." She went to give Cadell a quick hug. "Good luck."

He turned his startled expression first toward Tristan, then back to her. "Aren't you coming?"

"No." She glanced at Tristan, and he could've sworn something squeezed his heart. "I can do more good here."

Jacy enveloped Sha'Nara in a hug. "You have to come."

Sha'Nara shook her head. "I can't. Not now." She pried Jacy's arms from around her neck. "Someone has to explain this to your father." Entering the hatch, she paused to encompass them all in a weak smile. "Be careful."

Her voice caught on the words and she quickly disembarked. Tristan stared at the place where she'd been, unable to move, unable to think.

"You're not going to let her stay here, are you?"

Cadell's dry tone penetrated Tristan's cocoon of disbelief. He looked at his friend, then swung from the shuttle. "Sha'Nara."

She'd already started up at the narrow walkway around the bays. As he called her name, she froze, then slowly looked back. He hurried toward her, propelled by a force stronger than anything he'd ever felt before.

Upon reaching her, he could only stare at her, memorizing the contours of her face, inhaling her scent. "Come with me." He hadn't known what to say, the words emerged on their own.

Her eyes glistened with unshed tears. "I can't." When he would've protested, she placed her fingers over his mouth. "I have to stay here now. I feel it. It's important."

How could he argue with that? Lately her hunches had been frighteningly correct. "I . . ." He choked, not able to finish. He'd known all along they had no future, but facing it was another matter.

"Go now. Hurry." She started to back away, but he caught her hand and pulled her forward. Wrapping his arms around her, he kissed her, moving against her lips, plundering her mouth, conveying what he couldn't say aloud. .

A single tear streaked down her cheek when he finally released her, and he lifted his finger to remove it. "Remember me," he whispered.

She smiled sadly. "As if I could forget."

Hearing the shuttle engines in the background, he forced himself to return to the craft. Thankfully Cadell took charge of the departure. Tristan could only stare at the inner wall, recalling his last mental image of Sha'Nara.

He'd never see her again.

And he'd just realized he loved her.

Chapter Sixteen

Their journey back to the *Hermitage* was anticlimactic after fleeing the Alliance Headquarters. Tristan secretly longed to encounter a PSI Police cruiser. He needed a battle to relieve his pent-up tension. Though he saw several Alliance ships before they entered hyperspace, none of them challenged the shuttle.

Mael came to meet them in the landing bay, raising his eyebrows as Jacy stepped from the shuttle. "I thought the mission was to return the Director-General's daughter."

"We did." Cadell hugged Jacy to his side. "She decided she wants to stay with us."

The brief twist of Mael's lips indicated he wasn't entirely pleased with that turn of events. No doubt he had other plans for his son that didn't involve Jacy Vadin. "Perhaps that will be useful." Mael glanced at Tristan. "And Officer Calles?"

Hearing her name sent new waves of pain through Tristan. "She stayed." He started for the doorway, then paused. "The scroll imager exploded. We almost paid for that with our lives."

"Exploded? I knew it was old, but I didn't expect that." Mael hesitated. "Was anyone injured?"

"Not seriously. I was able to deflect the explosion." But only due to Sha'Nara's warning. Tristan gripped the edge of the doorway so tightly his knuckles whitened. "I'll be in my quarters."

Without waiting for an answer, he fled. To stay and watch Cadell and Jacy share their happiness would only accentuate what Tristan had left behind.

Upon entering his room, he first sat on his bed, then stood again to pace the small interior. His insides boiled with frustration. He shouldn't have left Sha'Nara behind. He could've forced her to come with them.

He visualized several scenarios involving Sha'Nara as she faced the Director-General and PSI Police Director—none of them pleasant. What would they do to her? Demote her? Imprison her? Kill her?

His throat constricted. He should've stayed with her even if it did mean his own death. What was she suffering now on his behalf?

Moving to his window, he gazed out into the star-scattered darkness and reexamined his earlier revelation. He loved her. Somehow, some way, this PSI Police officer had wormed her way under his skin and made him care. Worse. He couldn't picture a life without her. In just a few days, she'd become as important to him as breathing.

He loved a PSI Police officer.

Tristan gave a mirthless laugh. All he'd ever wanted was his own piece of land. But that had been before he met Sha'Nara and discovered her fire, her intelligence, her stubbornness. He couldn't have found someone more unsuitable if he'd tried . . . yet he wanted her, needed her with a fierceness that burned deep in his soul.

He turned from the window, and his gaze fell on his terrarium, left untended since Sha'Nara's arrival in his life. He picked it up and ran his hand over the smooth glass, trying to recall his desire for this land and the hope it represented. Instead all he could see was Sha'Nara holding the globe aloft during a fit of panic, then lowering it.

As he stroked the glass, he thought of the silkiness of her skin, the taste of her lips, the passion of her response. Gone. All gone.

In a sudden rage, Tristan hurled his terrarium to the floor, where it smashed into tiny fragments, the dirt and plants flying in all directions. He didn't care.

Returning to the window, he leaned his head on his arm. Without Sha'Nara, he didn't care at all.

"You may go in now."

At the words, Sha'Nara's heart rose into her throat. Nodding to her father's assistant, she approached Amyr's office. She'd carefully prepared what she wanted to say to her father with the hope of bolstering her courage, but that didn't stop her palms from suddenly becoming clammy as she entered the massive room.

One of the Alliance's top directors, Amyr commanded an office second only to that of the Director-General. Large dark furniture filled the room—a massive desk and chair, a long couch, conference table, and chairs. He could live in his office if necessary, and had on more than one occasion.

He stood behind his desk, his back to Sha'Nara, and didn't acknowledge her presence as she entered. She paused in front of the desk and waited. Her father kept no chairs by his desk as he didn't want people to feel at ease. His words came back to her with perfect clarity.

"Keep a person off balance, uncomfortable, and you'll always have the advantage."

Steeling her nerve, she decided she wasn't going to be the one off balance this time. "I won't apologize for what I've done," she said.

Amyr turned slowly to face her, his first glance indicating she was no better than the ever-present dust. "Just as well. An apology isn't about to clear you of treason."

"I didn't commit treason."

"You betrayed the Alliance. You betrayed your position. You betrayed me." He came around his desk until he stood in front of her. "What do you call it?"

"I call it correcting an injustice." Sha'Nara struggled to keep her knees from trembling. Her father's large size and closeness had always intimated her in the past. She refused to allow him to do it this time. "Tristan and Cadell had nothing to do with the explosion of the scroll imager. Remy had promised them safe conduct home. I merely ensured they received it."

"You defied my orders." Amyr didn't shout at her. He didn't need to. The icy tone of his voice worked just as effectively as impaling her on the blade of his knife. "They were scheduled for readjustment."

"I couldn't let you destroy their minds." She swallowed and plunged ahead. "Readjustment is a lie. I've seen it."

"They're *Scanners*." His tone indicated they were of no consequence.

"Then why they even bother with this farce of readjustment? Why not just kill them outright?"

"I'd much prefer that." Her father's reply sent a shiver down Sha'Nara's spine. "But Remy believes all creatures—even these mutants—deserve to live. The readjustment procedure placates him."

"What other lies have you told?" Clenching her fists, Sha'Nara paced the length of the room. "From personal experience I've learned Scanners aren't power-hungry. They represent no threat to the Alliance."

"I should've expected that from you."

She whirled to face him. "What does that mean?"

"You've slept with that Scanner, haven't you? Galeron."

Sha'Nara didn't answer, but she couldn't stop a blush from rising to her cheeks.

"You let yourself be swayed by sweet words and the touch of a man's hand. I thought I trained you better than that."

"It wasn't like that." Sha'Nara approached him. "Neither of us wanted—"

Amyr sliced his hand through the air, cutting her off. "It's of no importance to me. I'll be finished with all of them soon enough."

She caught her breath. "What?"

"Didn't you wonder why it was so easy to help those mutants escape?" He sneered. "I counted on you to behave as you did."

Her fingers went numb and she clasped her hands together. "Explain yourself. You planned for Tristan and Cadell to escape?"

"I saw your attachment to this man. I knew you'd help him."

"But . . . but why?"

"I had a tracking device planted on their shuttle. At this moment it's relaying the exact coordinates of their hiding place. I already have an attack team in place which will leave within minutes." Amyr rolled his fingers into a tight fist. "We'll eliminate this filth once and for all."

"No." Sha'Nara recoiled as if she'd been struck. "You can't do that." Her mind whirled with confusion. She latched onto the first excuse she could find. "Jacy . . . Jacy is there."

"She made her choice. It was the wrong one."

Sha'Nara could only stare at her father. She'd always known he was cold, but not so heartless. "Remy may not agree."

"Remy won't know until after the fact."

He would if Sha'Nara had anything to do with it. Holding back her anger, she met her father's gaze defiantly. "Is there anything else?"

"Yes." He grabbed her upper arm with his hand. "Consider yourself under house arrest. You'll be confined to your quarters until after this mission."

"And then?"

The smile he gave her held no warmth. "I may let you have a much closer look at how the readjustment procedure works."

Before she could do more than gasp, he yanked her to the doorway and signaled to two officers waiting outside. "Escort her to her room and secure the door. If she escapes, it's your head."

The officers took him seriously, each of them ensnaring one of Sha'Nara's arms, forcing her to walk in step with them. She didn't struggle. To do so would be useless.

Her thoughts reeled from the impact of her father's words. He would send her to be readjusted? After seeing the procedure, she had no doubt it could just as easily destroy her mind. He could do that to his own daughter?

Upon reaching her room, the officers tossed her through the door and secured her keypad, locking her inside. She barely registered that fact, already springing into action.

If she didn't move quickly, the Scanners would die. Tristan would die. Recalling his last kiss made her insides clench. She hadn't wanted him to leave, at least not without her, but she'd known she had to stay. Now she knew why.

As if that wasn't bad enough, she loved the farding man. Had loved him for some time, but had been too blind, too stubborn to admit it. How could she, when loving a Scanner was tantamount to treason?

Her father already believed she'd betrayed him. Too late she'd seen him for what he was—a man as power-hungry and bloodthirsty as he claimed the Scanners were.

She swallowed the lump in her throat. If he wanted to believe the worst of her, then she'd give him even more to base it on. The Scanners would not die if she could stop it.

At least she was a good PSI officer, despite what her father thought. Taking a seat before her terminal, she activated a program she'd developed that overrode any outside security measures—eliminating the lock on her comm program . . . and the one on her door.

With another few keystrokes, she accessed Remy's

suite. He had to be there. She'd heard he retired there as soon as he knew of Jacy's defection. The comm beeped several times with no answer. Sha'Nara was about to disconnect when suddenly Remy appeared on the view screen.

"What is it?" he demanded. At seeing Sha'Nara, his expression hardened. "What do you want?"

"To warn you." She ignored his bitter tone. "My father has ordered an attack on the Scanner ship." She waited for an reaction, but didn't receive one. "Jacy will be there."

That worked. Remy's eyes widened. "Why haven't I heard about this?"

"He doesn't plan to tell you until afterward."

"Amyr wouldn't do that."

Sha'Nara sighed. "I don't think either of us know him very well. He's capable of a lot more than I ever realized." She leaned closer. "Have you watched the readjustment video?"

"Video?" He looked surprised, then scanned the area. "I see one loaded."

"Jacy saw it and decided to return with Cadell. Why don't you watch it and see if you can always believe everything my father tells you?"

"And if I agree with Amyr?"

Sha'Nara hesitated. "Then you're not the man I thought you were." She broke off the connection. She'd done her part in warning Remy. Whether he acted on her warning was another thing.

She had to do something. She couldn't contact the *Hermitage* without knowing their comm frequency, but she did know where they were located.

Accessing her terminal again, she located her personal fighter craft parked in the transport building. Thus far, it hadn't been called into action. If she could get to it. . . .

Her door opened easily. To her surprise neither officer had remained to stand guard. Evidently they'd thought locking her in was enough to keep her prisoner. Wrong. A woman who'd been locked in her room once made sure she wouldn't suffer that kind of hell again.

Straightening her uniform, she kept her head high and tried to walk at a moderate pace toward the transport terminal. She even took the faster shuttle, blending in with the other PSI officers on board.

Sha'Nara leapt from the shuttle at her stop and raced for her fighter. Other PSI officers milled around, discussing their attack plans and preparing their craft for flight.

Fear rose, thick and heavy in her chest. If anything happened to the *Hermitage*, to Tristan, it would be her fault. She had to warn them.

"Officer Calles."

Someone spoke her name behind her, and Sha'Nara froze. She'd brought her laser, but could she use it on someone merely doing his job? Placing her hand near the weapon, she slowly turned to face the man behind her.

She frowned. Why did he look so familiar? She didn't recognize him, yet she did.

Trying to remember, she examined him closely. Slightly taller than herself and perhaps five years older, he was lean and differently dressed. Instead of the form-fitting suit worn by nearly everyone in the Alliance, this man had on loose-fitting pants and an even looser-fitting shirt, cut low to reveal his chest. His hair was a dark brown and wavy and fell to his collar.

The familiarity lay in his face. She'd seen the sculpted planes, high cheekbones, and square jaw before. Upon meeting his gaze, she remembered just as he spoke.

"I'm Dev Zdenek of Lander. You may remember me. You were supposed to deliver my fiancee to our wedding." He spoke without a trace of bitterness, but Sha'Nara couldn't help grimacing.

"I remember you. We've never met, but I've seen holos of you." She paused. "I'm sorry about Jacy."

"I understand she decided to return with the Scanners."

"Ah . . . yes." If Devon would only show some emotion, Sha'Nara might feel some sympathy for him. As it

251

was, his quiet tone made her secretly glad Jacy had escaped marriage to this man.

"And you're going there now."

Sha'Nara started. "I . . . I'm—"

"You helped the Scanners escape before. Now that Director Calles has ordered an attack on them, I would assume you intend to warn them. Isn't that correct?"

How did he know that? Sha'Nara gave up trying to deny her plans. Somehow this Landerite was one step ahead of her. "And if I am?" He wouldn't stop her. She'd make sure of that.

"I'm coming with you." Dev glanced over his shoulder. "We haven't much time to waste."

Who did this man think he was? "You're not—"

"Yes, I am." Moving swiftly, he caught her by surprise as he gripped her arm and led her into her ship. Once inside, he released her and examined the interior. "I can sit in the jump seat."

"You can't come with me. I'll get blamed for kidnapping you next."

"I'll vouch for you," he replied. "If we survive." He secured himself into the rear seat, then glanced at her, his expression giving nothing away. "Shouldn't you get moving?"

"Why do you want to go?" If he intended to harm Cadell or Jacy, Sha'Nara would vent him into space.

"I think I may be able to help the Scanners in their search for freedom." He lifted one eyebrow. "Shall we?"

Sha'Nara sank into her seat. Of all the answers she'd expected, that hadn't been one of them. How could he help?

Powering up her fighter, she examined the launch display. From what she'd heard, the first wave of attack was already in space. However, they'd be flying as a squadron, which would slow their approach.

With luck, if she made the hyperspace window, she'd get there first. Entering her code, she departed the terminal at the fastest speed she dared.

As she climbed the shimmering corridor, her comm

panel blinked at her. "PSI fighter, please identify yourself. Your launch is out of sequence."

She didn't reply, but increased her speed.

"Shouldn't you answer that?" asked Dev.

"Not if we want to survive." Shooting from the pathway, she spotted the first wave grouped near the hyperspace access point, undoubtedly waiting for a massive jump. Her heart hammered so loudly in her chest, she could barely think. With shaky hands she set the coordinates of her hyperspace controls.

This had to work. She wouldn't get a second chance.

Another call came through on her comms. Ignoring it, she pulled the lever toward her. The vibration caused by a close laser beam rattled her ship as it slipped into hyperspace and the view screen went black.

She'd made it, but how much time did she have?

Emerging from hyperspace, Sha'Nara found herself only a short distance from the *Hermitage*. As she approached, she searched the vastness of the surrounding space. No sign of the PSI Police troops . . . yet.

Selecting the short-distance comm frequency that Tristan had used earlier, Sha'Nara signaled the battleship. "This is Sha'Nara Calles requesting permission to dock."

"Permission denied."

Her chest tightened. "This is an emergency. Please."

For several moments she waited in silence, her throat clogged. If they denied her entry, could she still land? Probably not.

"Permission granted. Proceed to the bridge upon docking."

"Affirmative." She released her breath and guided her ship into the docking bay, aware of a strange sense of coming home. Not to the *Hermitage*, but to Tristan. Would he be there to greet her?

To her disappointment, no one awaited her in the landing bay. Had they all been ordered to stay away? She cast Dev a dry look and motioned for him to follow her.

He didn't move. "Do you know where you're going?"

"I know." She opened the door and stepped into the hallway. Still no sign of anyone. "You might want to stay alert. I'm not everyone's favorite person here."

"Then why do you defend them?"

"Because I learned I'd been wrong." And she'd learned to love. "This way."

"Then Scanners are not the scourge of the galaxy that the Alliance believes they are?" Dev sounded merely curious, but a strange note in his voice made Sha'Nara glance at him sharply.

"No, they're not." She signaled for a lift. "They're humans with advanced parapsychic abilities, nothing more."

"And the Alliance wants to destroy them because of these abilities?"

"Partially that," she admitted. "And because of the PSI Wars. Have you heard of those?"

"I've learned of them since my arrival at Centralia. As those wars took place over one hundred years ago, I would think they have no bearing on the present."

"Obviously the Alliance disagrees." Even an outsider saw the merit of setting Scanners free. Why couldn't Remy?

"Interesting."

Sha'Nara gave a short laugh. "You might say that." Boarding the lift, they rose to the A deck, then proceeded to the bridge.

Upon reaching the entrance, she spotted Mael standing by the main view screen. Only the normal bridge staff occupied the seats at the consoles. Where was Tristan?

"Mael?" She moved toward him.

He whirled to look at her, his expression definitely not welcoming. "Why have you returned here? I thought we were rid of your kind."

Sha'Nara stiffened, then lifted her head higher. "Get your ship's barriers up. I came to warn you. The—"

"Sha'Nara."

She spun around at hearing Tristan's voice, and

couldn't stop the smile that leapt to her lips. He stood in the entrance, his eyes dark with passion, his expression hopeful. He looked good . . . very good.

"Tristan, I—"

One of the bridge staff broke in, his voice quivering. "Mael, PSI Police ships are appearing out of hyperspace. At this rate, we'll be surrounded."

Sha'Nara looked at the screen. Hundreds of fighter craft were pouring from the hyperspace tunnel. She was too late. Despair washed over her. Too late.

"You led them here."

She jumped at Mael's angry words, and turned to see him aiming a laser at her, squeezing the trigger. Too startled to move, she could only stare at him.

"No." As Mael fired, Tristan jumped in front of her, absorbing the impact of the beam in her place. He fell to the floor motionless, and Sha'Nara immediately knelt beside him.

"Tristan, no." She touched his face, her heart threatening to rip from her chest. Tears burned at her eyes, and she fastened her accusatory gaze on Mael. "You've killed him."

Chapter Seventeen

Mael lowered his laser. "I didn't mean . . ."

Sha'Nara ignored him, returning her full attention to Tristan. The laser blast in his midsection had burned deep. Smoothing his hair away from his face, she felt for a pulse.

There it was—vague and uneven. Not good.

"Do something," she ordered. Why was everyone just standing around?

Dev surprised her by taking charge. Even this hadn't disturbed his unflappable demeanor. He turned to Mael. "I believe you have healers on this ship. May I suggest you get one up here immediately?" Glancing at the Alliance ships filling the view screen, he motioned toward the console operators. "Fire up the engines and prepare to take this ship out of here."

"It's not that easy," said Mael stiffly as he approached. He stared at Dev. "This ship is old and doesn't respond quickly."

Dev didn't flinch. "Then we should start all the sooner, don't you think?" His gaze flickered to the screen, then back. "I have no intention of dying today . . . unless you intend to surrender."

Mael stiffened. "Never."

"Then?" As if finished with that matter, Dev knelt beside Sha'Nara. She struggled to hold back her sobs.

"May I?" asked Dev. He felt for Tristan's pulse himself, then inhaled sharply, his eyelids flickering briefly.

That brief display of emotion dove deep into Sha'Nara's heart. "He can't die. He can't."

Dev briefly examined the scorch-edged wound. "This is bad. Where is that healer?"

"I'm here." A young woman raced onto the bridge and dropped to her knees beside Tristan. Ignoring everyone else, she studied Tristan's injury, then closing her eyes, she placed her hands over the gaping wound.

Sha'Nara couldn't help but feel dubious. She'd only briefly watched healers at work when the Scanners from Aktion had arrived, and had seen nothing to reassure her. Tristan needed more than this mental magic. His face had drained of color and his breathing grew rougher, more shallow. Without immediate immersion in a medtech unit, he'd die.

"Don't you have a medtech unit?" she asked.

The woman didn't reply, but Dev shushed Sha'Nara, his gaze still locked on the woman's hands. At one point, she gasped, her body jerking as if in pain, and he immediately placed his hand on her shoulder. To Sha'Nara's surprise, the woman calmed again.

Glancing at the wound, Sha'Nara caught her breath. She didn't know what she'd expected to see, but it wasn't a faint glow beneath the woman's hands. Looking closer, she could see the blast area didn't look quite as badly damaged. In fact, the edges of Tristan's skin were drawing together, melding without a sign of a scar.

Amazing. Just like medtech units. Sha'Nara stared at the young woman. Healing was a truly miraculous ability.

As Tristan moaned, Sha'Nara turned back to his face, surprised to see his color returning. She found his pulse point and sighed in relief. It already beat much stronger, more steady.

"What's going on?" Cadell's voice preceded his arrival on the bridge. For the first time Sha'Nara realized PSI fighters were firing on the battleship, which swayed beneath the blasts as if rocked by heavy waves. Mael stood by the control stations, issuing commands. Obviously the operators had listened to her and raised the barriers, or they'd have been destroyed by now.

"Tristan." Cadell stopped beside Sha'Nara, not recognizing her until she touched his hand. "Sha'Nara? What are you doing here? What happened?"

"I came to warn you about this attack." She aimed her glare at Mael. "But I didn't get a chance before they appeared. Mael assumed I had led them here and tried to kill me." Her voice lost its belligerence as she gazed down at Tristan. "Tristan jumped in front of me."

"Will he be all right?" Concern colored Cadell's words.

To Sha'Nara's surprise, the healer didn't answer as she continued to concentrate over Tristan, but Dev rose to study Cadell. "He'll be all right," he said. "She's managed to heal the worst damage and is focusing on the minor details now."

Cadell smiled, his relief obvious, and extended his hand toward Dev. "That's good to hear. I'm Cadell Ner and you are?"

"Devon Zdenek of Lander." He didn't take Cadell's hand, but pinned him with a steady stare. "I believe you know my fiancee."

For a moment Sha'Nara thought Cadell would forget to breathe again. Then he did so with a whoosh, withdrawing his hand and straightening. "She's decided she doesn't want to marry you."

"That remains to be seen."

A blast shook the ship and it rocked unsteadily. Sha'Nara tightened her hold on Tristan. Were they saving him only so he could die in this attack?

"Get . . . get engines . . . going." His eyes fluttered open as he gasped the words.

"Tristan." Joy bubbled through her veins. He was alive.

He tried to rise, but she pressed gently against his shoulders. "Don't try to move yet."

"Have to." He drew in a ragged breath. "Need to . . . need to get ship moving." The healer rocked back on her heels and he lifted a hand toward her. "Tamika, thank you."

"You should be fine with some rest." She looked drained, but managed a weak smile. "You can't rush into battle."

The ship shook again.

"I may have to." Tristan's voice grew stronger, and he struggled to sit up. After receiving a nod from Tamika, Sha'Nara helped Tristan into position.

He glanced from the view screen to the frantic operators and released an angry exclamation. "I have . . . strategy." He drew in a deep breath before continuing. "Why aren't they using it?"

Without waiting for an answer, he stumbled to his feet, and would have fallen if Sha'Nara and Cadell hadn't grabbed his arms. Forced to place his arms around their necks, Tristan wavered slightly, then balanced.

"Start all engines. Ignite off the main core if you have to," he ordered, his voice decisive. Operators snapped to attention. Almost at once, the massive battle ship vibrated beneath them. "Fire back only when necessary. Use the minor lasers and try to disable, not kill."

He paused to drag in a shuddering breath, and Sha'Nara wrapped her arm around his waist. "Don't overdo it," she said.

"I'll be all right." He returned his attention to the consoles. "Set coordinates for Tarragon V. That's close enough for this heap to make it, but out of their tracker range."

At his words, Sha'Nara stiffened. "There's a tracer on your shuttle. My father put it there."

Mael stood quietly beside them. At these words, he

motioned toward a nearby Scanner. "Find it and destroy it. Immediately."

"Yes, sir." The man hurried off and Mael approached Tristan.

"I . . . I'm sorry," Mael said.

Sha'Nara's jaw dropped. She wouldn't have thought those words existed in Mael's vocabulary.

Tristan nodded and squeezed Sha'Nara's shoulder. "Trust Sha'Nara. I do."

Mael gave her a brief nod, which she supposed meant he'd accepted Tristan's confidence in her. He didn't apologize to her, but she didn't expect him to. If their roles had been reversed, she might have reacted the same way.

"Engines are reaching full power." One of the console operators turned his frantic gaze on Tristan. "Can we go into hyperspace now?"

"No." Tristan watched the swarm of fighters outside, then lifted his hand long enough to point out a small gap. "Start us moving. Head for that gap. If they don't get out of the way, it's their problem."

"Where am I going?"

"Right now we'll build speed. We can't go into hyperspace without sufficient thrust behind us." He frowned. "This thing isn't maneuverable enough to head for the optimum launch window. We'll have to wing it."

"From what I've seen, I'll be surprised if we survive at all," Dev said suddenly, ensnaring everyone's attention.

"Who are you?" Tristan's frown deepened.

Sha'Nara started to answer. "He's Devon—"

Cadell joined her. "Zdenek—"

Dev finished. "Of Lander."

"Shibit!" Tristan's tone left no doubt of his feelings on that matter. "I don't need this right now."

A series of blasts set off several alarms, and Mael hurried to respond to them. "We have a breach on F deck." He touched a comm switch. "Evacuate all people from F deck and seal off the floor." After studying a brightly lit panel, he looked back at Tristan. "The ship can't stand much more of this."

"I need to see the controls." Tristan lurched forward, and Sha'Nara struggled to keep him upright. Though his voice sounded stronger, he still didn't look well. Her first urge was to drag him to his room and make him rest. As the ship shuddered again, she knew she couldn't. Everyone's survival depended on how well Tristan knew this ancient battleship.

"That's it, Bastian. Increase the speed slowly but steadily. Good." Tristan's gaze flickered between the view screen and the console. "Right, through that gap." As a PSI fighter went ricocheting away, Tristan nodded toward another operator. "That's it. Keep it up."

As the *Hermitage*'s speed increased, Tristan dropped his arm from Cadell's shoulders and reached out to trace the curve of Sha'Nara's face. Her heart instantly leapt into hyperspeed.

"I'm not sure this ship can make the leap," he said quietly. "Especially with all the hits it's taking."

"Do we have another option?"

He pressed his lips together. "If we stay here, they'll destroy us."

"I know." Surrender wasn't a consideration. With the readjustment procedure, it still meant death. "Then go for it."

He smiled sadly and turned back. "Keep going, Bastian. Almost there." He looked up and stiffened. A large battleship had taken a position directly ahead of them. "Bastian, maneuver around it. Now!"

"I'm trying." Sweat stood out on the young man's forehead. "The *Hermitage* is barely responding. Should I slow down?"

Tristan exchanged glances with Sha'Nara. She knew instantly what he was trying to tell her. All their options led to death now. The best one was to go out with glory. Swallowing the lump in her throat, she nodded at him.

He squeezed her shoulder in reply. "Continue to increase speed."

The distance between the ships lessened rapidly.

Sha'Nara's chest tightened, and she edged closer to Tristan. At this speed, the impact would be hard, quick, and definitely fatal.

Suddenly, at a point when Sha'Nara thought it too late, the PSI ship rose and allowed the *Hermitage* to sail beneath it. The bridge resounded with everyone's released breath as Sha'Nara tried to fathom why the PSI ship had moved. Had they panicked?

Tristan seized the moment. "We're at speed, Bastian. Put us into hyperspace."

The screen went black. The *Hermitage* shuddered slightly, then settled into a smooth glide. Sha'Nara relaxed, fighting the desire to throw her arms around Tristan's neck.

"Good job, Bastian." Tristan wobbled and strengthened his hold on her shoulders. "I think I'll retire to my quarters now." When Cadell approached, Tristan shook his head. "Sha'Nara can help me." He motioned toward Dev. "You can take care of him."

"Me?" Cadell looked as if he'd rather do anything but that.

"We should emerge in the Tarragon V system in about two hours." Tristan patted Bastian's shoulder. "Just park us somewhere far away from the trade routes."

Mael had already started organizing a team for repairs, and gave Tristan a brief nod as Sha'Nara helped him off the bridge.

Once they reached the lift, Tristan sagged against the wall. "I didn't think we'd make it."

"Neither did I." Tenderness overwhelmed her and she touched his face. "You saved us."

"Your warning saved us. The ship saved us." He gazed around the interior of the lift. "It held up much better than I expected." His lips lifted in a crooked grin. "I guess the Alliance builds pretty good battleships."

The lift stopped, and Sha'Nara helped Tristan toward his room. The lights flickered and many Scanners ran past, some in panic, shouting about damage to the ship, most on some apparent mission. All of them ignored Sha'Nara and Tristan.

Upon reaching Tristan's quarters, Sha'Nara led him inside and slid the door closed behind them. She tried to activate his lights, but they only reached the dim level.

"Doesn't matter." Tristan staggered to his bed and flung himself upon it. "All I want to do right now is sleep."

He needed his rest. Dark circles had formed beneath his eyes, and his face still hadn't regained its original coloring. Sha'Nara nodded. They'd have time later. "I'll come back—"

"No." Tristan pushed himself up on his elbows. "Stay with me. Please."

She approached slowly, her mouth suddenly dry. Even injured, he exuded a masculine presence. "Will you rest if I stay?"

"Much better than if you don't." He caught her hand and pulled her down to sit on the edge of the bed. "I thought I'd lost you. I don't intend to lose you again."

Warmth spread through Sha'Nara's veins at his words. "I won't go anywhere."

"Good."

Sitting beside him, she could make out the circle in his suit created by the laser blast. Burned material surrounded the edges, but the skin beneath it showed no signs of the earlier trauma. Stretching out her hand, she touched his abdomen.

"You almost died, Tristan." Her voice caught, and she had to regain control before she could continue. "You almost died for me."

"I had no choice. I love you."

She glanced at him in surprise. He'd said the words so quietly that she wasn't sure she'd heard right.

Capturing her hand between his, he pressed a kiss to the back of it, his gaze never leaving hers, his face filled with trepidation. Peace, desire, and joy mingled, building to a fiery blaze. He loved her.

She leaned toward him. "I love you, too."

Their lips met in a passionate reunion, fueling Sha'Nara's desire even as it added to her conviction that this was right. More than right. Meant to be.

Tristan moaned softly as they parted. "I want you so much, but right now I can barely sit up, let alone make love to you."

"Just being with you is enough." And it was. To touch him. To know he was alive. To bask in the knowledge that he loved her. Sha'Nara needed nothing else.

"Lie with me. Let me hold you." He moved over so she could stretch out beside him, her head pillowed on his arm. "Stay with me forever."

Sha'Nara snuggled closer. She couldn't promise forever, but for now . . . for now she wasn't about to leave.

The feather-light touch of kisses on her neck pulled Sha'Nara from the foggy depths of slumber. With a contented moan she rolled over and opened her eyes to look into Tristan's face.

Propped on one arm, he looked down at her with a seductive smile. "I wasn't sure you were really here," he murmured. "I thought I dreamed it."

"I'm here." Where she should be.

Tristan leaned forward to capture her lips beneath his in a slow, sensuous, enticing kiss. Sha'Nara groaned from the sudden onslaught of need his touch aroused.

Using his lips and tongue, he made love to her mouth with even, deliberate caresses that triggered a tightening from Sha'Nara's head to her toes. She tried to pull him closer, to increase the passion, but he resisted, pressing her arm back to her side.

He didn't lift his head until Sha'Nara's bones had dissolved to water, her skin screaming for his touch. Staring at him with hazy vision, she could barely speak. "Are you . . . are you well enough for this?"

"The short rest completed my healing." He pressed snugly against her side until she couldn't help but notice his hardness against her hip. "I want you, Sha'Nara." His husky tone reached deep inside her. "I need you."

He nibbled at her exposed throat, forcing her to struggle for air. "Do we have time?"

"We'll make time." Between words he continued to kiss her throat and face. "We're alive for now. Tomorrow we may not be. All this will come to a confrontation very soon. Now may be all we ever have." He drew back and met her gaze, his eyes dark with desire. "Let me love you."

She couldn't resist. She didn't want to resist. Reaching for his shoulders, she pulled him on top of her, reveling in the firmness of his body against hers as she sought his lips.

The kiss escalated as heat wrapped around them and fire blazed deep inside her. Between murmured endearments and hungry kisses, they removed their clothing until they could finally touch skin to skin. The intensity of their joining erased every thought but one.

She loved him. Now . . . and forever.

They found satisfaction together, a blending of passion that dazed them both. Contented, she snuggled against him. Only this man could make her feel so deeply, so completely.

Lazily she ran her palms over the lines of his body, the sculptured muscles of his abdomen, his chest, his shoulders. She leaned forward to nuzzle the tender skin beneath his ear. He inhaled sharply, pausing in his languid strokes over her hair.

As she stared at the shelf over his shoulder, she suddenly frowned. "Something's different." Realization dawned at once. "Your terrarium's gone. Where is it?" Tristan wouldn't lose his most precious possession.

"I broke it." The roughness of his tone brought her gaze back to his face. "Without you, my dreams had no meaning."

Her eyes watered at his confession. She'd never known that kind of love. Hadn't even known it existed.

Wrapping her arms around his neck, she pulled him closer to her. "And you, Tristan, are my dreams."

Later, as they showered together, they made love again tenderly, exploring each other's bodies, already knowing which spots to touch. By the time they started for the conference room, Sha'Nara had been truly well sated. Yet all it took was a look from Tristan to make her body tighten with need.

Upon entering the room, Tristan knew immediately his brief illusion of peace was gone. Mael, Cadell, and Jacy were there, standing side by side as they faced the new visitor. Devon Zdenek of Lander showed no sign of emotion, his expression placid. He glanced at Tristan and Sha'Nara as they entered.

"Good," he said. "You need to hear this, too."

"Hear what?" Though Tristan had no logical reason, he couldn't stop his antagonism for this man.

"I've just made the others an offer—a generous offer, I think."

Sha'Nara frowned. "What kind of offer can you make?"

"I believe I have some influence with the Director-General. After all, the Alliance is begging for Lander to join them." Dev went to study the expanse of stars outside the massive window. "I'm willing to talk to him on behalf of the Scanners."

"What do you mean by that?" This sounded too good to be true. Tristan saw no benefit for Dev out of this deal.

"I'll ask him to grant you freedom. That's what you want, isn't it?"

"That and a planet of our own."

Dev nodded. "Reasonable enough."

Tristan couldn't stop his muscles from tensing. "And what do you get from this?"

"A chance for my planet to join the Alliance. From what I've seen, this merger will make Lander into a very powerful force in the galaxy." Dev kept his expression bland, but something undefinable glimmered in his eyes. "Since we are behind most other planets technology-wise, we need this power and Alliance protection. As long as the Alliance is fighting Scanners, I doubt this union will take place."

"And that's it?"

"No, there's more." Slowly Dev turned and focused his gaze on Jacy. She moved closer to Cadell. "I want my bride."

"You can't be serious," exclaimed Sha'Nara.

"I'm very serious." Dev approached them again, a hard glitter in his eyes. "I was promised a bride. Once I accepted the idea, I found I rather liked it."

"Can't you find someone else?"

He turned his gaze on her. "Are you volunteering?"

Tristan stepped closer to Sha'Nara's side. "No, she isn't." This stranger wasn't getting Sha'Nara or Jacy. "We'll have to refuse your generous offer."

"Then you'll die." Dev said the words so matter-of-factly that Tristan recoiled. "It's only a matter of time, but I would say sooner than later."

"He is right." Mael grimaced. "After that last attack, the Alliance will be all the more determined to wipe us out."

"Then we'll fight back. I'll get better weapons." Tristan clenched his fists. He couldn't give in to Dev Zdenek.

"We have one fighter craft that's proficient." Mael moved to stand by Dev. "And it's a miracle the *Hermitage* survived the transfer here. It won't stand another attack."

In despair, Tristan knew the older man spoke the truth. If they faced another battle, they'd lose. He pressed his lips together, unwilling to admit it.

"Why Jacy?" Sha'Nara took the offensive now. "You know she loves Cadell. Why would you want a woman who wants another man?"

"She's young and very attractive." As Dev slid his gaze over Jacy, he left no doubt of his intentions. She blushed, while Cadell curled his fists, his muscles tight. "I need a wife and she'll do very well. Love isn't important."

"Then obviously you've never been in love."

"Perhaps not." Dev remained unflustered. "Take my offer or not. Either way, I intend to leave shortly." He started for the doorway.

"Stop." Jacy's quiet voice broke the silence.

Dev turned as Cadell grabbed Jacy's arm. "Jacy, no," Cadell cried.

Tears welled up in her eyes. "Don't you understand? Dev can help get your freedom. He can save your life . . . everyone's life."

"Without you, I have no life." The anguish on Cadell's face twisted Tristan's gut as well. He understood clearly. He couldn't give up Sha'Nara. Not now.

"Don't think about me or our feelings." She choked on a sob, refusing to enter Cadell's embrace. "Think about all the Scanners and how hard you've worked for this, how long you've struggled and hidden and died."

The passion in her voice tugged at Tristan. He had no idea she'd grasped the extent of their battle.

"If marrying Dev will stop all the killing, I have to do it. Don't you see?" Her tears flowed freely now, but Jacy made no attempt to wipe them away.

A myriad of emotions crossed Cadell's face—pain, love, understanding, and finally resignation. With a sigh, he nodded. "I do see." He glared at Dev. "But what if you're not successful? What if the Director-General doesn't listen to you any better than he listened to us?"

"Then she still marries me." Dev's coolness made Tristan want to wring the man's neck. He could do it with one simple thought. "The agreement is that I try."

"You might not try very hard either," Cadell replied. "If you have Jacy, it would benefit you to get rid of us."

"Not at all. If I make an agreement, I'll abide by it." Dev raised one eyebrow. "Will you?"

Cadell glanced at Jacy, who dropped her head. He closed his eyes briefly in pain. "If Jacy agrees, then I won't stop her."

"Excellent." Dev extended his hand toward Jacy. "Why don't we go someplace where we can be alone and talk?"

She jerked upright, then hesitantly placed her hand in his. As Dev led her away, Cadell stiffened as if wanting to go after them. Mael went to touch his son's shoulder and Cadell immediately went limp, his head bowed.

Tristan ached for his friend. Watching Jacy leave

with Dev reminded him of how fragile love could be. He stepped closer to Sha'Nara, wrapping his arm around her waist to bring him against him, noticing at once the tightness of her body.

As she leaned into his embrace, he realized her shaking chest came as a result of her attempt to hold back her sobs. "It's not fair." Her voice wavered. "How can he do that? How do we know we can even trust him?"

Mael fastened his gaze upon her. "At this point, we have no choice."

Chapter Eighteen

After much searching, Sha'Nara located Jacy in their previous quarters. Jacy had to listen. The younger woman couldn't sacrifice the love she and Cadell shared for Dev's vague promises.

Jacy lay flung across the bed, the dried tear tracks on her cheeks attesting to her distress. She barely moved as Sha'Nara entered the room.

Crossing to the bed, Sha'Nara sat on the edge of it. "Don't do this, Jacy. We'll find another solution."

"There are no other solutions." Jacy sat up and hugged her knees to her chest. "As it stands right now, the Scanners have been moved to the top of the destruction list. If Daddy puts the entire Alliance on this, they don't stand a chance."

Sha'Nara's heart sank as she heard Jacy put into words what she already knew. "I know. My father will be twice as determined to eliminate them now."

"If by marrying Dev I can get Daddy to change his mind, then I have to do it." Jacy drew in a ragged breath. "I'd rather have Cadell alive than never see him again."

Jacy was right. Though Sha'Nara hadn't expected the young woman to voice such wisdom, she accepted Jacy's reasoning. If it meant keeping Tristan alive, Sha'Nara would do the same.

Sha'Nara hugged Jacy. "I wish I could help."

"You can."

Sha'Nara looked at her expectantly, eager to lessen her sadness. Jacy bit her lip, then met Sha'Nara's gaze.

"Will you stand with me at my wedding to Dev?"

Stunned, Sha'Nara could only stare. She never expected to be asked to perform such an honor.

"It'll mean returning to Centralia," added Jacy. "You may not want to do that."

The thought of facing her father again sent chills through Sha'Nara, but she didn't feel that she could desert her one true friend. Yet what about Tristan? If she returned to Centralia, would she be able to find him again? Would she even be allowed to leave?

She hesitated, then glanced at Jacy. The younger woman watched Sha'Nara intently. This obviously meant a lot to her. "If my being there will help, then I'll come."

"Thank you." Tears welled in Jacy's eyes. "I'm so afraid of marrying Dev, of what it will mean. If you're there, then maybe I won't make a fool of myself."

Sha'Nara's heart constricted. She could well imagine Jacy's fears. Thus far, Dev had not given her the impression of being a reassuring individual. Would his kindness toward Jacy last only until Lander was firmly in the Alliance? How much patience would he have with his new wife?

"I'll be there," Sha'Nara repeated with more conviction. Jacy needed her support. Sha'Nara had escaped Centralia once. She could do it again.

When the door chimed, Sha'Nara went to answer it, surprised to find Tristan standing there. Her body warmed immediately, his presence triggering her awareness.

His gaze rested on her, darkening with passion, then moving over her shoulder to Jacy. "Dev is putting a message through to the Director-General. He says we all need to be there."

Jacy didn't move. "You two go ahead. I'll be along shortly."

Frowning, Sha'Nara glanced back. "Do you want me to stay?"

"No, go with Tristan." She swung her legs around. "I want to freshen up first."

Though Sha'Nara wanted to linger, Tristan took her arm and pulled her into the hallway. The door had barely slid closed behind her when he bent and kissed her, conveying more emotion with his lips than could ever be put into words. Love, passion, wanting, and more than a hint of desperation.

Lost at the first touch of his mouth, Sha'Nara responded with equal fervor. Who knew how long they could remain together? Or even remain alive?

She leaned against him, drawing on his strength. "Jacy's determined to go through with it."

"And Cadell is just as determined to honor her wishes." Tristan tightened his hold. "This will kill him."

"No." Sha'Nara drew back. "I think both of them are tougher than we give them credit for."

"Perhaps." Tristan didn't look convinced. "If Dev is unsuccessful, then both of them will have sacrificed their love for nothing."

"No, not for nothing." Tears threatened, but she blinked them back. "For everything." She turned away from Tristan before she gave in to despair. "Let's go."

Mael, Dev, and Cadell were already waiting on the bridge, the father and son across from the stranger. As Sha'Nara and Tristan entered, Cadell's gaze immediately went past them, obviously searching for Jacy. His features reflected his struggle to hide his pain.

"Jacy will be here in a few moments," said Sha'Nara quietly. She met Dev's curious look with a defiant tilt of her chin. "Do you think you can convince the Director-General to meet with you?"

"I'm certain of it." His unshakable confidence only irritated her. She wanted what he claimed he could do, but not at the cost of Jacy's happiness.

Jacy arrived soon after, her face scrubbed free of tear stains and a forced smile in place. After hesitating upon her arrival, she went to stand beside Sha'Nara, a position between Cadell and Dev.

Mael signaled the comm operator. "Put through the message."

As before, the receptionist barely acknowledged Mael before transferring him, though this time her expression was decidedly cooler, which Sha'Nara wouldn't have believed possible. She swallowed. That did not bode well.

Remy appeared on the view screen, every bit the highest authority in the Alliance. He no longer wore the concerned look of a father, but the stern features of a strict disciplinarian. Upon spotting Mael, he opened his mouth to speak, then closed it again when Dev stepped into the viewer range.

"Greetings, sir," said Dev.

"What are you doing there?" Evidently Remy hadn't missed the Lander representative.

"I came to retrieve my bride." Dev paused. "Upon meeting these Scanners, I believe they do have justification for their request, sir."

"They kidnapped my daughter."

"She came willingly this time." Dev glanced at Jacy, and she flushed. "And you almost killed her with that attack."

"I didn't order the attack." The Director-General grimaced. "In fact, I ordered it stopped once I learned of it."

"Your command came nearly too late. If not for Officer Calles' advance warning, this ship would've been destroyed . . . including your daughter."

"Officer Calles is there?" With a sigh, he shook his head. "I should've known." He met Dev's gaze. "What is it you're asking me to do now?"

"Meet with the Scanners as previously agreed. I will mediate."

"Why would I want to meet with them after they destroyed my conference room?"

"If you don't, then I'll return to Lander without joining the Alliance. As I recall, most of the benefits in this union are yours, not mine."

For once Sha'Nara enjoyed Dev's implacability. His set jaw indicated he wouldn't be swayed, an opinion Remy appeared to form as well.

"Then we'll meet," he said. "I assume Alpha Station Six will still work."

"I have no objections." Dev glanced at Mael. "How long?"

"Three hours."

Dev nodded. "In three hours, then."

"Agreed. Wait." Remy held up his hand when Dev would've terminated the call. "My daughter and Officer Calles will be returned to us there."

"No," cried Tristan, voicing Sha'Nara's instinctive reaction.

Dev ignored him. "They may not—"

Remy cut him off. "This is not open to discussion. Either the women are there or the whole thing is off."

"Very well. They will be there." Dev inclined his head slightly. "Sir."

Tristan barely waited for the transmission to break before he approached Dev, intent on wrapping his fingers around the man's neck. "Sha'Nara isn't returning to Centralia."

His attempt to intimidate Dev failed. The Landerite met Tristan's glare with a bland expression. "I've already said she will. If your goal of freedom is as important as I've been led to believe, then sacrifices will have to be made."

"So Cadell and I have to lose the women we love?" Tristan's gut churned.

Dev raised one eyebrow, his only display of emotion. "Yes, I suppose you do." He brushed past Tristan toward Mael. "How long will it take to reach this Alpha Station Six?"

"From this location, over two hours," said Macl.

"Then I'll need to leave immediately. Can Officer Calles pilot the ship?"

"I—"

Tristan didn't let Sha'Nara finish. "I'll fly the craft." He had no intention of letting her go off alone with this man.

"I'm coming, too." Cadell moved to Tristan's side, his tone equally defiant.

To Tristan's surprise, Dev nodded. "Very well."

Mael stepped forward. "If there are negotiations taking place, I believe I should be present as well."

"Your son can act in your stead." Dev started for the corridor. "Shall we go?"

Tristan caught Sha'Nara's arm before she could follow the others. "You don't have to return to Centralia. You didn't agree. Dev did."

Though she didn't respond right away, the sudden dampness in her eyes made his chest constrict. "I've already told Jacy I would return to Centralia with her."

She'd already agreed. He caught his breath. "Did you plan to tell me this?"

"Yes." Reaching out, she touched his face. "I just didn't know how."

No. It wasn't true. He couldn't have learned she loved him only to lose her again. "I won't let you go."

"I don't want to leave you, Tristan, but until we can find peace for Scanners, we have no future." Her voice trembled. "You know that as well as I. You're the one who helped me see it."

Shibit, he hated it when she was right. If the Director-General didn't grant the Scanners freedom, then Tristan would be forced to run again—never to live in one place very long, always hunted, never knowing when he would die. How could he put Sha'Nara in that kind of jeopardy?

He couldn't.

Ever since his family had been captured, he'd known

he had to survive alone. Nothing had changed that.

Except now he'd found someone he wanted to share a future with. A non-existent future.

"Will you be safe with the Alliance?" he asked. What if returning jeopardized her life as much as staying? He couldn't allow that either.

"If I return with the Director-General, I should be fine."

"And your father?"

The color drained from her face and he took her hand in his, silently offering his support. "I'll make him understand," she said. "I just don't know how yet."

"What will he do to you?" Demote her? Imprison her?

She avoided his gaze. "I'll manage." Lifting her head, she squeezed his hand. "No matter what, I won't give away the secret of the sound box."

"The what?" He blinked, uncertain he'd heard correctly.

"The sound box. I won't tell my father about it. I promise."

He stared at her. Mael's plan to erase that memory hadn't worked. He must not have touched her long enough. As his initial surprise ebbed, Tristan realized it didn't matter. He trusted Sha'Nara.

"Are you two coming?" Cadell's voice drifted down the hallway and Tristan grimaced.

Still clutching Sha'Nara's hand, he guided them toward the others. He'd always known in the back of his mind that their time was limited. He just hadn't expected it to end so quickly.

Or to be so hard to give up.

Under Tristan's guidance, the shuttle made it safely into hyperspace, but Sha'Nara still couldn't shake her unease. Forced to sit in the passenger seats while Tristan and Cadell piloted, she could at least watch him, study him, memorize every feature.

If only she had a chance to be alone with Tristan one last time. Everything had happened so fast, she longed to touch him again, to make slow overwhelming love, to experience the unique bonding they shared.

As if reading her mind, Tristan turned, his gaze traveling leisurely from her head to her toe. Sha'Nara's pulse quickened, her blood heated, her breasts swelled, her breathing became more erratic. Nestled in the far corner as she was, she fantasized about dragging Tristan back to join her. She could never get enough of his touch.

Suddenly she felt someone caress her face, fingers sliding over her chin and down her throat to brush gently over the tips of her breasts. Her gasp disappeared beneath an invisible kiss that shattered her senses.

Wide-eyed, she stared at Tristan. He gave her a slow, sad smile as she experienced another heartwarming kiss. Then he turned to face front again.

Her entire body vibrated with longing so intense she buried her fingernails into the seat's armrests. How could she possibly leave him? No one else could ever make her desire him, need him as Tristan did.

Remy had to free the Scanners.

If he'd watched the readjustment procedure, then maybe he'd be more willing to listen, maybe he'd believe them when they mentioned their inhumane treatment by PSI police.

She'd always considered the Director-General a fair and honest man. Jacy's involvement in these matters had no doubt colored his viewpoint, but he might be made to see. After all, he'd listened to her enough to verify the attack Amyr had initiated and cancel it.

They had a chance . . . slim, but a chance.

More optimistic than she'd felt in a while, Sha'Nara moved into a seat behind Jacy and Dev just in time to hear Jacy ask about the planet Lander.

"I believe you will like it there," Dev replied. "I have been told it resembles the planet Earth as it was several hundred years ago." For the first time, Dev's eyes lit up. "We have mountains, forests, lakes, oceans, plains, rich farmland, and numerous small communities."

Sha'Nara looked at him in amazement. "How have you managed to keep all that?"

"We don't have a huge population. In relation to most planets in the Alliance, we're infants. We don't even have our own spaceships, hadn't dreamed of traveling in space until an Alliance scout ship visited us."

"You've never been in space before?" asked Jacy in surprise.

"Not until my trip to Centralia. I admit I was very disappointed in that planet. All I could see of it were buildings, one upon another, blending into each other to form a solid mass."

He'd given an excellent description of the Alliance planet. Sha'Nara had spent very little time during her childhood away from Centralia, but she enjoyed any place that still had an abundance of plant life.

She eyed him suspiciously. He certainly had a lot of poise for someone who'd never traveled in space before. "Isn't this all new to you?" she asked.

"I learn quickly," he replied, his expression unchanging.

"Tell me more about Lander," said Jacy. "Have you traveled over all of it?"

"Much of Lander is still wilderness, unexplored, untamed. We have lots of room to grow and are doing so at a relaxing pace. For now, we have what we need. For the future . . ." He shrugged. "Who knows?"

"What do you do?"

"Usually the opposite of whatever my father wants." For the first time, a hint of a smile played about his lips. "Which is one of the reasons he thinks I should get married. He believes it will settle me down."

Jacy hesitated. "And what will I be expected to do?"

"Give me lots of sons, naturally."

Jacy paled and glanced down at her hands. Looking forward, Sha'Nara noticed how Cadell stiffened, his back unnaturally erect. To head off possible trouble, she stood and made her way to the front of the shuttle.

Tristan greeted her with a melting smile, but Cadell kept his gaze on the controls.

"He has no right to talk to her like that," he muttered.

Sha'Nara placed her hand on his shoulder. "If she's to be his wife, he has every right."

Cadell bowed his head. "I don't think I can do this, Sha'Nara. I know I promised to honor Jacy's wishes, but I can't bear to see him near her, touching her, talking of sons."

"I know." Her heart ached for him as well as herself. How could the four of them have found such glorious love only to be forced to give it up? "It's not fair, but life rarely is."

"I'm well aware of that."

Tristan reached out to touch Sha'Nara, rubbing his thumb over the back of her hand. Immediate tingles shimmered through her. She wanted to snatch her hand away—even this was too much when she knew she would have to leave him. But she didn't. Selfishly she enjoyed his gentle caress.

"Life has never been fair," he said quietly. "But I agree with Cadell. How can I let you go? I can't."

"You can't kidnap us again."

"Why not?" A gleam appeared in his eyes. "It worked the first time."

"I won't have you jeopardize your safety or what we're striving for. I think the Director-General may be persuaded to listen to reason. If we can just convince him—"

Tristan placed his fingers over her mouth, stopping her words, then gently ran one fingertip along her lower lip, triggering a new set of sensations throughout her. "He might listen." He removed his hand. "But the Director-General isn't about to give in. Not now. Not ever."

"I know him better than you." Sha'Nara didn't want to admit defeat. Only if the Scanners were freed would she and Tristan have any kind of chance at all.

"If he didn't hate us before, he hates us now. I'd bet my life on it."

At Tristan's dire pronouncement, Sha'Nara's heart dropped to her stomach. Staring out the view screen, she tried to recall her earlier enthusiasm.

Instead, a nagging sensation, almost as if someone was about to throw something at her, kept niggling at the back of her neck. She glanced around at Jacy and Dev, but they weren't even paying attention to her.

Looking back at the screen, she tried to focus on the irritation. She'd felt uneasy since she boarded the shuttle, but this . . . this grew stronger with each minute that passed.

"Are we almost there?" she asked.

Tristan examined the control panel and nodded. "Just a few more minutes until we exit hyperspace."

She leaned closer to the stars. Something . . . out there.

"What is it?" Tristan touched her arm.

"I'm not sure. I have a feeling. A bad feeling."

He frowned. "Another hunch?"

"In a way." As she continued to stare into space, she suddenly saw flashes of movement and jerked back.

"Sha'Nara." Concern filled Tristan's voice. "Is there something in hyperspace?"

"Not in hyperspace." But she could feel it now. Danger. Waiting. "But just outside."

Dev suddenly stood behind her. "Do we have any maneuverability when we leave this blackness?"

"Yes." Tristan and Cadell exchanged looks, then leaned toward the controls.

"Are we emerging from the designated launch window?" asked Sha'Nara.

Tristan's lips tightened as he nodded.

Sha'Nara held onto the edge of the control panel, unable to shake the sense of alarm. "Something's there. Waiting." Why couldn't she see something? How did she know this?

"Can we—?"

Waving his hand, Tristan cut Dev off. "Get into your seat and fasten your restraints. If nothing else, I've learned to believe in Sha'Nara's hunches." He glanced up at her. "Get in a seat. I know what to do."

Panic kept her frozen in place, unable to look away. The throbbing in the base of her skull became even more insistent. She needed to do something, but what? "Fast. Go fast."

"I can't do anything until we leave hyperspace." Tristan shook her slightly. "Get into a seat. Now."

Shaken from her daze, she started to back away, then stopped as the blackness gave way to the brilliance of stars surrounding a large, brightly lit space station. She barely noticed the station. Her gaze caught on the two objects hovering nearby.

She wanted to shout a warning, but couldn't. Words couldn't emerge from her constricted throat.

Two PSI Police cruisers waited. As she watched, they fired, the laser beams aimed directly at the shuttle.

Chapter Nineteen

Tristan immediately jerked the shuttle up, tossing Sha'Nara to the floor. His breath caught in his chest. He had no time to focus on her. The deadly beams skimmed beneath the ship.

As he struggled for control, more laser fire came at them. Calling on skills he'd developed over many years of evading capture, he twisted the unwieldy shuttle into a series of evasive maneuvers. They'd survived. So far.

"I'm okay. I'm okay." He heard Sha'Nara behind him, but didn't dare look around. Every second mattered.

More laser fire. More intricate dancing through space.

He didn't have enough room to try for a hyperspace launch. The PSI cruisers stayed close behind.

Cadell used the shuttle's limited lasers, but they made little difference. Tristan was too busy dodging to get into good firing position.

The space station grew nearer, but not close enough. They weren't going to make it. He should've known better than to trust the Alliance.

He dove sharply, tossing his heart into his throat. The shuttle couldn't take much more of this kind of stress. It had never been intended to be a fighter vehicle.

A laser seared the edge of the shuttle. Tristan banked quickly. An acrid odor reached his nostrils. Were they on fire?

"I'm on it," called Sha'Nara.

He didn't dare take his eyes off the view screen for even a second. Another sudden turn. The cruisers were learning his tricks. It was only a matter of time.

Two more ships flew toward them from the space station. Tristan inhaled sharply. They were done for now.

To his surprise, the new arrivals, displaying only Alliance markings, fired warning shots at the PSI cruisers. Not being on their frequency, he didn't hear what was said, but the cruisers abruptly turned away and soared into the stars.

"What now?" He didn't relax.

The Alliance ships positioned themselves on either side of the shuttle. They showed no signs of firing, but neither did they appear to be leaving. Tristan eyed them doubtfully. An escort?

To get them safely to the meeting with the Director-General? Or safely to their deaths?

He tried to change his heading, but the ships nudged him back. So much for having a choice. They were going to the station.

Sha'Nara joined him, the smell of smoke clinging to her. A black smudge adorned her cheek. "It's out," she said. "Don't worry."

"What was burning?"

"Just the panel liner. I added a sealant so I don't expect problems." She peered out the window. "What's going on now?"

"Good question. These ships appeared and ran off the others. Now they're taking us to the station."

"Maybe Remy sent them to insure we made it without any interference."

Tristan grimaced. "I doubt it."

Lights winked on, outlining an entry portal. Since

Tristan's guide ships left him no option, he steered the shuttle toward it. "Buckle up. We're landing."

The entry went smoothly, and he settled his ship on a lit docking area. Opening the hatch, he expected to be greeted by a laser, but found no one around.

"What now?" he asked. As one, they focused on Dev.

Dev started for the entry to the bay. "We find the Director-General." They met no one as they trooped through several twisting corridors. Had the Alliance taken over the entire space station? Tristan wouldn't put it past them.

The corridor narrowed as they approached a door at its end. Two Alliance officers stood on either side of the door, and waved Tristan and the others forward.

Tristan's muscles tightened. Was this where they'd be imprisoned or killed?

Wary, he made his way through the doorway first, and found himself in a small room furnished only with a round table and several chairs. Only one of the chairs was occupied.

Remy Vadin stood as Tristan entered, and motioned him further inside. "Have a seat."

The man's impassive face provided no clue to his thoughts. Settling into a chair, Tristan remained alert. He didn't trust the Alliance any more now than he had during the previous thirty-two years of his life. Only Sha'Nara had proven to be an exception.

She came to attention as she entered, and presented the Director-General with a salute before she took a seat beside Tristan. To his amazement, Jacy didn't run to her father as she had before. Instead she hung back, allowing Dev to present himself first.

"I hope you know what you're doing," said Remy, a note of warning in his voice.

"I believe so." Dev motioned Jacy forward. "Your daughter has agreed to become my wife as previously arranged. I trust the ceremony can proceed upon our return to Centralia."

Remy blinked, but disguised his amazement quickly.

"Certainly." He held out his hand toward Jacy. "Daughter."

"Daddy." She spoke so softly Tristan could barely hear her. "I do hope you're ready to listen now."

Capturing her hand in his, he pulled her forward for a hug. "It depends on what's said."

Cadell managed to avoid any type of greeting, taking the opportunity to sit beside Tristan. "Whatever kind of man he is, he does love his daughter," Cadell said softly.

"And Dev?"

"I get nothing from him. He's harder to read than anyone I've ever met before." Cadell frowned. "If only I could sense that he did care about Jacy, I might feel better about this."

Tristan continued to watch Remy and Dev as they took their places. "I doubt it." He knew how he felt about losing Sha'Nara. To know she would be with another man would be unbearable.

A thick moment of silence blanketed the gathering. Then the Director-General spoke. "Ever since I was a child I'd heard tales of Scanners and how they'd almost destroyed the Earth during their attempt to seize power. I grew up believing these people wanted only power and destruction, that their existence was a blight on our society."

Anger stirred low in Tristan's gut. He'd heard this a million times. Was the Director-General of the Alliance using it as an excuse for the mass obliteration of a race?

"From that background, I agreed with the rationale put forth by the PSI Police Director for his methods to capture and reeducate these people." Remy turned his gaze onto each of them, one at a time.

Tristan met the Director-General's gaze with defiance, not hiding his burning fury.

"But I fear I've been wrong."

At those words, Sha'Nara and Jacy gasped. Tristan's fury gave way to outright stupefaction.

"My daughter and a PSI Police officer, whom I have known since childhood and always trusted, both swear to me that these people can be trusted, that they aren't intent on taking over the Alliance as they once attacked the Earth." Remy smiled dryly. "I'll admit it does make me stop and think."

No one said anything. Tristan barely heard anyone breathing.

The Director-General continued his speech. "Then Officer Calles—Sha'Nara—tells me the readjustment procedure is not what she and I had been led to believe, that it maimed and killed instead of providing a simple removal of PSI ability."

Tristan glanced at Sha'Nara, his chest tight. Leave it to her to try and convince the Alliance's highest authority. How long had it taken him to persuade her?

"I admit I found this hard to believe. I've worked with Amyr Calles for years, and always found him trustworthy." Remy looked down at the table for a moment, then back up. "So Sha'Nara made a video for me of the procedure itself and I watched it."

He paused. "Afterward I wished I hadn't. Presented with such evidence, I had to face the fact that one of my loyal directors had been lying to me . . . for some time. Sha'Nara had told me of an impending attack on Scanners. I couldn't believe that either until after seeing the video. Once I discovered it was in fact happening at that moment, I ordered the attack stopped and recalled the troops."

"Just in time, too," added Dev.

Remy looked at Sha'Nara with a wry twist of his lips. "Your father and I had a rather heated discussion following that order. As a rule I don't tell my directors how to run their areas. I trust them to follow Alliance policy. Naturally, Amyr was upset that I canceled his attack."

"I can imagine," replied Sha'Nara.

"He saw it as his one chance to eliminate a good portion of the Scanner population and said as much." Remy sighed. "Elimination has never been part of Alliance policy. Even if Jacy hadn't been a part of your group, I could not have condoned such an attack."

"Then why were PSI Police waiting for us when we arrived here?" Tristan was tired of listening to this ruminating. He wanted answers. He wanted action.

"I made the mistake of telling Amyr I planned to meet with you. I'm assuming he decided that was a bad idea." Remy met Tristan's gaze. "I didn't send the PSI Police. When I saw what they were up to, I sent some of my own men out to ensure your safe arrival here."

"Are we prisoners or negotiators?" Though honesty rang in Remy's words, Tristan wasn't willing to trust the Alliance just yet.

"What I've been leading up to is that beliefs I've held my entire life are faltering. I can't promise anything will change, but I'm willing to be persuaded." The Director-General leaned forward. "Now it's up to you to convince me."

Inhaling deeply, Tristan glanced at Cadell and received an encouraging nod. "We are not the same people as our ancestors. For reasons unknown to us, they decided to use their abilities to seize control of Earth's government. From what history I do know, I believe all the rebels were killed, but all humans with PSI abilities then became suspect and were forced to flee for their lives. Today's Scanners are descended from these individuals who did nothing more than attempt to survive."

Remy nodded, providing the reassurance Tristan needed to press on.

"We have no desire to take control of anything other than our own lives. Our PSI abilities are nothing more than a part of who we are. They don't automatically make us dangerous."

Was he having any impact at all? The Director-General's face remained politely interested, nothing more. Tristan had to make him understand.

"I've spent my entire life hunted throughout the galaxy. My parents were captured when I was young and probably readjusted. I haven't seen them since." Fresh pain speared him as he spoke, and his voice thickened. "I've never been able to stay in one place for any length of time for fear of being found by PSI police. All I want—all any of us want—is freedom from being hunted and a place to call our own."

"I see." Remy's noncommittal answer made Tristan want to scream with frustration.

"You've always had a place to call home, sir." Tristan's anger caused him to clip the ends of his words. "How many times have you been hunted, threatened with destruction, simply because you exist?"

Sha'Nara quickly lifted her hand. "May I say something?"

The Director-General gave her the first honest smile Tristan had seen on the man. "Sha'Nara, I always thought you would break away from your father at some point in your life, but I never expected it would be like this."

She grimaced. "Believe me, I never expected it myself. When Jacy and I were first kidnapped, I honestly thought we'd be killed. I did everything in my power to escape."

"That's an understatement," muttered Tristan. She'd provided more challenges than taming a wild Anderian boar.

After sending him a quelling glance, she continued. "But while I was there, I began to see Scanners as more than the evil creatures we'd been taught they were. They're people, who live and love and hurt just as we do. They have families. They care about one another. In fact, the only difference is their special powers."

She pointed a finger at the Director-General. "Sir, the Alliance has gone about this all wrong. If we were smart, we'd welcome these people and learn how to put them to work in positions where their PSI abilities can help us. After a time everyone would see they can be trusted, that they're an asset."

The passion in her voice made Tristan smile. If he'd tried to make her think this way, he would've failed. That she decided to support them on her own made her that much more formidable. Remy had to be weakening.

"Interesting," Remy said.

"Sir, I don't think they're asking for too much," she added. "Freedom and a home are life's basic necessities and certainly within the Alliance's powers to grant."

"Perhaps." Remy glanced at Dev. "Mr. Zdenek, what have you to say? What makes you willing to jeopardize our agreement in order to support them?"

Tristan awaited Dev's reply even more eagerly than Remy. Why had this emotionless stranger decided to offer his help? What did he get out of it? Jacy?

"I only spent a short time with these people, sir, but I agree with Officer Calles' assessment. I saw no evidence that they desire control or offer a threat." Dev spared Tristan a quick look. "In fact, while we were under attack, nearly destroyed ourselves, Tristan did his best to ensure they didn't harm the attackers even while he all but performed miracles to keep us alive."

Surprised, Tristan sat back in his chair. He wouldn't have thought Dev had noticed anything going on during that chaos.

"In addition, I found them dedicated to this cause, so much so that they're willing to make extreme sacrifices if it will help." As if he'd mentioned them by name, Cadell and Jacy exchanged hurting glances.

"I find it difficult to believe that an Alliance which welcomed my planet so warmly and spoke of unity and peace would treat another race in this manner." Dev focused his steady stare on Remy. "Such treatment makes me reconsider my planet's decision to become a part of this organization."

"You have a valid point, Mr. Zdenek." Remy waved his hand to encompass the entire table. "In fact, you all present good arguments." He paused, furthering heightening the tension in the room.

Tristan clenched his fists. If this didn't work, they'd never have another chance, not in his lifetime at any rate. Feeling a warm touch on his arm, he opened his hand, then closed it around Sha'Nara's. Her support mattered more than he could admit. Without her . . .

A definite possibility.

Without her, he'd be lost.

Remy suddenly stood and leaned forward, placing his palms on the table. "I intend to order a discontinuance of Alliance policy toward Scanners. From this moment on, you'll no longer be considered dangerous or subjected to capture." He smiled. "Gentlemen, you have your freedom."

The words filtered through Tristan's mind, but reality took longer to set in. Freedom? They wouldn't be hunted any longer? He glanced at Cadell to find his friend looking equally incredulous. Jacy was smiling, while Dev's expression could only be described as smug.

"My father will never agree to it."

Sha'Nara burst his blossoming excitement before Tristan could celebrate. He'd forgotten. Amyr Calles wasn't likely to give up his entire directorate without a fight. Every Scanner was well aware of how powerful this man was. Did Remy realize it?

"I'm certain you're right," said the Director-General. "However, his is not the only opinion. I have to present this motion to the entire gathering of directors and ask for a vote."

"Why would any of them agree?" asked Tristan. All these people had grown up hating and fearing Scanners.

"Because you're all returning to Centralia with me. While en route we'll take what you've just presented and work it into a formal document. I'll call for an immediate meeting. With this document we'll create and your testimony, I feel certain a majority of my directors will agree with me."

Tristan turned to Sha'Nara. Was it possible?

A slow smile appeared on her face and she nodded. "The land," she whispered.

Tristan hesitated, turning back to Remy. "Is there any chance of finding a planet for us? Somewhere for Scanners to come together?"

Remy hesitated. "I don't have the power to give away a planet. They're already occupied."

"Isn't there a new discovery?" He couldn't keep the

urgency from his voice. He hadn't given up his quest for his own land . . . not completely.

Cadell joined in. "So long as it's inhabitable, we can make it work for us."

"Tristan, Cadell, I'd like to help, but at this point, I don't know of any uninhabited planets that don't deserve to be that way. I'm sorry." Remy grimaced. "You're all spread throughout the galaxy now. Does it make a difference?"

"We're spread out because that's the best way to hide." Tristan ran his fingers through his hair. "We have a couple hundred aboard the *Hermitage*—Scanners who have found us and stayed. We want to be a people together. Only among ourselves do we know there's no fear or hatred of who we are."

"I . . ." Dev started to speak, then stopped.

Everyone looked at him expectantly.

"I think the Alliance should reexamine their records." He finished his sentence, but Tristan received the distinct impression it wasn't what he originally intended to say. "Perhaps you'll have a planet you've forgotten."

"That's unlikely, but I'll send a message ahead to initiate such a search. They should have an answer for us by the time we arrive." Remy paused by the door. "I'll have my ship prepared for immediate departure. I trust you want this implemented as quickly as possible."

"Yes, sir." Cadell jumped to his feet.

"I'll leave one of my officers to show you the way." Remy consulted his chronometer. "We should be ready within half an hour."

After he left, Cadell fired his fist toward the ceiling. "Yes!" He grabbed the back of Tristan's seat. "Father will want to know this!"

"I'm sure we can contact him from the Director-General's ship. He can meet us at Centralia." Clasping Sha'Nara's hand, Tristan stood. "He'll never believe it. I don't believe it."

"You're free," repeated Sha'Nara. "You have a future." With her face irresistibly close, Tristan stole a soul-jarring kiss.

A future. He hadn't dared to hope.

He turned to share his enthusiasm with Cadell, then stopped as he caught sight of the agonized look his friend shared with Jacy, who stood beside Dev. Tristan's excitement dimmed. He had the opportunity now to build a life with Sha'Nara.

But his best friend had just lost any chance of happiness.

Their arrival at Alliance headquarters created even more of a stir than Sha'Nara expected. An entire ensemble of assistants, each trying to gain Remy's attention, fell into their group as they made their way to the Director-General's central area.

Though Sha'Nara caught only bits and pieces of the jumbled conversations, she gathered that all the directors were present for the hastily convened meeting. Her stomach knotted at the thought of facing her father again. He still believed her a traitor. No matter what their proposal said, he wasn't about to accept the Scanners—his hatred went too deep.

If only he didn't convince the others to feel the same way.

Upon reaching the central core, Remy directed them toward a massive conference room, remaining behind to confer with several more assistants.

Sha'Nara paused, her heart pounding, then opened the door and stepped inside. Cadell, Tristan, Jacy, and Dev followed. The directors leapt from their seats with exclamations of surprise. Amyr instantly started toward the comm panel.

"The Director-General knows we're here," she told him.

The coldness of his gaze raked over her. "What have you done to him? If you've—"

Remy breezed in behind them. "I'm here. We can get started." He went to take his seat at the head of the table.

Sha'Nara couldn't resist a grin at the astonished look

on her father's face. "What is the meaning of this?" Amyr demanded.

"If each of you will access your imager in front of you, you'll see a newly drafted document of peace. I'd like you to read it."

Approaching his seat, Amyr scowled at the lit imager built into the tabletop. "What does it say?"

"Read it and find out." Remy waved his hand at Sha'Nara and her friends. "Please take a seat. There are plenty here."

She had only taken two steps when fresh commotion erupted outside the conference room. Whirling around, she planted herself in front of the doorway. Tristan immediately came to her side.

The door slid open.

And Mael stepped into the room.

"I'm here and ready for a taste of freedom."

Chapter Twenty

Mael's announcement sent the directors into a flurry of conversation, each of them vying for Remy's attention. With a sigh, Sha'Nara ushered Mael inside. They hadn't needed his outburst at this point, not when Remy hadn't yet explained his intentions.

"Enough." The Director-General's voice rose above the chatter. "As I was saying before Mr. Ner arrived, I want you to read the proposal on your imager. Then I will open the table to discussion." He nodded toward Mael. "Please be seated."

Sha'Nara found a seat beside Tristan, and watched the directors' faces as they read. When the expressions reflected horror, even disgust, her stomach clenched. She should've known this had all been too easy. These directors would never approve the proposal.

As she expected, her father protested first. "This is insanity. You can't be serious."

Remy kept his features blank. "I am very serious. I see no reason to continue hunting Scanners when they no longer pose a threat to the Alliance."

"But they're barely human. They're killers, destroyers."

"Please give me specific examples of the killing and destroying in the past fifty years."

Sha'Nara glanced at Tristan. Hadn't they already been through this?

"I lost several men while capturing a group of Scanners on Regis Four. They had no qualms about injuring or killing my people." Amyr's face reddened with anger.

"Did this uprising take place before or after the PSI Police arrival?"

Taken aback, Amyr didn't reply. Remy glanced at Sha'Nara.

"The uprising came as a result of PSI Police actions to capture a group of Scanners hiding in an abandoned mine," she announced. "Six officers were injured, one killed." She frowned. "Twelve Scanners were killed and the rest taken for readjustment."

Her father cast her a look that threatened retribution, but she only lifted her chin defiantly. His days of intimidating her were over.

"I see." Remy nodded as if thinking. "And readjustment is nothing more than a death penalty, is it not?"

"Either a living death or permanent death. Given a preference, most Scanners would choose the latter," added Tristan.

"Try again, Amyr." A sharp glimmer in Remy's eye told Sha'Nara he knew exactly what he was doing. "Name an instance of Scanner uprising not instigated by the PSI Police themselves."

Sha'Nara could predict Amyr's next words. She'd used them herself.

"A Scanner named Roget tried to take over the government on Miniva Three. Only timely interference by my officers stopped him."

"I remember that," Remy said.

Tristan signaled for recognition. Upon receiving a nod from Remy, he cast Sha'Nara a wry smile, then began. "Along those same lines, three humans—Manderling on Delinor, Treadwell on Carpathia, and Smytheson on Earth—all engaged in revolts as well."

"I'm very familiar with Smytheson." A corner of Remy's lips twitched as if he held back a smile. "You're telling me this Roget was just an isolated incident among Scanners much as these other individuals were the exception among humans."

"Yes, sir."

Looking toward Amyr again, Remy lifted his hand. "Anything else?" When the PSI Police Director didn't reply, Remy extended his invitation. "Anyone?"

"What about the PSI Wars?" The Director of Technology cast an anxious glance at the Scanners in the room. "How do we know that won't happen again?"

"The PSI Wars were over a hundred years ago," replied Remy. "Any possible survivors of that bloodbath are long dead. If Scanners intend to lead a revolt, they'll do it whether free or not, as will any race in this galaxy. I tend to believe their assurances that this is not their goal."

"You believe them?" Amyr gave a derisive snort. "I find that incredibly naive."

"Perhaps I am naive." Remy narrowed his eyes and leaned forward. "I've believed my PSI Police Director all these years when he assured me readjustment did no permanent damage to these people, that they were reassimilated into society with ease."

Color drained from Amyr's face, then returned fourfold. A sudden surge of fear blossomed within Sha'Nara. He wasn't done, not yet.

Ignoring him, the Director-General continued to address his other directors. "I have talked with these people. My daughter and Officer Calles, who spent time with Scanners, will vouch for them. As they have shown no signs of the destructive tendencies we've all been led to believe in, I feel they have earned their freedom."

"But what will they do if they're free?" asked another director.

"This proposal binds them to the same rules and regulations governing all races in the Alliance. Alliance officers handle any infractions now, and will continue to do so."

"If we're going to set them free, why not require them to be readjusted first?" asked the Trade Director.

"No." Tristan, Cadell, Jacy, and Sha'Nara all spoke at once.

Remy motioned for quiet, then turned his attention to the Trade Director. "Toldof, unless you've been hiding something from me, I think you—all of us—have been sadly mistaken about what readjustment is and what it does. Officer Calles recorded a readjustment session for me. If you'll direct your attention to the imagers . . ."

After he keyed in a command, Sha'Nara's video appeared on the small screens, no less intense for being only a recording of events. She didn't want to watch, but neither could she look away. The horror held her, though her insides twisted into a tortured knot.

As the Scanner screamed, Jacy burst into sobs and Cadell immediately wrapped his arms around her. His face was pale as well. What kind of emotions was he reading now?

As the video finished, the directors looked as one toward Amyr. With a dark scowl, he pushed back his chair. "One less Scanner to worry about," he snapped.

A different kind of horror appeared in the directors' expressions now. Sha'Nara's tension eased. Maybe . . .

Remy shook his head sadly. "Regardless of how this turns out, Amyr, I will be removing you from your position. This malicious destruction is not the intent of the Alliance."

As the others cast disgusted looks at Sha'Nara's father, Remy continued. "Read the proposal again, gentlemen. Think about it. Ask all your questions. I intend to vote in fifteen minutes."

They had to be the longest fifteen minutes in Sha'Nara's life. Her father refused to read the document again. He sank into his chair and crossed his arms, his mind obviously unchanged.

The other directors were more flexible, turning their

attention again to their imagers, this time reading with interest and thought.

Remy circulated around the room, pausing to answer questions or point out a particular passage. As he passed Sha'Nara, he squeezed her shoulder in an encouraging gesture. Evidently he felt more confident than she did.

Nearing Mael, Remy extended his hand, and Sha'Nara jumped from her seat, almost as if pushed by an invisible force. From Tristan's surprised look, she knew he hadn't done it.

"I'm pleased to finally meet you in person," said Remy.

As Mael took the Director-General's hand, Sha'Nara stumbled forward, grabbing Remy to keep her balance, pulling the two men apart. Sha'Nara straightened. Why hadn't Remy tried to help her?

Glancing at him, she noticed a glassy quality to his eyes as he continued to look at Mael. "I admire the way you've led the Scanners," he said. "I may have a place for you here." He suddenly blinked, then smiled at Sha'Nara. "Are you all right?"

"Yes." Ensuring Remy moved on, Sha'Nara turned back to Mael, catching a glimpse of angry frustration before he carefully hid it. "Leave him alone," she ordered, keeping her voice low.

"I've done nothing." He even managed to look injured. "Your PSI Police mentality is at work."

Sha'Nara returned to her seat. Was her imagination seeing things that weren't there? When Mael had implanted words in her mouth, she'd known what was happening. Remy showed no indication that he hadn't meant what he said. She shook her head. Maybe it *was* her PSI Police mentality.

Tristan touched her hand. "What's going on?"

"Nothing." She gave him a wry smile. "Nothing."

Remy returned to his seat and called for a vote. Sha'Nara's breath caught in her throat as each director responded with an aye or nay to the proposal. Her father answered with a definite nay, followed by another nay from the Director of Technology.

Her stomach dropped, and she turned to Tristan in despair. They couldn't have come this far only to lose out now.

He redirected her attention to the voting. Aye from the Director of Resources, aye from the Director of Trade. In the end, five ayes to two nays. The proposal was accepted.

With a cry of happiness, Jacy threw her arms around Cadell's neck. Half afraid to believe it, Sha'Nara looked to Remy for reassurance.

He nodded and smiled. "I'll have the final document prepared immediately."

They'd done it. Turning to Tristan, she met his broad smile with one of her own.

Leaning forward, he caught her chin between his fingers and brushed his lips over hers. Excitement, happiness, anticipation, and desire mingled into an exquisite sensation she never wanted to lose. They had a future. They'd done it.

"I should've known that blood would tell."

At Amyr's bitter exclamation, Sha'Nara turned toward her father. He stood at the opposite side of the table, his glare designed to drive her to her knees.

Not anymore.

"What does that mean?" she asked.

"It means just that. You have their tainted blood. I thought I could contain it, but I failed."

"What?" She and Tristan cried out together as they jumped to their feet. Tainted blood?

"You're a Scanner, Sha'Nara." Amyr gave her an evil grin, the gleam in his eyes not quite rational. "All this time you've been killing your own kind."

She gasped, a chill spreading through her. "I don't believe you. How could I possibly be a Scanner?" Her eyes widened as a thought occurred to her. "Are you a Scanner?"

"No!" He drew back as if she'd slapped him. "Many years ago, when I was a junior PSI Police officer, still working my way up, I met a woman—beautiful, amusing, desirous. Her name was Mira. I made it my mission to take her to bed and succeeded."

Remy frowned. "Weren't you married at that time?"

"It didn't matter. I wanted Mira more than anything else I had."

Sha'Nara blinked. Her father? In love? Or merely in lust?

"Quite by accident I discovered she was a Scanner. The Scanner detectors had just been designed and I had one on me. It alerted on her." Amyr paused, caught in his memories.

"To my surprise she admitted to being a psychic. Then she tried to kill me." He scowled and his voice rose. "She tried to kill *me* after we'd just made love."

His lips twisted in an evil grin. "Maybe she'd had a vision and saw what was going to happen to her."

Words stuck in Sha'Nara's throat. Fortunately, Tristan voiced her question. "Why did happen to her?"

"I stopped her, of course, and had her readjusted."

Sha'Nara gasped. He could do that to a woman he'd loved?

"After her readjustment, I learned she was pregnant, so I kept her around. She didn't have much mind left, but with a body like hers, she didn't need one."

"Amyr!" Remy's exclamation contained the disgust Sha'Nara felt.

"In time she gave birth to a daughter." Amyr pointed an accusing finger at Sha'Nara. "You."

Black spots danced before her eyes and she gripped the edge of the table. Her mother had been a Scanner. *She* was a Scanner?

Glancing at Tristan, she met his sympathetic gaze. Psychic. He'd teased her about it and had been right all the time. That explained her hunches. She was psychic.

"Why . . . why didn't I know this?" she asked.

"I found it amusing to raise a Scanner child to destroy other Scanners. I made sure any sign of your ability was stomped down. You had only me. You believed whatever I told you. You trusted me." Amyr scowled at Tristan. "Until you met him."

Sha'Nara recalled buried instances from her childhood when any mention of knowing something ahead of time had been severely punished. Now her father's tirades against following her hunches made sense. No wonder she'd never been able to please him. "What happened to my mother?"

"She's dead."

Though he didn't admit it, she felt certain he'd killed her birth mother when she no longer proved useful. "What about Mother? My . . . your wife?"

"She's a weakling. We married to unite our families, but I quickly discovered she was barren. She was given no choice but to accept you."

Tears pricked at Sha'Nara's eyes. Now she understood her mother's reluctance to be around her, to show any kind of affection. The woman hadn't been her mother.

"You *are* a Scanner, Sha'Nara." Her father leaned forward to spit the word at her. "You've spent a better portion of your life destroying your own people. How does that make you feel?"

He wanted to see her destroyed, eaten with guilt. Sha'Nara stiffened her back, refusing to give in to something she had no control over. "It makes me wish I didn't have you for a father."

He snarled a reply, but she didn't hear it. Instead her attention caught on the corner of the room by Remy's seat. Nothing was there, yet . . .

Was that a shimmering?

Recognizing the voice in her mind for what it was, she gripped Tristan's arm and pointed. "Something . . . someone . . . there."

By the time Bran materialized, Tristan was already halfway over the table. Bran had a laser in his hand and aimed it at Remy.

Shouts erupted.

"No."

"Look out."

"Not yet."

Tristan tackled Bran as the man fired. The laser burst went wild.

The two men wrestled on the floor, punches flying. Unable to see Tristan, Sha'Nara started around the table, then froze at hearing her father's voice.

"It's time I took care of all my mistakes."

Turning, she found him aiming his laser at her, his intent clear. He had no love for her. He never had. Killing her would be only one more Scanner dead.

She raised her hands in a futile gesture to hold off the blow. "Father . . ."

The sound of a laser blast filled the room.

His eyes wide, Amyr looked down at the scorched hole in his chest, then sank to the floor as the life left his body.

Whirling around, Sha'Nara watched Remy lower his weapon, his features sad. "He would've killed his own daughter," he said in quiet horror. "I can't believe that."

Tristan smashed against the table, blood trickling from the corner of his mouth, then staggered to his feet. Sha'Nara saw the shimmering around Bran before Tristan did.

"He's getting ready to teleport again," she cried. "Stop him."

Snatching up Remy's vacated chair, Tristan hurled it at Bran. Although he'd begun to fade, it collided with his midsection, tossing him sideways to the floor.

Bran screamed—once, twice, then fell silent.

Making her way around the table, Sha'Nara inhaled sharply. Evidently Bran's dematerialization had stopped when the chair hit him. He'd reformed, but part of the seat enveloped his torso. He was definitely, horribly dead.

Tristan came to wrap his arms around her as Alliance officers flooded the conference room. "Bran must've thought he could destroy the Alliance this way," he said.

Closing her eyes, Sha'Nara buried her face against his chest, drawing on his strength, inhaling his uniquely masculine scent.

She never wanted to let go. Maybe now she wouldn't have to.

As officers guided everyone from the room, she reluctantly stepped away, but kept hold of Tristan's hand. They joined Remy by the doorway at the same time an assistant ran up to him with a hand imager. Glancing at it, Remy grimaced.

"Bad news?" asked Sha'Nara.

"It's about finding an available planet."

Though the directors had left, the others remained, focusing their attention on Remy.

"There's nothing. I'm sorry." He sighed. "Maybe in time."

"I have a suggestion." Dev stepped forward, amusement dancing in his eyes. "The Scanners can come to Lander if they wish."

"Lander?" From Dev's earlier description, she knew the planet had room, but why would he be willing to accept Scanners?

"Do you really want us?" asked Tristan.

Dev answering grin gave him an appeal Sha'Nara had missed before. As they watched, the imager floated from Remy's hand into Dev's.

Sha'Nara caught her jaw before it dropped, but Remy stepped backward in amazement while Jacy gasped.

"These PSI abilities, as you call them, are inherent in my people," said Dev. "We all have them. Scanners will be right at home on Lander."

"I've been to Lander." Remy shook his head. "I never guessed."

"You weren't meant to. Upon your arrival, we saw immediately you were different. Though flattered to be invited into the Alliance, we were cautious. After learning about how the Alliance hunted Scanners, I was not about to enter into any kind of agreement." Dev smiled at the Director-General. "You made the right decision. Lander will be glad to join the Alliance now."

"So that's why you helped us," said Cadell.

"In part." Dev turned his gaze on Cadell and Jacy. "And because I saw no reason for Scanners to be hunted. Your powers are natural to us. My only hesitation was over how badly you wanted this freedom. If it was only for power, as the Alliance claimed, then I wouldn't have helped. So I sought to find out how much you would sacrifice to achieve your goal. Power-hungry people would not be willing to suffer for what they want."

Cadell exchanged stunned glances with Jacy. "Then making Jacy marry you . . ."

"I have no intention of marrying Jacy." Dev sighed. "I fear her affections lay elsewhere."

The joyful incredulity that crossed Jacy's and Cadell's faces made Sha'Nara smile. When the two met in a passionate kiss, she leaned closer to Tristan. This was better than she could've dreamed.

Remy cleared his throat. "It appears I will have a different son-in-law than I expected."

Breaking away, Cadell stood tall before the Director-General. "With your permission, sir. I love Jacy more than life itself."

Spreading his hands, Remy grinned. "How can I argue with that?"

Remy left, and Jacy returned to Cadell's embrace as Tristan asked Dev about what to expect on Lander. Already Tristan had started thinking about the logistics of settling an entire race.

Leaving the men in their discussion, Sha'Nara hurried after Remy. She needed to know what role—if any—she had left. With her father dead . . . She shuddered, but couldn't summon much sympathy for the man who'd only used her as an instrument of revenge.

"Remy . . ." she said.

He'd stopped by Mael to talk. When Mael took one of Remy's hands, Sha'Nara's instincts kicked in again. Something was wrong . . . very wrong.

Closing the distance between them, she tugged Remy away from the Scanner leader. "What are you doing?" she demanded of Mael.

Remy staggered, forcing her to bear his weight. "I . . . feel . . . lightheaded."

Sha'Nara had never completely trusted Mael. What did he hope to gain by implanting Remy?

The Director-General's eyes were cloudy. "Give position," he muttered. "Second in command."

At his words, her heart skipped a beat and she faced Mael. "Put you in a position of authority? Then what? What's your plan, Mael?" She frowned. "I think you've been operating under a different agenda all along."

"I wanted freedom for the Scanners."

"And a position of authority?"

"It's the only way to ensure this doesn't happen again."

"I think we can trust Remy."

Mael scowled. "We can't trust any of them. I know."

Sha'Nara hesitated. Mael's vehemence indicated more than a simple problem of trust. "How do you know?"

His eyes flashed with anger. "Alliance people told me to trust them when they arrested me and my family, that we wouldn't be hurt. Then they separated Cadell and me from my wife." His features hardened. "They used her, then killed her."

"Orion's Sword." Sha'Nara shuddered. She'd heard stories of such abuse, but had seen none of it in her division. Of course, she hadn't known the truth about readjustment either.

Balling his fists, Mael aimed his glare at the staggering Remy. "I heard her screaming, but I couldn't get out of the room where I was locked. I tried . . . I tried." He paused, his thoughts obviously in the past. "At the first opportunity, I implanted them, forced them to kill each other while I escaped with Cadell."

He rounded on Sha'Nara. "Don't you see? I have to make sure I keep it from happening again. I have to destroy the Alliance."

"What is your plan, Mael?" she asked. Though she sympathized with his loss, his irrational rage against the Alliance made him capable of anything. "Did you plan to force Remy into putting you into a high-level position where you could control the Alliance, then destroy it?" Past doubts returned. "Did you intend to kill Jacy and me and make it look like an accident? Were you the one who sent Bran out in the Thorg ship?" Her eyes widened. "Were you the one who had him appear here to kill Remy?"

Amid the confusion of Bran's appearance, she'd heard the words "not yet." In Mael's voice.

"You'd planned to have Remy put you in a position of authority, then have Bran kill him, didn't you?"

"I'd like to hear those answers myself, Father." Cadell stepped forward, Tristan at his side. "*Did* you order Bran to shoot down Jacy and Sha'Nara's ship? Were you responsible for his appearance here today?"

Mael faltered, suddenly appearing older. "I did it for us. For all of us. We can't let the Alliance destroy us any longer."

"My life would've been over without Jacy and you sent Bran out to kill her?" Cadell stepped forward. Sha'Nara could feel his outrage. "We've already won our freedom. You're doing this for yourself, for revenge."

"Don't you see?" Mael pointed at Sha'Nara. "She knows too much. She has the knowledge to destroy us."

Tristan emitted a low growl. "You told me you could erase that memory."

Sha'Nara looked at Tristan in surprise. Was that why he'd looked at her so strangely when she mentioned the sound box?

"I don't have that ability. I only said I did so you'd let her go." Mael shook his head. "I'd planned for her to die, so it didn't matter."

"I trusted you."

Mael suddenly sailed across the room, only to be pinned by his shoulders against the wall. Tristan remained in place, his eyes bright with anger.

"I trusted you," he repeated. "And all this time you've been using Cadell and me to get the revenge you wanted. Not what we wanted. Not what was good for all Scanners."

Though Sha'Nara agreed with Tristan, his fierceness startled her. "Stop," she told him. "Stop now before you hurt him."

"He would've killed you." Tristan didn't look at her, but his voice broke. "And I would've been responsible."

"But he didn't kill me." She longed to touch him. "He can't manipulate any of us now."

Mael suddenly sagged against the wall.

Remy straightened, removing his weight from her shoulder. Shaking his head as if to clear it, he raised his voice. "Officers, in here!"

Three Alliance officers ran in from the conference room.

"Escort that man to a holding cell." Remy motioned toward Mael, then glanced at Cadell. "Will it hold him?"

"It should." Tristan frowned at Mael. The older man suddenly recoiled from an invisible blow, then sank unconscious to the floor. "Move him quickly. He can implant actions and words into people by touching them. Your men won't want to be near him if he's conscious."

Remy waved at the officers. "You heard him. Quickly."

Sha'Nara watched them remove Mael with a sense of relief. "I never did trust him," she murmured.

Wrapping his arm around her shoulders, Tristan hugged her close, grief etched on his features. He tried to smile. "Psychic?"

She admired his attempt to lighten the moment. Mael's deceit had to hurt him every bit as much as her father's had hurt her, maybe more. "Just a hunch," she replied.

"I'm sorry." Cadell's voice came out in a rasp. "I should've sensed something. I knew he wasn't the same after my mother's death, but I didn't realize. . . . I should've known."

Jacy grabbed his suit and forced him to face her. "He's your father. You had no reason to suspect he thought differently than you did."

"But—"

"It's not your fault, Cadell."

With a sigh, he enveloped her in a hug.

"Who does this leave in charge of Scanners?" asked Remy.

Tristan and Cadell exchanged glances. "Cadell is Mael's son," said Tristan.

"But you're the natural leader," Cadell said. For a moment his gaze held the mischievous glimmer Sha'Nara always associated with him. "I'm better behind the scenes."

"Very well." Remy came to stand before Tristan. "I'm appointing you Relocation Officer. You'll be responsible for coordinating with Dev the transfer and settlement of your people on Lander. All right with you, Devon?"

"I have no objection."

Sha'Nara grinned with pride. She had no difficulty in picturing Tristan as the leader of his people . . . her people.

"Sha'Nara, you're officially promoted to PSI Police Director."

"What?" She stared up at Remy. "But won't they be disbanded?"

"Of course, but it'll take time. I need you to oversee it for me."

"But . . . but . . ." She looked helplessly at Tristan, their plans shattering around her. "I'd planned to go with Tristan."

"I'm sorry, but I need you here." Remy assumed his leadership expression. "You're still an Alliance officer, Sha'Nara. Don't make me order you."

"But I'm only a Commander." At one time she would've desired this position. Now it meant nothing.

"You've worked closely with your father, enough to have familiarity with all aspects of the directorate. More importantly, you have a reason to work for disbandment. Another officer might be less inclined."

Tristan tightened his hold on her shoulders. "How long do you see this taking?"

"Not less than two months."

"Two months?" echoed Sha'Nara. "Then what?"

"You'll be assigned to another position until your commission is over or you decide to recommit."

Her heart sank. Her commission went for another three years. Would Tristan wait that long?

"I have no choice," she said finally.

"No, you don't." Remy squeezed her hand before he left. "I'm sorry."

Sha'Nara stood in silence, her heart breaking, her eyes misty with unshed tears. Of all the things she'd imagined to tear her and Tristan apart, she'd never expected it to be because they were both assigned leadership roles.

"Sha'Nara." Tristan spoke her name quietly.

Looking up, she realized everyone else had left. "I can't walk out on Remy. Not now. It would jeopardize everything."

"I don't expect you to." He ran his knuckles over her cheek. "You've worked hard for your career. I wouldn't ask you to give it up."

"Then you don't want me to go with you?" Doubts assailed her. Did he no longer need her now that he had his freedom?

"I didn't say that." He kissed her with restrained passion. "I want you with me every day for the rest of my life. I'll wait until you or I are free of our responsibilities."

"My commission has three more years." A single tear streaked down her cheek and he kissed it away.

"Then we should be well settled by the time you get there." He drew her close. "Sha'Nara."

She heard his pain and love in that one word, and closed her eyes against the overwhelming disappointment that threatened to destroy her. "I . . . I doubt if you'll have to leave until tomorrow," she said.

"Good." Tristan kissed her again, molding her close, his body hardening against hers.

Desire flamed to life. "I'll show you to my quarters."

At least they had tonight.

Chapter Twenty-one

Tristan glanced skyward as another transport ship maneuvered toward the landing field. Wiping sweat from his brow, he surveyed the hastily constructed spaceport. Not bad for three months' work.

Scanners had started arriving before the port was half finished, reaching their new home in a variety of aged spacecraft. Word had spread quickly throughout the galaxy of the Scanners' freedom. Every day brought new arrivals and new problems.

He didn't mind. It kept him busy. And as long as he was busy, he couldn't think of Sha'Nara. Some days he managed an entire ten-minute period without recalling her face, her touch, her voice. It didn't help that lilianas grew wild on Lander, their scent triggering memories of the woman he loved.

He'd learned that the PSI Police Directorate was being dismantled under her leadership—a job as demanding as his. Her infrequent, hastily compiled messages reassured him of her love, but only added to his need for her.

At the rate Scanners were arriving at Lander, he wouldn't be able to break free for another year . . . minimum. He'd never make it that long without her.

The transport settled on the landing pad. With a sigh, Tristan went to meet it. He tried to greet every new arrival in an attempt to ease their trepidation. Many had difficulty believing they were no longer hunted. Shibit, he had trouble believing it himself.

The passengers disembarked, their hesitation and excitement familiar to him by now. He shook hands, offered reassurances, and provided guidance on where they could register for Lander citizenship and apply for a land grant. Some didn't find it necessary to accept the Landerites' generous land offer, locating positions in the main city of Maat instead.

Thus far, Scanners had been welcomed with open arms as if they were long-lost cousins. Devon had never revealed his planet's origins. Maybe they were.

"Tristan." The transport pilot handed him a hand imager as he passed. "A message from Cadell."

"Anything from Sha'Nara?"

The pilot shook his head. "Not this time."

Tristan nodded and glanced at the imager. Remy had soon discovered the advantages to having an empathic son-in-law, and found Cadell a position as a mediator for the Alliance. Cadell loved it, almost as much as he loved his new wife. No doubt this missive contained more glowing reports of their new life together.

Though Tristan enjoyed hearing from Cadell and Jacy, he dreaded it, too. Their happiness only reminded him of what he'd left behind.

"Where am I to go again?" An elderly woman paused by his side, dragging his attention back to the work at hand.

"Let me take you to registration." He offered her his arm and started toward the large rectangular building.

They'd only taken a few steps when another roar ripped through the air. Turning, Tristan spotted a small Alliance cruiser landing beside the transport.

What now? He'd been visited twice before by Alliance

311

officers, and had ended up with more reports required than he could possibly handle. Fighting for freedom had been easier.

As one of his staff walked by, Tristan snagged the young man's attention. "Fedor, can you please show this woman to registration?" He aimed his thumb at the cruiser. "I'm afraid I'll be tied up again."

Fedor rolled his eyes. "Not more forms?"

Tristan grimaced. "Probably."

Making his way to the Alliance craft, Tristan wondered what new policy he'd have to follow now. The last one had added days of work to his already full schedule.

The door to the cruiser slid open and several Alliance officers streamed out. Moving to the rear storage areas, they began to unload large parcels. Tristan frowned. What was going on?

Another figure paused in the door, surveying the spaceport.

Tristan froze, squinting into the afternoon sun. He knew that figure, that deliciously red hair.

"Sha'Nara." He ran toward the ship, stopping only when she threw herself into his arms.

He found her lips immediately, reveling in their sensual softness. It had been too long . . . far too long. When they finally broke apart, breathless, she grinned at him.

"That should give my people something to talk about."

"Your people?"

She indicated the officers at the rear of the craft.

"What are they doing?"

"Unpacking."

"Unpacking what?" More forms, no doubt. At least having Sha'Nara deliver them was a bonus.

"A little of this, a little of that. Lander has agreed to let the Alliance set up an embassy here."

"An embassy?" Tristan frowned. Now the Alliance would demand his reports directly. Dismissing that thought, he drank in Sha'Nara's beauty. She looked better than he remembered and her hair was loose, the way he liked it. "How long can you stay? A few days, at least?"

She met his gaze, her face solemn. "I can only stay three years."

Her words didn't register until she broke into a blinding smile. "Three years?" Had he heard correctly?

Squaring her shoulders, she stepped back and tugged at her uniform, which he noticed no longer bore the PSI Police insignia. "You are addressing the first Alliance ambassador to Lander. You may call me Ambassador Calles."

Realization dawned. "Remy."

"Exactly. He's been working on getting this embassy in place since I began dismantling the PSI Police. I should've known he'd manage it so I could finish out my commission with you."

"Then you're staying?"

"Right here." A gleam danced in her eyes. "You're stuck with me, Tristan Galeron."

Joy burst forth in the sound of a laugh. "I couldn't ask for more." Except to get her home in his bed as soon as possible. "You are going to marry me, aren't you?"

"I'm counting on it. In fact, Cadell and Jacy are arriving within the week to be our attendants."

He laughed again, experiencing true happiness for the first time in his life. "I'm not waiting that long to take you home."

"Good. I'd have to attack you in your office if you didn't." She glanced toward the buildings nearby. "Any idea where we should take this stuff?"

"Take it to the holding shed. We'll find out from Dev where you're supposed to set up."

Sha'Nara went to issue instructions, then rejoined him. "I'm free for now. Let's go."

Strolling toward the registration building, Tristan couldn't stop a grin from covering his face. He had everything and more—a home, his love, his future.

"I just need to stop by the registration building for a moment."

"Then you'll take me home?" The husky sound of

Sha'Nara's voice sent the blood pulsing to his loins.

"Definitely. Wait until you see it." Steering her into the building, he grinned even more. "I've found the greatest piece of land."

Dear Reader,

Thank you for allowing me to share Tristan and Sha'Nara's story with you. Tristan actually had a brief role in *Sword of MacLeod,* my first futuristic. I was so intrigued by this human with advanced parapsychic abilities that I had to discover what adventures he had in his life.

Somewhere My Love takes place about a dozen years after Tristan's job with the privateers. I had an exciting time learning about the Scanners and their battle for survival. I had even more fun finding the perfect woman for this passionate Scanner. I hope you'll agree that these two individuals deserve each other and their once-in-a-lifetime love.

Lately, however, I've been wondering about Devon...

Writing is something I love to do, even with the distractions of an office manager job, three children actively involved in sports, two cats, a dog, and a wonderful husband. I also love to hear from readers. Please write me at: P.O. Box 4383, Biloxi, MS 39535-4383.

Karen Fox

Futuristic Romance

Love in another time, another place.

Daughter of Destiny

JACKIE CASTO

Winner Of The *Romantic Times* Reviewers' Choice Award

Never in his life has Raul known sensations like those he discovers when holding the sorceress Esme's delicate body in his hard, muscled arms. The throbbing ecstasy of those moments leaves him completely satisfied, yet the mastery he craves is still missing; the weapons he commands cannot compare to Esme's telepathic powers. Not until love transforms his heart will he understand his true place beside the daughter of destiny.

__52011-7 $4.99 US/$5.99 CAN

Futuristic Romance

Love in another time, another place.

The New Frontier
JACKIE CASTO

Bestselling Author Of *Daughter Of Destiny*

Raised to despise all men, Ashley has no choice but to marry when a cruel twist of fate sends her to the planet that is mankind's last hope for survival. There, colonists have one duty: Be fruitful and multiple. Forced to find a mate among the surly, women-hungry brutes, Ashley picks the one man believes will willingly release her from her vows.

A born warrior, Garrick is a man who's conquered all he's ever desired. But the rough-and-ready scout has neither the time nor the need for a wife—or does he? Before long, Ashley begins to wonder if Garrick will ever set her free from his tender grasp...or if she'll lose herself in the paradise of his loving arms.

__52071-0 $4.99 US/$6.99 CAN